Among Her Bones

Kate Serine

Cover art by Maria Spada

For Mom.

AUTHOR'S NOTE

This novel contains dark themes, adult language, sexual situations, elements of fear and suspense, emotional intensity, and moments involving grief and loss, as well as references to self-harm that may be distressing for some readers. Please read with care.

For more detail, please see the full content warning at www.kateserine.com.

CHAPTER ONE

"What do you mean, you're *evicting* us?"

I cradled my phone between my shoulder and my jaw, shifting my son Henry higher on my hip. His little body was hotter than it should've been as he nestled closer, his limp limbs making him feel heavier than he was.

"I am sorry, Ms. Dupont," the man on the other line replied. "With my client's passing, we have evaluated all his properties, and the one you are living is not even worth the upkeep."

I moved the phone to my other ear, hoping I'd misheard. "But—"

"Mama," Henry whimpered, patting my cheek, "my throat hurts."

"As Mr. Proffitt's attorney," the man continued, his voice bland, unconcerned, "I have been asked to advise in the disposition of his less valuable assets as his son is far too busy to handle it himself. Unfortunately, your location was never a desirable neighborhood and is getting worse, so I must sell the property before it is a total loss. Please understand—this is purely a business decision. You are no different from than any of the others being disposed of."

I hugged Henry a little closer, squeezing my eyes shut to rein in my rising panic. "Mr. Briggs, your client and I had an understanding. He lowered my rent until I could get back on my feet. I understand you're trying to do your job, but I just need a little more time—"

"Mama..."

"Shh, shh, baby," I consoled, tears blurring my view of his sweet face, flushed with fever. "I know. We're going to the doctor."

"I really am sorry, Ms. Dupont," Mr. Briggs told me, sounding almost sincere. "If there was another way..."

"There *is* another way!" I snapped. "You could honor Mr. Proffitt's promises."

"Ms. Dupont—"

"Where am I supposed to go?" I choked out, trying to keep the tears out of my voice and failing. "I work in a coffee shop making barely enough to pay what I already do. My five-year-old son is sick—I don't even know how I'm going to pay for a doctor's visit or any medicine he needs because my job's insurance sucks. And now you're kicking me *out*?"

Henry was crying quietly now, snuggling close to my chest. "Mama..."

Hopelessness squeezed my heart. My knees buckled, and I sank to the floor, cradling Henry in my arms, no longer pretending to hold back the tears. "I'm sorry, Mr. Briggs. I can't do this right now."

Not waiting for a response, I hung up and tossed my phone aside, then pressed my forehead into the heel of my palm, sobbing silently so I wouldn't upset Henry.

What the hell was I supposed to do? I'd vowed—*sworn* to myself—I'd never again be without a roof over my head, never let Henry feel the same gnawing fear and uncertainty I'd known as a child as my mother dragged us from shelters to friends' couches to shitty apartments that reeked of stale cigarette smoke and unrealized dreams. We'd never stayed in one place long enough to feel secure or know what it was like to have an actual *home*—or even understand what that word truly meant.

A few weeks after finding out I was pregnant with Henry, I'd moved into the little house—really just a one-bedroom box with thin walls that rattled when the wind blew—thanks to the kind old man who'd been a regular at the coffee shop. Montgomery Proffitt (or Mr. Monty as I called him) had been there for me ever since. He'd lowered my rent when the pandemic shut everything down, helped me with utilities when what little money I'd saved ran out, pushed me to finish my degree, even helped me find scholarships and grants to make it possible.

Mr. Monty had been my guardian angel.

And now he was gone.

A massive heart attack had taken him two months ago, according to Mr. Briggs when he'd first contacted me. I hadn't even known until after the funeral, so I never had the chance to say goodbye, no chance to thank his family for all he'd done. Since getting the news, I'd not only grieved for one of the few people who'd ever treated me with kindness and dignity, but I'd also lived in fear that his family wouldn't be as compassionate.

Turns out I'd been right to worry.

I sniffed and wiped my eyes with the back of my hand then shifted my now-sleeping son on my lap. "Okay. Okay," I murmured, squaring my shoulders, mind racing.

I'd figure something out. I always did. When my mom had kicked me out for being pregnant with Henry, I'd felt the same hopelessness. I'd dropped out of college with only a year left, but I'd found a job, a place to live at least—even if it wasn't much. I had survived then. I would survive now. We'd be okay, I told myself so emphatically I almost believed it.

My phone buzzed on the floorboards, the vibration traveling through the wood and up into my bones. I reached automatically for the device, but hesitated, my hand hovering inches away, not sure if I should answer, but at the same time knowing I had to. A chill rippled through me when I picked it up.

"Ms. Dupont?" asked a male voice I didn't recognize and yet was somehow vaguely familiar.

I cleared my throat, shaking off whatever had come over me. "Yes? Who's this?"

Before he could answer, a burst of pain flared behind my eyes only to immediately dull to a persistent throbbing.

Damn it. What the hell?

"This is Whit Proffitt," the man said, breaking through the lingering haze clouding my brain. "Montgomery Proffitt was my father."

My stomach sank.

Perfect.

“Don’t worry, Mr. Proffitt, your father’s attorney already told me that my son and I are being kicked out.”

“That’s why I’m calling,” he replied. “I just spoke to Mr. Briggs. He shared how his conversation with you went, so I wanted to call myself. I’m sorry for how he broke the news to you. It could’ve been handled better.”

“I don’t know how exactly that kind of news could be handled *better,*” I retorted. “No matter how you say it, I’m still going to be homeless.”

“Ms. Dupont—"

“I need to take my son to the doctor, Mr. Proffitt,” I interrupted, impatient to be off the phone. “I have to go.”

I hung up before he could respond, then got to my feet, groaning under Henry’s dead weight. I kissed his damp curls, then surveyed the dingy walls of our little house. Yellowing paint. Grease splatter baked in from decades of various renters’ fried chicken, pork chops, okra. Furniture thrifted or scavenged. Second-hand art. Almost everything I owned was someone else’s discarded trash I’d snatched up, pretending the mismatched styles were eclectic. The place was a dump, no question. It was no wonder Whit Proffitt and his father’s attorney were eager to offload it. But it was my *home.*

And I was losing it.

I closed my eyes and took several deep breaths, the last of the pain from my headache thankfully tapering off. Then I snatched up my purse and keys and carried Henry out to my old sedan. His eyes fluttered open briefly when I sat him in his booster seat, and he gave me a small, fever-weary smile that pierced straight through the dark cloud descending on me.

Whatever else was going on would have to wait until after the clinic. He was my top priority. Always. The rest was just shit to figure out.

An hour and a half later, I stepped out of the community clinic, medicine for Henry in hand and a knot in my stomach. The visit had cost more than I'd expected—because of course it had. But what was I supposed to do? I'd have to budget a lot tighter, maybe visit the church food pantry—something I hadn't done in a while. If it had just been me, I could've gotten by with bread and peanut butter. But my pride wouldn't fill Henry's belly.

"Mama, my throat still hurts," Henry rasped as I buckled him in, his voice so small it broke my heart.

"I know, baby," I murmured, kissing his forehead. "We're going to get you feeling better in no time. Should we get you some popsicles?"

He nodded, his lower lip trembling. "Orange, please, Mama."

I pinched his chin gently. "You got it."

I climbed into the driver's seat and turned the key. The engine chugged and whined, then fell silent. "No, no, no. Not now..."

I tried again. Same miserable sputter. Same refusal to cooperate.

I slammed my palm against the steering wheel, a strangled sound tearing loose before I could stop it.

"Mama?" Henry asked softly. "Are you okay? We don't have to get popsicles."

My heart broke right down the middle. I forced a smile over my shoulder. "I'm fine, baby. The car's being grumpy again. I'm sorry if I scared you. It's not about the popsicles, I promise."

My phone rang—shrill, insistent. I answered without looking.

"*What*?"

"Ms. Dupont—"

"Jesus, *really*?" I muttered. I brushed my hair back from my face and closed my eyes, emotionally exhausted. "Mr. Proffitt, I've got a sick kid and a broken-down car in front of the clinic. I really can't deal with this today."

"I think I might have a solution for you," he said quickly, before I could hang up on him again. "We have a property in Savannah that just became available unexpectedly. The building is still undergoing renovations, but the apartment is mostly furnished. I'll honor my father's arrangement for a few months. After that, we can figure something out."

I sat in stunned silence, staring out the cracked windshield at the waves of heat rising from the asphalt, blurring the path before me.

A solution.

My initial impulse was to not trust his offer. I could count on one hand the times someone's kindness to me hadn't come with strings attached. But panic squeezed my lungs, reminding me I didn't exactly have a lot of options.

"Ms. Dupont? Are you still there?" Mr. Proffitt asked, interrupting my warring thoughts.

I didn't immediately respond, still a little dazed by his offer, but then gave myself a mental shake. "Yes, sorry. I'm here. It's just...Savannah? I'd have to quit my job and find a new one. And I don't have anyone to watch my son. I can't afford childcare. My neighbor takes care of him now because I help her with groceries. I can't—"

"I'm sure we can help you find something in Savannah," he assured me. "It's the least I could do to make up for not being more sensitive to your situation."

"I don't know," I murmured. "Right now, I just need to get my son home—well, 'home' as long as it's mine."

From the backseat, Henry whispered, "Mama, can we still get popsicles?"

"Yes, baby," I told him softly. Then into the phone: "I'll think about your offer, Mr. Proffitt. I just...I just need a day or two."

"Of course," he replied. "I'll hold the apartment for now, just in case."

I hung up the phone before he could say anything else and turned the key again. The car chugged and coughed, then rumbled to life, taking pity on me this time.

I peered at Henry as he slept, his fever lower now that he'd had two days of antibiotics. Missing two shifts to stay home with him meant my paycheck would be a joke. But I'd had no choice. Ms. Reba next door couldn't risk catching anything at her age.

I kissed Henry's forehead and brushed his hair back from his face, then took a seat at the little kitchen table a few feet away. Whit Proffitt would be calling soon for my answer. Too bad I still didn't know what I was going to tell him. There was really only one option I hadn't already explored, and just the thought of it made me queasy as painful memories bombarded me. But I needed to be sure I'd looked into every possibility before accepting an offer from a complete stranger.

The devil you know...

I held my phone in both hands, staring at the number on the screen for several minutes, indecision making my heart pound. Finally, I exhaled hard and hit the call button.

"Screw it."

The phone rang. Once. Twice. No answer. I wasn't surprised—and was actually a little relieved.

I was about to hang up when a voice like sandpaper on concrete said, "Hello?"

My stomach dropped.

The last time I'd heard my mother's voice, she'd called me a whore and told me to get the fuck out. Hearing it again cracked open an old, festering wound that I'd told myself had scarred over when I'd cut her out of my life.

I swallowed hard. "Hi, Vivian. It's Zellie."

A long, heavy pause. "Well, you've got some nerve calling after all these years."

"You didn't want to talk to me," I reminded her, bristling. "You told me I was a sinner, that I was going to burn in hell. I didn't think you'd really welcome a call."

"And what makes you think I want to talk to you now?" A hacking cough erupted from her, choking the last word to little more than a gasp.

"You sound like shit," I said. "Are you still smoking?"

Another grating cough that ended on a rattle. "What the hell do you care?"

I repressed a sigh. I didn't. At least, I didn't *want* to.

"I didn't call to fight, Vivian," I said, trying to keep a lifetime of anger and bitterness out of my voice. "I just..."

"What?" she asked, her laugh a raspy, eerie cackle. "You in trouble again? Crawling back with your tail tucked 'tween your legs, begging for help?"

I should've known calling was pointless. For a moment, I'd wondered if maybe Vivian Dupont had changed, if perhaps she regretted how she'd driven me away and had missed out on her grandson, if maybe she'd take us in, just until I found something else. But I should've known how it would go. The woman who considered herself a "good Christian" because she went to church every Sunday didn't do kindness. Vivian Dupont only did scripture, punishment, and shame.

"I'm not begging," I told her, no longer the little girl pleading for scraps of affection. "And I'm sure as hell not asking you for anything ever again."

"Well, that's a switch." I could hear my mother flicking her Bic, lighting up another cigarette, and easily pictured her sucking in her first drag, her already sunken cheeks hollowing further, her eyes narrowed in habitual contempt.

"You know, all I ever wanted was for you to be my mother," I said, the words bitter on my tongue. "Apparently, that was just too much to ask."

Her derisive snort was loud in my ear. "I never wanted to be a mother. But God had other plans for me. 'I consider that our present sufferings are not worth comparing with the glory that will be revealed in us.' That's Romans 8:18. You'd know that if you'd ever listened to a damned word I said."

"For fuck's sake," I muttered, a familiar anger clawing at my gut. I made my decision. "Save your sanctimonious bullshit, Vivian. I'm just letting you know I'm leaving. Henry and I are moving to Savannah."

"Well, guess you'd better get to packing," she said flatly.

"Guess so." I laughed in a short, humorless burst. "And don't worry. You won't be hearing from me again."

Vivian started to say something, but whatever hateful comment she'd planned was cut off by another harsh cough.

I hung up.

Frowning, I replayed the conversation in my head, the familiar sting of rejection warring with resigned indifference.

I turned slowly, taking inventory of the contents of the tiny house. Not much to pack—Henry's toys, some clothes, a few boxes of books, the thrift-store art on the wall...

Just as well. The sooner I got the hell out of there, the better.

Still, the idea of starting over—leaving behind everything I'd managed to build, the meager support I'd gathered, the few friends I'd made—sent a wave of anxiety crashing over me.

I rushed to the kitchen sink and leaned against it, squeezing my eyes shut to fight the sudden urge to throw up. I didn't normally feel stress in my stomach. But it wasn't like anything was *normal* at the moment, so why should my body's reaction to my world falling apart be any different?

When the nausea subsided, I took a few deep breaths and opened my eyes. Through the tiny window, night settled over my little world like a shroud, the darkness pressing close, heavy with silence. The kind of silence that felt...ominous.

My mouth suddenly dry, I exhaled a shaky breath and grabbed a glass from the cabinet.

When I turned back toward the window, the glass slipped from my hand and shattered in the sink, shards skittering like tiny bones across the porcelain.

For a heartbeat, I couldn't move, couldn't breathe. I could only stare as two glowing silver eyes glared back at me through the reflection: a woman's face, pale and blurred at the edges, like an old photo negative. And those eyes locked on mine. Furious. Vengeful.

Her mouth opened in a silent scream, jaw unhinging wider than it should, and she rushed toward me, her fingers curled into claws.

Instinct snapped me free of my paralysis. I spun, bracing for her to be just inches behind me, to grab me, tear into me.

But the kitchen was empty.

No movement. No sound except for the hammering of my heart.

The window air conditioner clicked on, wheezing from its efforts to combat the spring heat, the suddenness of it shattering the silence and spurring me into action.

I lurched to the window, yanking the blinds down with shaking hands, the slats clattering into place, then stumbled across the room, checking other windows, locks, anything that could keep something out—even though I knew nothing *truly* could.

I flipped every light switch within reach. Warm light banished the darkness but still didn't seem bright enough when I pressed into a corner so I could see every inch of the room. Shaking, I slid to the floor and pulled my knees to my chest, arms wrapped tight, watching.

When nothing else appeared after several minutes, I squeezed my eyes shut and pressed my forehead to my knees.

The intruders.

They'd found me again.

They'd haunted me since childhood, no matter where my mother had dragged me. I called them *intruders* because they forced themselves into my awareness, but

I didn't know if they were ghosts, portends, or something else entirely. Vivian had called them demons and punished me whenever I mentioned them, convinced that it was my wickedness that drew them.

So many hungry nights, my grumbling stomach keeping me awake because Vivian believed fasting would "starve out" the demons. So many ice baths that left me gasping and crying because she insisted that making my little body inhospitable would send the demons away. So many prayer circles and "healings" from religious charlatans that were supposed to cleanse my soul...

So, I had closed myself to the intruders, forced them away, ignored the whispers, the messages, the shadows in the corner of my eye—until they no longer came.

Until now.

God. Damn. It.

A soft voice broke through my panic.

"Mama?"

Henry stood near the couch, eyes wide and scared, curls mussed from sleep.

"It's okay, baby," I assured him. "I just thought I saw something scary. That's all."

I leaned my head back against the wall, closing my eyes once more and taking a deep, calming breath. And then another.

His bare feet padded closer. Even though I expected him, I still flinched when he touched my arm.

"You'll be okay," he said, as if our roles had reversed. "Don't be scared, Mama."

I forced a smile and smoothed his curls from his eyes.

He sat down beside me, taking my hand in his. "I'll hold your hand," he whispered. "That will make it better."

My laugh came out trembly, edged with tears. "Thanks, baby." I pulled him into my lap. "That does make it better. How about if we snuggle for a little while until you go back to sleep?"

He nodded and curled against me, warm and solid, pushing the fear back into the familiar little box where I kept it buried.

When his breathing went soft and deep, I carried him to his bed and kissed his forehead.

As I exited his room, the kitchen light flickered—just once—and my stomach tightened. But nothing else stirred.

I found my phone where it had fallen earlier and dialed a number. It rang only once before a deep voice answered.

"Ms. Dupont?"

I swallowed hard, scanning the room, searching for anything that shouldn't be there.

"I accept your offer, Mr. Proffitt." My voice came out hollow, flat as I fought to keep it even. "How quickly can we move in?"

CHAPTER TWO

"Is that our house?" Henry cried from the back seat when we pulled up to the curb in front of the palatial old home in Savannah two weeks later.

I frowned as I took in the towering four-story mansion then double-checked the address on my maps app and the small metal sign identifying the home as a historic landmark.

Dawes House.

This was the place, but there had to be some mistake. There was no way Whit Proffitt had invited us to move into a house like *this* and only charge me the same rate I was paying for a tiny, rundown house in a dying neighborhood...right?

Mature trees surrounded the property, draped with Spanish moss that hung low, drooping in the muggy Savannah heat, giving the house an obscured, secretive air. The yellow stucco was chipping and crumbling in places and needed repair, but the edifice was still stunning.

The bottom level sat half submerged below street level behind a high wrought-iron fence, but I could see the top half of two sets of red double doors that opened onto a patio. The two main levels of the home each boasted balconies supported by thick columns that spanned the entire front of the façade, the peeling white paint giving it the appearance of a once-elegant home now softening into faded grandeur, yet still clinging to what once was even as long-hidden decay began to seep through the carefully curated exterior.

The top floor looked like it should've had a balcony too. A large set of doors opened inward, white curtains billowing in the breeze, but the occupant enjoying that breeze would've stepped out into nothing but air. I could picture a woman standing there, her back to the door, her hair lifting with the same breeze that rustled the curtains. In the next moment, she spread her arms and fell backward.

I gasped and shook my head, banishing the horrific scene. What the hell had *that* been? A glimpse of a past tragedy at Dawes House? A vision? Or just my overwrought nerves, inflamed by the stifling heat?

I decided not to explore the thought as none of the options were particularly appealing and surveyed the rest of the property.

Next to the massive house stood another building—a carriage house, if my research at the public library was accurate. Whit had told me there were eleven total apartments on the property, so one or two must've been in that building. Whereas the main house was imposing, the carriage house seemed...cold. Dead.

I shuddered from chilling vibe the carriage house threw off, grateful we weren't staying there.

"*Mama*," Henry said, impatient. "Can we get out yet? Is this our house?"

"Yes, baby," I said at last, still awed. "Yes, this is it. But let's go check in before we unload the car, okay?"

My hands were clammy as I opened Henry's door. The sweat sliding down my spine from the cloying humidity suddenly went cold, as if someone had whispered at the nape of my neck where my hair was pulled into a ponytail. I shivered, then wiped the perspiration from my hairline and tried to tamp down the nerves knotting my stomach.

Henry, unbothered, beamed with excitement, his steps bouncy as we approached the wide veranda. He hopped up each step, turning to me when he reached the top, eager for praise at what a big boy he was to jump up the steps so easily.

My nerves settled at his grin. He saw this move as an adventure—a brand-new place to explore. I just hoped that I'd made the right decision, that his joy signaled the fresh start I'd longed for, the one Whit had promised.

"Did you see me?" Henry panted. "I jumped up *all* the steps!"

"You sure did, baby," I confirmed, forcing a smile. "You're so big!"

"Big enough to go to school?" Henry asked. "Do I get to ride the bus now?"

"Yes! Won't that be fun!" I pulled him in for a quick hug, keeping my tone cheerful to hide the fact that sending him to school filled me with dread. "Just a few more months, kiddo."

I reached for the crimson door's knob, noting the colorful stained-glass panels, when the porch creaked. My head snapped toward the sound, my heartbeat spiking. An elegant white bentwood chair rocked slowly, the floorboards beneath creaking with the chair's rhythm.

What the hell…?

The door suddenly swung open, jerking the knob from my grasp, and a man strode out, barreling straight into me.

"Oh, shit, sorry, ma'am!" he cried, grabbing my upper arms to keep me from tumbling backward down the steps.

I tensed and reflexively brought up my arm to knock his hand away but stopped short when he released me quickly. "It's okay," I said in a rush, taking a half-step further from his reach. "No big deal. Excuse me." I gestured toward the door. "I'm the new tenant. I'm here to check in and get my key."

"You're Zellie Dupont," he said, scrubbing a hand on his thigh before offering it.

He didn't seem much older than me. His wavy, chin-length blond hair was already beginning to curl from the humidity, and well-developed muscles were visible through his T-shirt where it clung to his skin. A toolbelt slung around his hips looked more fashion accessory than functional, but the hand he still held out was callused, his nails showing proof of hard work despite his pretty-boy appearance.

I eyed him warily as I shook his hand. "Yes, that's me."

"I'm Chase Crawford," he announced as if his name was supposed to mean something to me. When I stared at him blankly, he added, "I'm overseeing the renovations, so you'll see me around here quite a bit."

I managed a tight grin. "Lucky me."

Henry tugged my hand. "Mama, are we going in?"

I lifted a brow at Chase. "I don't know. *Are* we?"

"Oh, sorry," Chase fumbled, pushing open the door and holding it for us. "You go right on in, little man. I've got your key inside here, Ms. Dupont. Whit wanted me to help y'all get settled."

I started to step over the threshold but paused, an uneasiness I couldn't explain rippling through me. I glanced toward the rocking chair—now still—and swallowed hard. A gust of wind rushed through the porch, setting it rocking again. I let out a shaky laugh, relieved to blame a breeze instead of one of Savannah's infamous ghosts.

But I still sensed *something*—an awareness squirmed beneath my skin, making my muscles twitch and my bones ache to run. I didn't know who this Chase Crawford was or if he truly had the authority to give me the keys. I would've been less anxious had Whit met us himself. As it was, I already felt like a charity case who was living here on borrowed time. And walking in now, I felt like...well, an *intruder*.

"C'mon, Mama," Henry urged, pulling my hand, hopping with excitement. "C'mon!"

"Sorry, sorry!" I laughed. "I'm coming." I shook off my apprehension and followed Chase inside.

The lobby area looked like it had once been a great hall, receiving guests for dinner parties and garden soirées. Just inside the door sat a heavy wooden reception desk that looked as old as the building, making the computer and flat screen monitor on it seem out of place. Chase rummaged through the top drawer and produced a set of keys, then grabbed a manila folder from the corner of the desk. My name was on the tab.

"Sorry," he said, holding up the folder. "I don't normally handle this. Iris is the one who welcomes new tenants and runs the building, but she's off today. She makes the most amazing peach cobbler you've ever tasted—you're gonna love it."

I'd lived in Georgia for several years but had never had peach cobbler, so my basis for comparison was nonexistent. Even so, the mention of it made my mouth water. Dessert had been a luxury Vivian never allowed— sugar led to gluttony, a deadly sin—so, I couldn't wait for Iris to share her famous cobbler. I might even have *two* helpings, just for spite.

"Y'all come on," Chase continued, motioning for us to follow him. "I'll give you the tour. We've got two floors completely renovated. Still working on the fourth floor—" He gestured toward the wide staircase with intricately carved banisters. "—and the first floor, which folks like to call the garden level. If it's half underground, then it's a basement, in my estimation. But it's never been labeled that way, so call it whatever suits you. No washer and dryer hookups in the apartments, so everyone uses the ones in the *basement.*"

He chuckled at his own joke, then gestured toward another set of stairs tucked back in the shadows. "Those lead to the lower level. Eventually, the basement apartment will be rented out, but it's empty at present. Now, on this level, there's one apartment down that hall there where Junior and Pearlie Johnson live. They're good people." He sent a grin over his shoulder at me. "Ms. Pearlie loves good low-country cooking and invites everyone over for dinner Sundays. It's my favorite day of the week."

"Do you know everyone here by their cooking?" I asked, finding I liked his lighthearted attitude.

He chuckled. "Well, boy's gotta eat, ma'am—especially one who can't cook worth a damn. Darn," he amended quickly, glancing down at Henry. "Worth a *darn*. Sorry about that. Not used to having kids around until recently."

"There are other kids nearby?" I asked, hoping Henry could make friends—something that was in short supply in our old neighborhood. What few people who'd still been around were older, too poor or too stubborn to move from a neighborhood, which had more houses boarded up and rotting to ruin than not.

"Well, a few kids, I guess," Chase said, pausing and drawing his brows together like he was mentally taking inventory. "There's a family a couple doors down got a little boy I've seen. And then there's Adelaide. She lives in this apartment here." He motioned toward the door on the other side of the lobby. "Her Mamaw June and Papaw Earl have custody. She's probably about the same age as your son. Sweet little thing." He winked at Henry. "She's got a headful of curls, too. Y'all could be cousins."

He led us past a bank of brass mailboxes on the wall to a set of heavy double doors that opened into an enormous room that looked like it had once been two. The area had a heaviness to it—the walls were painted deep green and the wood trim, like in the rest of the building, was rich mahogany that gave the impression of decadence and wealth. A few couches were arranged around the room that also held a pool table, a couple of large screen TVs, and a very expensive-looking card table covered in green felt.

"This is the common room," Chase explained. "Y'all are welcome to use it whenever you like. The Johnsons and Foresters play cards down here most evenings after dinner. Even Old Man Dean sometimes comes down to be sociable. He's up on the third floor."

I glanced at Henry to see if he was as nervous as I was now that we were inside the imposing house, but he was his typical happy, bouncy self, excited to see everything Chase showed us.

"Like a lot of these old homes in Savannah," Chase went on, leading us down a dimly lit hallway, "this place once belonged to a rich dude—prominent businessman in these parts—but it fell to ruin when his descendants moved on. For a few years back in the 1980s, Dawes House was turned into apartments for poor folks—"

He stopped talking abruptly and flushed, sending me an apologetic glance. Apparently, my arrangement with Whit wasn't a secret.

I gave him a tight smile. "Don't worry, Mr. Crawford. I'm well aware I don't have any money. Nothing to be embarrassed about."

"Sorry, all the same," he said with a nod. "But you're right—nothing to be embarrassed about. We all gotta have a little help now and then." He flashed that wide, charming grin and put a hand on his chest in mock solemnity. "Me, I like to rely on the good graces of my dear cousin Whit Proffitt, whose last name, it seems, was quite prophetic."

"Mr. Proffitt is your cousin?" I repeated, wondering if I'd heard right.

"Yes, ma'am," he said with a wink. "He prefers to leave all the dirty work on the properties to me. Thinks maybe it'll keep me out of trouble."

I laughed a little, unable to resist his roguish charm. "Well, I'm glad to see I'm not the only charity case."

He grinned again and gestured to an elevator. "Your chariot awaits."

I studied the rickety—albeit beautiful—elevator, then sent a side glance at Chase. "Are you sure that's safe?"

The conveyance looked more like a birdcage than an elevator. Its dark wooden panels on the bottom half were each emblazoned with some kind of insignia featuring a raven surrounded by filigree. The top half of the elevator was an actual cage of intricate bronze scrollwork and included a domed top sporting bronze statuettes of ravens mid-takeoff, as if carrying the elevator upward. The whole contraption looked old enough to be original to renovations a century ago.

Chase pulled open the door and stepped inside. "Yes, ma'am. And I'm sure you'll find it easier to get to the fourth floor than climbing all the stairs."

Henry bounded in and motioned for me. "C'mon, Mama!"

"Okay, okay, you two can stop ganging up on me." I said, stepping in.

Chase pulled the door closed and pressed the button. There was a loud *clunk*, and the elevator slowly began to creep upwards, creaking ominously as it inched along.

"Oh, yeah," I murmured. "Totally safe."

Chase chuckled. "Now, Ms. Dupont, do you think I'd put you and this handsome young man in danger on your very first day in this fine establishment?"

I had no idea what Chase Crawford would do. He was charming, handsome, maybe even a little bit wicked in all the good ways—but I didn't trust him. Not yet. Certainly not with the safety of my son. I let his question go unanswered. It was probably meant to be rhetorical anyway.

The elevator dinged as we passed the third floor.

"Is Mr. Dean the only tenant on this floor?" I asked, changing the subject.

"Nope," Chase answered. "Three apartments on the third floor. You've got Billy Wayne Wright and his wife Kitty. And then there's Ms. Netty and her full-time nurse, Merilee Vaughn. Pretty sure Ms. Netty came with the house. Not quite all there anymore, but she's a feisty old gal."

"And Merilee?" I prompted.

Chase flushed slightly. "She's young, pretty. You'll like her."

Clearly, he did. I suppressed a grin as the elevator jolted to a stop on the fourth floor.

Chase pushed open the door to reveal a dark hallway lit only by a single bulb hanging about midway down the hall, the others burned out or not working, and the open door at the far end with the white curtains I'd seen from the street.

"It's dark up here," I noted, reluctant to step out. I'd never been a fan of darkness, thanks to the intruders. I'd slept with the light on for years, trying to keep it a secret from Vivian when I could, taking the punishment she doled out when I couldn't.

"Sorry about that," Chase said in a rush, striding from the elevator and disappearing into the semidarkness, making me think he must've been the one who'd opened the door to nowhere. A moment later, more sunlight spilled into the hallway. "Hadn't had a chance to finish opening things up."

The sunlight revealed the reason why the hallway was so oppressive. The burnt-orange paint on the walls made the corridor feel claustrophobic. The paint peeled in places to reveal the plaster wall beneath, glimpses of white that were like quick gasps of untainted air.

"Are you adding more lights?" I asked, pulling Henry closer. "And I gotta be honest, the door at the end of the hallway makes me nervous. There's nothing to prevent Henry from falling out if he got too close."

Chase had opened another door at the other end of the hall, creating a welcome cross-breeze in the stifling heat. "Yes, ma'am," he answered. "I'll get these light fixtures back up today so you have some more light. There's supposed to be a locked wrought-iron gate on that door like on the other one. I'll see where that might've gotten to and take care of it as soon as possible." He turned to Henry. "You promise me you'll stay away from that door until I can get the gate back up, alright?"

Henry nodded. "Yes, sir, I promise."

Chase tussled Henry's dark hair and winked. "Atta boy. See, Mama? He'll be fine until I can fix it."

I eyed the door again, still uneasy. "What about the apartment on the basement level? Could we just stay there instead?"

"Afraid not," Chase said. "It's completely torn up. The new crew will be here Monday to get started on the renovations. There's still some work needed on your apartment, but it's livable, so Whit asked me to put you up here."

I tried to set aside my hesitation, determined not to let Henry see that I was starting to regret my decision.

It's only temporary, I reminded myself.

And, besides, it wasn't like I had any other choice *but* to make it work until I had saved enough money to move again.

I nodded without much enthusiasm. "Okay. So, which one is ours?"

"That one there." Chase gestured to the door farthest down the hall, but at least it was the one nearest the door with the gate. "Sorry about the heat up here. The duct work is being worked on, so only the lower floors are air-conditioned right now. I've set you up with some window units until we get it taken care of."

I swallowed hard, thinking about how hot it already was. And it was only late spring. It'd been hard enough at our little house, but getting through a Savannah summer with only window units on the fourth floor of an old house...

My feet dragged a little as I followed Chase. "Do you have an ETA on when that will be finished? Henry has asthma. Summer can be tough on him."

But asthma was only one of the issues that plagued my son. The inexplicable, persistent anemia led to countless appointments, ER trips, a suppressed immune system, and days when he was too tired to function like a normal, healthy kid. Heat just made his exhaustion worse. But I couldn't say anything more or the tears I was holding back would come spilling out.

"I'll see what I can do," Chase promised, the look in his eyes a little too close to pitying for my liking. He unlocked the door and swung it open. "Here you go."

I stood in the doorway, wide-eyed. "I...I thought this was being renovated. I mean, I didn't think..."

Chase chuckled. "That'd be this nice?"

Sure, the walls had yellowed with age and needed new paint, and the area rugs were worn and threadbare in places, but the living room immediately inside the apartment was in great shape, all things considered. Chase went to the windows across the room and pulled open the heavy drapes, revealing the air conditioning unit. He turned it on, checking that it was secure.

With the drapes open, I could get a better look at the apartment. The furniture was covered in sheets, but as Chase went around the room, pulling them off, revealing heavy (and no doubt expensive) couches, side tables, a coffee table, lamps with stained-glass shades, it was like I was watching a magician's stage show. It was all too surreal.

"Mr. Proffitt mentioned that the apartment was mostly furnished, but I didn't expect this much," I said, taking it all in.

Chase pulled off the last sheet, revealing a credenza over which hung an ornately framed mirror. "Yeah, the previous tenant left all this here. We haven't had a chance to do anything with it."

"Did they leave recently then?" I asked. "Mr. Proffitt said the apartment became vacant unexpectedly."

Chase shrugged. "About a month ago, I guess. Just up and left. Didn't take much—just clothes mostly. Skipping out on rent, if you ask me."

I glanced around once more, seeing it differently this time. I'd left behind the furniture at the tiny house I'd rented, giving some of it to my neighbor and some to charity. Whit assured me he'd dispose of the rest. We'd brought what had meant something—the *personal.* So I was baffled by the previous tenant's ability to just pick up and leave *everything.* Books, artwork, plants (now dead). There were even baubles and knickknacks that looked sentimental—amateurish clay fingerbowls made in a kindergarten art class, Disney World souvenirs. Not really the kinds of things you just discard on a whim.

Or maybe that was just a rich-person thing. Growing up, I'd never left any of my meager belongings behind if I could help it. Anything nice or meaningful from Vivian was rare and performative. Like when she was putting on a show of how good a mother she was. So maybe I was more attached to *things* than I should've been. But even when Vivian *was* skipping out on rent, we'd load up the car or a friend's van in the middle of the night so we could still take our personal things.

"Mama, can I see my room?" Henry asked, tugging my hand to get my attention.

I looked at Chase. "Is it safe for him to look around?"

"You go right ahead, buddy," Chase said. "Everything's solid in here. We'll get in to paint and repair the cracks in the plaster soon. The rugs need replacing, but that can wait a bit. You've got hardwood in the bedrooms. Looks rough, but the boards themselves are good—not rotting or anything."

I shook my head in disbelief. "Is there a kitchen? Bathroom?"

"'Course," Chase said. "Kitchen's through there." He gestured toward the arched doorway off the living room. Then he pointed toward the short hallway off the other side of the room where Henry had gone exploring. "Bedrooms and bathroom are down that way. You go ahead and take a look around. I'll start bringing up your stuff."

"Oh, you don't have to do that!" I said quickly. "We really didn't bring that much."

Chase winked. "Well, all the more reason for me to take care of it. Y'all get settled." He set the manila folder and keys on the credenza. "I'll just leave all this here for you to look over. The code for the front door is in there, too. Be back in a few minutes."

"Thanks," I called after him, bemused. The apartment was far better than I'd dared hope. The first person I'd met was as friendly as I could ask for. If they were all as welcoming as Chase, it was going to be hard to leave when Whit decided it was time for us to go. But, for now, I wasn't about to complain.

Starting to feel cautiously happy with my decision and maybe even a little excited, I went to find Henry to get his reaction.

"Henry?" I called, heading to the first bedroom. "Where are you, baby?"

I peered inside, taking it all in. Everything in this room was covered in sheets as well and was thick with shadows. "Henry?"

I heard him giggle in the next room and smiled, turning to go see what he found so amusing. When I poked my head around the door jamb, I saw him sitting in the middle of the floor, playing with a pile of action figures he'd apparently dug out of a toybox I could see just inside the open closet. All the sheets had already been removed from the furniture—a simple twin bed, dresser, and bookshelf filled with children's books. The drapes were open, revealing a small air conditioning unit in the window.

The paint on the walls was chipped and worn down to plaster in some places and the white paint on the ceiling curled up in one corner where I guessed there'd been a leak. Across from the closet, a large crack spanned a good portion of the wall, but it was still an improvement over what Henry had had in the one little bedroom at the old house.

Henry giggled again, drawing my attention back to him.

"What were you laughing at?" I asked, coming in and turning on the air conditioning unit. It kicked on with a loud whir, the cool air blasting me in the face and chilling the sweat that had accumulated beneath my hair. I closed my eyes, briefly enjoying the artificial breeze.

"The funny pictures in the closet," Henry answered before returning his attention to the action figures. "I'm gonna get you this time, Doc Ock! No way, Spiderman!"

My heart filled with such happiness at seeing my son enjoying our new home, that the tears stinging my eyes weren't tears of frustration for once. Blinking rapidly before Henry could see them, I went to the closet to see the pictures he'd mentioned.

Several crayon drawings were taped to the back wall of the walk-in closet. One showed a little boy stick figure holding hands with a mommy and daddy stick figure and a house with smoke coming from the chimney. A sweet little family scene. The next was a child's rendition of what I suspected was supposed to be Spiderman.

"Hey, Henry, which of these pictures did you think were funny?" I asked, frowning at the sweet drawings—drawings I wouldn't have parted with for anything if they'd been Henry's. In fact, I had a whole folder of them in one of the boxes in the car.

Henry scrambled to his feet and ran to the closet. "Not those," he said, pointing to the ones on the wall. "The ones in the desk."

On another wall of the closet sat a little desk just the right size for a child. It had a top that lifted like an old-timey school desk I'd seen once in an antique shop, and initials had been scratched into the corner—*DP*.

I grinned, running my fingertips over the carved letters, wondering if they belonged to the little boy who had apparently stayed in this room before his parents had skipped town.

"Here," Henry said, lifting the desktop. He pulled out a stack of crayon drawings and handed them to me.

The first couple of drawings *were* cute. A puppy making a silly face. A bunny with green ears and a purple nose. More attempts at various superhero characters—a happy-looking Hulk and a broadly grinning Thor. But the next in the stack showed a stick figure of a child with curly blond hair—the little girl downstairs, maybe? Or was it a little boy? Hard to tell. Next to the child figure was a stick figure of a woman with long dark hair. Her eyes were black circles, and her mouth was a squiggly line, making her appear angry.

Definitely *not* a happy little family scene...

The next drawing was even more disturbing. The angry woman again, but this time, she held a knife that dripped with blood. Next to her was the child, its head of golden curls lying on the ground at the woman's feet.

"Jesus," I murmured, horrified by the disturbing drawings. "What the hell?"

Whatever had been going on with the previous tenants, one thing was certain—their kid was deeply troubled.

"Maybe we should put these somewhere safe in case he comes back for them," I suggested, hoping Henry had only seen the first few.

Henry's mouth turned down in a pout. "But David said I could have them."

I paused in gathering the papers, my brows drawing together in confusion. "Who?"

"David," Henry told me. "The little boy in the closet."

My flesh prickled with goosebumps and the hair on the back of my neck rose, but I forced a smile, ignoring the sudden closeness of the closet.

"Well," I said, gathering up the rest of the papers and steering Henry out before closing the door, "I'll put them up for a while. If he doesn't want them back in a couple of weeks, you can have them."

Henry shrugged. "Okay. Do I still get to play with his toys?"

I took in the room again, making note of more toys than I'd originally noticed. "Are all these toys David's?"

Henry sat back down on the ground to continue playing. "Well, kinda. They were someone else's, but now they're his. He said he'd share them with me if I shared mine with him."

I shuddered, suddenly colder than what the little air conditioning unit could cause but immediately chastised myself for being freaked out by what Henry had told me. We hadn't even been in the new apartment for an hour, and I was already allowing what had happened at the old place with the intruder to put me on edge. Henry just had an active imagination. That was all.

"Is David your new friend?" I asked, willing to play along.

Henry nodded. "Yep!"

I experienced a pang in my chest, feeling for the millionth time that it was my fault Henry didn't have any friends. I'd berated myself I don't know how many times, my mom guilt in overdrive: If only I'd been able to afford to live in a better neighborhood, maybe he wouldn't be so lonely. If only I'd tracked down his father and asked for his assistance. If only, if only, if only...

But this was a fresh start for both of us, with a chance to make new friends. I'd never had many friends growing up thanks to our frequent moves and had made up a few imaginary friends too, so I wasn't going to take that away from Henry if that's what he needed right now to cope with the changes in our life.

"Well, I hope I get to meet him sometime," I said, sitting down on the floor with Henry and leaning forward to squeeze his hand. "But, hey, I have an idea—maybe we can go meet Adelaide once we get unpacked. Wouldn't that be fun?"

Henry shrugged. "I dunno. David says he doesn't like Adelaide."

I frowned. "Why not?"

He shrugged again. "He says she doesn't ever talk to him, so he doesn't like her."

A whisper of a breeze at the back of my neck chilled me to the bone once more. Except the air conditioning unit was directly across from me, not behind me.

"Hey, y'all!"

I started so hard every muscle in my body contracted.

"I brought little man's toys first," Chase called, his voice growing closer as he came down the hall toward us.

Embarrassed by my overreaction, I scrambled to my feet and snatched up the stack of drawings as Chase entered with the box of action figures, toy cars, and stuffed animals.

He paused in the doorway, flicking a glance at the papers in my hands. "Everything okay?"

"Yeah," I said with a nervous laugh. "Yeah, it's great. Just taking a look at Henry's room. I still can't believe they left all this behind."

Chase set the box down and took the room in. "Never know what people will do when they're backed into a corner."

CHAPTER THREE

I'd finished tucking my few clothes into drawers while Henry went down for a nap and was trying to figure out where to hang the artwork I'd brought with us when someone knocked on the apartment door. I opened it to see a slightly hunched elderly man with a shock of wild white hair and narrow, pale-blue eyes.

"May I help you?" I asked, ignoring his scowl.

"I don't like crumb snatchers," he said without preamble, "and I hear you have one. I'd prefer *not* to hear him running around at all hours of the night, keeping me awake."

"You must be Mr. Dean," I replied. "Well, no need to worry, Mr. Dean. Henry doesn't run around all night. He's in bed by eight o'clock. Is there anything else I can do for you?"

In reply, Mr. Dean grunted and shuffled away, leaving me shaking my head.

"Nice to meet you, too," I murmured.

So maybe not all *my neighbors were going to be friendly.*

I barely closed the door and had turned away when a loud pounding rattled it again. Irritated with the crochety old man, I shot a glance toward the hallway where Henry slept then yanked open the door.

"Listen, Mr. Dean—"

My words died on my tongue. The hallway was empty. I poked my head out farther, looking down the hall one way and then the other. At each end, the white curtains billowed in the cross-breeze, lifting and falling in a graceful dance.

As I peered down toward the end with the missing gate, the curtains lifted again, and just for a heartbeat, revealed a pair of bare feet before the sheer material drifted down, settling upon what appeared to be the figure of a woman.

"Be careful!" I yelled, rushing out of my apartment and toward the figure. "You'll fall!"

But I'd only gone a few steps before the curtains lifted once more, revealing nothing but the open doorway. I stopped short, suddenly finding it difficult to move. "What the hell?"

Pushing through my momentary paralysis, I slowly backed toward the apartment, my eyes never leaving the curtains as they continued to flutter. As soon as I reached the door, I pivoted and grasped the doorknob with both hands, but it refused to turn.

Locked.

With Henry asleep inside.

"Shit!"

Instinctively, I patted my hips, immediately reminded that my sundress had no pockets. *Of course.* But even if it had, I now recalled the key was still on the credenza.

Right next to my phone.

I groaned and pressed my forehead to the door.

Shit, shit, shit.

I tried the door again, just in case I hadn't turned the knob hard enough, but it refused to budge. I slammed my palm against the door several times, hoping it might wake Henry so he could let me back in.

"Henry?" I called, pounding again. "Wake up, baby. Come let Mama in!"

I pressed my ear to the door, listening for movement, but heard nothing but the soft *thwap* of the curtains in the breeze. I tried twice more, but sometimes when Henry was asleep, a freight train running through his bedroom couldn't wake him.

I cursed again and leaned back against the door. The buzz of a saw droned somewhere outside. I rushed to the gated door and wrangled the curtains out of the way to see if maybe the noise was Chase working down below. But the yard was empty.

"Damn it," I spat, sending a conflicted glance toward the apartment. I'd have to go hunt down Chase to get him to open the door. But what if Henry woke up while I was gone? What if he went wandering out of the apartment to look for me? What if he saw the barefooted woman, too, and got too close to the open door? What if—

"Stop it, Zellie!" I ordered aloud, pushing the intrusive thoughts out of my mind. The longer I waited, deliberated, imagining the worst-case scenarios, the more likely it was that Henry might wake up.

I hurried toward the elevator, glancing around nervously, not eager to encounter the person whose feet I'd seen earlier. I was a few steps from the elevator when a door creaked open behind me, bringing me up short. I swallowed hard. My stomach twisted with fear as I forced myself to turn around.

Our apartment door stood open, the stained-glass lampshades spilling dim, jeweled light into the hallway.

My steps were slow, hesitant as I approached the doorway. My heart pounded in my ears, the pulsing *woosh* of my blood drowning out any other sound. I tried to swallow again, but my mouth had gone dry.

When I reached the doorway, I peered cautiously inside. "Henry?"

No answer.

I placed my palm on the door and eased it open, then scanned the living room.

Nothing.

Relief loosened the knots in my stomach. "Nice, Zellie," I muttered. "No more scary movies for you."

I turned to close the door. And screamed.

A woman in a white nightgown stood inches away, a crimson stain across her abdomen, her bedraggled black hair caked with grime, her bare feet muddy. But it was her eyes—sunken black pools of darkness—that terrified me most.

I slammed the door, my hands shaking violently as I secured the deadbolt, then stumbled back several steps, tripping over myself and landing hard.

"What the fuck?" I screeched, my throat tight with fear.

"Mama?"

I screamed again, my head snapping toward Henry's voice.

"What's wrong, Mama?" Henry asked from where he stood in the hallway, his bottom lip trembling. "What happened?"

I glanced at the door, half expecting the woman on the other side to burst in, then scrambled to my feet and rushed toward Henry. I scooped him up and hurried to the credenza, grabbing my phone.

"It's okay, baby," I managed, my voice thin. I used my free hand to try to make the call, but the phone slipped from my fingers and landed with a thud on the floor.

With a little strangled sob, I sank down with Henry and snatched up the phone, hitting the number I'd added just that morning. As it rang, Henry studied me with wide eyes and then wrapped his arms around me and gave me a tight hug.

"It's okay, Mama," he whispered. "David says he's sorry. He won't lock you out again."

My breath caught in my chest, and I leaned away from Henry. Now it was my turn to study *him*. He offered me a sweet smile, his face one of pure innocence, then kissed my cheek and hugged me again.

What the actual fuck *was going on?*

"Hello? Ms. Dupont? Zellie?"

Hearing my name snapped me out of my shock. "There's someone up here," I blurted, knowing I sounded hysterical and not giving a damn. "There's someone in the hallway!"

Whit Proffitt wasn't what I expected.

When he showed up at my door, Chase in tow, I was taken aback by how different they were. The men seemed to be roughly the same age, but unlike the suave golden boy with the easy grin, Whit's hair was as dark as his somber expression as he peered down at me, taking in every inch of me with disconcerting scrutiny, a frown furrowing his brow. Something flickered briefly behind his dark eyes—surprise, maybe?—but he recovered quickly.

"Are you hurt?" he asked by way of greeting.

The depth of his concern brought a flush of heat to my skin. "No," I said, shaking my head. "I'm okay. Just freaked out."

"Stay here," he ordered. Then to Chase, "You start in the basement."

As Whit made his way down the hall, I noticed that unlike his cousin, who ambled with the unconcerned confidence of someone who'd never worried about being noticed, Whit moved as quietly and as gracefully as the shadows. There was nothing lacking in his confidence. It was more like he didn't *want* to be seen.

He was how I'd often imagined the Byronic hero in a novel by one of the Brontë sisters, a Mr. Rochester or a Heathcliff—but hopefully without the toxic manipulation or destructive rage. It was a good thing he was my landlord; otherwise, he would've been exactly my type (not that I'd really even dated enough to *have* a type, but still...).

While Whit left to search the floor below, I leaned against the frame of my apartment door, hyperalert and nervously nibbling the skin at the edge of my thumb as I waited. Several minutes later, he returned, his arms raised at his sides in a shrug that seemed a little bit apology, a little bit concern.

"I'm not seeing evidence anyone was here," he said. "I checked out the other apartment down the hall and the other floors, but no one's here that shouldn't be."

"Someone *was* here," I assured him in a harsh whisper. "I didn't imagine it. She was right outside my freaking door!"

Chase had sauntered up during the exchange, his thumbs casually hooked in his pockets, completely unconcerned by what I claimed. "I'm sure my cousin isn't saying you imagined it," he replied. "Just saying that maybe you misunderstood what you saw. This is an old house. Odd noises, shadows everywhere and all that."

I pushed off the doorframe with a huff, suddenly feeling gaslighted. "Right."

Chase grabbed my elbow as I turned to go inside the apartment, but when I sent an alarmed look to where he held my arm, he immediately let go. "Sorry," he said, raising both hands and glancing at his cousin before taking a step back. "Didn't mean to scare you. It's just that it's been a long day for you and your little guy."

"Sure," I replied, dismissing him with a wave of my hand. "Thanks."

"Ms. Dupont—*Zellie*," Whit said, his voice going deeper when he said my name. "I'll personally check all the exterior doors and make sure they're locked. No one should be able to get into the building without a door code, but we'll check our security cameras outside, make sure someone didn't sneak in somehow."

I nodded. "Okay. Thank you."

He stepped toward me and said more gently, "If anyone *was* in here, they're gone now. You don't need to worry."

The nearness of him was distracting as I tried to determine if he was just placating me or if he genuinely believed what he said. Finally, I decided on the latter. "I hope you're right."

He offered what I figured was supposed to be a reassuring smile, but it didn't quite seem to fit. But my heartbeat still quickened.

Misreading my hesitation to go back inside the apartment, his brows furrowed in concern. "Is there something else? Do you want us to look around in the apartment as well?"

"No, it's okay," I said with a shrug, not even sounding convincing to myself. "I'll be fine. Like Chase said, old building and all that."

Whit gave me a curt nod and turned to go, but Chase grasped his upper arm and stopped him before he could take a step. "Hey, here's an idea," Chase announced. "Zellie, why don't you and Henry come hang out in the game room tonight? I'll order some pizza, see if any of the others want to come meet you all. I'm sure we can even persuade my delightfully loquacious cousin to join us. What y'all think?"

"I don't know..." I hedged, catching the exasperated look Whit sent his cousin. "We still have a lot to do."

"It'll be there tomorrow," Chase assured me. "Plus, it'll give you a chance to get to know June and Earl since Henry will be staying with them when you're working."

Whit cursed under his breath.

I shook my head, not understanding. "Wait—what? What are you talking about? I haven't found a job yet, let alone childcare."

Chase glanced between Whit and me. "Oh. Sorry. I just figured Whit had talked to you about it."

I sent Whit a pointed look as I replied to Chase, "Your cousin sure likes to make decisions for other people without their input."

Chase chuckled and smacked Whit on the back. "Yeah, he's always been a bossy son of a bitch. Thinks he's quite the fixer of everyone's problems. But he's a good guy. Just used to people doing what he says, that's all. Ain't that right, Cousin?"

Whit's dark eyes flashed with annoyance, and he looked like he could murder his outspoken cousin. "Someone has to keep you all in line, *Cousin.*"

I straightened and raised my chin defiantly. "Well, I'm not most people, Mr. Proffitt."

Whit's lips twitched as if he was suppressing a grin and inclined his head in what I took to be an apology. "I'm beginning to see that."

Something about the way he said it brushed warm across my skin, kicking up my heartbeat another notch.

Chase's eyes sparkled with amusement. "So, about that pizza?"

I studied them both for a moment before making my decision. "Okay. And thank you. We'll see you downstairs later."

"Ms. Dupont—"

I closed the door before Whit could say another word and leaned against it, squeezing my eyes shut. I didn't know what scared me more—the fact that Whit and Chase hadn't seen anyone or the fact that I *had.*

I hadn't imagined it. I knew that for damned sure. That woman had been there, and she'd needed help. She'd either been injured or had injured someone else if the amount of blood on her nightgown was any indication.

In hindsight, I realized I probably should've called the police instead of reaching out to Whit. I honestly couldn't even have said why I'd called *him*, of all people, and hadn't just called the police. This certainly wasn't how I'd wanted to meet my new landlord and benefactor for the first time. He probably already thought I was a pain in the ass. Now I'd just confirmed it. But having the police descending on the place when I'd only been there a few hours didn't seem like the best way to make friends with my neighbors either.

"Mama?"

I started at the sound of Henry's voice. "Oh, my gosh!" I said with a laugh. "I about jumped outta my skin!"

He laughed. "I got you, Mama!"

I scooped him up and gave him a tight hug. "You sure did! Now, how about we finish unpacking? And later we can go share some pizza with our neighbors."

"Yes, ma'am!" Henry agreed. "Not the frozen kind of pizza?"

I shook my head. "Nope, not the frozen kind. The pizza place kind."

Henry wiggled to be put down. "Then I gotta go put away my toys."

He ran to his room, his little feet pounding on the hardwood.

Mr. Dean will be thrilled.

"Too bad, you grumpy old man," I muttered, grabbing a box of books near the built-in bookshelves. They flanked a gorgeous brick and stone fireplace, which I supposed was just ornamental at this point. Just as well. The air was thick and humid, making my clothes cling to me even with the air conditioning unit running full blast. There was no way in hell I was going to think about a fire in the fireplace anytime soon.

Still rattled by the mysterious woman—and by the darkly handsome Mr. Proffitt—I focused my attention on unpacking.

As I arranged my books among those the previous tenant had left behind, I handled each one lovingly, running my fingertips over the covers and spines, a sense of peace coming over me. Books had been my lifeline during my childhood and certainly still were. I'd read everything I could get my hands on, making weekly trips to whatever library was close by. And this precious collection was a variety of titles from classics to science fiction to romance to poetry—books I'd bought at garage sales, library sales, thrift stores...wherever I could find them and whenever I'd had a couple of bucks to spare. A few had been gifts from Vivian when she remembered to get me a present for my birthday or Christmas—sweet, wholesome titles that "wouldn't corrupt the soul."

I lifted out my children's Bible and flipped through the pages, shaking my head at the melodramatic illustrations of Noah's ark with a rainbow arching over it, blinded Sampson using the last of his strength to destroy his enemies and himself in the process, a very Euro-Jesus in long robes speaking to a group of wide-eyed children gathered around him.

I set it on the shelf and picked up my other Bible, a gift from Pastor Ted, the preacher my mom had zealously followed for a while during her Protestant phase when I was a pre-teen. Ted had liked to hug me a little too much, but Vivian had hung on his every word, never questioning a thing he said. Even at that age, I'd suspected that Vivian had been having an affair with the supposed man of God and pillar of the community during their private Bible study sessions.

I wasn't sure why I'd kept the Bible all these years, except that it was a book and I kept them all. And maybe because it was a reminder of how I *wasn't* going to live my life, sleeping with people to get something out of them, and then moving on, ignoring what was going on with my own kid instead of facing uncomfortable truths.

When I finished unpacking the books, I went to the kitchen to put away the little bit of food I'd brought with us—mostly cereal and snacks for Henry. There'd been no way to bring perishables, so we'd finished off the last of the milk and yogurt that morning before setting out to Savannah. I'd have to get to the market yet that day—a prospect that always induced soul-killing anxiety.

I pulled up my banking app to check my balance and did a few quick calculations in my head to figure out how much would be left after buying what we needed. A familiar sinking feeling in the pit of my stomach sunk a little deeper than usual. I'd been paid my last check at the coffee shop, plus a little extra for my unused vacation time, so I would have enough for a week or two, barring any emergencies. But it wouldn't last long.

The light pounding of tiny feet running on the hardwood in the living room drew me out of my thoughts. I called over my shoulder, "Henry, baby, please don't run! You'll disturb our neighbor, Mr. Dean."

Instead of answering, he ran across the room again, giggling.

"Henry James Dupont!" I scolded. "What did I say?"

When he just giggled again in response, I huffed and strode into the living room, hands on my hips. "Young man—"

But the room was empty.

Frowning, I glanced under the credenza, behind the couch, to make sure my mischievous five-year-old wasn't hiding from me, determined to scare me again. But he was nowhere to be found.

"Henry?" I called as I headed toward the bedroom. "Where are you, baby?"

When he still didn't answer, my chest grew tight with panic.

"Henry!"

"Yes, ma'am?" he said, coming out of the bathroom. "I was going potty. And there are more toys in the bathroom! Do you want to see?"

I stared at him, baffled. If he'd been in the bathroom, then who'd been running around the living room and giggling?

"Um, sure," I said with a shake of my head and a forced smile. "The people who lived here before left a lot of cool stuff, didn't they?"

"Yes, ma'am!" he said, grabbing my hand and pulling me into the bathroom. He pointed to a basket of tub toys and foam letters that would stick to the side of the tub when wet. "Look, I can spell my words when I take a bath. And there are little boats and alligators and squirty fish!"

I couldn't help smiling at Henry's excitement. I'd bought him a few bath toys at the dollar store, but these were much nicer than what I'd been able to afford. There were even waterproof books we could read together while I was giving him a bath.

But as grateful as I was for the things the previous family had left behind, it somehow seemed wrong to use them. What if they came back? What if they wanted to get all the stuff they'd left behind? What was I going to tell Henry?

Sorry, baby, I'd love to buy you toys, but...

No. I'd figure it out if they ever came back. No sense borrowing trouble. I'd done everything I could to shield Henry from the knowledge of just how tight money was, and I'd continue to do so however I had to. And when I finished my classes and got my degree, I'd get a good job and a better place to live and toys that didn't fall apart after a few weeks.

A loud clatter made us both jump and turn toward the bathtub. A plastic shelf that had held soap and a couple of bottles of shampoo had fallen from the wall, scattering its contents across the bottom of the tub.

"What the heck!" Henry cried.

"Careful, mister," I said, tousling his curls.

"That scared my bejeepers, Mama," Henry said, panting theatrically, palm against his chest.

I laughed. "You mean it scared the bejeepers out of you?"

"No, ma'am," he said, solemnly shaking his head. "They're still in me. I can *feel* 'em."

I laughed again, forgetting my worries and allowing myself to enjoy my son's unintentional humor. "Okay, if you say so. Why don't we just throw this stuff away? We'll get you some new soap and shampoo and maybe even some bubble bath. Sound good?'

"Yes, ma'am!" he said, his excited grin returning. "Can David use it too?"

I cleared my throat, which had gone tight at the mention of Henry's new "friend" and glanced over my shoulder to the empty hallway. "Uh, sure. Yeah."

"He's not in the hallway," Henry told me, rolling his eyes as he grabbed my hand and led me out of the bathroom. "Let's check my room."

My skin prickled in warning, and I resisted, pulling him toward me. "You can tell him later. Let's go to the market so we can get back in time for pizza."

As I ushered Henry from the hallway, I sent a glance over my shoulder again, half-expecting to see someone standing behind me. From the corner of my eye, for just a fraction of a second, I thought I noticed the shadows shift slightly, growing darker, longer, creeping closer.

Not waiting to see what happened next, I scooped up Henry, ignoring his protest, and rushed to the apartment door, praying nothing was waiting on the other side.

CHAPTER FOUR

"You live here?"

I turned from juggling two grocery bags and the slip of paper with the front-door code Chase had given me. A guy holding a stack of pizza boxes stood at the bottom of the steps.

"Yeah," I said. "I can let you in to drop those off. I assume they're for Chase Crawford?"

"Yes, ma'am." He hurried up the steps and somehow took my grocery bags from me without dropping the pizzas. I keyed in the code, shielding the numbers with my hand—just in case the pizza guy wasn't quite the gentleman he seemed.

"Where you want me to put these, ma'am?" the guy asked.

I glanced around the lobby, looking for other tenants, but no one else was around. "Uh, just there on the desk, I guess."

"Yes, ma'am," he said with a nod, setting the boxes on the corner of the desk, casting a nervous look around, then handing me back my grocery bags and rushing for the front door. "Y'all have a good night."

"Weird," I murmured, thrown by his urgency. He'd looked like he couldn't wait to get out of the house as he raced down the steps "like his hair was on fire and his ass was catchin'," as my elderly neighbor Ms. Reba used to say.

I could relate. Maybe he sensed something, too. Unfortunately, unlike him, I couldn't run away.

Determined not to let my imagination run wild in the old house, I took Henry's hand and headed toward the elevator. Henry reached for the button just as the doors slid open, revealing a young woman dressed in workout clothes and running shoes, dark coils of hair framing a beautiful face.

She offered Henry and me a friendly smile as she removed her earbuds. "Hi there!" she greeted, stepping out of the elevator. "You must be Zellie. Chase told me we had new folks moving in."

I returned her smile. "Hi. Yeah. I'm Zellie Dupont, and this is my son Henry."

"Would you like some help with those bags?" she asked, taking one from me before I could respond and stepping back inside the elevator. "You're up on the fourth floor, right?"

I shook my head as we stepped into the elevator, delighted and a little confused, not used to having help. "Yeah, thanks."

"I'm Merilee Vaughn, by the way," she told me after Henry pressed the button. "I live on the third floor, right below you."

"I thought Mr. Dean lived below us," I replied.

Merilee offered me a mischievous grin. "Met him already, have you?"

I laughed, deciding I liked Merilee, particularly the playful twinkle in her eye that made me think she was the kind of person everyone would want for a best friend. "Came banging on my door earlier," I admitted. "He wanted to make sure my 'crumb-snatcher' wasn't running around all night. Because that's what five-year-olds do—run around all night. It's quite a party at our place."

Merilee chuckled. "That sounds like Mr. Dean." As the elevator doors opened, she added, "He likes to complain about everything, but he's harmless."

"Have you lived here long?" I asked.

Merilee shrugged slightly in response to my question. "Hmm, long enough. Seems like forever."

"Mr. Crawford told me you're a nurse," I said. "And that you care for a woman who lives here."

Merilee shook her head with a grin. "That's our Chase—he's quite the talker. Give him an audience and he'll jaw all day." She strode toward my apartment, calling over her shoulder, "But, yes, I look after Ms. Netty. She's a handful sometimes."

I unlocked the door and was a bit startled when Merilee walked right in like we hadn't just met and headed straight for the kitchen.

"Mama, can I go play in my room?" Henry begged, clearly bored.

I nodded, distracted by the woman currently putting away my groceries. "Um, yeah, sure, baby. Go ahead."

When he scampered off, I made my way to the other room. "Thank you, Ms. Vaughn, but you don't have to do that. I can manage."

Merilee closed the refrigerator door and smiled. "First, it's Merilee. Second, I'm sure you can."

The warmth of Merilee's kindness seemed to fill the room, and the uneasiness that had hung over me like a storm cloud lifted. For the first time since we'd arrived, everything felt a little...lighter. "Thank you. I do appreciate it."

"That's what neighbors are for, right?" Merilee asked. "Help each other now and then? Now, I'm gonna get my run in before Ms. Netty wakes up. You need anything, I'm just downstairs."

After Merilee left, I went looking for Henry. As I stepped into the hallway, I heard him chatting away and rubbed my arms to smooth the goosebumps rising on my skin.

"But she seems nice," Henry said as I neared his door. "I like her... You shouldn't say that. Mama says no one should say 'hate'."

I leaned against the wall, listening, curious to hear what was going on in Henry's imagination.

"I won't," Henry whispered. "I'll be careful."

At this, I shoved off the wall and strode into the bedroom. "Careful about what?" I asked, grinning so Henry wouldn't think he was in trouble.

He still started, guilt flickering across his face. "David says that I need to be careful around Ms. Merilee. He doesn't like her."

I sat on the bed and pulled Henry to me. "Well, that's just silly. You saw how nice she was to us and how friendly."

Henry nodded. "Yes, ma'am. But I want to still be careful."

"You, know, Ms. Merilee is a nurse. Is David maybe just afraid she'll give him a shot? Or a transfusion?" I asked, knowing well Henry's nervousness about this very thing every time he had a doctor's appointment. Unfortunately, thanks to his chronic anemia, both shots and transfusions were common occurrences. "Maybe he just doesn't like needles."

Henry pressed his lips together as if considering the possibility but then slowly shook his head. "No, that's not it. He won't tell me anything else. He doesn't want to talk about it."

I gave him a quick hug. "Well, that's okay. He doesn't have to until he's ready. Now, let's go grab some of that pizza and meet the rest of our neighbors."

When we entered the game room, Chase was already there, handing out slices of pizza to several people I hadn't met yet. A tall, slender woman with stark-white hair pulled up into a ponytail immediately came forward, hand outstretched. Her complexion was fair and flawless, and her blue eyes sparkled with vivacity. She was dressed in jeans and a simple white button-down but if I had to guess, that "simple" outfit cost more than my entire wardrobe.

"Come on in, darlin'," she said, her voice soft and filled with warmth. "You must be Zellie."

I shook her hand, a bit taken aback by her effusive welcome. "Yes, ma'am. Hi."

The woman took my hand in both of hers and gently patted it. "So good to have you here. We miss having young folks around. I'm June."

My brows briefly knit together. *Young folks? Chase and Merilee couldn't have been that much older than me.*

Before I could think more on it, June gestured toward a handsome, fit man with steel grey hair and chiseled features who was reclined casually in an easy chair, highball already in hand. "That's my husband Earl."

In chinos and a golf shirt, Earl looked like he belonged at the country club, not the game room of a historic apartment building. He got to his feet and raised his glass in greeting. "How do, honey. You come on in and make yourself at home."

I glanced between them, astonished at how youthful the couple seemed. If not for their hair, I would've put them thirty years younger.

"Nice to meet you," I finally managed. "This is my son, Henry."

June bent and placed her hands on her knees so she was at Henry's eye level. "It is *so* nice to meet you, Henry. You're going to be visiting us during the day while your mama is at work. Won't that be *fun*? My granddaughter Adelaide will be so *excited*!"

"Where is Addie?" Chase asked. "I thought she was just in here."

June waved a hand dismissively as she straightened. "Oh, she's outside. Can't keep that girl indoors! Henry, would you like to take your pizza outside on the patio and eat with Addie?"

He glanced up at me to gauge my reaction before nodding. "Yes, ma'am."

"Henry, stay in the yard," I ordered, nervous about letting him out of my sight so soon.

"Don't worry, Zellie," Chase said, taking my elbow to guide me over to the table. "You've got lots of eyes to watch out for him. Time for you to rest easy for a bit."

The tension slipped from my shoulders. I hadn't realized how tightly they'd been bunched into knots until that moment. "Thank you," I said, tears in my eyes, suddenly feeling less alone for the first time in a long while.

He gave my arm a squeeze before handing me a plate. "All right now," was all he said before stepping away.

I couldn't say why that simple phrase almost undid me. Maybe because, for just a few minutes, I wasn't carrying the weight of everything on my own.

"You all getting started without us?"

I looked up from my pizza to see an older couple entering the room. The woman who'd spoken was probably close in age to June, based on her close-cropped, white hair, but she too looked ageless.

Oversized, gold earrings, a statement necklace, a tennis bracelet, and an enormous diamond ring glinted in the early-evening sunlight, creating a halo of light around her. There was precisely zero chance that any of it was high-quality costume jewelry. No gold plating in that room. And the loose, flowing ensemble she wore was in a bright print every bit as bold as I imagined she was. If June carried herself with graceful poise, the woman who'd just entered commanded the room like a queen.

"We know better," June said with a bright grin. She greeted the woman with a hug as if she was a long-lost friend and not a neighbor who lived just down the hall. She then turned to me and gestured with a thin, pale hand. "Pearlie, honey, this lovely young woman right here is Zellie Dupont. Zellie, this is Pearlie Johnson."

I set my plate aside and smoothed the front of my sundress, which suddenly seemed inadequate for the impromptu gathering. The women of Dawes House that I'd met so far were beautiful, fashionable, clearly used to finer things and probably fancier food than pizza.

Pearlie had an air of wisdom and kindness about her, but when she turned her attention to me, I could see in her dark eyes that beneath her grandmotherly persona, she had an edge that could slice through bullshit like a hot knife through butter. Even so, her smile appeared genuine when she reached out both hands and came toward me to grasp mine, lifting my arms away from my sides as if to get a better look at me.

"Well, now," she drawled. "Aren't you a pretty little thing? I think you'll do quite nicely."

I frowned again, confused by what she meant. "Sorry?"

"As a neighbor," she clarified, her smile never faltering. "You don't look like you eat enough to keep a bird alive, though! Well, don't you worry about it, baby. We'll fix that."

I forced a smile—which seemed like the thing to do—but my stomach tightened, and my mouth was too dry to respond. So, I nodded and gave a small laugh, like someone who'd just walked into a joke at the punchline but didn't want to be the only one who didn't get it.

"Pearlie, give the girl a little room to breathe," a deep male voice said on a chuckle. "She's barely moved in—I think putting some meat on her bones with your fabulous cooking can wait a day or two, honey."

Pearlie laughed and swatted the air dismissively at the man who'd entered the common room with her. "Oh, go on, Junior. I'm just being welcoming."

She gave my hands a squeeze then took the cocktail Earl handed her. She didn't say a word but gave a curt nod of her head, simultaneously thanking and dismissing him.

Watching, I thought this must've been what it was like when a CEO enters a room—charming and warm and no doubt that she's in charge. Her husband, by contrast, was like the churning wake her powerful presence left behind—tall, immediately likable, quick to laugh or make a joke with Earl or the others.

Even though I still felt like the poor kid peering into the window from the outside, it wasn't for a lack of hospitality on their part. Every one of them was eager to make sure I was comfortable, that I'd had enough to eat, that I had enough to drink, especially Earl who seemed to be the de facto Dawes House bartender (and who I discovered was very generous with a pour).

I checked on Henry, who was sitting at a bistro table under a shade tree, laughing and chatting merrily with a pretty little girl with blond, curly hair. She was wearing a surprisingly fancy pink party dress, her legs swinging happily. I'd just turned to accept the blessedly cold drink Earl was handing me when I sensed a dramatic shift in the atmosphere.

Everyone seemed to stiffen at once, and I swear the temperature in the room dropped by a few degrees. Ridiculous. I knew it even then. And yet that's what it was like as all heads turned to the doorway to see Whit standing there, looking even more out of place than I felt.

He swept the room in a glance, his expression unreadable. Not waiting for an invitation, he sauntered in and strolled along the perimeter with what would've seemed like nonchalance if not for the charged energy filling the air. He scrutinized each face as if he could see straight through to their darkest sins.

I glanced at Chase, uneasy for reasons I didn't fully understand. He winked and got to his feet, raising his glass to greet his cousin. "Well, as I live and breathe, if it isn't the illustrious Whit Proffitt. C'mon on in, Cousin! Wasn't sure you were gonna make it, but I'm sure glad you did. Ain't that right, y'all? Watcha drinkin', Whit?"

Pearlie came forward, taking his hands in hers and kissing his cheek. "How are you, baby? We haven't seen you much."

"Pearlie," Whit said by way of greeting. "Good to see you." He nodded toward Pearlie's husband. "Junior." He then turned to June and Earl, who were not as thrilled to see him as Chase and the Johnsons. "June. Earl. I'm glad to see you've met Zellie."

June forced a smile and busied herself with the pizza boxes. Making more of an effort, Earl and Junior greeted Whit warmly, slapping him on the back as men do, their voices outwardly friendly, but I still sensed something just beneath the surface, a tension that had been pulled taut to the point of snapping just a moment before and hadn't quite faded.

Chase strolled over and thrust a double scotch into Whit's hand. "Thought you might could use a sip."

Whit took the glass, but his gaze searched for and held mine. Then he broke away to answer a question Junior had asked about some sport score that I can't now be bothered to remember.

But I do remember Whit's glance flicking my way again. It was fleeting, just a glance, but it was enough to make the room feel too warm, too crowded. Pearlie was saying something about Sunday, but I just nodded, not really hearing.

Breathe, Zellie. Breathe.

Afraid I was about to pass out, I excused myself from Pearlie and stepped onto the patio where Henry and Adelaide were giggling together over some secret joke.

When he saw me, Henry hopped up and scurried over, jumped up and down a couple of times, squeezing my hand.

"I want to dig things up with Addie!" he announced. "Can I, Mama?"

I shook my head, puzzled. "What kinds of things?"

"In the flowers," he said, irritated with having to explain. "Addie said she found *bones.*"

"Bones!" *What the hell?* "What kind of bones?"

"Pirate bones!" Addie exclaimed, hopping off her chair and joining Henry to grab my hand, both of them bouncing with excitement.

I hesitated, taking in the walled garden—beds teeming with flowers, trellises braided with vines and climbing flora, the air thick with their perfume. An artificial stream flowed over rocks, under an arched white footbridge, and pooled in a small pond. I hadn't seen anything so beautiful since a field trip to the botanical gardens in middle school.

"I dunno," I said. "You probably need to ask if it's okay to dig in the flowers. Someone's done a lot of work out here."

"Oh, it's okay," Addie said with a shrug, shoving her unruly curls off her face only for them to fall back into her eyes. "My Mamaw June lets me dig all the time. I have my own shovel and everything. I can share with Henry."

I had the distinct impression I'd been out-maneuvered by—what?—a six-year-old?

"Please, please, pleeeease," they pleaded, drawing out the last *please* like waiting for my answer was torture.

I laughed, happy to see Henry had already made friends with Addie. Unable to resist their eager faces, I nodded. "Okay, okay. But you'd better change your dress, Addie."

Permission granted, Addie pivoted and dashed toward the house. Henry turned to follow, but stopped short, his shoulders drooping a little. He didn't have the same energy as his new friend. Instead, he hurried back to the table, snatched up the rest of his pizza, and finished it off, ready for when Addie returned.

A few minutes later, Addie burst from the house in shorts and T-shirt, shovel and plastic pail in hand. They hurried to a mostly barren flowerbed that must've been the area reserved for Addie's projects.

Grinning and not ready to go inside to whatever tension was brewing among the residents, I sat down on a wrought-iron bench and closed my eyes, listening to the children play. The scape of a small shovel against dirt. The faint *tink* of metal against stone. Water burbling under the little bridge.

"Mind if I join you?"

Whit's voice startled me. I hadn't even heard him come out.

I sent a glance his way—which apparently was invitation enough because he sat down beside me. I could only stare, baffled. He must've noticed my confusion because he grinned, a crack appearing in his stony façade.

"Did no one tell you staring was impolite, Ms. Dupont?" he teased.

I shook my head and chuckled, embarrassed. "Sorry. I wasn't expecting company. Especially not—"

"Especially not me?" he finished for me with a sly smile.

I looked to where Henry and Addie played and leaned forward, gripping the edge of the bench. "We don't exactly travel in the same circles, Mr. Proffitt."

He scoffed, a short, dismissive sound. "Be grateful for that."

"Be grateful that everyone here at Dawes House might as well be wearing shirts made of hundred-dollar bills while I'm relying on my landlord's charity to keep my son and me off the street?" I asked. "I'll trade you."

After a beat, he said, "I'm sorry. That was insensitive."

I sighed. "It's okay. I'm just tired. Long day. I shouldn't snap at you. You've been more accommodating than a lot of landlords would be."

"More than you expected, if our first conversations are any indication," he said. "I'm not used to people hanging up on me."

I groaned and let my head hang between my shoulders for a few seconds before meeting his eyes, squinting a little from the light filtering through the trees. "And yet you're still sitting here talking with me."

The corners of his mouth twitched with amusement. "A little rejection now and then can be good for the soul."

I shook my head, confused by his attention. "So...why exactly did you come out here? Seems like you could've collected enough rejection from the other tenants to last you a while."

He nodded, the humor gone. "I apologize for the tension when I arrived. You weren't the only one concerned about me taking over for my father. Old family dispute. Nothing for you to worry about. They like you. You'll do fine."

I frowned. *There's that phrase again...*

Before I could think more on it, he settled back, draping his arm over the back of the bench, stretching out long legs in tan linen pants, and crossing his ankles.

The leather summer loafers he wore probably cost more than my rent, but he wasn't showing them off, I could tell. Old money carried wealth with effortless indifference that eluded those who were new to luxury and extravagance. Being a barista wasn't my ideal job, but it certainly had given me the opportunity to observe all kinds of people.

"How did you meet my father?" Whit asked abruptly.

From the flowerbed, the shovel scraped stone, the sound a tinny rasp.

"Oh...uh..." I hesitated, not sure what all I should share. "He'd been a regular at the coffee shop where I was working, so I'd seen him a lot. But we didn't really start talking until the day my mom threw me out for getting pregnant with Henry."

"Hmmm." That was it. Just that little musing sound. I wondered if there was more he wanted to say, but when he didn't, I continued.

"I was in a panic about where I was going to live, what I was going to do," I told him. "But I didn't have any time off—and I clearly was going to need every penny—so I was at work, trying to keep from crying. I wasn't very successful. Mr. Monty asked me if I was okay, and I lost it."

He nodded as if understanding what I was saying. But for all his ease with me then, he still struck me as someone with carefully guarded secrets.

"Mr. Monty immediately asked my manager to excuse me from work," I continued, "offered to pay for my missed wages, and asked me to join him for breakfast so he could hear the rest of the story and offer me privacy from my co-workers." I laughed a little and shook my head. "I was so upset and feeling so hopeless, I didn't even think about the fact that I could've been getting in the car with some predator."

Whit turned his attention to where the kids were playing and simply said, "Indeed."

I wasn't sure what to make of his commentary, so I continued. "Mr. Monty was so kind to me, so caring. He told me I could stay at one of his properties, that I could move in that very evening. He would've done much more for me, I'm sure, if I'd asked, but I'm not someone who takes advantage of the people who give me a chance, Mr. Proffitt."

"I'm glad to hear that," he said. "I admit, I had my doubts when I first heard about you. I actually thought he might be the father of your son."

"You can't be serious!" I cried, louder than I'd intended. Henry and Addie lifted their heads from their play in surprise. I smiled and waved to assure them everything was fine and then said more quietly through clenched teeth, "What the hell are you talking about?"

"My father had a habit of collecting damaged young women, Ms. Dupont," Whit explained. "He was quick to come to the rescue of vulnerable women and then marry them. I suspected that my father intended for you to be the next Mrs. Proffitt."

I shook my head, refusing to allow this man I barely knew to tarnish the gilded image I held of his father. "No," I said, leaving no room for him to argue. "Mr. Monty wasn't like that. He was my guardian angel."

"My father was no angel," Whit assured me, speaking the words like they left a disgusting taste in his mouth. "And I don't know you, Ms. Dupont. Not really."

"Well, I'm not the kind of person who would sleep with my landlord just to get a sweet deal on my rent, Mr. Proffitt." A tremor ran through me, but my voice stayed even. "So, if that's what you were expecting when you offered for me to move into Dawes House, you can fuck right off. And I'll be out by morning."

I stood, intending to storm off with Henry and never look back, but Whit caught my fingers, gently, yet firmly enough to startle me.

"Ms. Dupont—" The pressure on my fingers increased ever so slightly. "—please don't go. I didn't mean..." He exhaled in a frustrated huff. "You might've noticed I've got a talent for saying exactly the wrong thing. I'm sorry for implying that you could be taking advantage of my father. If anything, I'd put the blame on *him* for taking advantage of *you*."

His gaze drifted from my face, down my arm to my fingertips where his thumb brushed my skin. Then, as if he'd forgotten he was still holding them, he abruptly let go and cleared his throat, shifting away on the bench so that he was no longer looking at me at all.

I studied him, trying to understand what it was that had just passed between us. My skin was oddly cold without his touch. I sat back down. For a while, we sat without saying a word, listening to Henry and Addie's chatter, a chorus of bullfrogs joining them from near the pond.

"I wish you would call me Whit," he said abruptly.

I was taken aback by the request. "Uh...okay. Sure. And you can call me Zellie. No need to be formal. I mean, you can't be that much older than I am."

He didn't respond, taking cover behind that stony mask again. When he finally spoke, the topic wasn't at all what I expected.

"My father was obsessed with his legacy," Whit said. "He was fixated on having children. I'm the only son still living and not exactly the heir he imagined. That's why I thought...what I thought. I've had quite a few stepmothers, Zellie. But after meeting you and hearing your side of things, I think perhaps my father saw something in you that reminded him of someone else he knew once. You even look like her a bit, except her hair was darker, didn't have any of the red in it that yours does."

"Mr. Monty never mentioned anyone," I told him. "What happened to her?"

"She took her life when she discovered she was pregnant," Whit said, his tone flat, matter of fact.

"Oh, my God," I gasped. "I'm so sorry."

I didn't ask for any additional details and Whit didn't offer them. It was none of my business. Monty's motivations—for helping me or for marrying however many women he'd married—were his own. I wasn't there to judge.

I thought about my own life as we sat there in silence, listening to the peaceful sounds of the spring evening, watching the lightning bugs begin their nightly dance as the sun sank lower.

How different things might have been had I lived in a different time. The desperation that Mr. Monty's friend? sister? lover? must've felt to resort to something so extreme... I'd chosen to keep Henry when I found out I was pregnant. But I'd *had* a choice—at least at that point.

"My mother threw me out when I got pregnant," I told him. "I tarnished her image with her church friends. She called me a sinner, a whore. Demanded to know who the father was."

"Did the father not offer to help you?" Whit asked.

I shook my head. "He didn't know. I..."

I shifted a little, not sure why I was sharing so much when I still barely knew Whit, had no idea if he'd judge me like others had. Maybe it was the quiet of the evening, the peacefulness that surrounded me there in the garden, peace that had eluded me my entire life. Whatever the reason, the words came out as easily as if I was talking to a trusted friend.

"I didn't know his name. A one-night stand—which isn't my style, by the way. I don't remember the details, can't really even tell you what he looked like. But I know he was wonderful. Tender. Kind. And for that one night, I loved him intensely."

Whit stared at me, a range of just barely noticeable expressions washing over his face as if he didn't know what to say.

I laughed a little, embarrassed at waxing poetic. "Sorry—I've been reading too much from the Romantic period, which isn't *romantic* at all. It's mostly tragic really."

He tilted his head, curious. "The Romantic period?"

I shrugged. "Books, poetry... It's probably my favorite literary period." I noticed his surprised expression and added, "Might come as a shock to you, Whit, but even us poor folks can read."

"Well, you sure do have a way of making me feel like I need a crowbar to pry this foot out of my mouth," he replied, shaking his head with a laugh. "Zellie, I think you might be just the one to keep me humble."

I lifted a brow at him. "Happy to oblige. Any other ways I can cut you down to size?"

He held up his hands as if warding off my attack. "No, no! I think that's enough for one night!"

We grinned at each other until the intensity of his gaze brought warmth to my cheeks, and I looked away. Was I seriously *flirting* with him? After just swearing up and down that I wasn't about to sleep with him to get a break on my rent? Way to reinforce *that* message.

Time to call it a night.

"Henry!" I called. "It's time to go in, baby!"

Henry and Addie both shouted a long, melodramatic, "Nooo!"

"Adelaide, you listen to Ms. Zellie," Whit said, his tone gentle but firm.

Addie mumbled a resigned "Yes, sir" before brushing her curls out of her face, leaving a muddy streak across her forehead. I smothered a grin, deciding I already adored the quirky little girl.

The kids jogged over to us, Henry lagging a little behind, panting heavier than I liked.

Yeah, definitely time to go.

I stood and lifted him up on my hip. "I'm sure you'll see Addie again soon," I promised, smoothing his curls, damp from the humidity. "Now, tell Addie and Mr. Proffitt goodnight."

"Bye, Addie," Henry said, stifling a yawn. Then he held out a hand to Whit. "Goodnight, Mr. Proffitt."

Whit solemnly shook his hand. "Goodnight, Henry. I hope we get the chance to see each other again soon."

Whit held open the door, but I paused before stepping inside. "I don't know what I would've done if Mr. Monty hadn't helped me."

Whit studied me for a moment before saying, "I have no doubt you'd have figured out something."

"Maybe," I said softly. "But I think you might be more like your father than you realize."

"I'm no saint, Zellie," Whit insisted, something in his voice telling me that was half confession, half promise.

He stood so close I could feel the heat of him warming the space between us. I looked up into his eyes—dark, hypnotic—and something inside me tightened in a way I hadn't experienced in years. I realized I actually *liked* this quiet, mysterious man. More than liked him. And the pull between us was undeniable, palpable. And dangerous.

If Henry and Addie hadn't been there, if the murmur of voices from the game room hadn't cut across the moment, I don't know how the night might've ended. And judging by the way he looked at me, he felt the same.

I drew in a steadying breath, gathering the scent of the evening air into my lungs, focusing on that instead of the nearness of Whit Proffitt, and forced myself to turn away. When we stepped inside, conversation halted and several curious faces turned to us. Merilee was among them now, I noticed. Her knowing grin grew, and she winked—at me or at Whit, I couldn't tell.

I cleared my throat and smiled politely. "Thank you all for such a warm welcome. And, Chase, thank you for organizing this. It was wonderful. I'm really happy to be here. But if you'll excuse me, I need to get this little guy to bed."

Everyone burst into cheerful chatter and goodnights. Pearlie wrapped me in a motherly hug and ordered me to come see her if I needed *anything.*

As I carried Henry toward the elevator, I let the warmth of my new home envelop me. But beneath it, Pearlie's words echoed, raising questions I wasn't ready to ask just then.

She'll do just fine...

CHAPTER FIVE

Two days after moving in, I'd just tucked Henry into bed after reading "just one more" story when Whit texted that a friend of his family wanted to talk with me about a job. A job. Really, the man was unbelievable. If I hadn't desperately needed work, I might've resented his help, even considered it interference—like when he'd arranged for childcare with someone I'd never even met. But instead, I was grinning like a teenager getting a text from her crush.

Stupid, stupid, stupid.

I sent a brief, businesslike reply thanking him for the lead and promising to follow up, then looked up the business online. It was a used bookstore and coffee shop appropriately called Ever After Coffee and Books. It was perfect, exactly the type of place I'd always dreamed of working.

Damn it all.

"Mama!"

I sighed, already knowing what was coming. Henry was relentless when it came to his bedtime reading. I couldn't blame him, though. He came by it honestly. And I knew these times would be gone all too soon, so I always caved.

"What's up, baby?" I called, walking back down the hall to his room. "You're supposed to be going to sleep. No more stories tonight."

But when I entered the room, Henry was fast asleep, blankets tucked beneath his chin, gripped in his little fists, his eyes buttoned up tight.

A chill ran along my spine like a thousand squirming spider legs. I crept in, trembling as I scanned the shadows, praying I wouldn't find anything, that maybe Henry had just called out to me in his sleep.

Thankfully finding nothing, I sank down onto the foot of Henry's bed, willing my pounding heart to slow down, reassuring myself that it was fine.

Shaken, but forcing the unusual incident out of my mind, I went into the bathroom and started a bath, opening the frosted window a crack when the room grew a little too warm, but not wide enough to let anyone walking by get a bit of a peep show.

I'd never had a tub big enough at our little place to take a bath and relax. Once, at an old farmhouse Vivian and I had stayed in for a while with one of her boyfriends, there'd been a huge clawfoot tub where I'd soak for an hour at a time, draining a little water and adding more when it got to be too cool. The rest of the experience staying there was total shit—Vivian had made sure of that.

The guy—Mike—had been one of the good ones. A loving boyfriend to her, a rare father figure to me. One hell of a difference from what she usually shacked up with. I'd actually let myself hope that we could stay, be a real family, maybe even get a dog or something *permanent*. But Vivian picked fights with Mike all the time, drank too much and threw empty Jack bottles at his head, tried to drag me into the middle of it and then would call me an ungrateful whore when I took his side.

One time, Mike bought me a jacket that I'd wanted and gave it to me for my birthday. Vivian was beyond pissed. She and Mike had quite the screaming match over that one. And she marched the jacket out to the burn pile and set it on fire.

We left the next day. That was the first time I ran away. I went back to the farmhouse, begged Mike to let me stay. But I was fourteen, so Mike did what any decent guy would've done and called the cops. CPS got involved for a while.

Yeah...if I'd ever hoped to have any relationship with my mother, I'd pretty much blown that. She tolerated me afterward, still let me stay wherever she was staying. But I'm pretty sure she only kept me around because it made her situation more pitiable and consequently easier to con people into thinking she was a good mother just trying to make ends meet and take care of her daughter.

Bitch.

I stripped out of my clothes and sank down into the steaming water, forcing all thoughts of Vivian out of my head, just letting the heat warm the frozen parts of me, the dark, shadowy parts of my past that I tried to keep locked away, so the cold truth didn't burn so much.

I closed my eyes and let my arms float, wondering if this was what flying was like—weightless, carefree, no worries about what fresh hell was waiting for me the next day. One day I would know. I'd get out from under the fear and hopelessness that gnawed at me whenever I thought about how I was failing my son. Failing myself.

Soon.

I could feel something coming, something that would change my life forever. It was like I was poised on a precipice, peering down into a vast, haze-shrouded cavern, not knowing what was hidden from my sight, but knowing there was something so much better just out of my reach. I was just going to have to take the leap.

I lay there, fantasizing about the home I'd make for Henry—maybe a little place out in the country like Mike's farmhouse where Henry could be healthy and happy and run and play with all the friends he would make, and we'd *definitely* have a dog, maybe three.

The water had just reached the temperature where I'd either have to end my little respite from reality or add more hot water to stave off real life for just a little longer, when the bathroom door creaked.

My eyes snapped open. I turned, expecting to see Henry in the doorway, maybe needing a drink of water or a trip to the toilet—we'd gotten past the bedwetting stage a year ago, but he sometimes still had to get up in the middle of the night.

But no one stood there.

"Henry?" I called softly. "Is that you, baby?"

Silence.

Unnerved, but not yet frightened, I let out some of the cooled water and turned on the faucet, definitely needing that warmth to get rid of the chill making my skin creep. The door had probably just blown open a little thanks to the slight breeze coming through the cracked window. Completely reasonable explanation. I'd left the door open a little so I could hear Henry if he needed me. Next time I'd make sure to close it.

I don't know how much longer I lay there, but I do know I was drifting off to sleep when I sensed someone else was in the bathroom. "Henry, baby, you should really knock—"

My words died on my lips when I opened my eyes. There was no one there. But in the middle of the floor on the tile was a puddle of what I first thought to be water—which would've been weird enough considering I hadn't been out of the tub, and nothing seemed to be leaking—but then I realized it was thicker, the edges not spreading out the way water would.

I sat up slowly, surveying the entire bathroom, looking for...I don't know what. I tried not to let my imagination run wild, but that was next to impossible. I stood and grabbed my towel, wrapping it around me and stepping out of the tub to get a closer look at the puddle.

I knelt and touched it. Thicker than water as I'd suspected, almost the consistency of hand soap but didn't lather when I rubbed my fingers and thumb together.

"What the hell?" I murmured, frowning at the substance.

The instant the words left my lips, the bathroom door slammed, the sound echoing off the walls like a gunshot. I cried out, starting so violently I lost my balance and pitched forward into the puddle, my hands sliding out from under me. I landed hard on my left elbow, sending pain shooting up my arm to my shoulder.

Groaning, I rolled over to my back and lay there for several seconds, squeezing my eyes shut to breathe through it. When the pain from the impact diminished to a dull ache, I slowly got to my feet and grabbed a towel from the bar on the wall to wipe up the puddle before I had a chance to slip again.

I tossed the towel in the hamper and turned toward the sink, half-expecting to see an intruder's monstrous face in the mirror like in basically every horror movie ever, but to my relief I saw only my own face, eyes wide with fear and confusion, not sure that made me feel a whole lot better.

So much for my relaxing bath...

I turned back to the tub and gasped, covering my mouth to stifle the scream that rose in my throat. A woman floated in the tub, long red—or maybe blond—hair fanned out in the water gone dark with blood. She lay there, eyes wide, vacant, gazing into nothingness. As I stared, unable to move, she sank slowly and vanished. The water cleared in an instant.

Then the trembling began—starting in my legs then climbing upward through my abdomen, my arms, my head... The combined violent jostling of the contents of my stomach when I fell and the shock of what I'd just seen was too much. I lurched toward the toilet, barely making it in time before I vomited with such explosive force that the water splashed up onto my face and hair. My muscles seized, and I heaved again, the acid from my stomach burning my throat, my nose.

Too weak and shaky to do anything but collapse onto the tile floor in the fetal position, I lay there, sobbing—but quietly so as not to wake Henry—the image of the dead woman playing over and over again in my mind.

Who the hell was she?

She wasn't the same woman from the hallway who I'd come to suspect wasn't an intruder of the corporeal kind after all. And she wasn't a figment of my imagination, of that I was certain. Had she died in my apartment? This house? Or had she just latched onto the first person she thought might see her? Not every intruder who showed themselves to me had anything to do with where I was. Sometimes, it was almost like they just finally sensed an opening to tell their story and jumped right through.

And I freaking hated it.

But there was something different this time, something darker and heavier than what I usually experienced, a suffocating pressure that compressed my lungs, making me gasp for air between sobs. Maybe it had nothing at all to do with the specter in my bathtub. Maybe it was the realization that I was trapped, that there was nowhere I could go, nowhere I could escape to—at least not yet, not when I didn't even have two nickels to rub together. Who knew how long it would take to get back on my feet.

Before, when I lived with Vivian, I'd always just known we'd be leaving soon, that Vivian would be picking up stakes and moving on to the next temporary crash pad, and that the intruders would rarely follow. But this time, despite my bravado with Whit, I had to stay where I was. I had no money, no options except living in my car or going to a shelter. And I had sworn that I would never do that to Henry.

I clenched my jaw and pushed up until I was sitting, my back against the vanity, and closed my eyes to keep the world from spinning. Taking several slow, deep breaths, I focused on the image of my son's sweet face, his smile, the absolute trust in his eyes when he looked at me, knowing that I would never let him down, that I would make everything okay.

I sniffed and wiped the tears from my cheeks, then forced myself to get up and stand on my still-shaky legs. This time when I peered into the tub, there was nothing but the clear—and by now cold—water. I reached down to let out the water, but hesitated, my fingers hovering just above the water's surface. But then I took a deep, bracing breath and plunged my hand in to pull the plug. The tub gurgled as it drained, the sound oddly chilling, making me shudder.

"Stop it, Zellie," I ordered, shaking my head to clear the images that flooded my brain.

I turned on the shower, adjusting the temperature until it was nearly scalding my skin, then discarded my towel and got in so I could rewash my hair and face to remove any residual vomit and toilet water. I paused briefly to look around the bathroom again, making sure that I was alone once more, and pulled the shower curtain closed. I quickly rewashed then stood beneath the water, trying to infuse some warmth into my bones.

It didn't help.

Finally, I gave up trying.

Panic and fear gripped my heart in a ruthless grasp. I wanted to grab Henry and run, get the hell out of the apartment to somewhere else. But where was that? My mother's?

Yeah, right.

One of my new neighbors?

Who's to say the intruders wouldn't find me in their apartment?

Whit Proffitt?

God, no.

He already thought I was a charity case that he was obligated to put up with for the time being. The last thing I needed was to show up on his doorstep—wherever that was—and beg for his help. *Again.*

I was stuck there. Trapped—at least for now. My only chance to escape whatever the hell I was experiencing at Dawes House was to get the money I needed to support myself and my son as soon as I could. Until then, I just hoped that seeing the spirit of a dead woman in my bathtub would be the worst of it.

Except deep in my gut, I knew that it wasn't. I could feel a darkness creeping closer, a heaviness closing in.

I checked in on Henry one last time before climbing into my own bed. The mattress was softer and more inviting than I'd remembered. As I drifted off to sleep, I decided I'd meet the family friend Whit had mentioned to talk about the job at her bookstore. And as soon as I had enough money saved, Henry and I were getting the hell out of Dawes House.

CHAPTER SIX

"I don't want to go," Henry complained as we made our way across the foyer. "Can't I stay here and play with Addie?"

"No, baby," I told him. "I haven't talked to Ms. June. I'm not going to just show up at her door and ask her if you can stay and play. That's rude."

"Well, good morning, y'all."

I started, having not expected anyone to be in the foyer that early in the morning. My head snapped toward the soft, purring voice.

The woman at the front desk offered us a friendly smile. "I'm sorry, darlin'," she said, standing and coming around the desk to greet us properly. "Didn't mean to startle you. I'm Iris. And you must be Zellie and Henry. I was told you moved in while I was away. I'm sorry I didn't get a chance to meet you all last night at supper. I live over in one of the carriage house apartments if you ever need anything. I tend to keep to myself as I prefer my private business to *stay* private. But no need to be a stranger."

Iris was statuesque, blond, beautiful, and oozing sex appeal—not at all the older woman I was expecting based on what I'd heard about her. She seemed overdressed for her position at Dawes House in what had to be an expensive suit, and her five-inch stilettos added to her already impressive height. I'll admit, I stared at her, dumbfounded, for what was a very awkward, uncomfortable ten seconds before I could manage a pathetic response. "*You're* Iris?"

She laughed—a very pretty, musical laugh—and gestured toward her nameplate on the desk. "Last time I checked."

Embarrassment burned my cheeks. "I'm sorry," I managed. "You're just not..."

"What you expected?" she finished with a milder echo of her lovely laugh. "I get that a lot. Now," she said, shifting her focus to Henry, "where are you off to this morning? You are looking very sharp, darlin'."

Henry grinned, enjoying the praise. "We have to go to the bookstore. Mama has a job interview."

"You don't say," Iris drawled, turning her smile on me, clearly expecting for me to share more.

"Whit has a family friend who's looking for someone to work at her store—Ever After Coffee and Books," I explained.

Iris pressed her palms together with a delighted gasp. "Oh, you'll love it. Dottie is a doll! She recently lost her manager—just up and quit with no notice. She's going to be so excited to meet you!"

"Thanks. I hope so." I gave Henry's hand a little tug. "C'mon, baby. We have to get going. I'll be late."

Iris regarded Henry like she was sizing him up. "You don't want to go to a boring job interview with your mama, do you? Listen to grown-ups talk about books and coffee and inventories?"

"No, ma'am," Henry said, shaking his head.

Iris looked at me with a twinkle in her blue eyes. "I don't think Addie and Ms. June are back from their errands. Would you like to stay with me while your mama is away?"

Henry's face brightened. "Yes, ma'am!"

"Oh, that's so kind of you, Iris," I began. "But—"

She waved away my words with a dismissive gesture. "My pleasure!"

I offered her a brief, tight smile. "I appreciate it, truly. But I can't pay you, Ms. Iris."

"Don't you worry about that." She reached out her hand to Henry, who happily accepted it and skipped around the end of the desk. "He can work it off by keeping me company. We don't get many visitors who need my assistance, as you can imagine. And when Ms. June and Addie get back, we can go for a visit. I guarantee Ms. June won't mind this little man coming to play for a while."

I hesitated, still uncertain. I didn't know this woman at all, had never met her. Hell, she might not have even been who she said she was. I was just opening my mouth to politely decline when the front door opened, spilling sunlight into the foyer.

"Mornin', y'all!" Chase stepped in carrying several cans of paint and sporting his usual grin. "You're looking particularly lovely, Ms. Iris."

"Flatterer," Iris teased.

Chase turned his attention to me. "Where y'all off to this morning?"

Iris answered before I could get a word out, "Zellie is going to visit Dottie Shay about a job, and Henry is going to stay with me for a bit until Ms. June and Addie get back."

"Well, that sounds like a good plan to me," Chase said, giving Henry a wink, then added, "Don't you worry, Zellie—Iris will take good care of your boy. You'd best get going. Probably easiest to walk to the store. Just cut right through the cemetery and you'll be there in no time!"

Still torn at the prospect of leaving Henry but needing to leave so I wasn't late, I hesitated. "Are you sure, Ms. Iris? I don't want to impose."

"Not at all, darlin'," she assured me. "You go on now. Henry and I will be just fine. We're all family here, honey. We take care of our own."

Henry beamed and waved, perfectly content with me leaving him with Iris. "Bye, Mama!"

I gave him one last hug and kiss and ordered him to mind his manners then hurried out the door before I could change my mind.

I walked a few blocks, turning down a beautiful tree-lined street that offered a little shade from the bright morning sunshine. The humidity was already starting to make the air thick and sticky, but a light breeze skimmed over my skin, offering just enough relief to pretend it wasn't going to be miserable by noon. I cut through Chippewa Square, one of Savannah's smaller green spaces, and paused to take in the loveliness before continuing a few more blocks toward Colonial Park Cemetery.

I stopped at the entrance.

Of course, the shortcut would be through a cemetery...

I took a deep breath and let it out slowly, steeling myself for what was to come, and tried to surround myself with a protective bubble in my mind, doing what I could to keep anyone from getting my attention, latching on.

Cemeteries were never my favorite places. Too many spirits reaching out, trying to get my attention. And this one was the oldest in Savannah, dating back to the 1700s—a long time for the dead to grow restless, more frustrated, more insistent.

As I stepped through the gates, the weight of the place settled over me. Desperation and sorrow clung to the air, particularly that of the thousands lost to yellow fever epidemics, buried in mass graves with no records and no tombstones to remind anyone they lived and died here.

But even those whose lives were memorialized with headstones or buried in one of the above-ground red brick tombs had no one left to visit them, generations gone since the last of the burials here. Now, their only visitors were tourists with cameras, hoping to maybe catch a glimpse of a restless soul.

As I passed a small group of tourists who'd gotten an early start, I suddenly sensed someone watching me. I glanced around but saw only a handful of other people in the cemetery, none of whom were remotely interested in me and all very much alive. Still, dread crept along the back of my neck, urging me to get going. I quickened my pace, making a mental note to go the long way on my return, cemetery shortcuts be damned.

A flicker of movement drew my attention.

Standing behind one of the tombstones was the woman from the hallway of Dawes House—her long, black hair bedraggled and matted, her nightgown soaked and stiff with blood.

Her eyes locked onto mine, the darkness I saw there drawing me in, surrounding me with a preternatural coldness that chilled me to my core.

Then she pivoted and ran.

"Wait!" I called, chasing after her but not able to keep up as she disappeared around the east wall of the cemetery where dozens of headstones leaned against the brick. Out of breath and confused by the strange encounter, I slowed and scanned the area, trying to determine where she could've gone.

When I turned back, one of the names on the headstones caught my eye.

Susanna Dawes Proffitt.

Next to it, a smaller headstone for an infant.

Josiah Proffitt.

I stared in disbelief, stunned by the coincidence. But *was* it a coincidence, or had she led me here? And, if so, why? What was she trying to tell me by leading me to a set of headstones for members of the Dawes and Proffitt families who had died two centuries before?

My phone buzzed, jolting me. I had ten minutes before my appointment at Ever After. Shaking, I forced myself to turn away from the headstones and hurried out of the cemetery. The moment I stepped through the gates, the oppressive weight lifted.

I collapsed onto a bench and took some time to compose myself, smooth my hair, still my hands. As soon as my pulse had slowed and I could breathe normally, I headed to the bookstore, smiling when I spotted the sign above the doorway. It was exactly as whimsical as the name promised.

A bell chimed as I entered, drawing the attention of the lone patron perusing one of the shelves. She spared me only a glance before turning back to the rows of fantasy novels. I lifted my gaze to take in the shop and was transported straight into a fairytale. Greenery draped the entire place, intertwined with twinkling fairy lights. Dragons and pixies peeked out from among the foliage. Gnomes crouched behind the stacks. Even the furniture—bistro tables, oversized armchairs, comfy couches—looked like they'd been salvaged from a storybook.

"Good morning!" a cheerful voice called, accompanied by a rapid *clack, clack, clack* of heels on the hardwood.

An older woman hurried toward me, her long yellow-white hair pulled into a side ponytail. She balanced precariously on her purple high-heeled sandals and seemed right at home among the eclectic décor in her zebra print capris, gaudy, bedazzled shirt, and numerous bangle bracelets. She wore enormous dangling earrings the same shade of purple as her shoes and a glass bead necklace that had been looped twice so it rested against her chest where her tanned skin puckered into wrinkles from decades of too frequent sunbathing.

"Good morning," I replied, unable to suppress a smile. "I'm looking for Dottie Shay."

She flapped her hands in excitement as she hurried toward me. "Oooooh!" she sang, drawing out the sound for several seconds. "You must be Zellie! Come in, come in, come *in*!"

I was obviously already in, but I shook her hand. "Yes, I'm Zellie Dupont. Whit Proffitt said you might have a job opening."

"Oh, yes!" Dottie cried. "I am so pleased to meet you. Let me show you around!"

She pivoted and hurried in the other direction but came to an abrupt halt and looked back at me over her shoulder. "Wait—do you need coffee? I need coffee. It's far too early to discuss such things without coffee. Yes, coffee? Cream? Sugar? Oh, I'll just guess. Come on, honey!"

Not waiting for my answer, she tottered off again, motioning for me to follow.

I giggled, not sure what to think about the odd woman, and hurried after her. She flitted around the store, showing me the different sections, pointing out all the reading nooks and warning me not to let teenagers hang out in them too long so they didn't get up to any "hanky panky." Then she led me into the little coffee shop that was tucked into its own alcove. It was just as eclectic as the rest of the store—mismatched chairs and tables, odd pieces of wall décor—but here, twinkling stars hung from the ceiling.

"So, what do you think?" she asked, clearly proud. "I'm in sore need of the help! It doesn't look busy now, but trust me, I've got more customers than I can handle."

"I love it," I told her truthfully. For the first time in a very long time, I felt... peaceful. I had no doubt that Ever After would be a haven until I could find somewhere else to live.

Dottie flapped her hands in excitement again and hugged me like we were long-lost friends. "I'm so glad!" she gushed. "My last manager was such a dear, but not very dependable, unfortunately. She was around your age, in fact. Lived at Dawes House, too, so it wasn't just me she left high and dry."

I frowned, my stomach sinking. "She lived at Dawes House? I didn't realize..."

"Oh, yes," Dottie affirmed, nodding vigorously, her giant earrings and ponytail bobbing. "She and her little boy, Jackson. She was quite a sight the last week or two—not sleeping, barely eating. That poor girl looked a *mess*! And troubled. Couldn't concentrate on anything. Hardly a surprise when she up and left without a word. I suppose she *was* a little flighty now that I look back on it."

Flighty? Coming from Dottie, that was saying something. I liked her immensely, but she was definitely unique.

We sat and enjoyed our coffee together—well, I enjoyed the coffee; she mostly talked about her favorite books, her life in Savannah, favorite musicians...pretty much anything and everything without much logical progression or timeline. I managed to get in a few short answers to her questions to me before she shifted topics again.

Eventually, she realized the time. We worked out my schedule, she handed me a key to the shop, and then she hugged me again before sending me on my way. "Bye, now, honey! You be careful. I don't want to lose another manager before she even *starts.*" She laughed at her joke and tottered back inside, leaving me standing on the sidewalk, charmed but a little baffled by the whole experience.

Grinning to myself as I walked back to Dawes House, I took the long way around the cemetery just as I'd planned, though I still found myself sneaking glances, worried the darkhaired woman might appear again. Thankfully, nothing moved in the shadows.

But as I approached the front porch of Dawes House, the similarities between me and Dottie's previous manager hit me all over again, slowing my steps. What *had* happened to her and her son? Had she seen the same things I had? Or was it something else entirely? A toxic ex? A mental breakdown?

A sudden wave of nausea washed over me so violently I doubled over, pressing my hands to my belly with a groan. Sweat prickled my forehead and between my shoulder blades as another wave hit me. Before I could catch my breath, the nausea hit me again, harder this time. Weak and trembling from the pain ripping into my stomach, I stumbled to the steps and sat down just as my knees gave out.

What the hell?

I bent over, putting my face in my lap and wrapping my arms around my knees, fighting to keep my breakfast and Dottie's coffee down as saliva filled the space beneath my tongue in ominous warning.

Then, as abruptly as it started, the nausea vanished.

I stayed hunched for a few seconds, taking slow, deep until my stomach unclenched. When I finally lifted my head, I closed my eyes and drew in the fresh, warm air, letting it fill my lungs. An electric saw whined nearby—one of Chase's or a work crew's, I guessed. Traffic droned in the distance. Voices of people walking down the sidewalk drifted on the breeze. Not too far away, the bell from the Cathedral Basilica of St. John the Baptist began to chime. And then the most precious sound of all—children laughing—floated to my ears, bringing the grin back to my lips.

I recognized it immediately as belonging to Henry and Addie.

Eager to see what they were up to and share my news, I went around to the back courtyard. There they were, partners in crime, digging happily in the little dirt plot—searching for pirate bones, presumably—while chatting away about the episode of *Bubble Guppies* they'd watched that morning before coming out to play.

"'Morning, Zellie darlin'," June greeted me, waving a dirty, gloved hand, a garden trowel clutched in the other. Dressed in jeans, a short-sleeved cotton smock, and a floppy sun hat with a wide brim, she looked like she should've been hosting a trendy DIY gardening show.

"Well, don't you look pretty as a peach!" her husband added from where he knelt by an azalea bush. He still somehow managed to look like a man who belonged on a golf course instead of digging in the dirt.

"Thank you, sir," I said, heat creeping into my cheeks, not used to compliments.

"Mama!" Henry cried, running toward me to give me a hug, only to be intercepted by June, who scooped him up with a laugh.

"Oh, no, you don't, little bit," she said, holding up one of his muddy hands before his eyes with a smile. "You don't want to get your mama's dress all dirty, do you?"

Henry cackled, turned to me, making a monster face, fingers curled into claws. "I'm a mud monster, Mama!"

I shook my head. "You sure are! Are you and Addie helping or making a mess for Ms. June and Mr. Earl to clean up?"

June set Henry down. "Oh, he's no trouble at all. It's good for Addie to have someone to play with."

"Thank you so much for looking after him, Ms. June," I gushed. "I really appreciate it. I start my job with Ms. Dottie tomorrow, so I'll be able to pay you soon for watching him."

Earl scoffed as he stood and brushed the dirt from his gloved hands. "Nonsense! You don't owe us a thing. We're all family here, Zellie."

Everyone kept saying that, but the concept seemed so foreign to me. Family that actually cared for one another, looked after each other, not expecting anything in return?

"Earl, honey," June said softly, apparently sensing my discomfort, "why don't you go ask Pearlie to bring out an extra glass for Zellie? Pearlie's making her famous lemonade and some sandwiches, Zellie. Why don't you join us and tell us all about meeting Dottie? She's quite the character."

I hesitated, but then I glanced at Henry who was once more digging happily beside Addie. "Thank you, Ms. June. I'd be happy to."

June smiled. "Lovely. I'll just go freshen up and be right back."

A few minutes later, she emerged looking completely refreshed, this time wearing a flowing, fiery-red sundress that somehow looked both elegant and casual. Just a few steps behind her, Pearlie appeared, also casually elegant in bright yellow, carrying a silver tray with lemonade and glasses, Earl following with another silver tray piled high with finger sandwiches.

"Children," Pearlie called, "go wash up now."

"Yes, ma'am!" they chimed, hopping up and racing inside.

Pearlie set the tray on a bistro table and smiled at me warmly. "Well, look at you," she said. "You look like the world's been lifted off your shoulders, Zellie."

"She's going to be working for Dottie Shay," June supplied before I could answer. "Isn't that wonderful?"

"Yes, indeed!" Pearlie agreed. She then added with a wink, "I think that deserves a celebratory lemonade."

Earl took a glass for himself and raised it slightly. "I'll let y'all enjoy your refreshments. I believe Junior and I have a golf game to get to." He dropped a kiss on June's head. "Bye, darlin'. Zellie, you enjoy that lemonade. Ms. Pearlie's is the best around."

"Yes, sir," I promised, "it's delicious."

And it was. I'd never tasted any lemonade like it—the perfect blend of tart and sweet and some other underlying taste that I couldn't quite place. Mint, maybe? Or maybe it just tasted better because I actually mattered to the people here.

"Now," Pearlie said, handing me a plate with sandwiches already selected, "tell us all about your visit with Ms. Dottie."

I recounted my somewhat surreal experience with Dottie Shay until June called Addie and Henry to her and ushered them inside to clean up and get ready for nap time.

"He's having such a good time playing with Addie," I told Pearlie. "It's been a long time since I've seen him with so much energy." I didn't add that high energy usually meant a hospital visit was coming.

"Well, I'm glad you all are settling in," Pearlie said, topping off my lemonade. "If there's anything you need, you just let your Aunt Pearlie know, all right?"

I blinked at her in surprise. *Aunt Pearlie?* I couldn't help but smile. The thought warmed me in a way I wasn't prepared for. "Yes, ma'am. Thank you."

She leaned back in her chair and laced her fingers together, studying me. "You look like something's eating at you, Zellie. What's on your mind? Nervous about the new job? Ms. Dottie's a bit eccentric, but I'm sure you'll get along just fine."

"Oh, no, ma'am," I said quickly. "It's nothing like that." I wasn't about to share what had happened in the cemetery, but I still wanted to find out what I could about the intruder I'd now seen twice. Trying to sound nonchalant, I replied, "Could you tell me more about the history of Dawes House? About the family?"

Pearlie gave a short laugh. "The Dawes family? That's a better question for Ms. Netty. I'm old, honey, but that woman's *ancient*."

"But you know some of the story, right?" I pressed carefully. "You must've heard things living here as long as you have."

She didn't immediately respond, regarding me through slightly narrowed eyes as if weighing whether to share what she knew. Then she said, "Fairland Dawes made his fortune in shipping. Piracy, some would call it. From what I've heard, he ran his home with a strong hand—much the same way he ordered his men around on his ship. His family obeyed him without question. Story goes he married off one of his daughters to a wealthy foreigner—that'd be Whit Proffitt's ancestor—but the poor girl died in childbirth. So, he married off another daughter, Eliza, to the same man. The two families became the wealthiest in these parts."

"What happened to the other daughter? Eliza?" I asked.

Pearlie sighed. "She drowned when she was pregnant with her second child. Her first child survived. And Josef went on to have other children, of course. The Proffitts were the first to renovate Dawes House after it was rebuilt. It's been passed down through the family ever since."

"Rebuilt?" I repeated. "What happened to the original house?"

"Burned down," Pearlie said. She took a sip of her lemonade then added, "Fairland Dawes perished in the fire."

"You said Whit's ancestor did renovations on the new house," I prompted. "What did he do?"

"Oh, he did quite a lot over the years," Pearlie said. "Hard to know what he did and what those who came after him contributed. I do know he added the fourth floor. It had originally been an attic, I believe, but he turned it into living space."

"An attic?" I repeated. "Well, that certainly would explain the lack of duct work. So...did Whit grow up here?"

Pearlie paused before nodding slowly. "Of a fashion. Lived here at various times over the years." Her eyes sparkled with mischief as she added, "Always was a handsome young man, too."

I flushed at her knowing grin. "I'm sure. Was Whit's mother Mr. Monty's first wife? Whit said he'd had a lot of stepmothers."

Pearlie didn't answer right away as if choosing her words carefully. At last, she said, "No, she was not one of his wives at all. She was one of Montgomery's *projects.*"

Ah. There it was. Whit apparently wasn't the only one who'd wondered if I was Mr. Monty's sidepiece.

"But I think that's Whit's story to tell, honey," Pearlie added. "I imagine he'll share more if he sees fit."

Eager to steer the conversation away from whatever nerve I'd apparently touched, I circled back to the story of the Dawes women. "The first daughter you mentioned who married the foreign gentleman—was that Susanna?" Pearlie's brows lifted in surprise, so I quickly added, "I saw her headstone in the cemetery. And there was an infant's as well—Josiah."

Pearlie nodded. "That's my understanding."

"Do you know anything about a boy named David who lived here?" I asked.

"Where did you hear about David?"

I hadn't realized June had returned until she spoke behind me. "Henry found drawings in the closet of his room," I told her. "They look like they were done by a child around Henry's age. He keeps talking about a boy named David, and the initials DP are carved into a little desk. I assumed he was the one who drew them. But Ms. Dottie said the previous tenant's son was named Jackson."

June joined us, but her manner noticeably more aloof. "I'm sure I don't know a David. Although, I suppose there could've been a David who lived here at some point over the years—common enough name. Or perhaps he's just a figment of Henry's imagination, Zellie."

I had to concede her point. "I'm sure you're right," I admitted, smiling politely. "But I can't shake the feeling that something happened to the woman and boy who lived in our apartment before us. The things she left behind..."

I left the thought unfinished, and neither June nor Pearlie prompted me to continue, so I let it go. Thankfully, Henry and Addie reappeared in the doorway, breaking the tense silence that enveloped our little party.

"We're ready, Mamaw June," Henry announced, trying to stifle a yawn.

Mamaw June?

"I think it's time to go to *our* apartment," I told him, standing and offering a grateful smile. "Thank you again for the lemonade and sandwiches. And the conversation."

"Anytime, darlin'," June replied, although something behind her smile felt off.

"Why don't you and Henry join us for dinner at my apartment tonight, Zellie?" Pearlie suggested. "We can all celebrate your new job."

I shook my head, already worried I had imposed too much. "Thank you, Ms. Pearlie, but I couldn't—"

She waved away my protest. "Nonsense. We'll see you at six."

There was nothing for me to do but nod and thank them again. By the time we reached our apartment, Henry was already half asleep and getting heavier in my arms with each step.

When did he get so big?

"C'mon, baby," I said, setting him down in the bathroom and grabbing a washcloth to remove the remaining dirt on his face. "Looks like you missed a few spots."

"I don't want to take a nap," he said around a yawn. "I'm not tired."

I arched a brow. "You're about to fall over, Henry. You have to take a nap, especially when you play this hard. You know what will happen if you don't get enough rest."

He nodded. "Yes, ma'am."

The effects of his condition and I were old friends. I'd spent too many long nights and days to count battling the headaches, dizziness, weakness, irritability... As I tucked him into his bed, I noticed his flushed cheeks, which would've looked healthy on any other child. But I grabbed the thermometer and took his temperature, just in case.

"I'm fine, Mama," he grumbled, already drifting to sleep.

And he was. At least, his temperature was. It was probably just the effects of playing outside in the warm weather. I'd have to remind June to put sunscreen on him next time, even if they are playing mostly in the shade.

I entered the living room to grab a cookbook from the shelf—no way I was committing the cardinal sin of showing up to dinner empty-handed—when I thought I heard voices, low and bitter.

I frowned and stepped closer to the door, listening intently. It wasn't coming from the fourth floor—too muffled and far away. I eased open the door and poked my head into the hallway. The arguing stopped. But in its place was a woman's heartrending sobs.

I grabbed my keys and stepped into the hallway, searching for the source, but the crying had already faded by the time I shut the door behind me. For several minutes, I stood still, listening. But the only sound was the flapping of the curtains at either end of the hallway and the quiet whistling of the breeze.

CHAPTER SEVEN

I could smell something mouthwatering before I even reached Pearlie's door and worried my deviled eggs wouldn't be worthy of being on the same table. But I should've known better than to doubt the Johnsons' hospitality. When Junior opened the door and saw the glass casserole dish of halved eggs filled to overflowing with a truly unexceptional concoction of whipped egg yolks, mayonnaise, vinegar, and paprika, he rubbed his palms together in anticipation.

"Is that some deviled eggs? You must've read my mind, Zellie," he said, taking the dish. "I have been wanting some deviled eggs all day. Come on in, come on in!"

I don't know what I'd expected, but stepping into their apartment was like walking into a museum curated by someone with impeccable taste. Their walls were adorned with African art that ranged from ancient relics to more modern art. Their furniture belonged in a design magazine, a blend of elegance and comfort, both modern and antique, with dark wood, bright fabrics, and clean lines. I was almost afraid to let Henry loose among such expensive pieces.

Junior set my eggs out on the dining room sideboard next to fried green tomatoes, cheddar biscuits, mac and cheese, salad, and a relish tray piled high with gourmet olives, marinated mushrooms, cherry tomatoes, and pickles. A moment later, Chase emerged from the kitchen carrying a serving tray with two roasted chickens and an abundance of potatoes, carrots, and parsnips.

"What'd I tell ya?" he asked with a wink. "Dinner at Pearlie's is always a treat."

"It all smells amazing!" I admitted, wondering when I'd last had so many choices in one meal. And just how many people Pearlie planned to feed.

My question was soon answered when June, Earl, and Addie arrived carrying desserts.

"Is this all of us?" Junior asked when Pearlie exited the kitchen carrying a pitcher of sweet tea. "Merilee not coming?"

"All for tonight," Pearlie replied. "Merilee's tending to Ms. Netty and Mr. Dean, who are both feeling poorly. Iris already had dinner plans, and Billy Wayne and Kitty weren't up to it."

There was one person missing whose absence I definitely noticed. There was a void in the room without him there.

"Is Whit coming?" I asked, trying to sound disinterested.

But Pearlie's grin told me I'd failed. "He'll be here any minute."

True to Pearlie's prediction, Whit arrived moments later, looking as stiff and uncomfortable as he had our first night at Dawes House. Everyone greeted him warmly except June, who continued to give him the cold shoulder. If I'd known any of them better, I might've asked why. But my questions were swept aside by an amazing dinner and lively conversation.

I don't even recall most of what was said. I just remember being *happy.* I hadn't felt that welcome and part of a family—a *true* family—since living at the farmhouse. Even June softened a little, laughing at something Chase said that had us all rolling.

At one point, I realized I was just sitting there, smiling, watching all of them, so grateful. I didn't even notice my eyes had filled with tears until the soft pressure of a hand on mine beneath the table drew my attention to Whit beside me.

I managed to smile and gave his hand a small squeeze before blinking rapidly, clearing the tears, then excused myself to go check on Henry and Addie, who'd rushed off after dinner to play.

I peeked into the living room to see them sitting together on the floor, playing with a collection of stones that Addie had arranged in a circle. In the center was a little pile of what looked like bones from the board game Operation.

I frowned. "What are you two playing?"

"Tell the Bones," Henry replied, holding up one of the tiny bones. "These are the pirate bones we dug up, Mama!"

Addie brushed her hair off her face and looked at me with eyes that seemed far too wise for a six-year-old. "We have to tell the bones to either stay dead or come back to life, Ms. Zellie."

I stepped into the room to get a closer look, keeping my voice gentle when I asked, "And how do you tell them to come back to life?"

She held up a tiny watering can that looked like it might've belonged to one of her dolls or maybe the gardening set she'd mentioned before and pretended to pour something over the bones. "You just sprinkle them with the special water that makes them grow back together."

"Maybe you two should play something else," I suggested, concerned that the game was a little too morbid for Henry and might give him nightmares. "Henry, you brought some books. Why don't you and Addie look at those instead?"

I hung out long enough to see them pack the stones into a little pouch Addie had and dig through the puppy backpack with floppy brown ears that held some of Henry's books. When I returned to the dining room, I was mortified to find the table already cleared and Pearlie pouring coffee from a silver pot.

"Thought we'd lost you," Earl teased.

"I'm so sorry," I said, slipping back into my seat and accepting the cup Pearlie handed me.

"Never mind him, baby," she said, sending Earl a look that only made him chuckle. "You came back just in time for dessert."

"You do *not* want to miss Ms. June's buttermilk pie," Chase assured me, taking a large bite for emphasis.

I'd barely taken my first bite when Junior leaned forward. "So, Zellie, Whit says you love books. Got a favorite?"

I glanced at Whit. His lips twitched into the hint of a smile before he turned his attention to his pie and his cousin's inane prattle. "Yes, sir. I *do* love books," I answered. "But a favorite?" I grinned. "Do I have to pick just one?"

And that's how I found myself drawn into a lively conversation with Junior, hitting on pretty much everything from Chaucer to Jane Austen to Stephen King. I didn't realize how much time had passed until I looked around to see everyone had gone but Whit. Henry had passed out cold, face down on the couch, sleeping harder than I'd seen in a while.

"Oh, I'm so sorry, Ms. Pearlie!" I exclaimed, jumping up. "I shouldn't have stayed so long. I've been a horrible guest."

"Now hush," she said, waving away my apology. "I don't shoo out family."

This time, I couldn't stop the grin at her calling me family. But that happiness fractured a little at the thought of eventually leaving Dawes House. I turned away quickly and bent to scoop up Henry, groaning a bit at the unexpected weight of his limp, sleeping body.

"Allow me."

I looked up to see Whit standing beside me. He gently took Henry under the arms and lifted my son so that Henry was draped over his shoulder, arms and legs dangling.

"I...uh..." I stammered, not used to anyone stepping in to help. "Thank you."

"Here you go, baby," Pearlie said, thrusting a stack of leftovers into my hands. "You take these for you and Henry. You won't have to worry about supper after your first day of work tomorrow."

"Thank you, Ms. Pearlie," I said, my vision blurring again with those damned tears.

On impulse, I threw my free arm around her neck in a brief hug. Pearlie hugged me back then gave Whit a pointed look, something unreadable passing between them.

Whit and I didn't speak in the elevator. I was already self-conscious and embarrassed about my emotions being on full display that evening, betraying just how starved for friendship—for family—I really was. And I was afraid if I looked at him just then, I'd completely fall apart.

When we reached my apartment, I paused, thinking I heard crying again. "Do you hear that?" I asked, scanning the hallway.

Whit shook his head. "Hear what?"

I listened for a moment longer before unlocking the door. Once inside, I quickly put away the leftovers and returned to the living room to find Whit still holding Henry, waiting patiently.

"Sorry," I whispered, reaching for my son. "Let me take him." I started for the hallway but paused and looked back. "Thanks again, Whit. For everything."

He shoved his hands into his pockets and gave a terse nod, his brows drawn together in something of a frown. "My pleasure."

When I returned from getting Henry into his pajamas and tucking him in, I was startled to see Whit on the couch—not relaxing, just perched on the very edge of the cushion, hands clasped, posture tense.

He rose immediately when he saw me. "Apologies," he said, shoving his hands back into his pockets in what I was beginning to realize was his tell when he felt awkward and uncomfortable. "I wanted to make sure you were okay before I left."

"Because I'm hearing things as well as seeing things, you mean?" I teased with a small grin.

This earned an actual smile. "I never said that."

I shrugged. "Didn't have to. I saw it in your face. But I'm not hearing things. I *did* hear arguing this afternoon and then a woman crying. I'm certain of that."

"Ah," he said, nodding. "I can solve that mystery for you. You likely heard Billy Wayne and Kitty. They have a volatile relationship."

Determined to get at what Whit *wasn't* saying, I asked, "Is Kitty in danger? Should someone check on her?"

"I'm not aware of any danger," Whit assured me. "Just arguing and screaming at each other, most likely over Billy Wayne's wandering eye, if I had to guess. But if it concerns you, I can look in on her tomorrow."

It wasn't entirely reassuring, but I nodded anyway. "Thanks."

We stood there together in silence for a moment before he finally gestured toward the door with his thumb and said, "Better get going."

I walked him to the door, suddenly feeling awkward again. He paused in the doorway, studying me, brow furrowed.

"Zellie—" he began, but he bit off whatever it was he'd wanted to say. "Goodnight. Call me if you need anything."

I nodded. "I will," I said softly. "Thank you, Whit. For everything."

He gave me a curt nod then headed toward the elevator. I watched him go, then shut the door and leaned against it, closing my eyes as I recalled the gentle pressure of his hand on mine earlier, the comforting gesture that made my heart skip a beat and my breath hitch, and wishing I could silence the voice inside me that whispered in warning.

In my dream, I was running barefoot through the trees, the branches smacking me in the face, clawing at me, cutting my skin. I glanced behind me, terrified of what followed in the darkness, my fear propelling me forward though my lungs burned and my muscles ached. My long white nightgown snagged on a branch and for one brief, panicked moment I thought I'd been caught, but the fabric ripped, and I kept running—

A slap to the face startled me awake. I bolted up and covered my left eye, which throbbed and watered from the impact.

"What the hell?" I spat, furious.

The hand that had struck me was small, a child's hand. Heart pounding, I searched the darkness with my good eye, looking for Henry.

Why would he do that? Was he sleepwalking? Playing some strange prank?

It wasn't like him at all.

I threw back my covers and stormed to his room, intending to find out what the hell he was thinking, but he was sound asleep, his covers kicked off to expose one bare foot, one arm dangling over the side of his bed.

My stomach twisted.

If it wasn't Henry...

As I stood there, the implications of what had just happened made those tighten, and a wave of nausea swept over me. I raced to the bathroom, barely making it in time.

What the hell was with me?

I had never experienced nausea so easily as I had lately—not since I was pregnant with Henry. And I knew for a fact that morning sickness wasn't even a remote possibility.

By the time I could stand again, tears of frustration blurred my vision as I looked at my reflection in the mirror. The flesh around my eye was puffy and swollen, and the white of my eye was now pink from burst capillaries.

Taking a steadying breath, I turned around and leaned against the vanity, my hands gripping the edge so tightly my knuckles ached. I swallowed hard, preparing for what I was about to open myself to.

"David?" I whispered. "Was that you? Why did you hit me? What are you trying to tell me?"

I waited, listening, not knowing if the intruder would show himself or communicate—or if he even could.

"You don't have to hit me to get my attention," I assured him. "You can reach out to me in other ways. You could blink the lights or knock or..." My mind raced, searching for alternative methods. "You could turn on one of Henry's toys."

I stood motionless for several minutes, every muscle taut, waiting, but nothing else happened. Relieved and disappointed all at once, I returned to my bed. I lay there in the darkness for a little while, too amped up to sleep, too afraid of what might happen as soon as I closed my eyes. Finally, I switched on the bedside lamp.

It's ridiculous that we think leaving the lights on will neutralize any threats that lurk in the shadows. If a spirit has the power to attack in the darkness, they can attack when the lights are on. Trust me. Still, it was a small comfort that would perhaps let me get a little more sleep.

As I drifted off, the sound of crying came through the vents.

I hadn't even met Kitty yet, but my heart was breaking for her. Maybe she, too, didn't have the money to leave and find something better. I squeezed my eyes shut, trying to keep from absorbing her anguish and making it my own. Eventually, the crying stopped and the house was quiet again.

CHAPTER EIGHT

The next morning, I dropped off Henry with June for the day, but instead of heading straight to the bookstore, I took the elevator back up to the third floor and went to Billy Wayne and Kitty's apartment.

The woman who responded to my knock opened the door only a crack, just enough to reveal one pale blue eye. But even with that glimpse of her, Kitty seemed small. Frail. Frightened.

"Good morning," I said softly, in case Billy Wayne was still inside. "I'm Zellie Dupont. I just moved in and thought I'd come introduce myself."

She stared at me like she was waiting for me to say more, then gave a tight nod. "Mornin'."

When she didn't shut the door in my face, I cleared my throat, checking the hallway before lowering my voice. "Kitty, I heard you crying. Are you okay? Do you need help?"

Kitty's eye widened. She opened the door just a little bit more—just enough to see her face, drawn and hollow, cheeks sunken, the skin beneath her eyes dark with lack of sleep or crying...or illness.

"Please don't say things like that," she whispered urgently. "You don't understand."

"Kitty," I said gently, "if you need help there are places you can go, people who can get you on your feet, and Billy Wayne won't be able to hurt you again."

She shook her head vehemently. "It's not like that. Please, just don't concern yourself with my affairs. *Please*. It's better for you if you just leave it alone."

Before I could say anything more, she closed the door.

Taking the hint, I left Dawes House and walked toward the bookstore, trying not to think about my neighbor who was so clearly scared of...*something*. But the image of her gauntness troubled me for days. Weeks, even. Haunted me so much that Dottie pulled me aside at the end of my shift one evening.

"What's eating at you, Zellie?" she asked, blinking at me through cat-eye glasses that made her eyes look cartoonishly large.

I considered how much to share before asking, "Dottie, if you knew someone was in trouble, would you help them—even if they didn't want you to?"

She nodded sagely. "A vexing dilemma. Dreadful. What does your intuition tell you? You must listen to what you know on a deeper level, honey. Don't trust your head *or* your heart. That's just for motivational posters." She tottered away from me to help a customer, calling over her shoulder, "Toodle-oo now, honey."

I stared after her, bewildered by her quirky yet somehow sage wisdom, before shaking my head and closing the café. But before I left for home, I dialed a number on my phone. My intuition was screaming that something was dreadfully wrong with Kitty Wright. And I'd be damned if I was going to just stand by and watch her slip through the cracks.

I didn't see the police car until I was only a couple of houses away from Dawes House. Several neighbors had come out onto their porches to see what was going on, concerned expressions doing little to mask their morbid curiosity. A woman holding a snow-white bichon in her arms offered me a sympathetic smile as if to reassure me that she wasn't being nosey—she was merely *curious*.

I heard voices before I stepped inside, but nothing prepared me for what I saw in the foyer. A sturdy, muscled man stood with his arm around Kitty who was smiling as they chatted with a policeman. Kitty laughed at something the man said and patted her very round, very pregnant belly.

They were a picture of domestic bliss.

Kitty's smile faltered when she saw me. She shot me a brief glare, her eyes narrowed, before turning back to the officer. "I'm so sorry you had to come out this way because of some silly anonymous call, Officer. The caller must not have known what she was talking about. I'm perfectly fine, as you can see! Just tired. This little fella has been kicking me something fierce."

The officer chuckled and tucked his palm-sized notebook into his shirt pocket. "No worries, ma'am. I'm sure they had good intentions. Had to come check it out. You understand."

"Of course!" Kitty assured him. "I *have* been so emotional—nerves, I guess. So it's possible someone heard me crying and just misunderstood."

"My wife was the same way when we were expecting our first," the officer commiserated. "Don't you worry, Mrs. Wright. I'm sure everything will be fine."

I watched the performance from beside Iris's desk, trying to keep my mouth from falling open in disbelief. They were faking it—whatever *it* was. What Kitty was going through wasn't just a case of jittery nerves. It was fear wearing a phony smile. And Kitty's fury when she glanced at me again confirmed it. And complicated it.

The man—who I now realized was Billy Wayne—extended his hand to the officer. "Thank you, sir. Glad you cared enough to look in on my beautiful wife."

As the officer passed me, he nodded in polite greeting. The second the door shut behind him, Kitty pegged me with another venomous glare, Billy Wayne adding one of his own.

Only then did I realize several other residents of Dawes House had gathered in the foyer during the Wrights' exchange with law enforcement. Each of them gave me a disapproving look before slipping wordlessly back into their apartments.

They knew it was me who'd called in the anonymous tip. I didn't know how. But they knew.

"Don't worry."

I jumped at the sudden voice behind me. Merilee sat on the edge of the front desk, legs elegantly crossed. She unfolded them and approached with slow, deliberate grace, then placed her hands on my shoulders.

"They'll come around," she said, her tone sympathetic. "We're all a family at Dawes House. And we want you to be *part* of that family. But there are certain rules you just can't break, Zellie-girl."

She gave me a pointed look as she drifted away toward the hallway that led to the elevators. I stared after her, wondering what in the hell that was supposed to mean and why it sounded like a warning. Or a threat.

I stood in the center of the foyer, alone, for a few more baffled minutes, not understanding what had transpired.

"*Run!*"

The faint voice whispered, harsh, urgent near my ear, a warning so sudden I flinched and snapped my head around, hoping to catch a glimpse of the speaker.

A burst of icy breath—now in the other ear.

I whipped around in that direction. But the foyer was empty. The shadows stretched long and menacing across the floorboards as the sun slowly sank to the west, the sunlight that had been so vibrant now growing muddy and bland.

Around me, the air grew heavy, thick. It pressed in on me, weighing down my limbs, making it difficult to move, impossible to breathe. I clutched my chest, my lungs burning, fighting for air. Panic dug its claws into my skin, slashing, shredding, pulling me apart bit by bit. I tried to scream, plead for help, but no sound came. I stumbled forward, arm outstretched, grasping desperately for anything, anyone—

"Zellie!"

The pressure and panic instantly lifted. I gasped, air slamming into my lungs so hard my body arched backward, and I would've fallen had someone not caught me. Strong arms pulled me close for one steadying moment before guiding me to the game room and easing me into one of the plush velvet chairs.

"Slowly, slowly..."

I closed my eyes, forcing a long inhale, then another, releasing each breath slowly until the room stopped spinning. When I opened my eyes, Whit was kneeling in front of me, holding my hand, his thumb stroking lightly over my skin. His brows were drawn tight with worry.

And then a flash of something else, warm, electric, shot through me. My breath hitched. Embarrassment burned my cheeks.

"Oh, my God," I muttered, yanking my hand away and trying to stand, only for Whit to gently guide me back down.

"Give it a few minutes," he insisted. "Just breathe. Make sure you're steady."

I nodded, still anything but steady but not wanting to sit there feeling like an idiot any longer than I had to. "I'm good," I lied, forcing a smile. "I need to go pick up Henry. June will be wondering where I am."

Whit shrugged. "June can wait. You want to tell me what happened?"

I hesitated, debating, but then shook my head. "It was nothing. Just a panic attack. I'm fine."

He gave me a disbelieving look but didn't press. Instead, he went to the alcohol cabinet and poured a finger of what appeared to be brandy and handed it to me. "For your nerves."

I didn't typically touch hard liquor, but when I took a sip, the warmth of the amber liquid as it slid down my throat had a surprisingly comforting effect. I took another sip before handing him the glass.

"Thank you," I murmured, mortified all over again.

Only then did I notice he was wearing a slate-gray suit—not the casual clothes I'd grown used to seeing him in during his increasingly frequent visits to Dawes

House when we'd walk the garden paths or sit on what had become our favorite bench while watching Henry and Addie play.

He must've come straight from the office or some important meeting. And here I was fainting like some melodramatic Victorian heroine who'd had a "great shock" over—what? Calling in an anonymous tip about one of my neighbors and pissing off half the building? Being terrified of disappointing people who'd started to feel like family? Or, I don't know, maybe it was the phantom voice that had whispered *run* in my ear.

Pathetic, I thought bitterly. *Was I really that needy? That easily scared?*

Irritated with myself, I stood abruptly, but my head swam again. I reached out blindly for something to steady myself.

Whit's hand found mine immediately. "I've heard of someone being a lightweight, but..."

I opened my mouth to protest his assumption, but when I caught his gaze, I saw a sparkle of humor there. "You're teasing me."

His expression immediately shifted into its customary seriousness. "I'm sorry. I shouldn't—"

"No, no!" I interrupted in a rush. "I didn't mean that in a bad way. I just..." I sighed, words failing me. "I'm not really used to anyone..." I let my words hang there, not sure how to characterize this particular void in my interpersonal relationships. I didn't have many friends. Certainly not anyone who teased me or was playful with me in any way, honestly, even when I was a kid. Even my friends from the old coffee shop had been careful around me, maybe sensing there was something different. Or maybe I just gave off a vibe that kept people at a distance.

I shook my head, clearing away thoughts of how Whit had so quickly filled gaps I didn't know existed. Heat crept into my cheeks. I cleared my throat. "Anyway, thank you for your help. Really. I think I'm okay now."

Despite my assurances, Whit stayed close, valiantly absorbing June's barbed glances as I picked up Henry from her apartment. And he stayed at my elbow when we made our way to the elevator. And he stepped inside with us, pressing the button for the fourth floor before I could insist for a third time that I was fine.

When we reached my apartment, Whit slipped off his suit jacket and draped it over the back of the couch before rolling up his shirt sleeves. "What would you like for dinner, Henry?" he asked with a grin. "Spaghetti tacos?"

Henry burst out laughing. "Yuck! No!"

Whit looked up at the ceiling as if thinking. "Hmm... How about fried frog legs and turtle soup?"

Henry gasped. "No way! That's *gross*!"

Whit rested his hands on his hips. "Okay, then you tell me, sir—what sounds good?"

Henry's eyes lit up. "Chocolate chip pancakes!" He grabbed Whit's hand and pulled him toward the kitchen. "C'mon! I'll show you where everything is."

Whit shot me an amused glance and winked. "We've got this."

I sat in the living room for several minutes, stunned, listening to the concerning clattering and banging around of bowls and skillets and to Henry's laughter—his big, heartwarming belly laughs—as Whit apparently committed unspeakable culinary crimes.

Henry shrieked with laughter. "No, Mr. Whit! Not like that!" Another cackle. "Oh, my gosh!"

Smiling, I finally went to the kitchen door and burst into laughter.

There was pancake batter on the counter, the wall, the floor... An unreasonable number of dishes were already piled in the sink. Whit's suit pants—which I imagined were extremely expensive—were splattered with pancake mix, and a smear of batter was on his cheek.

Henry turned to me, beaming with amusement, hair spiked with a glob of drying batter. "Mama! I don't think he's done this before!"

Whit grimaced apologetically. "I'm afraid Henry is correct. Cooking isn't my forte."

I shook my head, not bothering to suppress my amusement as I entered the kitchen and waved him aside. "Let me show you how it's done, Mr. Proffitt." I squeezed between them, my hip brushing against Whit and making my stomach flutter. Struggling to ignore how close he stood, peering over my shoulder into the bowl, I added more mix to the soupy batter. "Wow…this is…"

"A disaster?" Whit supplied.

I turned to look at him and our eyes locked. The air shifted, growing charged as we both seemed to realize how his body crowded mine in the small kitchen. Our smiles faded. He leaned closer. His eyes dropped to my lips then back up to my eyes, and my heartbeat thudded against my ribs, my breath growing shallow. And when he placed his palm lightly on the small of my back, my eyes fluttered shut on a sharp exhale.

"Mama!" Henry said, tugging my shirt. "Don't forget the chocolate chips!"

My eyes snapped open, and I quickly shifted my attention to my son. "Don't worry, baby. I won't forget. Where are they?"

"Here you go." Whit held out a bag of chocolate chips, his eyes still burning as his gaze met mine. "I think I have what you need."

Oh, I thought, flushing, that delicious, tempting warmth flooding my veins, *I have no doubt you do…*

I was surprised to see Whit sitting on the couch when I returned from giving Henry a bath and tucking him into bed. Well, *sitting* wasn't exactly accurate. He was perched on the very edge of the cushion, hands laced together, shoulders stiff, his expression tense and unreadable. Just like the last time he'd hung around after I thought he'd already left.

"Hi," I said, stopping short, my curiosity evident in my tone.

He stood immediately, offering me the tentative, careful smile he used when he wasn't sure where he stood with me. "I cleaned up my mess in your kitchen," he said, jerking a thumb over his shoulder toward the crime scene. "I hope you don't mind me still being here. I wanted to make sure you were okay before I left."

I shook my head. "No, no...It's okay. I appreciate your concern. I'm just...not used to anyone looking after me."

"Well, you don't have to worry about that now," he assured me. "You have all of us at Dawes House to look after you."

All of us?

As much as I wanted to believe that the residents of Dawes House meant what they said about being a "family," the truth hit me hard and fast: there was only one person's attention I cared about. One person whose concern breathed life into something broken and frail in my heart. But it wasn't anything I had the right to ask for or even hope for. Not when I had no idea whether it would continue as soon as I found a new place to live.

"Thanks, Whit," I said. "I really do appreciate how welcoming everyone has been—well, until today. I really screwed up."

He frowned. "What do you mean?"

I sighed and leaned on the back of the easy chair, picking at a loose thread rather than meet his gaze as I explained what had happened with Billy Wayne and Kitty—her fear, the police call, the foyer performance. When I got to the part about Merilee's odd comment, I glanced up to see an angry expression flicker across Whit's features before smoothing into his usual stoic composure.

"I don't blame any of them for being pissed," I said quickly. "I would be too. I took what Ms. Pearlie and the others said at face value, got too comfortable here, but I'm not family. I haven't been here long enough to get involved with anyone's business. And I won't be here much longer anyway. Maybe a month or two tops.

I'll be gone as soon as I can, and then you can rent this place to someone who can actually pay you."

I lifted my eyes fully this time, holding his gaze, needing him to see that I meant it and that I wasn't going to impose on his kindness any longer than I had to. And I now realized I had to leave before I came to care for him more than I already did. Because the pull toward him was stronger than anything I'd experienced before. Strong enough to scare me. Strong enough to shatter my fragile heart.

Something in my expression must've betrayed my inner turmoil because Whit grabbed his jacket from the back of the couch and crossed to the door without a word, but he paused when he grasped the doorknob and turned back to me. "Zellie, don't worry about what happened earlier. There are dynamics among the residents that have nothing to do with you." He opened the door and stepped into the hallway before adding, "I hope you'll stay. For as long as you need to."

I shook my head, not wanting to be just a charity case. "Whit, I—"

"I'd like you to stay," he interrupted, the way he held my eyes stealing the breath from my lungs.

I tried not to read into what he said or what I saw in his eyes, but the warmth I'd known before when he and I were side by side in the kitchen came back in a rush, and I swallowed hard, finding it impossible to speak.

When I didn't answer, he turned away and shut the door behind him.

I stood where I was, my mind racing with questions I wasn't sure I wanted to answer, when icy breath hissed in my ear—the same voice I'd heard in the foyer.

I spun around. Nothing. But I *felt* her. Felt her fear. Her rage. Her desperation.

"Please leave me alone," I whispered. "I don't know what you want from me. Just leave me alone!"

The energy dissipated instantly, and the humidity of the Savannah evening clung to me again, suffocating despite the window units rattling away.

I rushed to the door and turned the deadbolt, knowing it would only keep out the intruders of the flesh and blood variety, but it still offered the smallest sliver of comfort.

Not ready to sleep—certainly not ready to face whatever waited behind closed eyes—I curled up on the couch where Whit had been sitting moments before. The upholstery still held the scent of his clothes, his aftershave—clean, warm, masculine.

I turned on the TV, willing the soft flicker of light and the low murmur of voices on the legal drama to distract me from the memory of how good his arms felt around me. And how empty the room now was without him.

CHAPTER NINE

In my dream, I was running barefoot through the trees, the branches smacking me in the face, clawing at my skin, slicing little lines of fire into my arms and legs. Terror gripped me so completely I couldn't think of anything except escape, getting away from the darkness pursuing me. I cried out as my nightgown caught on a branch and tore, but I didn't stop. I just kept running.

This time, my dream wasn't interrupted by David's slap. This time, I was lucid enough to know I *was* dreaming, that I wasn't myself. I was witnessing events from the perspective of the woman in my dream, suffering the sting of the branches against her skin, the rocks that cut into her feet as she ran, the suffocating humidity that lingered after a recent storm. The intensity of her fear...

I glanced over my shoulder repeatedly until the trees thinned and the shape of a house rose before me in the moonlight. My father's house, my childhood home. As the clouds parted, the moonlight grew brighter, allowing me to see the house more clearly.

Dawes House.

Through her I knew it was Dawes House, but it wasn't the house I lived in now, but a version that belonged to another century, and it stood alone on the grounds, predating the Victorian neighborhood that now occupied the land. But I knew it instantly—*she* knew it. The surge of hope that rushed through her—through me—nearly buckled her knees. Safety was only a few strides away.

I sprinted up the steps and pounded on the door with my fist. "Father!" I screamed, my throat burning, my voice ragged. "Father, please! Let me in!"

A moment later, someone opened the door—not my father, but a very pretty young woman in a nightgown similar to mine, clutching a shawl around her to preserve her modesty, her blond hair hanging loose around her shoulders.

The blond woman looked familiar to me as I observed the scene, but I couldn't place her...

"Susanna?" she cried. "What on earth are you doing here? What's wrong? Come in, come in! You'll catch your death!"

Crying, shivering, I stumbled inside and into her arms, babbling unintelligibly. As she guided me to the front sitting room, I caught a glimpse of my reflection in the hall mirror.

Of course, it wasn't me at all. She was younger, maybe eighteen or nineteen, her dark hair wild and tangled. Blood streaked her cheekbones, scratches ran down her throat, across her chest, along her arms.

"What in the name of God is all that racket!" came a booming voice, footfalls heavy as the speaker stormed down the stairs.

I was more terrified then than I had been when in the woods running for my life.

I rushed toward him, clasping my hands as if in prayer. "Father! Please don't make me go back! Please, I beg you!" I clutched at his nightshirt, tears of desperation streaming down my face, burning my wounds. My knees gave out as the last of my strength drained away, and I collapsed at his feet. "Please!"

His hand fisted in my hair, and yanked—hard—dragging me toward the door.

I screamed with pain and fear, struggling to get my feet beneath me. "No! No! Father!"

"I will have none of this," he snarled. "You will return this instant, or I will drag you there myself."

"Help me!" I begged. "Eliza, please! Don't let him send me back. Please!"

But no help came. The young blond woman—Eliza—cowered in a corner, trying to look as small as possible.

"No daughter of mine will break her vows," my father roared, hauling me onto the porch. Fear and panic twisted my stomach. A wave of nausea hit me so hard, I couldn't stand. I doubled over, retching.

He shoved me down the front steps, disgust twisting his face as he towered over me. "You will obey me and return to your husband, Susanna" he spat, "or you are dead to me, to this family. Do you understand? I will not suffer this humiliation!"

"I cannot!" I sobbed. "He is the devil! He will drag me down to hell with him if I return!"

Before my father could respond, the sound of hooves and carriage wheels cut across the night. My father stomped down the front steps and grasped my arm, yanking me to my feet as the carriage came to a stop.

"Fairland," came a deep, accented voice from inside the carriage.

My father gave the speaker a curt nod. "Josef."

"I suspected I might find her here," Josef Proffitt drawled, his voice smooth and even. "Thank you for retrieving my beautiful bride before harm befell her." He leaned forward, extending his hand. His face was still half in shadow, more ominous for the concealment. "Come, my love. We have much to discuss."

My father dragged me to the carriage and forced me in. "Do not return to this house," he ordered through clenched teeth. "You are only welcome here on the arm of your husband."

I trembled so violently, I couldn't find my voice to protest. All hope I'd had of escape vanished. I slumped back against the seat and turned my head toward the porch—toward Eliza. She stood beside our father, her gaze fixed on Josef, her cheeks flushed, her eyes unnervingly bright.

Foolish girl. She adored him, the devil beside me. Wanted him for herself. One day she'd see him for what he truly was.

I didn't look at my husband until we reached his home a couple of miles away. He, too, said nothing, sitting there in stony silence, his fury palpable. When we arrived, he was eerily gentle as he helped me out of the carriage, then led me up the steps and into the house.

It was then that the light of the lanterns dispelled the shadows, and his face came into full view. And when he turned his eyes down to me, there was no kindness, no warmth, no empathy. Only darkness so deep it seemed bottomless.

I screamed.

Not the dream me, not Susanna. *Me.*

The dream tore away as I came fully awake, but the terror didn't. Josef Proffitt could've been Whit's brother. The likeness was uncanny—except for the soulless darkness in his eyes. It chilled me to my bones, and the shivering I'd experienced through Susanna clung to me, a coldness that burned inside my chest.

Part of me believed Susanna was showing me her history, begging me to understand the warning she couldn't voice. But another part of me whispered doubt, reminding me that years of pain, desperation, and frustration the dead experienced when trying to communicate could warp memory, taint the truth.

But one thing was certain. Susanna had been afraid of her husband. Deeply, hopelessly afraid.

There was no more sleep for me that night. Every time I began to drift off, another jolt of terror snatched me back. When my alarm finally went off, I stumbled into the shower, letting the hot water pour over me, trying to give the warmth time to eradicate the icy center that continued to make me shiver, even when the steam had grown thick and suffocating in the closed room.

Henry was particularly bouncy and talkative as he got ready to go to Ms. June's, which only served to drain what little energy I'd scraped together and to pile on fresh mom-guilt. I knew I should've been grateful that he was so full of life despite his condition, that I was being selfish for not finding joy in that moment. He was happy. And that should've been enough. At least, that's what I kept telling myself as I led him downstairs to Ms. June's apartment.

But part of me also knew I was being unrealistic. I was his mom, not a saint. I had the right to be exhausted after doing this on my own for so long and from now dealing with interrupted sleep and amped up adrenaline from never knowing what freaky-ass thing was going to happen next.

So between my tangled emotions and my bone-deep exhaustion, I wasn't in the best headspace when I turned down the hall to Ms. June's apartment and saw Whit and Chase in a heated argument, voices low, harsh. I couldn't make out what they were saying, but I heard my name more than once.

"Mama, let's go!" Henry tugged my hand, urging me forward. I hadn't even realized I'd stopped until then.

At the sound of Henry's voice, the argument came to an abrupt conclusion. Chase didn't miss a beat, turning toward us with his signature easy grin.

"Morning, Zellie! Hey there, buddy," he called, raising a hand. "How y'all doing?" Before I could answer, he clapped Whit on the back and added. "See you later, Cousin. I'll get back to you on those numbers."

Whit sent him an irritated look that was completely lost on Chase who was already sauntering away, whistling as if he didn't have a care in the world. But *I* saw it. And Whit knew it.

"Everything okay?" I asked softly, cautiously, fearing that hearing my name meant that I had something to do with Whit's stormy expression.

He nodded. "Yeah, it's fine. Chase is frustrated that I haven't squared away the contractors for the fourth-floor renovations. Plans are behind schedule. He had to get rid of the latest crew when they tore down the wrong wall in the basement, so they obviously haven't started upstairs."

"Oh," I said, realizing how I fit into the conversation. "I don't want us to be the source of a disagreement between you and your cousin. Just do what you need to do. Henry and I will be out of the way most of the day during the week. Contractors won't bother us."

Whit offered me a smile that seemed forced. "Well, I hope that's true seeing as how I'll be the one doing the work."

I shook my head, not understanding. "What do you mean?"

"We need to move ahead with repairs on the other apartment while I put out bids, so I'm moving into that unit. I'll handle the work myself." His smile faded, his expression becoming more serious, almost uncertain. "Hope you're okay with me being your neighbor for a while."

"Well, there you are!" Ms. June announced, her voice loud in the hallway. She opened her door wide, arms outstretched.

Henry immediately released my hand and ran to her, giving her a tight hug when she scooped him up and planted a kiss on his cheek.

"I was wondering when this sweet boy would get here!" June crooned. "Breakfast is ready, honey-pie. We'd best get you fed before it gets cold."

Henry turned toward me, his beaming smile warming my heart—and tugging at it more than a bit—as he waved to me. "Bye, Mama!"

"Bye, baby," I said, forcing a smile. "You be good for Ms. June." I lingered there a few seconds after the door closed, fighting the urge to barge into the apartment and take him to work with me. I was halfway to convincing myself that Dottie wouldn't care if I brought Henry to the shop when Whit touched my arm lightly.

"He'll be okay."

I nodded. "I know. He loves Ms. June and Mr. Earl and has such a great time playing with Addie. It's just..."

Words lodged in my throat. Why did it feel like I was losing him? It made no sense. It wasn't like Henry hadn't gone to a babysitter's before. So why did I feel so anxious, so sad?

Whit's fingers drifted down my arm until they reached my hand and gave it a brief squeeze. "You're not being replaced, Zellie."

I blinked away tears. Whit had put into words the fear I hadn't even fully admitted to myself.

"He calls her Mamaw June," I said. "He's never had a grandma before. I should be grateful. I know that. It's just hard to see him light up like that around someone else, after it's been just the two of us for so long."

"C'mon," Whit said, gesturing toward the foyer. "Why don't I give you a ride to the bookstore so you're not late." I started to decline his offer, but before I could he added, "I'll even treat you to the best coffee in town on the way."

I huffed a little laugh and nodded. "Thanks, Whit. I'll take you up on the ride, but I doubt Ms. Dottie would appreciate me walking in with coffee from a competitor."

"Fair point," he said with mock solemnity. "Then perhaps I should come in and sample yours."

"Sample my—" I repeated, then flushed. "Oh! Coffee!"

The corner of his mouth lifted in a wicked little grin. "Yes, coffee. In fairness, I suppose I shouldn't crown anyone the best until I've tried yours."

I opened my mouth to provide an appropriately saucy comeback when his phone rang.

His expression darkened immediately when he saw the number. He silenced the call.

"Everything okay?" I asked.

"Family business," he said, his tone tight. "I might have to take a raincheck on the coffee."

"Yeah, sure. Of course! Anytime," I said with a shrug even though I couldn't help being disappointed.

When we reached the bookstore, Whit hopped out first and quickly made his way to my side, opening the door before I could, and took my hand to help me—completely unnecessary but devastatingly effective. My heart hammered as he pulled me a little closer before shutting the door behind me.

"Thanks," I managed, breathless.

His eyes held mine as his thumb smoothed over the back of my hand.

The early morning breeze danced across my skin, sending a shiver through me. Well, it was partly due to the breeze. Suddenly shy and awkward at the way my body reacted to the closeness of him, I whispered, "I should go."

Before I could change my mind, I hurried to the shop, fumbling with the key until I finally got it in the lock. When I glanced back, Whit still stood where I'd left him, watching to make sure I got inside safely. He gave me a soft yet heart-stopping smile and lifted a hand before getting in his car.

"Hi, Ms. Dottie!" I called, cheeks still warm. "It's just me!"

Quick, muffled footsteps—more than one set—padded on the floor above where Dottie kept an apartment. A few minutes later, Dottie descended the back stairs, smoothing her side ponytail and tugging at her bedazzled shirt.

"Good morning, honey," she said, without meeting my eyes. "You certainly are *punctual*."

"Yes, ma'am," I said, unable to suppress a grin. "Where would you like me to start this morning? Inventory?"

She fluttered around a little aimlessly as if trying to look busy. "Oh. Oh, yes, Zellie honey. I think that would be just fine. You go right ahead."

I headed to the back of the store to where we kept all the supplies for the coffee shop. I'd barely stepped inside when low voices floated through the doorway. Dottie's voice was obvious. The other belonged to a man. Curious, I poked my head out just in time to see the back door closing.

I wasn't about to pry, so I was surprised when later that afternoon during a lull, Dottie came clacking into the coffee shop, glancing over her shoulder as if making sure no one was around.

"Zellie honey, I need a word." She leaned in and whispered with exaggerated precision. "I'd like to keep my...*visitor* between us, if it's all the same to you. We have too many nosy old busybodies in this town. I don't need them poking around in my affairs."

"Yes, ma'am," I assured her. I gave her a conspiratorial wink and added, "Your secrets are safe with me."

She patted my hand. "You're a good girl, Zellie. I'll be sure everyone knows that."

As she tottered off on her heels, I frowned after her, confused. "She'll make sure everyone knows I'm a 'good girl'?" I muttered. "What the hell is that supposed to mean?"

CHAPTER TEN

I hated the basement of Dawes House.

It was dark and creepy as all old basements are, but this was on another level. Whit was absolutely right to forbid anyone from living down there.

Some of the space was under construction. Framed-out rooms and half-finished hallways created even darker corners than usual. Other sections seemed untouched for decades. The timber used for support beams groaned with age. Forgotten possessions lingered like abandoned memories, the remnants of lives left behind—an antique wooden wheelchair, an old hobby horse, a child's rusting bicycle, lanterns, long-unused gardening tools. An enormous black heating oil tank loomed in the far corner, cold and obsolete since the house was converted to electricity.

But one of the most unnerving relics—the one that always made my blood run cold—was the well set into the floor. Layers of stone stacked in a circle formed its lip, a heavy wooden lid secured over the hole with a rusted padlock. Piles of construction debris sat on top of the lid as if someone had tried to bury the damn thing.

"I don't like it down there, Mama."

Henry pressed close to my side as we stood at the top of the basement stairs. Even with the light on, the bottom was lost to shadow.

"I know, baby," I told him. "I don't like it either. But I have to do laundry."

I put off laundry days until it was absolutely necessary, but with the late-spring heat settling over the city with its full force now, nothing could be worn twice.

"I don't *want* to go in the basement!" Henry whined, tugging my hand, trying to pull me away.

I blinked at him in disbelief. "Excuse me?" I cautioned. "You don't take that tone with me, young man."

"I'm not going!" He yanked again, harder, the force of it sending me stumbling.

"Henry!" I cried, dropping the laundry basket to catch myself. "What's wrong with you?"

He broke down completely then, sobbing loudly, his head thrown back, his mouth wide open as he wailed, "No! No! No! No!"

I knelt in front of him and held his arms. "Stop it, Henry," I said as calmly as possible. "I need you to stop crying and use your words. Baby, please—"

"Can I be of assistance, honey?"

Iris stood just a few feet away. Henry was crying so loudly, I hadn't noticed her approach.

"It's okay," I told her, sitting down on the floor and pulling Henry into my lap, rocking him a little to quiet him. "He's scared of the basement. I'm so sorry. He never has tantrums like this."

Iris gave me a sympathetic smile. "No problem, honey. We all have rough days. Isn't that right, Henry?"

Henry sniffed, took a shaky breath, and nodded.

"Why don't you let him come sit with me for a spell?" Iris offered. Before I could respond, she extended her hand to him. "Would you like to come sit with me at my desk, sweetheart?"

He nodded and launched himself from my lap, taking her hand then turning back, giving me a guilty look as if realizing he should've asked first.

"It's okay," I said with an exhausted sigh. "Go ahead with Ms. Iris this time." I got to my feet. "Thank you, Iris."

"Of course," she said, waving away my gratitude. "We all need a hand now and then, especially someone like you without anyone else to help her. You go on and tend to your laundry. We'll be up front when you're finished."

I watched them walk down the hall, grateful and unsettled at once. I hadn't missed her pointed reminder that I had no one but the Dawes House "family." Maybe they had forgiven me for the call about Kitty. Or maybe this was yet another way of reminding me to stay in line. Because I needed them.

I lifted my laundry basket again and turned to face the basement stairs, my mouth going dry. The first step creaked ominously as I started down.

As soon as I reached the bottom of the steps, I fumbled in the darkness for the light switch on the wall, heart kicking against my ribs. Finding it, I flipped on the lights to the main hallway that led to the laundry room, relieved when most of the bulbs instantly blazed to life, only one flickering a few times before finally joining the others. These were the big floodlights that people put on their houses that came on whenever they detected motion and then would shut off after a while, making it a race against time to reach the laundry room before being plunged into darkness once more.

I waved my hand in front of the sensor again to give myself more time—the damned things never stayed on long—and hurried forward, trying to keep my mind from imagining anything down there with me. But almost immediately the hairs on the back of my neck rose and my skin tingled with the undeniable sense that I wasn't alone.

I stepped into the laundry room just as the hallway lights clicked off, plunging me into darkness. My panic spiked hard. I waved my hand wildly, activating the laundry room sensor.

Not wasting a second, I went to one of the washing machines and began sorting the clothes. When I glanced over my shoulder to the doorway, the light blinked out. My gut twisted with fear.

“Damn it!” I muttered, waving my hand across the sensor, reactivating it, then turning back to my laundry. “I hate this freaking basement.”

Seconds later, the lights turned off again.

“Shit!” I cried, more irritated than frightened this time. With a huff, I waved my hand again, turning the light back on. “Screw this.”

I grabbed a couple of the small loads, and threw them in, hoping the colors were similar enough and the clothes old enough that they wouldn’t bleed and create a whole load of tie-dyed laundry for Henry and me.

I was just adding the detergent when the lights went off a third time.

“Are you freaking kidding me?” I demanded, angrily waving my hand across the sensor.

The light flicked back on.

And the woman in the bloody nightgown was inches from my face.

She opened her mouth hellishly wide in a silent scream, her face twisting with raw fury.

A ragged scream ripped from my throat. I stumbled back, tripping over my laundry basket and slamming into the wall hard enough to crack the plaster.

The lights died again.

Choking on sobs of fear, I scrambled blindly, but something caught my hair and yanked, dragging me back down. I screamed again thrashing wildly, twisting, fighting to get free of whatever—or whoever—grasped my hair.

Panting, terrified, I waved both arms wildly trying to activate the motion sensor.

When the lights came back on, I was alone again.

The tug on my hair ended instantly, my scalp stinging but free.

I lurched to my feet and spun around, breath sawing in and out of my chest. Relief nearly buckled my knees when I saw my hair had caught on splintered wood, the rotten laths behind the plaster having given way when I fell.

I waved a hand in front of the sensor, just to be safe, and leaned against the dryer, bent over, dragging air into my lungs and trying to calm the hammering in my chest. Just as my heartbeat approached its normal rhythm, a shadow fell across the doorway.

I straightened with a shaky gasp but then let out a short, relieved laugh when I saw Pearlie standing there with a laundry basket on her hip.

"You alright, Zellie?" Pearlie asked, rushing to me and setting down her basket so she could take my hands in hers. "You look like someone just walked over your grave."

I flinched internally at her choice of words and nodded, forcing a smile. I wasn't about to tell her what had just happened.

"I'm fine, Ms. Pearlie," I lied. At her concerned frown, I added with a thin laugh, "Really. Just embarrassed. The light went out and startled me. I tripped over my own laundry basket."

Pearlie chuckled and reached for the light sensor, sliding a switch at the bottom. "There now," she said, patting my arm. "That'll keep on the lights while you're in here. Just slide it back to the middle when you're done."

Embarrassed I hadn't figured that out sooner and possibly prevented the horror I'd just lived through, I quickly started my load. Pearlie chatted as she loaded her own laundry in the second machine. But her words didn't register.

All I could think about was the dead woman's silent scream...

Apparently, during our laundry room conversation, I'd agreed to come to a birthday party for Mr. Dean, of all people. I hadn't seen more than the occasional glimpse of him since he'd visited on our first night to roll out the welcome mat, but it wasn't like I'd made any effort to be neighborly either.

And, although I couldn't imagine anyone wanting to spend time with the cantankerous old man, let alone host a party for him, I couldn't refuse the invitation from Ms. Pearlie. She'd been kinder to me than my own mother ever had, so I wasn't going to insult her by backing out.

Figuring everyone else would be dressed up for the special occasion, I found a consignment shop near the bookstore during my lunch break and managed to buy a dress for me and a cute little shirt and tie for Henry. My paychecks from Dottie weren't much—not with what I needed to save for a down payment on an apartment. But it was something. And I refused to be like my mother. I wouldn't deny my son something special now and then when I could afford it. I just wouldn't.

"Look at you!" I said, adjusting Henry's tie, tears pricking my eyes as pride swelled in my chest.

He cupped my face with his little hands and kissed my cheek. "Thanks, Mama! I look like Mr. Whit!"

I laughed. "You sure do. Very handsome."

"Maybe I should wear it to school then," Henry said, suddenly very serious. "So everyone will know that I'm five and old enough to ride the school bus."

"We'll see," I replied, suppressing a smile. "You might change your mind by the time school starts."

I hadn't been wrong about everyone dressing up. They all looked like they were heading to the opera or a museum gala or some other fancy event. Even in my new dress I felt underdressed. But no one noticed. They were too busy doting on Henry and making a fuss over him. I faded into the background, content to sip on my lemonade in the corner. Which is probably why no one noticed me when I wandered into the living room where Henry and Addie had been playing during our first dinner at Pearlie and Junior's apartment.

"You promised."

An elderly woman in a wine-colored lace evening gown and perfectly matched leather pumps that looked like ones she might've worn as a young woman, clutched Whit's hands from where she sat in her wheelchair. Her voice was thick with tears as she added, "Your daddy promised it was my turn. I was supposed to be next!"

"I'm sorry, Ms. Netty," Whit told her, his tone sympathetic.

At that moment, Merilee glanced up and saw me. She bent to whisper something to Whit, then gave me a bright, carefully placed smile.

"Hey there!" she said cheerfully. "I'm going to take Ms. Netty back to our apartment. I think the party might be a bit too much for her."

I stepped aside as she began to wheel Netty past, but the older woman grabbed my hand, her grip surprisingly strong.

"Don't trust these people," she rasped. "They're lying to you, girl. Run now while you can!"

"Now, Ms. Netty," Merilee chided with a condescending smile. "You're going to frighten our Ms. Zellie. We want her to stay, don't we?"

"No!" Ms. Netty shrieked, shaking her head vehemently, her voice stronger than it had been, the cloudiness in her eyes briefly clearing. "Run, girl!"

I watched them disappear down the hall until I sensed Whit at my elbow.

"Poor Ms. Netty," he murmured. "She gets confused so easily these days."

"Is she always like that?" I asked, dread twisting inside me, unnerved by her warning.

Whit sighed. "Most days."

I turned to face him. "What did she mean 'her turn?'"

He swirled the ice in his drink and downed the last of it before responding. "Like I said, she's confused." He abruptly held up his glass. "Going for another. Would you like one?"

I shook my head. "No. Thanks. I'm good."

But before Whit could top off his drink, Junior poked his head in. "Come on, y'all!" he said, waving at us to follow. "We're gonna take this party outside. June's worrying herself to death that no one's eating Mr. Dean's cake."

I raised a brow. "Outside? Isn't it too hot? The frosting on the cake will melt."

Whit chuckled. "Guess we'll just have to eat quickly."

He gestured for me to exit the room before him, then placed a hand on the small of my back, gently guiding me from the room. It was an innocent enough touch, but it still sent a rush of heat through my body. I tried to hide the shiver that followed. But the subtle increase in pressure from his fingertips told me he'd noticed...and maybe even felt it too.

"Mama!" Henry shouted, having already shed his tie. "We're going outside! Papaw Earl put up a swing for me and Addie!"

Papaw Earl, was it now?

June smiled down at him and ruffled his hair. "He sure did! You'd best go try it out, little prince!"

Little Prince?

"That's awesome, baby!" I gushed, forcing excitement into my voice. "I'll be right out."

Henry pivoted and ran outside, June behind him. I reached out to grab Whit's arm before he followed.

He turned, frowning. "What's wrong?"

I hesitated, considering my words. Finally, I managed, "I just...I appreciate all the kindness from June and Earl, but I'm worried they're going to confuse Henry. He's not their grandson. I mean, when we leave..."

I didn't continue, remembering what he'd said the other day about hoping I'd stay. He knew exactly what sentence I'd left unfinished.

His expression shuttered, that familiar guardedness slipping back into place. "Even if you leave Dawes House, I hope you won't disregard us. There are people here who care about you and Henry."

I swallowed hard, working up the courage to ask, "People like you?"

His eyes searched my face briefly, and his voice was deeper, softer when he confirmed, "People like me."

We stood there for a long, charged moment before the sound of singing drifted across the yard, drawing my attention away from the warmth of his gaze.

I frowned. The melody tugged at some distant corner of memory, familiar, but out of reach. "What is that song?"

Whit cleared his throat and stepped back, retreating to Junior's liquor cart and pouring himself another drink. "Old blessing song."

I moved to the open door that led from the Johnsons' apartment to the back garden. "What language is that?"

"Uh...not sure," Whit said with a shrug. "Old English, I think. Or maybe Gaelic."

I laughed. "What happened to *Happy Birthday*?"

He grinned, visibly relaxing again. "Yeah, well, if you want to sing *Happy Birthday* to Mr. Dean, I'm sure he'd just glower at you for the duration of the song and not hold it against you for the rest of the night."

I rolled my eyes. "Does the man *ever* smile?"

Whit took a sip of his drink and then shook his head. "Not that I've seen." He gestured toward the door. "But there's a first time for everything, as they say. Better not miss it."

I followed him outside and instantly hit a wall of heat. Thick, damp humidity wrapped around my lungs, making it difficult to draw a breath. Within moments, sweat began to creep along the nape of my neck. I scanned the yard to make sure Henry wasn't suffering the same discomfort, but he was happily spinning on the rope swing Earl had hung earlier.

A grunt near my shoulder drew my attention. Mr. Dean glowered at the children as they played, clearly disapproving of their presence.

"Had a swing like that when I was his age."

I blinked, surprised to see him standing there, let alone talking to me. "Really? That must've been fun."

He grunted again. "Fell off and broke my arm in three places. My mother was so upset that my father cut down the tree and burned it for firewood."

And *there* was the Mr. Dean I was familiar with. "Henry and Addie seem to love it," I offered. "Henry's doing so much better now that he has someone to play with."

Mr. Dean glanced at me and made a dismissive noise. "That'd be June and Pearlie's doing."

I wasn't sure what that meant or how to respond. So, I cleared my throat and changed the subject. "Are you enjoying your birthday party?"

"A lot of nonsense," he grumbled. "Don't need a party. Need to be about fifty years younger. Why would I want to celebrate getting even older? Bullshit, if you ask me."

I glanced around, hoping someone would come rescue me from the conversation, but they were all occupied elsewhere—either playing with the kids or enjoying another cocktail while chatting with the others. Even Whit was now talking quietly with Merilee who had returned. A brief, sharp pain stabbed me in my chest at seeing them together, but I shoved it aside.

"Well," I said to Mr. Dean, exasperated by his attitude, "if you didn't want a party, you should have said so. I doubt they would've gone to all this trouble if they'd known you didn't want it."

He stared at me and shook his head like I'd said something profoundly stupid. "I'm eighty," he said. "It's tradition."

With that, he shuffled away toward Ms. Pearlie, who was waving him over to a tray of tiny silver goblets. Then Pearlie clapped her hands, calling for everyone's attention.

"My beloved family," she called as Earl picked up the tray and began handing out the drinks. She placed a hand on Mr. Dean's shoulder. "Our dear Mr. Dean has reached his eightieth year. Tonight, we toast him and bid him well as he takes his next journey."

I accepted the goblet Earl handed me. He winked. "Don't worry, darlin'," he whispered. "It won't kill you."

I gave him a weak smile and turned my attention back to Pearlie.

She glanced around the yard as if looking for someone and then a smile curved her lips. I turned to see who'd arrived and was surprised to see Billy Wayne and Kitty, the latter heavily pregnant and dangerously pale, leaning on her husband's arm as if she was nearly too weak to walk. Earl immediately handed goblets to both of them.

The only one missing at this point was Ms. Netty.

Pearlie raised her goblet again. "As we enter, so shall we depart."

Every resident raised their goblet, repeating Pearlie's words. I quickly raised mine, murmuring the odd toast a beat late, and watched as they all tossed back their sherry in a single swallow—except Kitty who only took a tiny sip before handing hers to her husband to finish.

"Drink up, buttercup."

I flinched and turned to see Merilee standing beside me, grinning.

"Is this the way you all usually celebrate birthdays?" I asked before obediently downing the sherry. It wasn't like I knew what a normal birthday celebration was supposed to be except for what I'd seen on TV or read about in books, but this couldn't have been typical.

"Not every year," Merilee replied. "Just the big ones. When we come of age and when we turn eighty."

"Why those?" I asked.

Merilee lifted her empty goblet, signaling Earl for a refill. "Coming of age is obvious, isn't it? That's when everything changes. You're no longer bound by childish rules. You're free to *be* without apology, to truly experience it all without reserve—love, joy, pleasure, desire, sex." She gave me a wicked grin. "You *do* remember what sex is like, don't you?"

My cheeks burned. And not from the sherry. I wasn't about to divulge anything I wanted or needed or had (or hadn't much) experienced. Luckily, before I could respond, Earl showed up to refill both our goblets before moving on to chat with Billy Wayne and Iris, Kitty having gone back inside.

Merilee reached up to curl a tendril of my hair around her finger and gave it a playful tug, her grin never faltering. "You need to learn to have some fun, Zellie-girl. Life doesn't always have to be so *serious*."

She tapped her goblet to mine and tossed back her drink then looked at me expectantly. I only took a sip this time, letting the liquid roll around on my tongue, savoring the flavor. It was delicious—a blend of spices and fruit and other flavors that reminded me of a mulled wine I had once at a Christmas party. But it wasn't like I had a broad basis for comparison. I never drank much. With Henry's medical condition, I couldn't afford to be even a little tipsy in case we had to make a trip to the ER.

"What d'you think, Zellie?" Earl called from across the yard. He was looking at me intently, gauging my reaction.

I stiffened at the attention, self-conscious at being singled out. "It's delicious. Thank you, sir."

"Made it ourselves, June and I," he said proudly. "Thought you might enjoy it."

I finished off the drink and scanned the yard for Henry, suddenly a little light-headed. "Henry? Time to go, baby."

He wasn't on the swing. I glanced around the yard, my heart pounding when I didn't immediately see him.

Shit, shit, shit...

"Henry!" I shouted, the world spinning, anxiety surging.

"Zellie?"

I ignored whoever spoke, turning in a panicked circle. "Henry, where are you?"

Someone gripped my shoulder and said my name, but I only dimly registered the information until that same someone grabbed my upper arms and gave me a little shake.

"Zellie."

I blinked rapidly. Whit's concerned face swam into focus. "Where's Henry? He's gone."

Just then, Henry and Addie burst out of the house, June right behind them. Each child held a sippy cup and was happily drinking whatever was inside.

Relief washed over me. I broke away from Whit and rushed to Henry.

"Baby, you have to tell me where you are," I told him, crouching down in front of him. "I was so worried!"

"I'm sorry, Zellie," June said. "I should've checked with you. The children wanted their smoothie. I didn't see the harm in giving them one."

I looked up at her, not understanding. "What smoothie?"

She smiled down at Henry. "Honey, you and Addie go drink your smoothies at the table and rest for a minute."

I stood slowly as Henry hurried off with his friend, then turned back to June. "What's going on?"

June gave me a patient look that only served to piss me off. "Zellie, darlin', don't be so alarmed. The smoothies are perfectly safe—just fruit and yogurt and some vitamins and herbs to help them stay healthy. It's all natural and perfectly fine."

I shook my head. "How do you know?" I demanded. "You have no idea how what you're giving him might interact with his medications."

June waved away my concern as if it were inconsequential. "There's nothing in there that could do harm. And he's been healthier since he started drinking them, hasn't he? Look at all the energy he has!"

"That's not your decision to make," I told her, struggling to keep my tone even.

June took my hand in both of hers and stepped closer, her expression softening. "Let's face it, darlin'," she said softly, "he has some catching up to do. After all, you haven't been able to provide the most high-quality food for Henry, given your situation and all."

My mouth fell open. All I could do was blink at her, too stunned to immediately respond.

"It's not your fault that you couldn't afford better," she continued, her patronizing tone getting under my skin. "But we're your family now so you should let us help you."

"Henry," I called, my eyes not leaving June's. "It's time to go." Then, through clenched teeth, to June, "How *dare* you question my ability to take care of my son? I am a *good* mother!"

She patted my hand. "Of course, you are, darlin'. You've been doing the best you could. Montgomery should've let us help you sooner."

Henry bounced to my side and handed June his cup. "All done, Mamaw June!"

"You sure are!" she gushed. "You'll have to tell your mama how much you like your smoothies."

I shook my head and let out a thin, incredulous laugh at her audacity to keep from being impolite. "Let's go, baby."

I dragged Henry away without another word, my mom-guilt tearing my heart apart. June wasn't wrong. I *hadn't* been able to afford the best food or to make everything from scratch with all the best ingredients the way they seemed to at Dawes House. But damn her for insinuating Henry's health issues were because I didn't have money. Damn her to hell.

"Zellie!" Whit called after us, but I didn't stop until he caught up to us in the foyer. "Please don't be upset with June," he said gently. "She means well."

I sent him a wry look. "Oh, I'm sure."

He reached out to touch my arm just as the elevator door slid open. I jerked away, but clearly not taking the hint, he stepped inside with us.

"Are you coming to play at our house, Mr. Whit?" Henry asked, grinning broadly with excitement, still buzzing from sugar or smoothies—or whatever June had slipped into that cup.

Whit sent me a quick glance, then shook his head. "Probably not tonight. I'm just going to stay and talk with your mama for a little bit."

"Go get ready for your bath, baby," I told Henry as soon as we entered the apartment, forcing a tight smile, though indignation still vibrated in my veins.

As soon as Henry disappeared down the hall, Whit exhaled and dragged a hand through his dark hair before finally meeting my eyes. "I'll talk to June. But think it over, Zellie. You might change your mind. There's old knowledge that has been passed down, preserved for generations. Things modern medicine has forgotten."

"I don't doubt it," I said. "And, trust me, I'm open to anything that can *safely* treat Henry's condition. But June had *no right* to treat him without my permission."

Whit nodded. "You're absolutely right. She should've checked with you first."

"And *shaming* me because I'm poor?" My voice cracked, tears stinging behind my eyes. "I already feel like a failure half the time for not being able to give Henry everything he deserves. I sure as hell don't need someone like June making me feel even worse!"

Whit stepped closer. "You're a great mother," he assured me. "You can't help your circumstances, Zellie. You've done everything you could to try to create a better life for you and Henry, even if the options weren't great." He grinned. "You certainly didn't want to move into Dawes House and have to deal with *me*, if I recall correctly." His voice softened. "But here you are."

I wasn't quite sure how I felt about everything he'd said about June's intentions or about my abilities as a mother. But he was right about one thing—I *hadn't* wanted to move into Dawes House. But I'd had no choice.

And now here I was, standing in front of this enigmatic, mysterious man, his kindness and friendship so much more than I'd ever expected. Whose presence soothed something raw inside me. Who stirred longings I'd buried years ago.

Whit's eyes searched mine—hopeful, questioning, unguarded.

And my pulse quickened, breath catching as I whispered, "But here I am."

CHAPTER ELEVEN

This must be what hell feels like...

That's all I could think as I checked the date on my phone, confirming it really *was* only June. I stood in front of the window air conditioner in my bedroom in nothing but a thin tank and even thinner pajama shorts, cursing the sticky night air that that refused to let me cool off even with the chilled air blasting me in the face, lifting my hair, needling at the sweat that clung to every inch of me, sweat that soaked my clothes and bedsheets the second I tried to sleep. Making a mental note to press Chase for an ETA on the central air installation, I wiped the back of my neck and went back to my bed, praying the sheets were cool enough for another attempt at sleep.

I was staring up at my ceiling fan, watching the lazy rotation, considering getting up again to check whether the AC was *really* on the highest setting, when my phone rang. Frowning, I reached for it. My stomach dropped when I saw the caller ID.

Vivian.

What horrible thing did she want to accuse me of that couldn't have waited until morning?

My first instinct was to send the call to voicemail, but I hesitated when I glanced at the clock and realized that it was after 2 a.m. Even when Vivian was off the wagon, she didn't have a habit of drunk dialing me anymore.

Hating that I even wondered whether she might actually need help, I took a deep breath, bracing myself, and answered. "Hello?"

Static washed through the line, thick and garbled, but I thought I caught my name somewhere inside the white noise.

"Hello?" I tried again. "Vivian? I can't hear you. We have a bad connection."

"Listen!" Vivian burst through, her voice shrill with panic. But the rest came through in broken, lurching fragments. "Need— tell— God— found— hear— devil—"

And there it was.

Clearly, she was calling to give me the same sermon as always—well, more a variation on a theme, really. But, had to hand it to her, calling in the middle of the night, definitely added a certain flair. I shook my head, angry that she would pull this shit. Why call me like this now? Why call at all?

"Vivian," I said loudly, hoping my voice broke through the static, "I can't understand you. You're breaking up."

The noise swallowed whatever she said next, the words unintelligible. Then there was just a flat, persistent hiss.

But I still listened, despite myself, knowing that if it really were an emergency, I'd never forgive myself for hanging up on her—or anyone in such a situation. The line didn't improve.

After another few seconds, I exhaled hard, exasperated. "Vivian, I'm hanging up."

I hit the button, tossed the phone aside, then flopped back onto my pillow, turning and shifting positions until finally finding a cool spot on the sheets. I was just dozing off when my phone rang again. I groaned, snatching it up from the bed beside me.

"What do you want, Vivian?"

Only static answered.

Frowning, I checked the screen. No name this time. Just a string of zeros.

"What the hell?" I murmured. My heartbeat jumped. My mouth went dry as dread crept along my skin, and I slowly lifted the phone to my ear. "Who is this?"

A hellish screech exploded through the speaker, the sound so shrill it seemed to penetrate my skull and pierce my brain. I yelped and threw the phone away, clutching my head with both hands as pain flared behind my eyes.

"Damn it!" I cried, blinking through tears. I glanced around the room, searching for my phone and found it on the floor near the bed.

Shaken by the strange call, I lowered one bare foot until my toes touched the floor. The boards creaked as I put more weight on my foot and then lowered the other. I eased down into a crouch next to the bed and reached slowly for my phone, then froze, my fingers still a few inches from it.

The line was still connected. Static hissed and crackled from the speaker, what sounded like fragments of urgent whispers trying to force their way through.

I stared at it, torn, not sure I wanted to know who was on the other end. But, my curiosity winning, I stretched my fingers toward it.

Without warning, a hand shot out from the darkness under the bed and clamped around my wrist.

I screamed and jerked back, trying to break its hold, but the grip tightened. Fingers mottled gray with decay, nails bloody and jagged, as though they'd clawed their way out of the grave, dug deeper, refusing to let go.

Another scream tore loose from me, and I pulled harder, fighting to get free. A second hand emerged, palm flat on the floor, pushing down on the boards, dragging its body forward. Silver eyes glowed in the darkness, then a wide grin peeled back putrid lips as a half-decomposed face slid into view.

Another ragged, terrified scream ripped from my throat.

My bedroom door slammed open, banging into the wall as Henry rushed in, eyes huge. "Mama!"

My head snapped up, fear for him overriding everything else. I opened my mouth to tell him to run—

But the corpse's grasp abruptly released me. The thing dissolved into the empty shadows beneath the bed. Gone.

I scrambled backward until I hit the wall. My chest heaved as I gulped in air.

Henry threw himself against me, wrapping his arms around my neck.

"It's okay, Mama," he whispered, his little hand stroking my shoulder.

I pulled him close in a tight hug, my gaze fixed on the darkness beneath the bed, trembling, waiting, half-expecting those silver eyes to flicker back into existence.

When I finally convinced myself she was gone and my brain could focus on what had just happened instead of my own horror, I realized there'd been something familiar about the intruder's face. But it'd been too dark and the face too decomposed to place it. Was she the screaming woman? The woman in the bloody nightgown? Her hair was too dark to be the one in the bathtub.

"Was that the woman in the basement?" Henry whispered as if reading my thoughts.

I pulled back, frowning at him in confusion. "What woman?"

His little body shuddered, and he buried his face in my shoulder. "The angry one."

I smoothed his curls. "I don't know, baby. Is that why you didn't want to go in the basement with me?"

He nodded. "I don't like her, Mama. She scares me."

"Well, you don't have to go down there anymore," I promised. "I'll go by myself."

Henry pulled back and looked up at me with tears in his eyes. "But what if she hurts you?"

Good question.

"She won't," I assured him, knowing for a fact that she definitely *could*. Dark bruises had bloomed around my wrist the moment she'd let go but then faded away seconds later. "Sometimes when a person is angry, they just need to tell someone."

"But, Mama," Henry said, his voice small. "What if she's angry with *you*?"

I wrapped my arms tighter around him, eyes drifting to the darkness under the bed.

Shit. That was a damned good question.

I didn't sleep much the rest of the night even though Henry and I decided to camp out in the living room on the couches, closer to the door if we needed to escape. Every time I dozed off for more than a minute or two, I jolted awake, convinced someone was in the apartment with us. But each time, the room was empty. Whoever had been under my bed was gone.

More than once, I checked the balance in my checking account as if money might magically appear and give me enough for a deposit on another apartment. But after I paid for groceries and Henry's medications and medical bills and other bills that I was behind on and desperately trying to catch up, there wasn't much left to move over to my savings. No matter how many times I did the math, no matter how many times I tried rearranging things in my head, the answer didn't change. It would be a few more months, at least.

We could make it a few more months, right? Just a few months. Then whatever haunted Dawes House could fuck off and bother someone else.

Of course, as soon as I thought that another realization hit me. The intruder who'd attacked me at our little house wasn't native to the property. She'd come from somewhere else. Had she been a warning? A premonition of the ghostly women I was to encounter? A portend nudging me away from Dawes House? If the last one, then that little clue would've been nice to freaking know at the time. If being a harbinger of doom had been the intruder's goal, she'd done a piss-poor job. Instead, she'd scared me straight into what I'd thought was my only option.

By the light of the day, when things seemed relatively normal, it was easier to compartmentalize. I had a job that I loved. A group of people who cared about

Henry and me. Surely, I could tough it out a few more months. It wasn't like we were visited every night, right? We just had to make it a few months...

I had an easier time selling that idea to myself when it was just me I was worried about. But when Henry began to show signs of exhaustion over the next few days, the skin beneath his eyes sunken and dark, his newfound energy and happiness from playing with Addie fading, his bones beginning to ache once more, the desperation to find another place to live came rushing back with a vengeance.

It had been a week since the last incident when I was awakened from a deep sleep by Henry calling for me, his voice taut with fear. I bolted to his room and flipped on the light, chasing away as many shadows as possible.

"What's wrong, baby?" I asked, catching him in my arms when he practically launched himself out of the bed.

"Someone was hurting David," he said, hiccupping around sobs. "I saw it!"

I sat down on his bed, still holding him, smoothing the damp curls from his forehead. "It was just a nightmare," I said gently. "I'm sure David's fine."

Henry shook his head vehemently. "No, he's not. She was stabbing him!"

My blood went cold.

Dear God...

"Want me to look around your room?" I asked, part of me praying he'd say no. When he nodded, I tried to seem unbothered as I sat him down on his bed and only hesitated for a few seconds before opening his closet door. Thankfully, it held only what belonged there. Nothing lurking. Nothing watching.

I scanned the rest of the room—no shadows out of place, no intruders making themselves known.

"It's all good," I told him, giving what I hoped passed for a reassuring smile.

"Under the bed," he whispered, his voice tight, thready, his fear causing him to shrink into himself. "You haven't checked there yet."

Shit.

My smile faltered for a heartbeat, but I pasted it back on. My stomach clenched as I knelt down beside his bed. I swallowed hard, lifted his comforter, and glanced underneath. An errant sock. A few action figures. Nothing else.

Thank Christ.

"All clear."

He didn't look convinced. "Can I sleep in your room?"

Considering what I'd just gone through a few nights ago in my room, I was stunned he wanted to be in there at all. But if it made him feel better and helped us both get some sleep, who was I to say no?

"You bet," I said, standing and lifting him into my arms.

As we stepped into the hallway, I flicked off his light. I'd only taken two steps when the lamp clicked back on, soft yellow glow spilling out into the hallway. I froze. Then I turned back, scanning the room. Nothing. I flipped the switch off again.

The light snapped back on.

Henry buried his face in my shoulder with a whimper. Irritated, and more than a little afraid, I spun around and glared into the empty room. With a huff, I flipped the light back off.

"Don't worry, baby," I murmured, rubbing his back. "There's nothing there."

Three pointed taps on my shoulder assured me otherwise.

I gasped, fear lancing through me as I whirled around.

No one was there.

"Fine!" I snapped at the empty doorway. "I get it. You're here. Now leave him the hell alone."

Without another word, I hurried to my room and locked the bedroom door behind us. It was a useless measure, sure. A locked door wasn't going to keep out a spirit who was intent on being noticed, but maybe the illusion of a barrier would be enough to keep us from being haunted by nightmares.

Whether in our dreams or in the putrid, rotting, decaying flesh...

CHAPTER TWELVE

"Who's that?" I asked Henry one afternoon while we sat at the kitchen table with his playdough. On his mat was the figure of a person with yellow hair. "Is it Addie?"

He shook his head without looking up, still pressing tiny buttons onto the shirt. "It's David."

"Ah," I said, nodding. I tapped the table beside the playdough version of David. "I like his shirt."

Henry grabbed the can of brown playdough and pinched a couple of pieces from the can and began molding them together. "It's a jacket. He wears a jacket. This is the wrong color, but David likes it."

"A jacket?" I echoed. "Very nice. Are those shoes you're making?"

Henry nodded.

"Do you want to see what I'm making?" I asked, keeping my tone light.

He shrugged. "I guess."

I blinked at him. "You *guess*? Where are your manners?"

He heaved the long-suffering sigh of a much older person before answering. "Yes, ma'am."

I gently touched his arm. "Hey, what's going on with you?"

He shrugged again.

"Did you have another nightmare?" I pressed.

"No, ma'am," he said, setting aside David's shoes and sliding off his chair. "I'm tired. Is it okay if I take a nap?"

"Sure, baby." I watched him go, frowning. Maybe it was time to call his doctor, see if he needed a treatment.

I started cleaning up, pulling apart my own creation and putting the pieces in their cans. I reached for Henry's, but I stopped short, my blood going cold. Playdough David's head had been ripped off and set to one side. And strips of red playdough crossed the abdomen like wounds.

"Sweet Jesus," I breathed. I hadn't even seen Henry make the gruesome changes. When the hell had he done that? I could've sworn that the head was still attached when he left the table.

Unnerved and concerned that Henry's nightmares were infiltrating his waking hours, I quickly tore the figure apart and sorted the pieces into their respective color cans then sealed each container and pushed them together into a neat cluster in the center of the table.

I stared at them, my thoughts going back to the first day in the apartment and the drawings hidden away in the desk that had depicted a crazed woman with a knife and a decapitated child. I'd assumed the child was a little girl, thinking it was Addie because of the yellow curls. Could it have been David?

I pushed back my chair and started for the kitchen doorway, intending to go find the drawings and take a closer look, when something hard nailed me between my shoulder blades. I yelped in surprise and spun around just as a can of playdough hit me in the chest. I grunted, but before I could react another can flew off the table, whistling past my head to slam against the doorframe.

"Stop it!" I snapped, my fists on my hips. "Stop it right now, David! Throwing a tantrum isn't helping anything. I'm trying—"

The doorbell rang, cutting me off.

"I'm trying," I repeated to the empty room, softer this time. I hurried to the apartment door and opened it a crack to make sure my visitor was of the corporeal variety.

I sighed with relief when I saw who it was, then slid the chain free and opened the door. "Hi."

Whit's eyes narrowed with concern. "Everything okay? Should I come back later?"

I pushed my hair back from my face with my forearm and shook my head. "No. Sorry. It's been a...weird day."

He lifted a few grocery bags, offering a tentative grin. "I brought you dinner."

I stared at him for a few seconds, not comprehending. "Did we...I didn't know..." Heat flushed up my neck and burned my cheeks as I realized I was in my ripped jean shorts and a too thin tank, bra-less because of the rising temperatures as Savannah crept toward summer.

"Sorry—I should've called first," he said. "I moved some of my stuff into the apartment down the hall so I can start on the renovations and wanted to proactively apologize to you and Henry for any noise."

"Uh, thanks," I said, still rattled by the experience in the kitchen and now taken off-guard by Whit's unplanned visit. "Come on in." I gestured to the kitchen. "Feel free to take the groceries in there. I'll...uh...be right back."

I hurried to my bedroom and stripped out of my shorts and tank, swapping them for a sundress and quickly raked my fingers through my hair before pulling it up into a messy bun so I at least looked somewhat presentable.

"Sorry," I called, heading to the kitchen, "I wasn't expecting anyone, so it's kind of a mess..."

My words trailed off as I entered the room.

Every cabinet door and drawer gaped open. The refrigerator also stood wide open. A bottle of ketchup had been emptied, the contents splattered across the floor and cabinets as if someone had stood in the middle of the room and shaken the bottle indiscriminately.

"What the hell?" I breathed. I looked at Whit, who stood in the middle of the chaos looking equally baffled. "Whit?"

He shook his head. "It was like this when I came in."

I closed my eyes and drew in a deep breath, letting it out slowly to hold back the tears that stung the corner of my eyes. Apparently, David's tantrum with the playdough was just a warmup.

When I opened my eyes, Whit had set the groceries aside and grabbed a roll of paper towels.

"You don't need to do that," I said, carefully stepping around the ketchup on the floor to take the roll of paper towels. Tears of frustration and exasperation and helplessness and a jumble of other emotions spilled onto my cheeks despite my efforts to hold them back. "I'll get it."

I tore off a wad of paper towels and ran them under the faucet. I'd just started to the counters when Whit's hands settled on my shoulders.

"Leave it," he said, gentle but firm. "I'll take care of it."

I turned to him. "I'm not letting you clean up my apartment, Whit," I snapped. "You've done enough for me. Jesus—I'm not completely helpless!"

He stepped back, raising his hands. "I never said you were helpless. I'm sorry if I've ever made you feel that way." He moved aside and let me work, not interfering while I finished wiping up the mess.

When I threw away the last of the paper towels, he asked, "What happened?"

I hesitated, weighing how much I could tell him—how much I *should* tell him—about what had been going on without sounding unhinged. I didn't want his pity. Not for me. Not for Henry's health. But I needed someone to talk to, someone to tell me it would be okay.

And I wanted that someone to be him.

I turned away and began closing the cabinet doors so I wouldn't have to look at him. "I'm worried about Henry," I said, starting with the safest topic. "He's struggling again. I'm taking him to the doctor this week. We're probably looking at another transfusion. But those only work for so long."

"If you're worried about the medical bills—" Whit began, but I cut him off.

"No," I said. But of course, I was. "I'll figure that out somehow." A bitter laugh slipped out. "What's one more payment plan, right?"

"Zellie—"

I shook my head. "It's fine, Whit. I'm just tired." I closed the final cabinet door and leaned against the counter, suddenly feeling the weight of...*everything.*

"All the more reason to accept help where it's offered," he said from where he stood across the room, his arms crossed over his chest.

"I don't mean to be rude," I sighed. "I'm just not used to having help. I appreciate everything you've done for Henry and me—what *all* of you have done for us."

He gave me a crooked grin. "Well, I hope you're still grateful after dinner. You saw my last attempt at cooking."

I laughed, the sound half-hearted, betraying my exhaustion. "Well, it can't be worse than what I just cleaned up. David's in rare form today."

He blanched at my words. "Who?"

Damn.

I hadn't meant to tell him about anything going on with the intruders. Henry and I had grown so comfortable talking about David that it just slipped out.

"David," I repeated. "I originally thought he was Henry's imaginary friend, but...I think he's a ghost. We've had a lot of weird things happening."

Whit's frown deepened. "Weird how?"

I waved a hand dismissively, vaguely noting he hadn't even questioned the "ghost" part of my statement. "Oh, you know...the usual. Lights turning on and off, feeling watched, stuff moving on its own, noises..." I laughed, trying to make light of it, not yet ready to share the more horrifying events. "All the usual activity you see on those reality TV ghost shows."

His eyes narrowed—not with disbelief, but more like quiet, searching concern, as if he was trying to figure out if there was more that I wasn't telling him. And because there was *a lot* more I didn't want to tell him, I turned away and started unpacking the groceries. "So," I said looking over my shoulder with a smile, "what's on the menu tonight?"

Henry rallied during dinner, animatedly chatting with Whit about TV shows and books Whit clearly knew nothing about but still listened to Henry as if he were the most fascinating person in the world, asking questions and commenting on Henry's vivid descriptions. But as the evening wound down, Henry started to complain about his bones hurting.

"You must be growing," Whit said. "Where does it hurt?"

Henry rubbed his knees, wincing, and then pointed to his shoulders, arms, hips.

"C'mon, baby," I said, picking him up. "Let's get your medicine and a warm bath."

"I'll clean up," Whit said, rising to gather the dishes.

I shot him a grateful look then took Henry to the bathroom to get him ready for his bath.

"Mama, I don't like this," he whimpered, his voice thick with tears. "I don't want to hurt anymore."

I sat on the floor and pulled him into my lap, rocking him for a little while. "I know, baby," I murmured, my own tears blurring my vision. The helplessness pressing on me was suffocating. There was nothing worse than seeing my baby in pain and not being able to relieve it. I would've taken on his pain myself in a heartbeat. But with that not being an option, all I had were the tools the doctors gave me.

Those aren't the only tools, my conscience whispered.

An hour later, Henry's pain medicine and warm bath had helped enough that he was able to sleep.

I didn't expect Whit to still be there, but when I entered the kitchen, he was just wiping down the counter.

"Thank you," I said, my weariness evident in my voice. "I appreciate you doing this."

He slung the damp dish towel over his shoulder and narrowed his eyes, studying me again. "You look exhausted."

I laughed. "Thanks."

He gave me a wry look, tossed the towel aside, then took my hand and pulled me to him, wrapping his arms around me. I melted into him, slipping my arms around his waist and pressing my cheek to his chest.

God, it felt so damned *good* just to be held, comforted for once, to feel like everything was going to be okay. I don't know how long we stood this way. But for just that short space of time, I wasn't scared or overwhelmed or alone.

At some point, Whit rested his cheek against the top of my head. His arms around me tightened. And what had been a comforting hug suddenly became something more. My fingers splayed on his back, feeling the corded muscle beneath his shirt.

There was a shift in the air between us, a charge that ignited. His heartbeat accelerated, matching my own. Our breath synced, shallow, quickening. A warmth unfurled inside me, want and hunger and longing I hadn't experienced in years. *Desire*. Pure and unmistakable. I *wanted* him. *Needed* him.

His hands drifted down to my hips, his fingers curling into fists, gripping the fabric of my sundress. In my mind, I saw him pulling it over my head, tossing it aside, kissing me breathless, taking me right there on the kitchen table...

In reality, he let out a low, strangled groan and stepped back, putting distance between us. His gaze stayed fixed on the floor, as if meeting my eyes might break something open.

"I should go," he practically growled, his voice rough.

A shiver raced through me at the deep rumble of his voice. "Whit—"

Before I could tell him it was okay, that I wanted him too, he strode from the kitchen without looking back. A moment later, the apartment door closed.

I gripped the back of a chair to keep from sinking to the floor, holding on until the rush of warring emotions I experienced at where things had *almost* gone and then his abrupt departure had passed.

When I could feel my knees again, I drifted into the living room, hoping I'd see him sitting there on the couch, his back stiff, his hands clasped like before. But he wasn't there. And a great, gaping hole opened up in the center of my chest.

"Oh my God," I groaned, dragging my hands down my face. "Get a grip, Zellie."

As I showered, I tried not to think about how his arms felt around me, the heat of his body against mine, how badly I'd wanted to feel his kiss, how longing had surged through me, how I burned for his touch. But the fantasy that had played in my mind in the kitchen replayed in my head, leaving me gasping and shuddering as my hands explored my body as I imagined his would.

But it wasn't nearly enough.

I fell into a fitful sleep, my dreams haunted by fantasies of Whit instead of nightmares. Which was almost worse. The dreams of Whit were torture. I woke several times, tangled in my sheets, drenched in sweat, until finally exhaustion dragged me under.

I didn't feel the bed shaking at first. But as I slowly came awake, I realized my mattress was shifting, moving horizontally in a slow rhythm as if someone was standing beside the bed, pushing the side of the mattress. And then it abruptly stopped.

I lay still, staring at the ceiling, muscles tensed, adrenaline spiking, preparing me for fight or flight as I waited to see what would happen next. Minutes passed. Nothing.

My eyes drifted shut again.

Then something grabbed my leg and shook me so hard that my left hip rocked up off the mattress.

I bolted upright with a gasp, my heart slamming against my chest, fully expecting someone to be standing near my bed. For a fraction of a second, I thought I saw a shadow slinking along the wall. I clicked on my bedside lamp.

No one.

I blew out a shaky breath and ran my fingers through my hair.

"What a freaking night," I muttered, extricating myself from my sheets, and swinging my legs over the side of the bed.

I glanced at the clock.

3 a.m.

I groaned. "Seriously?"

That's when I heard Henry whimpering.

I launched to my feet and raced to his room. "Henry?" I said, flipping on his light as I burst inside. "Baby, are you okay?"

He was thrashing around on his bed, writhing in pain.

"Oh, God," I breathed, rushing to scoop him up. I somehow managed to find my shoes and my keys despite my panic. By the time we were halfway to the elevators, Henry's whimpers had turned into agonized moans.

"It's okay, baby," I said, stabbing the down button. "It's okay. Mama's got you."

"Zellie?"

I glanced behind me to see Whit, hair mussed, barefoot, wearing only jeans and T-shirt, sleep still clinging to him.

A strangled sob was all I could manage.

Whit pivoted instantly and ran back toward his apartment. The elevator doors opened, and I rushed in, punching the button for the main floor.

When the doors slid open again, Whit was already waiting.

How the hell had he gotten downstairs so fast...?

"I'm driving," he said, jogging ahead to open the front door.

The drive to the ER was a blur. All I could remember was sitting in the backseat of Whit's car with Henry in my arms while Whit drove at breakneck speed.

Oddly, there was no wait in the emergency room. Henry received pain medicine and was admitted to a room in minutes.

And then I lost all sense of time.

There was only the endless waiting while the doctors worked to figure out what was causing Henry's pain. They sedated him, transfused him, poked and prodded and scanned him. And all I could do was sit by his bed, questioning every choice I'd made, berating myself for not doing something more—whatever the hell that would've been.

Finally, after what I deduced to be two days based on the number of trays of food that had been brought to me but which I hadn't eaten more than a few bites, Henry started to improve. A day later, we were discharged with still no official diagnosis but lots of sympathetic smiles and well-wishes.

"I need to give you my address and insurance information," I told the patient coordinator who brought us our final paperwork. "We didn't have a chance to do any of that when we arrived."

She smiled. "No need. That's already been taken care of. Your friend gave us your contact information."

"Oh," I said. "Okay. Do I need to pay my co-pay before we leave, or will you just bill me?"

She gave me another smile. "No, that's been taken care of."

"What's been taken care of?" I asked, shaking my head in confusion.

"The bill." She turned her clipboard to me. "Just sign here," she said, tapping the x on the release form with her pen before handing it to me.

My mind still trying to wrap my head around the fact that the bill was paid, I did as instructed.

She patted my shoulder when I handed back the clipboard. "You take care now, you hear?"

"Yes, ma'am," I murmured. "Thank you."

"I'll send the nurse in to wheel Mr. Henry to the car," she told me. "Your ride is already here."

I blinked at her, confused. I hadn't called anyone.

Whit must've arranged that too. Part of me bristled—here he was once again arranging things without consulting me first. But another part of me, the very tired, worn-down part of me, felt a rush of gratitude and pleasure. I'd needed help, and he'd been there.

But when the nurse rolled Henry out to the patient pickup area, it wasn't Whit waiting for us. A man I'd never seen before stood next to a sleek, black sedan, dressed in a black suit and chauffeur's cap.

"Now, that's a nice ride," the nurse said as we approached the car. "Look at you going home in style, little man."

Henry grinned up at him and bumped the fist the nurse held out. "Bye, Darnell! Thank you for taking care of me!"

"I'd say 'anytime'," Darnell told him, locking the chair's wheels in place, then pointing a finger at Henry, "but I don't want to see you back here anytime soon, you got it?"

Henry's smile broadened. "Yes, sir!"

"I'm sorry," I said to the driver, "there must be some kind of mistake."

"Are you Zellie and Henry Dupont?" he asked. When I nodded, he opened the back door. "Then there's no mistake, ma'am. Mr. Proffitt instructed me to pick you up and deliver you to Dawes House."

I could only stare at him in disbelief, but Henry had already climbed into the car and was buckling into the booster on the seat behind the driver. "C'mon, Mama!"

I slid into the backseat, uncomfortable with the extravagance. "I'm surprised Mr. Proffitt didn't pick us up himself," I told the driver. "I didn't even know he had…" I paused, not sure what the correct term was for the man driving the car, so I finished with "this car."

The driver smiled at me in the rearview mirror. "Yes, ma'am. He typically only uses the driving service for business, but he was called away to New England this morning and wasn't able to come for you himself."

"New England?" I repeated, wondering what business he had that far north.

"Yes, ma'am," the driver replied. "He'll be using the service up there for his needs. Little out of my territory."

The car was silent for the rest of the drive to Dawes House. As the driver pulled up to the front of the house, a new wave of panic hit. What was the protocol after getting dropped off by a driving service? Did I tip? Say something? I'd never even taken an Uber. How was I supposed to know how to deal with *this*?

"I'm sorry," I said quietly as soon as Henry started up the sidewalk to the front steps. "I don't know how this works. Am I supposed to tip you? I don't have any cash…"

He smiled reassuringly. "No, ma'am. No need. Mr. Proffitt has already taken care of that."

We were barely inside the building when Pearlie and Iris rushed toward us, offering hugs to both Henry and me, gushing about how glad they were that Henry was okay and that we were back home, safe and sound.

"Iris," Pearlie said, taking Henry's hand, "I'm going to go up with Zellie and Henry to make sure they're settled. Could you please let June know that I'll be a little late to our afternoon tea?"

"Of course, Ms. Pearlie," Iris agreed. She gave me a sympathetic smile. "Just let me know if there's anything you need, Zellie."

I nodded and allowed Pearlie to take the lead as we made our way to the elevator. When we reached the apartment, she opened the door and ushered us in.

I frowned, surprised that the door was unlocked. I must not have locked it in my haste to get Henry to the hospital. Or someone had unlocked it while we were gone. Either way, it made for a stunning homecoming.

The house was filled with vases of flowers that looked like they were cut from June's garden. And several bouquets of balloons in bright colors and themes that reflected the TV shows Henry had discussed with Whit at dinner the other night filled in some of the remaining empty space.

"Look, Mama!" Henry cried, his face beaming. "Look at all the balloons!"

"You'd best go look in your room, Henry," Pearlie told him with a wink.

His eyes went wide, and he hurried off down the hall as fast as his still-healing body would allow. "Oh, my gosh!" he shouted from his bedroom.

I glanced at Pearlie who just smiled knowingly and gestured toward the hall. "Go on."

When I stepped into Henry's room, I gasped. The cracks in the walls and ceiling had been repaired, the entire room repainted. And on Henry's bed was a new teddy bear and a stack of books tied with a ribbon.

I shook my head in disbelief. "How...? Who did all this?"

"Well, now," Pearlie said from just behind me. "Who do you think? But I believe the books are a get-well present from Dottie Shay."

My heart swelled with such emotion I thought it might burst. Words failed me. But apparently that was okay. Pearlie just slipped her arm around my shoulders and gave me a hug.

"Thank you so much, Ms. Pearlie," I finally managed, wiping tears from my cheeks. "I don't know how I can thank all of you for this."

"Oh, don't thank us," she said. "Whit had three crews in here fixing things up. We just handled all the flowers and food."

"Food?" I asked, my brows drawing together.

"Oh, honey," she said with a laugh. "What kind of neighbors would we be if we didn't smother you in food in your time of adversity? You'll probably want to freeze some of it. Iris made enough peach cobbler to feed an army!"

We left Henry perusing his new books, and I walked Pearlie to the door, still stunned by everything they'd done to welcome Henry home. Before she could go, I threw my arms around her and hugged her tightly.

"Now, now," she said, patting my back. "It will all be okay, baby. Don't you worry."

I nodded and released her, blinking back fresh tears. "Yes, ma'am."

She turned to leave but paused and faced me again. "Whit is a good man," she told me. "But he wouldn't have done this for just anyone, Zellie."

My cheeks grew warm, remembering what Whit had told me about his father. I prayed Pearlie didn't think I was playing Whit just to get what I could from him and then would take off in the middle of the night.

When I said nothing, she patted my cheek. "Well, I'll let you get settled. You'll definitely be more comfortable now, but let us know if you need anything. Whit will be back in a few days."

I went to check on Henry and only then realized the window air conditioning units were gone. There was a soft click, and a rush of cold air hit me in the face.

How in the world had Whit managed to get the air conditioning installed while we were gone? That must've been one of the work crews Pearlie had referenced.

Grinning, I sat down on Henry's bed and texted Whit:

Thank you. For everything.

I added a heart emoji and sent it before I could change my mind.

A few seconds later, he responded with just a terse:

You're welcome.

My heart sank a little, realizing I'd been hoping for something more personal. Maybe I'd misread things. Maybe he'd just taken the opportunity to do repairs while we were out of the apartment and there wasn't anything else behind it.

After reading a few books with Henry and settling him down for a nap, I finally made my way to the kitchen and laughed. Food was piled high on the counters, in the freezer, in the refrigerator… I hadn't known there *were* so many casserole recipes. And in the refrigerator door were seven sippy cups filled about halfway with a mixture of some sort.

A note was taped to the first: *One per day. Add yogurt.*

Smoothies.

There was no message of rebuke from June, no "I told you so." Just instructions she knew I would now follow. My pride wasn't worth Henry's pain.

I sighed and picked up one of the cups, gave it a shake, then set it on the counter so I could give Henry one with his supper that evening. I still didn't know exactly what was in the concoction June had been giving Henry without my knowledge, but it had clearly helped him.

Exhausted, I went to my own bedroom and stretched out on the bed. That's when I noticed a book on the bedside table that hadn't been there before. Frowning, I picked it up, running my fingers over the cover. It was old but well cared for. I opened it and stared at the cover page, unable to believe what I was holding: a first edition volume of poetry by Lord Byron.

Later, as I gingerly paged through the delicate tome, my phone buzzed with a text notification. My heart lifted when I saw it was Whit again.

I hope you enjoy your present. From my personal collection.

I look forward to discussing with you.

Grinning, I curled onto my side and dozed off while reading the poems I loved so well.

Maybe Pearlie was right. Maybe everything would be okay after all.

CHAPTER THIRTEEN

"Help me, please," I sobbed, banging my fist on the door of the little shack in the woods. "Help me!"

The old woman who came to the door wore her gray hair in a single long braid that was draped over her shoulder, a woolen shawl wrapped around her in the cold autumn night. "What do you want, child?"

I looked behind me, afraid of who might be following. I licked my lips, dry from my escape. "You must help me. I've...I've heard you can help me take care of...things."

She stepped aside and beckoned me in. "You shouldn't say such things aloud."

My hands shook as I held them up, pleading. "Please, you don't understand. I can't have it. It's evil. You must take it."

"Evil?" the woman repeated. "How can it be evil?"

"Please, just help me before he finds me," I begged.

She studied me for a long moment then sighed. "I know who you are," she said. "Your husband and father are very powerful men. If they find out what I've done for you...

"They won't!" I swore. "Please."

She had just turned to a cabinet filled with bottles and vials when a horse approached, hoofbeats drumming the ground, harness clinking. I whimpered, my fear and desperation flooding me with panic.

Frowning, the woman turned back to the door and then sent me a disapproving look. "Did you lead him straight here?" she demanded. She pulled back a ragged blanket that served as a curtain to reveal a small bedroom. "In here."

I rushed toward the room, but before I could hide, the front door flew open so violently, it slammed the wall, rattling the glass on the shelves.

My eyes widened with panic as my father strode into the cabin, his eyes blazing with fury.

"Get out of the way, witch!" he barked.

The woman stepped in front of me. "Your daughter is a grown woman," she said evenly. "You have no right to be here."

His face flushed darker. "No right? Her husband demanded that I return her or our arrangement is forfeit. And he *has every right to prevent your hellish interference."*

She laughed, not the least intimidated by my father. "You men," she said, shaking her head. "You treat your women like chattel, to be bought and sold at your whim, and then demand they bear your children without a thought of the cost." She laughed again, the sound mocking and angry. "Well, when it suits you, anyway. You are the worst of hypocrites, Fairland Dawes. On Sunday, you'll rant against the help I provide, and then on Monday bring your mistress to my door."

Ignoring her, my father shoved her aside and seized my wrist, dragging me toward the door. I pulled against his hold, casting the woman a silent plea for help, but she could only look on with a sorrowful expression.

When he delivered me to my husband's home, Josef wasn't there to greet me. Instead, he'd sent his women—those whose beds I knew he visited on the nights he didn't come to mine. They had been nothing but cruel to me since my arrival, eager accomplices to my husband's demands.

They dragged me up the stairs to my room and locked me in. I don't know how many days passed—one? two? I was weak from hunger and sorrow when Josef entered. He stood at the door, his hands clasped behind his back, and glared at me for several minutes in disapproving silence.

"You clearly do not care to be in this house with me," he finally said, his tone flat, emotionless. "I am therefore returning you to your father's. You will have the baby there. The child will then be delivered to me."

I stared at him, unable to speak, not knowing what to say. Finally, I whispered, "What will you do with me?"

His brows lifted. "Do with you? Nothing. You were never anything to me. Your father may dispose of you how he will."

"Dispose of me?" I breathed. "What do you mean?"

"I will have the others pack your things," he said, ignoring my question. "A servant will take you to your father. I want nothing more to do with you."

"I know who you are," I said, narrowing my eyes. "You have everyone fooled, but I know. And I will tell anyone who will listen!"

He said nothing, merely turned and closed the door behind him.

"I know!" I screamed after him. "You evil bastard! I know*!"*

My eyes snapped open at the sound of breaking glass. I bolted upright and scanned my room. Not seeing anything to explain the noise, I swung my legs over the side of the bed and hurried into the hall to search the rest of the apartment. I peeked into Henry's room first. He slept soundly, hugging his new teddy bear tightly, completely undisturbed.

I then went to the bathroom and flipped on the light.

The mirror had been smashed, shards of shattered glass scattered on the sink and floor. Only one triangular piece still clung to the mirror's backing.

Careful to avoid stepping on the glass, I crept into the bathroom toward the sink, searching for what would have caused the mirror to shatter. But there was nothing out of place.

I focused my attention on the mirror itself. My reflection peered back at me from the remaining fragment, but something was wrong. Instead of wallpaper behind me, there was only darkness.

Frowning, I leaned closer until my reflection filled the glass. For a split second, a shadow slid across my face, obscuring my own features, making me look like someone I didn't recognize. Curious, I leaned closer still, until only my left eye filled the glass.

I studied the flecks of green and gold. Nothing seemed wrong, nothing unusual. The colors I'd seen every day for my entire life were just as they should be.

Then the reflection blinked.

I cried out in surprise and stumbled backward, stepping on slivers of the mirror, cutting my feet, leaving smears of blood as I scrambled to put distance between me and the image in the mirror.

When my back hit the wall, I stood there, shaking, my heart hammering, staring at the shard that had blinked. But whatever had stared back at me from the mirror didn't return. I waited, my eyes scanning the bathroom, fearing what might happen next.

When nothing else occurred, I squeezed my eyes shut, drawing in several slow breaths until my pulse resumed a normal rhythm. Calmer now, I opened my eyes, taking in the glass glittering at my feet, the blood on the floor where shards had cut my soft flesh in my haste to get away from what was behind the mirror.

As I bent to pick up a piece of glass, the window above the bathtub sprung open with a crash that rattled the pane.

I yelped in surprise and nearly fell but caught the edge of the vanity. Cursing under my breath, I crept to the tub and hesitantly peeked over the side. No drowned woman appeared, so I stepped into the tub and reached up to close the window. It wouldn't budge.

"Damn it," I muttered, thumping the frame, trying to jar it loose. I braced, pulled down again, groaning with the strain. "Come on!"

It gave all at once, slamming down. My bloody feet slipped on the porcelain, my head cracking against the windowsill as I fell.

Moaning, I tried to sit up, but the world spun, and I slid back down, breathing through the pain. As the initial pain began to ebb, dulling to a persistent throb, I suddenly realized cold water lapped at my hips.

What the hell?

The tub was filling. Fast.

I forced myself to sit up to turn off the water that I must've turned on when I fell. My vision swam before me, making it difficult to see. I blinked through the blur, pawing for the faucet. My fingers found the knob and curled around it. I tried to twist it, but it wouldn't budge.

I grasped with both hands, straining. "Shit!"

Instead of fighting to turn it off in the icy water, I swung my leg over the side of the tub and started to climb out, but something grabbed my hair and yanked, pulling me under.

I thrashed, fighting to get free. Each time I broke the surface, it dragged me back down. I kicked and flailed, desperately searching for something to hold onto. My lungs burned, screaming for air.

No! No! Not like this! I can't die like this! Henry can't find me—

And then it let go.

I exploded up, gasping for air, and somehow managed to haul myself out, then collapsed on the tile, shaking, too cold and terrified to move. But after a few moments, I forced myself up on my knees and reached for the faucet to turn off the water before it overflowed the tub.

Disbelief froze me where I knelt.

The water had already stopped flowing, the tub empty.

I turned to look behind me.

The shards of glass were gone, the mirror intact.

The only proof that anything had occurred was the pulsing ache in my head where a sizeable lump was beginning to rise and the cuts on the bottoms of my feet.

Fighting the dizziness from what was likely a concussion, I managed to peel off my wet clothes and grab a towel from the linen closet. The cuts on my feet weren't deep, but there were enough that I dug out sterile gauze and medical tape from the cabinet and bandaged them.

I limped toward my room, wincing a little with each step, and flinched when I passed the full-length mirror. Ugly purple and yellow bruises were beginning to form on my shoulder. I let the towel drop and examined the rest of me, new marks mapping every place my body ached.

Fear and desperation pressed heavy on my chest as I realized what could've happened had I not been able to escape. What could've happened to Henry if I'd drowned. Who would've taken care of him? Certainly not my mother. God—growing up with her would be worse than anything at Dawes House.

No matter what Whit had said about wanting us to stay, I couldn't put my son or myself at risk any longer than I had to. I just hoped he could understand that when I finally had enough saved to move out—and that the intruders tormenting us would stay behind.

The cuts on my feet were gone by midday, as mysteriously healed as the mirror itself, making me think they, too, were just a paranormal manifestation. But I was still nursing a headache and bruises that afternoon. Those were *definitely* real.

I slipped into my pajamas early and booted up my hand-me-down laptop to look at what class I needed to sign up for in the fall, hoping to focus on something other than events at the house for as long as my aching head would allow.

I'd only just signed into the student portal when Henry started singing.

I smiled. His little voice immediately quieted my fear and despair. I peeked into his room to see him sitting on the floor, arranging stones in a circle on the floor. Next to him lay a small green velvet bag that looked like it probably contained even more stones.

"Where did you get those?" I asked, wishing the pain reliever I'd taken would hurry up and start working.

He jumped at the sound of my voice and turned wide eyes to the doorway where I stood.

"I'm sorry!" I said quickly. "I didn't mean to scare you. I just heard you singing and thought I'd see what you were up to."

Henry blinked at me a couple of times as if trying to comprehend what I was saying but then held up one of the stones for me to see. "Do you like my rocks, Mama? Mamaw June gave them to me. She said I could have them."

I lowered myself beside him, wincing when my bruises protested. "Those are really cool. I hope you thanked Ms. June."

He nodded enthusiastically. "Yes, ma'am!"

"What are you doing with them?" I asked, picking up one of the polished stones to study the gold striations that ran through the white quartz.

"Making a circle like Addie," he said. "But I don't have bones, so I'm using my extra stones."

I kept my tone light when I asked, "Are you playing the game Addie taught you? Was that the song you were singing?"

"Yes, ma'am," he said, swapping out a couple of the stones for ones that were in the bag. "I don't know all the words yet."

"Well," I said, picking up several of the stones from the circle and putting them in the pouch, "why don't you play something else instead? Or I can sing songs with you, if want."

He gave me a pouty look but put the remaining stones away. "Yes, ma'am."

When Henry eventually grew bored with playing with me, I told him to go pick out a snack and I'd let him watch his cartoons. As soon as he scampered off to the kitchen, grinning, I tucked the pouch of stones in the top drawer of my dresser and covered it with some clothes.

There was technically nothing wrong with the gift from June, but something about the stones—and the game Addie had taught Henry—made me uneasy.

"What happened to your head?" Henry asked me later, casually swinging his legs as we sat at the kitchen table eating some of the mixed fruit and finger sandwiches our neighbors had dropped off.

I touched the lump on my forehead, glad to find it wasn't hurting quite as much as it had been, the pain reliever finally taking effect. "I slipped in the bathroom and hit it," I told him. "Did you hear me fall?"

He shook his head. "No, ma'am." I reached for one of the sandwiches as he added, "But I saw the sad lady."

I frowned. "The sad lady?"

He nodded. "She cries a lot."

I set the sandwich on my plate, no longer hungry. "Why is she crying? Did she tell you?"

"No, ma'am." He shook his head again. "She just cries and holds her stomach. Maybe she's got a tummy ache. Or maybe she's cold 'cause she's wet and is giving herself a hug."

The woman in the bathtub.

He'd seen her too. And yet, he didn't seem scared at all.

"Do you know her name?" I asked. "Did she ever tell you?"

He nodded and popped a grape in his mouth. After swallowing, he said, "Eliza."

Goosebumps rose along my skin. "What does she look like?"

He shrugged. "She has hair like Addie's. And a fancy dress."

"Fancy how?"

He made wave motions with his arms. "It's flowy."

"Have you seen her anywhere else?" I asked, dread making my throat tight.

But he shook his head. "Just here. She said this was her house."

So, had Eliza been behind the mirror and the bathtub incidents? Was she trying to tell me her story, or was she trying to get rid of me? She had given birth to one child but had drowned when pregnant with a second. Did she resent that my child and I still lived?

“Does she scare you?” I asked, taking his little hand in mine, my guts twisting with guilt. I hated that he’d inherited my cursed ability. “Does she ever try to hurt you?” .

He shook his head. “No, Mama. Not Eliza.”

I frowned. “I know the angry lady in the basement scares you. Does anyone else?”

He hesitated but then nodded.

“Who, baby?” I asked. “Who scares you?”

He leaned in and cupped his hand around his mouth as if sharing a secret, then whispered, “The lady in the wall.”

CHAPTER FOURTEEN

Several days later, my conversation with Henry was still troubling me—mostly because I didn't know who he was talking about. Who was this woman in the wall? Why could he see her and I couldn't?

"Zellie, darlin'," June asked, "are you feeling alright? You haven't eaten a bite of my tomato pie."

"No one makes one better," Earl said with a wink. "Secret's in the bacon."

I forced a smile. "I'm sorry, Ms. June," I replied. "I've not been myself lately."

"Well, then, you'll definitely want to try some of these fried oysters, Zellie," Merilee said with a sly grin. "They're the cure for what ails you."

"Oh, now," Pearlie scolded, "you leave the poor girl alone, Merilee. She's had a rough time of it."

I flushed at Merilee's insinuation about the oysters' reputation as an aphrodisiac and risked a glance at Whit, praying he hadn't heard her. But he was rapidly typing on his phone, his brows drawn together in a deep frown. Whatever the subject, it must've been urgent if he was willing to risk incurring Pearlie's wrath for using his phone at the table. Earlier, I'd caught a glimpse of a message from someone identified only as CP, and it had led to the same dark, shuttered expression he wore now.

Fresh from his business trip up north, he seemed worn down—fatigue in the slump of his shoulders, tension in his jaw. And the way he stayed locked on that phone told me whatever he'd been dealing with hadn't gone well. Even when he finally set the phone face-down beside his plate, agitation clung to him like a shadow.

But then he looked up and caught me watching him. His eyes held mine, and something in his expression cleared, softened, as if a weight had slipped from his shoulders. Relief flickered across his face, subtle but unmistakable, like he hadn't *truly* come home until that moment.

I broke our shared gaze first, but I'm sure he saw the small, secret smile tugging at my lips.

"You *are* looking peak-ed, baby," Pearlie pressed, her words cutting across our moment. "Are you sleeping? Should Henry comes stay with June or me for the night, let you get a good night's sleep?"

"Thank you, Ms. Pearlie," I said sincerely. "But I don't think that will help. There have been some...disturbances in my apartment."

Whit shifted slightly in his chair. "Junior, could you please pass the cornbread down this way?"

"What kind of disturbances?" Junior asked, absently passing the plate of skillet cornbread to Whit.

I hesitated, mulling over whether to say anything. I'd gone over it many times in my head since the events in the bathroom, realizing I needed help to deal with what was going on, even if it was just permission to do a cleansing or bring in a priest for a blessing. As much as I would've liked to help the women who were tormenting Henry and me, I couldn't deal with this on my own any longer.

I took a deep breath and blurted, "I think my apartment's haunted."

There was complete silence as each of them stared at me, their expressions impossible to read. Then, almost in unison, they laughed.

All but Whit.

"Oh, honey," June said, patting my hand. "It's Savannah. *Everywhere* is haunted."

"Lord," Chase added. "I thought you meant we had rats or something. I was about to be worried."

They chuckled again and returned to their food.

I scanned their faces. Not a single one of them looked surprised or even concerned. Did they already know about the women? About David? When I'd asked Pearlie and June about him before, they'd waved me off like Henry had imagined his new friend.

Sensing my bafflement, Merilee leaned over and gave me a hug with one arm. "Don't worry, Zellie-girl. We've all seen a ghost or two in our time."

I glanced at Whit. His gaze locked with mine again, steady and unflinching, as if silently assuring me in his quiet, attentive way, that he understood my concerns, that he could feel the panic just under my skin even from several feet away and wasn't about to dismiss it so easily.

Of course, unlike the others, he'd witnessed an incident first-hand. He'd seen the kitchen after David had torn it apart.

So then why didn't he say anything? Make them understand that this wasn't something I could laugh off like they did?

Then I realized—maybe because I hadn't been completely honest with *him* about the seriousness of the situation. I'd waved it off, downplayed what had been going on because I didn't want him to think I was crazy.

I dutifully ate my dinner and tried to pay attention to and enjoy the after-dinner conversation as we moved out to the patio so Henry and Addie could play and so Junior and Earl could enjoy the cigars that their wives refused to allow them to smoke indoors. Merilee made her excuses after a while and left with a plate of food for Ms. Netty, with Chase in tow with food for Billy Wayne and Kitty.

"I'm surprised not to see Billy Wayne and Kitty here," I told Pearlie. "And I haven't seen Mr. Dean since his party."

"Mmhmm," Pearlie replied, nodding. "Kitty's having some complications, so she's keeping mostly to her bed. And Billy Wayne is working extra shifts at the docks, from what I understand from Iris."

So maybe I wasn't the only one at Dawes House who wasn't living comfortably. It seemed odd that Iris would be privy to the Wrights' financial situation, but I supposed it made sense for Iris to know everyone's comings and goings since she ran the apartment building. But there was still something odd about what Pearlie shared that nagged at me.

"And, well," Pearlie continued, "Mr. Dean has never been particularly social in his old age. He was quite the catch back in the day, but he didn't handle aging very well. Some people don't, I suppose. Vanity knows no boundaries."

"Here you go, y'all," Earl called, rubbing his hands together in anticipation. "Bringing out the good stuff for a little after-dinner digestif tonight, Junior?"

Junior chuckled and held up a decanter of a deep purple wine. "You're gonna have to try this elderberry wine, Zellie," he said. "It's my own recipe."

"You shouldn't force it on her, Junior," Whit said, his tone taut with disapproval.

I cast him a confused look but then smiled at Junior. "I'd be happy to try it!" I told him. "I've never had elderberry wine."

"There you go!" Junior said to Whit.

I politely accepted the glass of wine he handed to me and took a sip, letting the delicious liquid flow down my throat.

"You might want to let that breathe," Whit said softly near my ear. The nearness of him, the warmth of his breath, brought goosebumps to my skin.

I took another sip to divert my attention from the effect he had on me. "This is unbelievable," I said, licking an errant drop from my lips. "I don't think I've ever tasted anything like it."

Something flared in his eyes, but he dropped his gaze before I could catch more than a glimpse. "Yes," he said, savoring a sip from his own glass. "Junior is quite the artiste. But don't overdo it. His wines are particularly strong if you're not used to them."

Despite Whit's warning, I somehow found my glass refilled time and again and finally had to set it aside to keep from being tempted.

I don't recall being tipsy. It was more a sense of peaceful euphoria and hyper-awareness. The flowers in the garden were brighter and more vibrant than I'd ever seen. The breeze kissed my bare arms, the light caress both sensuous and erotic. I could hear every sound with disorienting clarity—the crickets chirping, the noise of traffic a few blocks away, the tolling of the bells at the Cathedral. No, "tipsy" isn't the right word for what I experienced. I had never tried drugs, but I imagined this is what it was like to be "tripping balls."

And through it all, I was acutely aware of Whit—his voice, his warmth, his scent, the way his hand hovered near the small of my back, close enough to make my pulse spike but not touching me until I leaned in the tiniest bit. And then the slight pressure of his fingertips as he curled me into him stole my breath.

"Are you alright?"

I turned toward the voice and had to blink a few times before her face came into focus.

Pearlie.

"Um...yes, ma'am," I managed even as my skin grew warm, becoming so unbearable, I wanted to strip down naked and plunge into an ice bath to try to slake the heat ravaging my body.

"Hmm..." Pearlie mused. "You don't look fine, baby. I think maybe you've had too much of Junior's wine. It can be a bit strong for first-timers."

"Which all of you knew," Whit pointed out, his tone harsh, accusing. I thought I saw him peg the others with a furious glare. "I'm taking Zellie back to her apartment."

"She shouldn't be alone," June warned. "Not in this state."

"Don't worry," Whit snapped. "I'll look after her."

"Henry," I called, my voice sounding like I was talking in slow motion. "It's time to go, baby."

"Why don't you let him stay with me tonight?" June offered with a comforting smile.

"No, no," I said, shaking my head. "It's okay. I don't want to impose. I just need to...sit down for a...for a few minutes."

"Nonsense," June said. "Henry? Do you want to spend the night with Mamaw June, honey?"

Henry came running over, Addie on his heels. "Yes, ma'am! Can I, Mama?"

I was about to protest, but the world tilted, and I grabbed Whit's arm to steady myself. "Sure," I told Henry, nodding carefully, the simple movement disorienting. "Yeah, that's okay."

Henry gave me a tight hug and a kiss on the cheek before scampering off to play. My heart ached a little at how quickly he'd taken June up on her offer. But before I could call him back to me and tell him I'd changed my mind, Pearlie took my hand in both of hers.

"You'll be just fine," she said with a comforting smile. "All just part of the process."

I frowned. "Process? What do you mean?"

"Take good care of her," Pearlie ordered, giving Whit a significant look that I found puzzling even in my current state.

Whit pulled me tighter against him, keeping his arm around my waist to support me as he led me into the house.

"I'm sorry about this," he said as we made our way to the elevator. "I should've paid closer attention. I didn't realize they'd given you so much."

I let out a small, giddy laugh. "You tried to warn me," I said, searching for the button for the fourth floor among the multiple, blurry buttons that swam before my eyes. "It's not your fault."

"The effects should wear off in an hour or so," he assured me, pressing the correct button for me. "I'll sit with you until they do."

Sitting with me was the *last* thing I wanted him to be doing with me. The fire in my body raged, making me want to peel off my skin for relief. But in my mind, I pictured us tearing at each other's clothes in a frenzy, reckless, impatient to join our bodies together, to feel skin upon skin.

I shook my head to banish the dangerous images and stepped away from him to give myself some space. "Is it hot in here?" I panted. "I can't breathe. It's so hot..."

The doors opened to my floor and not a moment too soon.

"So freaking hot..." I muttered, tugging at the collar of my shirt as we made our way down the hall. But finding that insufficient to relieve me, I pulled it over my head and tossed it onto the floor.

"No, no, no," Whit said in a rush, grabbing up my shirt and hurrying me to my door. "Not out here. We'll cool you down inside."

As soon as we entered the apartment, I kicked off my shoes and started unbuttoning my shorts. "What the hell is wrong with me?"

He stilled my hands with his, firm but careful. "Easy," he said, his voice tight. "Let's get you in the shower."

I lifted my eyes to him and grinned. "Sounds fun. Want to join me?"

Somehow, I could hear his breathing become shallower, his heartbeat quickening. He swallowed hard and squeezed his eyes for a beat as if the sight of me tormented him. "No," he finally managed. "Not like this."

I stepped closer and popped open one of the buttons on his shirt, my grin growing. "Are you sure...?"

He put his hand over mine, pressing my palm against his chest briefly before his fingers curled around mine, and then headed toward the hallway, pulling me after him to the bathroom.

While he turned on the shower, his back to me, I stripped out of my shorts, the heat unbearable.

When he glanced back, his breath caught before he averted his gaze.

"Jesus," he ground out, his voice thick. He cleared his throat, keeping his eyes trained on the floor when he extended a hand to help me into the shower. "Cool off in here for a while. I'll be right outside if you need me."

And what if I needed him now?

I stepped toward him, taking his hand. "Whit," I said, his name saying everything I wanted to but didn't know how to voice.

At this, he looked at me—really looked at me—conflict showing in his eyes, a struggle between apology and...longing. "I'm not going anywhere. I promise."

He then moved past me and out of the room, pulling the door mostly closed, but leaving it open just enough that I knew he could hear me if I called.

The first touch of the water stole my breath no doubt colder to me than it actually was. I don't know how long I stood there under the water, letting it soak my hair, cool my skin. I leaned against the tile and let my forehead rest on my folded arms. As the heat finally dissipated, a bone-deep exhaustion took its place, hitting me so hard, I had to grasp the windowsill to steady myself.

I shut off the water and grabbed a towel, my teeth chattering as I hastily dried off. Shivering, I wrapped my bathrobe around me and hugged myself, trying to ward off the chills wracking my body.

"Whit," I called, my voice shaking.

He was there in an instant, gathering me close, his warmth wrapping around me. He tucked me under his chin, his palm rubbing slow circles on my back, his touch so careful, so tender, it made my throat tighten.

"You'll be okay," he murmured against my hair. "C'mon, let's get you something hot to drink. That'll help."

I laughed weakly as he ushered me to the living room. "Just make sure there's no booze in it. I never realized I was such a lightweight."

After I settled on the couch with a warm blanket, he brewed tea and helped me to hold it for the first few sips, his hands covering mine. When my eyes began to droop, he set my mug aside and found a thicker blanket, draping it over me before resuming his seat beside me.

"I'm so sorry," I told him, stifling a yawn. "I never get like this. What in the world was in that wine?"

When I sagged sideways toward him, he put his arm around my shoulders and drew me in. Despite the lingering haze clouding my mind, I noticed that I fit against him perfectly as if we'd been made for one another.

"Rest now, sweetheart," Whit said, his voice soft. He pressed his cheek to my damp hair and held me a little tighter. "I'll sit with you until you're asleep."

Except I didn't *want* to fall asleep. I wanted to stay awake, sink into the warmth of him, the comfort of his arms.

But his heartbeat was steady and strong and soothing under my ear, and sleep took me anyway.

The air was heavy.

Pressure weighed on my chest, squeezing my lungs, forcing me awake with a gasp.

My eyes snapped open to search the darkness that seemed just a little too thick, too...aware.

Whit had gone, but I couldn't shake the sensation that someone was standing just out of my sight. The apartment suddenly felt claustrophobic, full, and yet vastly, endlessly empty like some great cosmic void had opened up in its center, sucking out its soul. Or maybe it was just the after effects of the wine.

I clicked on the lamp next to the couch where I still lay and scanned the living room once again now that the soft light illuminated the small space. But that solitary lamp seemed to cast more shadows than it dispelled. It flickered. Once. Almost imperceptible. I stared at it, waiting. But it didn't happen again.

Convinced the flicker had been nothing more than a normal surge of electricity, I shoved aside the fleece blankets Whit had draped over me and sat up, disjointed memories of what had happened playing in my head.

Groaning, I pulled my hand down my face.

What the hell had come over me? It's not like I'd never had a drink before. But a couple of glasses of elderberry wine and I was totally wasted. Worse, I had completely thrown myself at Whit. Which was nothing like the real me.

I just hoped he didn't think less of me, that I hadn't derailed things between us before there was even anything *to* derail. But considering the way he'd bolted from the bathroom, maybe I'd misread him. Maybe the heated glances, the charged moments were all in my head. Maybe all along he'd just been trying to be a good friend.

With another groan, I flopped back against the couch cushions, covering my face while the full force of my embarrassment washed over me.

I owed him a huge apology.

A soft creak in the corner of the room, like a single floorboard under a cautious step, brought my head around. Seeing nothing, I glanced down at my phone on the coffee table.

3 a.m.

The Devil's hour, Vivian had always called it. No one would be up at this time unless they were up to no good, she would say.

"Welp, guess you were right about me, Vivian," I mumbled.

I stood up, intending to go to my bedroom, when I thought I heard a quiet clatter—like when Henry rustled through his Lego bricks, looking for a specific piece. I held my breath for a few seconds, listening for the sound again, cold creeping along my skin, raising goosebumps on my arms.

When only silence followed, I heaved a sigh of relief and continued toward my room, but something drew me to Henry's bedroom instead. I cautiously entered, searching for the source of the noise, but nothing looked out of place. If anything, the room seemed oddly still. Like it was holding its breath.

A few minutes later, I'd thrown on my favorite pajama pants and shirt, making a mental note to check the thermostat's settings. The apartment was freezing, but the AC hadn't kicked on since I'd woken up.

And then I heard the clatter again.

My breath caught in my chest. I *knew* I'd heard it that time.

A soft scrape followed, like something being dragged across the hardwood.

Part of me wanted to just shut and lock my bedroom door and ignore what might be in Henry's room. Another part of me wanted to storm in there and confront whoever—*whatever*—it was, banish it from the apartment. And then there was the tired, frightened part of me that just wanted to run from the apartment, grab Henry from June and get the hell out of there even though I had nowhere to go.

I paced my bedroom rug in agitated designs and chewed my bottom lip, weighing my options. Finally, I made my choice.

I crept toward Henry's room. This time, my blood ran cold.

In the center of the floor, a robotic toy dinosaur advanced straight toward me, the mechanical clicking and whirring producing an eerie cadence. I was so locked on the dinosaur I nearly missed the flash of movement at the foot of the bed. With a gasp, my gaze snapped in that direction.

The pale face of a young boy peeked out, his eyes wide, startled, his body low to the ground like he was on his hands and knees. But as soon as our eyes met, he ducked back, frightened, like I was the one haunting *him*.

I flipped on Henry's light and rushed to the other side of his bed, but the boy had vanished.

"David?" I called. "Was that you? You can talk to me. It's okay."

But the room was still. The dinosaur had abruptly halted mid-stride as if its animus had been snatched away.

I took a deep breath and got down on my knees, my maternal instinct to help David warring with my fear. I grasped Henry's comforter, my hand shaking as I hesitated, not sure I wanted to see what was under the bed. I closed my eyes and took a slow, steady breath. Before I could imagine what might be lurking there, I snatched up the comforter and dropped my upper body to peer beneath.

I laughed in a nervous burst of sound.

Empty.

"Thank God," I murmured.

I rested my forehead on the floor, waiting for my muscles to recover from the rapid release of adrenaline. When I thought my legs could once more support me, I pushed back up to my knees. Just as a hand came down on my shoulder, the fingers digging into my skin.

I screamed and launched to my feet, whipping around to face the intruder, but no one was there.

"Fuck this," I spat.

Pausing only long enough to grab my phone, I hurried out of my apartment, not sure where I was going until I was in the hallway, running toward Whit's door. The hall lights dimmed and brightened as I passed them, creating a strobe effect that made my shadow's movements jerky, oddly out of sync with my own.

It took only seconds to reach Whit's door but felt much longer. I knocked softly but urgently, glancing over my shoulder, praying nothing had followed me down the hall.

Oh, God...what if he doesn't answer?

I knocked again, harder, sending another look over my shoulder, my panic building.

The lights blinked three times in rapid succession. The bulb at the other end of the hall burst, shrouding the path in darkness.

Shit.

Just then I caught a glimpse of my shadow on the wall nearby.

It hadn't followed me all the way to Whit's apartment, stopping several feet behind me, perfectly still.

Watching.

Waiting.

Oh, my God.

Too terrified to move, I could only observe helplessly when my shadow rippled, and the silhouette of a woman stepped away from the wall to turn toward me.

"Zellie?"

I jumped, inhaling a jagged breath as my attention snapped back to Whit's door. I was so relieved to see him standing there, I wanted to throw myself into his arms. But I could only stare at him, trembling, eyes wide, suddenly forgetting why I'd come.

He stood in the doorway, his lids heavy with lingering sleep, dark hair mussed. He was barefoot and wearing only a pair of jeans slung low on his hips, probably having just thrown them on when I pounded on his door.

His concerned gaze drifted from my face to my shaking hands.

"Are you okay?" he asked, his voice rough from sleep. His eyes flicked past me, just for a second, like he was checking for something in the shadows. "What's wrong? Do you want to come in?"

I blinked a couple of times, then checked the hall behind me again. But it wasn't necessary. I could already feel that it was empty. The heaviness had lifted the moment Whit opened the door.

I gave myself a mental shake and cleared my throat. "I'm sorry," I said. "I shouldn't have come. I just..."

...am a victim of multiple ghosts who are terrorizing me?

"I just...I wanted to...apologize," I stammered, still too shaken to think coherently. "I mean, for earlier. But I guess also now for waking you up at three in the morning." I vaguely gestured at his bare chest and torso. "Obviously."

He shook his head. "Zellie—"

"I don't want you to think that I was throwing myself at you to get something in return," I said in a rush, cutting him off. "I'm not that kind of person, Whit. I hope you know that. Despite what happened earlier."

The muscle in his jaw twitched. "There's no need to apologize, Zellie," he said, his voice quiet, tense. "It wasn't your fault."

His words were comforting, but there was an undercurrent of something else. Frustration? Anger? With himself? With *me*?

My heart sank and tears pricked the corners of my eyes, my emotions worn raw. "I should go."

I turned away, but his fingers caught mine. "Wait."

His touch trailed along my palm as he released my hand, lingering just a second too long when he reached my fingertips.

I swallowed, the brief contact still burning on my skin.

"Zellie, I never want you to feel obligated to me in some way because you live at Dawes House. I hope *you* know *me* well enough now to understand that." He took a half step toward me to lean on the doorframe, so close to me I could feel the warmth of his body, and dropped his gaze to the floor, exhaling slowly as if taking the time to carefully consider his words before lifting his head, his gaze locking with mine, his already dark eyes growing even darker as he rasped, "I only turned you down earlier because you weren't thinking straight tonight."

I searched his face, gauging his sincerity. Then, my voice little more than a whisper, I spoke the words that I knew could change everything between us. "I'm thinking straight now."

He went completely still for a long, torturous moment. Then he lifted his hand, hesitating just a beat before the back of his fingers skimmed along the line of my jaw, his touch light, almost reverent. When he reached my chin, he gently tipped my face up. He flicked a glance down to my mouth then lifted his eyes back to mine, questioning. I nodded, my lids drifting shut as he slowly bent to press his lips to mine.

It was a sweet kiss, tentative, just a light brush.

But it ignited a powder keg of desire.

In one swift motion, his arms wrapped around me, pulling me tight against him as his mouth captured mine, possessive, demanding. One kiss led to another and another until all else faded away, until all that existed was the heady desire that stole my breath.

At some point, we moved inside. He shoved the door shut then lifted me, his hands grasping the fabric of my shirt when I wrapped my legs around his waist. Then my back was against the wall and we was pressing kisses to my jaw, my neck.

I whispered his name and dragged his face back to mine, eager to get lost in his kiss again.

I don't know how much time passed. I don't know when he carried me to another room and lowered me to his bed. There was only his mouth and his hands as they explored my body, his touch gentle, patient as his hand slipped beneath my shirt, caressing my back, smoothing along my ribs, over my hip, pressing me closer. When his thumb skimmed across my nipple, I gasped, the contact sending a lance of heat straight to the core of me.

He immediately stilled and pulled back. "Should I stop?"

I shook my head vehemently. "God, no."

He still hesitated, so I covered his hand with mine, guiding him down along my belly to the waistband of my pajamas.

"Touch me," I breathed. "Please."

When his fingertip brushed against the bud of nerves, so tender, so careful, I moaned, arching against his hand, needing more.

He hissed a curse and then his mouth was on mine again, his breath ragged as he then broke away, to watch me as his touch brought me closer and closer to release, only to back me down again then drive me toward that blissful precipice until I couldn't take it anymore, my moaning growing louder, more fevered as his finger slid inside me and then a second and his thumb continued to caress. I panted, grasping his sheets in my fists, when sensation overtook me. My cry of release filled the room.

I was still burning, still aching as his thrusting fingers slowed again, backing me back down to a simmering desire that would soon need to be released again. He brushed his lips against mine, then kissed my cheek, my temple, before finding my mouth again.

When he lifted his head to gaze at me, I took his face in my hands. "I want you. All of you."

A grin tugged at the corner of his mouth. "Oh, we'll get there," he assured me. "But not yet. I want to take my time with you, Zellie. I want you to know how beautiful you are, how precious you are to me."

With this, his touch became more insistent. I gripped his shoulders, gasping as he made good on his promises. And then there was only pleasure. And love. Such intense love, it enveloped me, cradled me, filled my soul.

Much later, when we drew one particularly languid kiss to a close, he lifted his head to gaze at me and brushed a lock of hair from my eyes. Neither of us said a word. There was no need. He rolled to his side, pulling me against him, holding me close.

"Should I walk you back to your apartment?" he asked eventually.

"Are you asking me to go?" I replied.

His arm tightened around me. "No," he said. "I'm asking you to stay."

I curled into him. "Then I'll stay."

Held in his arms, I fell into the most restful, peaceful sleep I'd ever known, feeling truly loved, truly safe for the first time in my life.

CHAPTER FIFTEEN

Feather-soft fingertips trailed down my arm, so light, so gentle, as the caress stirred me from my sleep. I grinned, thinking I could get used to waking up this way every morning. I opened my eyes to tell Whit exactly that, but the words died on my lips.

Inches from my face was a putrid, rotting face, twisted with rage. She opened her mouth in that terrifying, silent scream.

I yelped, scrambling backward over the top of Whit's legs, so anxious to put distance between me and the screaming woman, that I went too far and fell off the bed, slamming my shoulder into the floor. Pain shot down my arm and up my neck, but I rolled onto my knees just as strong hands gripped my upper arms.

I screamed and struggled to get away, until arms wrapped around me, drawing me close, trapping my own arms to keep them from lashing out.

"Zellie!"

I immediately stopped moving and looked up to see Whit's concerned expression, a long scratch along his cheek. "Whit," I whispered. "Oh, my God. I'm so sorry!"

He touched the scratch, smearing a few drops of blood. "It's fine. What happened? What's wrong?"

Sobbing with relief, my fear and frustration spilling out in my tears, I opened my mouth to tell him everything about the screaming woman, the dreams of Susanna, all of it. But, for some reason, I just shook my head and managed to pull myself together before saying, "Nightmare."

It wasn't a lie. Not really.

He took my face in his hands and searched my eyes as if he knew I wasn't telling him the whole truth. But instead of calling me out, he merely wiped my tears with his thumbs and kissed my forehead. "It's okay now," he murmured against my skin. "I've got you."

"I'm so sorry," I said, resting my cheek against his chest.

He tucked me in closer. "Zellie, no more apologies," he insisted. "You have nothing to be sorry for."

I wasn't so sure. It seemed like a damn big imposition to be living off of his kindness and generosity and waking him up at all hours.

"Well, I'll try not to keep waking you up by screaming like a banshee and falling out of bed," I assured him.

He pulled back enough to grin down at me, a wicked twinkle in his eyes. "So, does that mean you plan on spending a lot of time in my bed?"

My cheeks burned, but a thrill of desire made me shiver. "I suppose it does."

A slow smile curved his lips. "I like the sound of that."

He kissed me, long and slow. I savored every moment, clinging to him, not wanting to draw away from the safety of his arms. But later as we lay together, the sunlight streamed through his bedroom window, inching closer and closer to his bed as the time stretched on, and something told me this perfect peace couldn't last, that I should be suspicious of something so beautiful. Nothing good in my life except Henry had ever lasted.

"I should go," I said, an ache in the center of my chest growing as I spoke the words. "I need to get Henry from June and Earl."

"Why don't I get him while you get ready?" Whit suggested.

I rolled over to face him. "Ready for what?"

He propped himself up on his elbow. "I'd like to take you and Henry out to breakfast—and Addie, too. They're thick as thieves it seems. Maybe go down to River Street if you haven't been yet."

"Whit, you don't have to do that," I insisted.

His brows came together in a frown. "Do what?"

"You don't have to take us out, spend money," I said. "It's okay if we just keep things between us."

"Ah," he said, nodding. "You think I'm trying to buy your affections by ingratiating myself with Henry and spending money on you."

I shrugged. "I just...I want things between us to be genuine."

His expression instantly became aloof.

I covered my face with my hands with a groan. "Damn it. Now I've offended you."

He heaved a sigh. "No, not offended. Zellie, I have a shit ton of money. It's ridiculous, really. But what good is it if I can't make the people I care about feel special?" He pulled my hands away. "You deserve to feel special. Will you let me prove that to you?"

I studied his handsome face, still not daring to believe that someone like Whit was lying there beside me, that he truly cared about me and my son and that I wasn't just a piece of ass that he'd cast aside when someone better came along. After all, one night—and morning—of incredibly passionate make out sessions did not a relationship make.

But he seemed sincere.

I nodded. "Okay."

Sometime later, he walked me to my door and kissed me so tenderly I felt adored for the first time in my life. Already missing him, I watched him walk back to his apartment, waiting until he reached his door and turned back to offer me a smile. Just then, a cloud must've passed over the sun for the shadows in the hallway grew darker, briefly obscuring him so that he was a mere shadow himself.

And then he slipped inside his apartment, and the cloud lifted, bright morning sunlight spilling into the hallway once more.

I shivered, the moment feeling like a warning that something dark was waiting just outside the periphery of my understanding. But I shook it off and entered my own apartment, relieved to find that the heaviness that had been there the night before had lifted.

I hurried to get ready and was just strapping on my sandals when the apartment door flew open and Henry came running in, a bright smile on his face.

"Good morning, Mama!" he said, hurrying to me to throw his arms around my neck in a tight hug.

"Good morning, baby," I said, kissing his cheek and brushing his curls out of his eyes. "Did you have a good time with Ms. June and Mr. Earl?"

He nodded enthusiastically. "Yes, ma'am! And Mr. Whit said if I hurried up and got dressed and brushed my teeth, we could go get pancakes!"

"Well, you'd better get going," I said, but he was already running to his bedroom before I'd even finished my sentence.

I chuckled and turned to the open door to where Whit stood. "What can I say? He loves pancakes."

He strolled in and pulled me into his arms then shrugged. "Seemed like a good option considering our disastrous attempt at making pancakes." Then he dipped his head to brush a kiss to my lips. When the kiss ended and he drew back, his eyes took on a hungry look. "You look amazing."

I flushed and hastily stepped away from him when a rapid patter of footsteps alerted me to Henry's return. Henry paused when he entered the room and glanced between the two of us. But then his smile grew, and he hurried to me and grabbed my hand and then Whit's and dragged us toward the door.

"C'mon, guys," he said. "We can't keep Addie waiting!"

I laughed at his grown-up turn of phrase and glanced over to see Whit grinning, looking truly relaxed and happy.

Addie was practically bouncing with excitement when we exited the elevator, earning a mild rebuke from June to mind her manners. June then sent a questioning look at Whit who completely ignored it.

"Y'all have a good time," she called as Whit and I hurried to keep up with Henry and Addie. "We'll see you later!"

"Can we, please, Mama?" Henry asked, pointing toward the ice cream shop as we drove back toward Dawes House that afternoon.

"Are you serious?" I laughed. "Henry, how can you still be hungry after breakfast *and* lunch *and* the fudge Mr. Whit bought you and Addie?"

"Maybe he has a hollow leg," Addie added matter-of-factly, pushing back her curls with both hands. "Mamaw says we must have a hollow leg because she doesn't know where else we put all our food."

I chuckled, turning around in my seat to look at the two of them. "You might be right," I told her, grinning. "Are you wanting ice cream, too, Addie? I don't want you guys to get upset tummies. Your mamaw won't be happy with me if you get sick from too much junk."

Addie shook her head. "I won't get sick. I just eat peppermint and ginger when I have a tummy ache. Mamaw grows it in her kitchen."

I glanced at Whit, realizing I'd never actually been inside June and Earl's apartment. "Really?"

He nodded. "She has a third bedroom that doubles as a greenhouse, but most of the herbs she grows in the kitchen."

I don't know why that made me uneasy, but I shoved it to the back of my mind to think about later. "I guess it's okay to get ice cream, if Mr. Whit is okay with it."

"Coming right up!" he announced, making a U-turn and heading back toward the ice cream shop.

When we'd all finished off our ice cream, we loaded the kids back into the car. I wasn't surprised to see them fast asleep in their booster seats within minutes of being back on the road. Apparently, Whit had noticed it at the same time because he reached over to take my hand and brought it to his lips.

"Thank you for this," he said, his voice low, warm.

"I should be thanking you," I told him, lacing my fingers loosely with his. "You didn't have to get them every souvenir they asked for, you know. It really is okay to tell them no, especially as we *live* here."

He shrugged and smiled. "I enjoyed it. I haven't spent much time with Addie. I realize now what I've been missing out on."

I thought that was a curious comment to make, especially considering the tension between him and June, but he admittedly hadn't been around Dawes House much before Mr. Monty died, it seemed. So maybe he just had never had a chance to be around the little girl.

I leaned my head back and closed my eyes, enjoying the warmth of the sun on my face. "Thank *you*, Whit."

His thumb smoothed over my skin. "Should I just drive around for a while? Let the kids nap?"

I nodded, happy to just be together.

We drove around Savannah and then to Tybee Island, thankfully heading back to Dawes House before Henry and Addie realized we were near the beach. That would have to be an adventure for another day.

"What's brought that smile to your stunningly beautiful face?" Whit asked.

I laughed. "Stunningly beautiful? Wow, you're going to be great for my ego." I turned in my seat so that I was facing him. "I was just thinking that we'd have to come back to the beach sometime with Henry and Addie. I'm sure they'd love it."

He smiled. "I think they would. And I love that you're making future plans for us."

As we pulled up to Dawes House, the happiness we'd enjoyed all day was immediately dampened by an ambulance parked out front.

"Kitty?" I asked. "I hope nothing's wrong with her or the baby."

Whit shook his head, his jaw clenched, his hardened, aloof expression back in place. "No," he said, his tone terse. "It's not Kitty."

As we sat in the car, two EMTs exited the house with a gurney, a sheet covering the occupant's face.

"Oh, God," I breathed, reaching for Whit's hand.

"It's Mr. Dean," he said, his voice flat, expressionless as the EMTs loaded the body into the ambulance and slammed the doors.

I turned my attention back to him, frowning. "How do you know?"

He shook his head and released my hand to unbuckle his seatbelt. "I just do."

Before I could respond, Whit got out of the car and opened Addie's door, rousing her just enough to lift her into his arms. She sleepily blinked a few times then put her head back down on his shoulder.

I started to get Henry out of the car, but Whit called out, "Just leave him, sweetheart. I'll be back in a minute to help you."

I nodded, not really used to needing help, but my knees went weak, my stomach aching at the thought of Mr. Dean's passing.

Neither of us spoke as Whit and I made our way into the house a few minutes later. Inside was just as silent even though the residents had all gathered in the game room. I glanced in as we passed. They seemed more solemn than sad. There were no tears for Mr. Dean. Perhaps a testament to his irascible personality. But it seemed odd to me that the same group who had so happily celebrated Mr. Dean's birthday did not in any way mourn his death.

Once Henry and I were settled, Whit dropped a distracted kiss to the top of my head. "I should go," he said abruptly. "I need to talk to the others about Mr. Dean."

I nodded. "Okay. Let me know what the arrangements are."

His brows twitched together briefly. "A funeral, you mean? I doubt there will be one. He didn't have any family around."

"What about *this* family? Here at Dawes House?" I asked. "You all keep telling me that we're family here. Why would you not hold a memorial service, at least?"

Whit's expression softened, and he took my hand, pulling me to him. "You're right," he murmured. "Of course, we'll do something for him."

He kissed me once more, gentle and lingering this time, but still seemed distracted. I watched him as he strode toward the elevator, puzzled by the tension in the air at Dawes House. Maybe Mr. Dean didn't have any life insurance, and they were concerned about how to handle his burial. Or maybe they were worried about who might take over his apartment.

"Mama, did Mr. Whit leave?"

I started at the sound of Henry's voice and spun around, forcing a smile. "Hey, baby. Yes, he had to go. Did you have fun today?"

Henry nodded and climbed up on the couch. "Yes, ma'am. Is Mr. Whit your boyfriend now?"

I laughed in a short burst, surprised by the abrupt question. "Well, I...uh...I don't know. We'll see what happens." I sat down next to him. "Would it be okay with you if he was?"

Henry shrugged. "Sure. I like him even though he's super old."

"Super old?" I laughed. "He's not that much older than I am! Am I super old?"

Henry giggled. "No! Not *super* old..."

I scoffed with mock offense. "What?! Oh, you're gonna get it, mister!" I said, tickling his belly.

He screeched with laughter and leapt from the couch, running away to his bedroom. I started to call out to him not to run because Mr. Dean wouldn't like it but caught myself.

"Mama," Henry called, giggling. "You can't get me!"

I hopped up and rushed toward him, my eyes narrowed and fingers curled. Henry cackled with delight and started to close the door on me, but I caught him up and twirled him around before plopping him down on his bed and falling down beside him.

I gave him a big hug. "Mama loves you."

"I love you, too!" he said. "Addie doesn't have a mama anymore, but she said it'd be okay if you were her mama."

My heart broke for the poor little girl. Chase hadn't really said what had happened to her parents, just that June and Earl had custody. "Well," I said, "luckily, Addie has her Mamaw and Papaw."

"But what if something happens to them?" Henry asked.

I shook my head. "Like what?"

"I dunno," he said with a shrug. "Like a fire."

I sat up, concerned about where all this was coming from. "What's got you thinking on all this?"

He sighed. "Sometimes I have bad dreams."

"Oh, baby," I said, pulling him onto my lap and rocking him a little. "I know. But you can always tell me when you have a nightmare, you know that, right? I don't want you to think about horrible things like that. Okay?"

He nodded. "Okay." He sighed and then added, "Mama, I had one the other day."

"Do you want to talk about it?" I asked. "It might help."

He sighed again. "I dreamed about our day today."

"Well, that's a good dream, isn't it?" I said. "We had a lot of fun."

He nodded. "It was a good dream until the end. That's when Mr. Dean died."

My stomach sank like a great boulder had dropped, dragging it down. "What?"

"Mama," he said, his face scrunched up with the gravity of his question, "*did* Mr. Dean die today?"

CHAPTER SIXTEEN

I heard the screaming first. Then a cacophony of voices shouting instructions. And then came the crying.

"Mama, what's wrong?" Henry asked, his voice edged with fear.

I shook my head. "I don't know, baby. You stay here and watch cartoons, and I'll take a look."

It'd been relatively quiet in the couple of weeks since our outing with Whit, but this wasn't an intruder trying to get through to me by reliving some horror from the past. This was one of the residents of Dawes House.

I hurried out of the apartment and realized the screaming was coming from the floor below us. I raced down the stairs and nearly ran into Ms. Pearlie and Merilee.

"What's happening?" I shouted so they could hear me over the screams.

"Kitty's in labor," Merilee said in a rush, brushing past me to get to Kitty's apartment.

"Isn't it a little early?" I asked.

Pearlie turned me back toward the stairwell. "Don't worry, honey. We've got it under control. Merilee is doing everything she can."

"Shouldn't Kitty be at a hospital?" I demanded.

"I'm sure Merilee will call if she needs to," she said, her voice maddeningly calm. "Just go on back to your apartment."

Clearly not welcome, I returned to the apartment to find Henry sitting on the couch, clutching his teddy bear.

"It's okay," I assured him, turning up the cartoons to drown out the noise from below. Eventually, the screaming stopped. I kept checking my phone, hoping to receive a text with an update from Merilee or Ms. Pearlie of June or—hell, *anybody*—but nothing came.

Finally, I tucked Henry into bed for the night, glad it was quiet but worried sick about Kitty and her baby.

"Mama," Henry said as I pulled his comforter up to his chin. "Did somebody else die?"

"No, baby," I said quickly. "I'm sure they're fine."

He slid down in his bed, his face half-hidden under the comforter, his eyes wide, anxious.

"Do you want me to stay with you until you go to sleep?" I asked.

He nodded, scooting over to make room for me. I settled in beside him and leaned back against the wall, smoothing his hair. It wasn't long before his breathing slowed, deepened. I smiled, relieved he didn't seem to be too shaken by the events of the evening. Not wanting to disturb him by getting up, I closed my eyes, letting myself drift.

I'd only intended to rest for a moment, but when I jolted awake, the room was thick with shadows cast by the full moon.

I'd been sleeping so soundly that I wasn't sure what had awakened me. Then I heard it—a thin scraping. Like rats in the walls, but longer, slower. Deliberate.

Careful not to disturb Henry, I eased out from under him and rested his head gently on his pillow, then stood in the middle of the room, listening. I tried to locate where it was coming from, but the sound saturated the room, everywhere at once. I shut my eyes, straining, listening more closely.

There it was again.

Scriiiiiiitch

I took a step to my right, and the scratching grew marginally louder, so I opened my eyes, letting my sight adjust to the darkness, and turned toward Henry's closet.

My throat grew tight. I forced myself forward, wincing when the floorboards creaked and casting a quick glance back at Henry to make sure he was still asleep. Assured that he was, I leaned closer and pressed my ear against the closest door.

The scratching was louder now.

I swallowed, grabbed the doorknob, then took a deep, bracing breath and flung open the door.

The closet stood empty.

Thank, God.

I'm not entirely sure what I'd been expecting to find, but there were no monsters lurking there. It had to be mice, I told myself. My imagination must've assigned something more to the sound, something more deliberate and human. I made a mental note to ask Chase to call an exterminator in the morning.

Sighing, adrenaline still buzzing in my veins, I closed the closet door and turned back to Henry—only to find him awake and alert, holding his blankets up to his eyes. Before I could urge him to go back to sleep, a quiet creaking of hinges sounded behind me.

An icy quiver shot down my spine.

"She's coming," Henry whispered, his eyes huge with terror. "Mama..."

My heart hammered as I slowly turned toward the closet. The door inched open, the foul stench of rotting flesh flooding the room. I gagged, swallowing hard. As I stared into the shadows, too terrified to move, the darkness shifted.

Henry whimpered.

I saw her eyes first, glowing silver with fury. Then her face emerged, twisted with rage. She crawled toward us like a spider, limbs cracking and snapping at the joints like dry kindling. Her mouth worked silently, screaming words I couldn't hear. Her head twisted in mad, jerking motions like poorly edited movie clips, disjointed, too fast then too slow.

"What the fuck!" I cried, scrambling onto Henry's bed and gathering him into my arms as she moved ever closer, blocking the doorway. "What the hell do you want?"

Her head snapped toward Henry. Her eyes narrowed. She screeched something unintelligible then lunged at us, sharp, jagged nails curled into talons.

I screamed, clutching Henry close to my chest and curling around him to protect him from the spectral assault, bracing myself to feel the searing pain of her claws digging into my skin, ripping flesh from my bones.

But no attack came.

After a deep, shaky breath, I dared to open my eyes.

The room was empty. The closet door was closed.

Henry was sobbing into my chest, clinging to me, making it awkward to jump off his bed and race from his room with him in my arms. But I did, not waiting one damned second longer to get the hell out of there.

I hurried to my room and slammed and locked the door, backing away until I bumped into the mattress.

"Shh, shh..." I soothed Henry, rubbing his back. "It's okay, now, baby. She's gone."

Sweet Jesus...was that *the woman he'd seen? Was she the one that scared him?*

"I don't like her, Mama," he hiccupped.

"I don't either," I whispered, still shaky. "You're sleeping in here tonight."

"Is she coming back?" he asked, his voice small.

"No," I promised. "Not tonight."

"But what if she does?"

I held him tighter and rocked gently. "Don't worry, baby. I'll stay awake to make sure you're safe."

I jerked awake, instantly feeling guilty for falling asleep after promising to stay awake. But my guilt quickly morphed into confusion. Instead of being in my bedroom with the door locked, Henry and I were back in his room, sitting on the bed in the exact same positions we'd been in before the woman appeared.

What the hell...?

"Henry," I whispered, gently shaking him. "Henry, baby. Time to wake up."

He stretched and blinked up at me then rubbed his eyes. "Is it time to go to Mamaw June's?"

"No, not yet," I told him. "Are you okay?"

He sat up and nodded. "Yes, ma'am."

"You sure?" I pressed. "That was pretty scary."

He frowned in confusion. "But it was okay when you kept me company. I wasn't scared anymore."

Now it was my turn to frown. "What about the woman in the wall? The one who came out of the closet?"

His eyes widened. "Oh, yes, ma'am. She's scary!"

"I know," I said carefully. "I saw her last night. Don't you remember?"

He tilted his head. "What do you mean?"

My mind raced, reviewing everything from last night. Had I *dreamed* it? Was that why we were here in Henry's room? Because we'd never left it?

I forced a smile, brushing his curls off his forehead. "Nothing. I guess I was confused. How about we get you ready for Ms. June's since we're already awake?"

While Henry watched his cartoons in the living room, I stood in the shower, letting the water run over me, hiding the tears that slid down my cheeks as silent sobs shook my shoulders.

The dream—if it was a dream—had felt so real, so terrifying. The woman in the wall. The crawling. The stench. Now it made me question the other dreams I'd had about Dawes House, Susanna... Was any of it true? Were they memories? Or nightmares built from fear and fragments of history? What about the other encounters? Were they real? Hallucinations? Had I lost the ability to tell the difference between fiction and reality?

If so, where did that leave everything? The family I'd found here—the first I'd really ever known? Was I planning to run from the only people who truly seemed to care about me, about my son, because of my overactive imagination? Had Vivian been right all along? Was this all something I'd created in my mind? Or the influence of something dark and sinister that Vivian sensed before I ever did?

And what about Whit?

Was my impression of things accurate? Or was that just my imagination as well? I couldn't deny I was falling hard for him. Had already. But was it genuine? Could I trust any of what I felt for him? Or was I just infatuated with the idea of him, of someone who actually treated me kindly and made me feel safe for the first time in my life?

A tentative knock interrupted my spiraling thoughts. "Cartoons are over, Mama!"

I wiped my face quickly and smoothed my wet hair back. "I'm almost finished, baby! Go ahead and get dressed!"

My eyes were still swollen and red when I dropped Henry off to June an hour later, but she had the grace not to comment.

Dottie, however, was less subtle.

"Lord have mercy!" she exclaimed when I walked into the bookstore. "You look like something the cat dragged in." Her eyes twinkled wickedly. "I'm not one for gossip in general, but I might make an exception if a certain eligible bachelor I know is why you look exhausted."

My cheeks burned at Dottie's insinuation. But I shook my head with a little laugh that sounded devoid of mirth. "Nothing so tantalizing, Dottie."

Her expression softened into concern. "Oh, darlin'," she murmured, taking my hand and leading me to one of the comfy couches in a nearby reading nook. "Come tell me all about it. We've got time before the store opens."

I intended to tell her I was fine, but the words started spilling out before I could stop them. And I told her about all if it—the hauntings, the premonitions, the dreams, the fear of leaving, the fear of staying, the fear of losing the fragile sense of safety and security Henry and I had finally found.

"And what about Whit?" Dottie asked gently.

"What about him?" I replied, trying to sound casual.

She smiled knowingly. "I see the look in your eyes when you say his name. You're proper smitten."

"It's that obvious?" I groaned. "I didn't mean for this to happen, Dottie. I really didn't!"

"Of course, you didn't," she said, giving my knee a comforting pat. "It's just the way of things. No accounting for what the heart wants, Zellie. But it's *most* important to listen to your *soul*—it knows the way. What does your soul whisper to you when he's nearby, accidentally brushes your hand, kisses you until you can't breathe, like you're the only woman in the world who matters?"

Shocked by Dottie's directness, heat crept up my neck. "It tells me I love him," I whispered. "I feel like I have forever, like I was just waiting to find him."

She smiled. "There now. *That's* the truth. So, what are you going to do about it?"

I shook my head. "I don't know. My head's telling me to be careful, that I'm just bound for heartbreak."

She sighed wistfully. "Oh, my girl. The heart can be fooled as easily as the mind. But don't you think it's time you had a little happiness? It's not living if you shut yourself off from what you feel—the good and the bad. Open yourself up to the possibilities of what could *be* instead of dwelling on what has *been*."

"What about the hauntings?" I asked. "These women? What do they want from me?"

She exhaled, the sound heavy with sorrow, perhaps reliving old wounds of her own. "There are those who die without ever being heard, Zellie. These women were silenced then, and scream in silence now. They need a voice. Or they will never know peace. You know what it feels like to be denied a voice in your fate, darlin'. Don't deny these poor souls theirs."

CHAPTER SEVENTEEN

I didn't expect her to call again. But there was no mistaking Vivian's raspy voice cutting through the static on the line.

"What do you want, Vivian?" I asked, holding the phone between my ear and shoulder as I tried to shift ground beef from the skillet to the pot of sauce that was bubbling over, leaving splatters across the stovetop.

"Darkness," she said, fear threading her voice. "There's only darkness."

Here we go...

"I'm fine, thanks," I said, not bothering to hold back the sarcasm. "How are you? So good to hear from you, as always."

Whatever she said next broke apart into garbled noise. Thinking of what had happened the last time she called, I shuddered and glanced over my shoulder toward the kitchen doorway, half expecting something monstrous to come charging through, ready to rip me apart and consume my soul.

"Where are you?" I asked, frustrated with the horrible connection. If she was going to call, I might as well hear what imaginary sins she thought I'd committed.

"Listen!"

That one word came through, urgent and clear.

I heaved a sigh. "I *am* listening," I told her. "I've *always* listened to everything you ever said, even when I shouldn't have. Do you have any idea what your constant hatefulness did to me, Vivian? What your inability to get your shit together cost me?"

A crackle of static was the only response. Of course, she had nothing to say. And why would she? She'd never cared about what harm she inflicted. Why start now?

I listened for a few more seconds, but nothing came. "Okay, great. Good talk. Thanks for calling." I hung up and tossed the phone aside just as the pot of boiling spaghetti foamed over, the water hissing angrily as it hit the burner.

"Shit!"

I yanked the pot off the burner and flipped the knobs to OFF. Between the sauce splattering everywhere and the noodles boiling over, the kitchen was a disaster.

"Of all nights..." I muttered, glancing at the clock.

Whit would be there any minute, and I hadn't even had a chance to do anything with my hair or makeup. Not that spaghetti with sauce from a jar was all that special or anything close to what he was probably used to, but I hoped the invitation meant something.

"Mama!" Henry called. "I need help!"

I hurried to his bedroom where he'd been playing with Legos. "What's up, baby?"

He sat in the middle of his floor, surrounded by loose Lego pieces. "I can't get up!"

I gave him a look. "Seriously? That's the emergency?"

"There's no place to walk," he said. "They hurt my feet when I step on them."

I shook my head. "Just put away the pieces."

"I tried, but David keeps dumping them again."

I put my hands on my hips and said sternly, "Knock it off, David. Henry has to pick up his room. You're welcome to help with that, but no more dumping Legos." I turned back to Henry. "There. He should behave now. I'll help you scoop."

A few minutes later, we'd put all the bricks in the bucket when the doorbell rang. And the smoke alarm started blaring.

"The garlic bread!" I groaned, scrambling to my feet and rushing to the kitchen, where smoke seeped out of the oven. I turned it off and grabbed a dish towel to fan the alarm.

Whit appeared in the doorway. "Need some help?"

I grimaced as the alarm started beeping once more. "Yes, please!"

He reached up, popped the smoke alarm off the wall, and removed the battery. The ear-splitting beeping immediately stopped. "Remind me to put that back up before I leave."

I blew a lock of hair out of my face. "Thanks. That was supposed to be garlic bread, but I'm guessing it's charcoal now."

He chuckled and pulled me into his arms. "Turns out I'm a fan of charcoal."

"Well, lucky you! Because I have a confession." I glanced behind me at the stove. "I really only ever cook the kind of stuff that Henry eats, so I might've misled you when I invited you over for 'dinner'. I'm not sure it'll be edible."

He shrugged. "Not about the meal. I'm here for the company. Aside from the Sunday dinners at Pearlie and Junior's, I usually eat alone. So, I will take your spaghetti and garlic bread charcoal briquets if it means I get to see you."

I was smiling when he kissed me, but my grin faded as the kiss deepened. The sound of Henry's feet pounding down the hallway brought an abrupt end to the moment.

Whit groaned softly and kept his back to the doorway as Henry barreled in. "How about I help you finish this up?"

I couldn't help a little wicked grin, having a pretty good idea why he was keeping his back to Henry.

"I'll help, too!" Henry announced.

I intercepted him before he reached the stove and lifted him up. "I'm sure Mr. Whit appreciates the offer, but I could really use your help with something else."

Despite the sad excuse for dinner, Whit dutifully ate a full plate and scraped the burned parts off his garlic bread, winking at me across our little table as he took a bite. We spent the rest of the evening playing Candy Land, watching Henry's favorite cartoon, and reading three bedtime stories before I finally called it.

"I think Mr. Whit needs a break," I said, tucking Henry's comforter around him. "It's time for you to go to sleep."

"But Mr. Whit is good at all the voices!" Henry protested.

Whit beamed as he tousled Henry's curls and then offered his fist to bump. "We'll read more stories next time. You gotta mind your mama."

"Yes, sir," Henry said, bottom lip jutting out.

When I finished tucking Henry in, I came out to the living room where Whit was sitting on the couch—not perched on the edge in that aloof posture I'd seen so often. He was actually *lounging*.

He held out his hand and pulled me down beside him when I offered him my fingers. I snuggled against him, closing my eyes, inhaling the scent of him, enjoying just being held.

"You okay?" he asked after a moment. "You seem far away tonight."

I nodded. "Yeah. Vivian called today."

"Your mom?" he replied. "I didn't think she wanted anything to do with you or Henry."

"She doesn't," I said. "She only calls when she wants to remind me what a horrible spawn of the Devil I am and how I'm going to burn in hell."

"Hmm. Seems extreme." His arm tightened around me. "I'm pretty sure the Devil isn't your father."

I lifted my head from his chest. "Care to tell *her* that? I haven't been able to get through."

He gave me a grin—cockeyed and boyish in a way that reminded me of Chase. It was the first real family resemblance I'd ever seen. "Happy to set her straight."

"Thanks." I sat up and kissed him.

It was meant to be a brief embrace, but then he was pulling me onto his lap so that I was straddling him, kissing me—passionately, urgently. I gasped when he released my lips to press kisses along my neck, my shoulder, the hollow of my throat. Then his mouth found mine again. His hands smoothed over my back, pressing me closer. My skin was flush, burning for his touch. When his fingertips brushed along the inside of my thigh, I shuddered and rose up on my knees. His hand slipped under the hem of my shorts, his questing fingers making me bite my lip to keep from crying out.

"Is this okay?" he asked.

I nodded and let my head fall back. "God, yes..."

And then I was lost on a wave of pleasure, all the world slipping away until there was only that moment, only ecstasy.

"I wish you didn't have to leave," I said as we stood in the doorway of my apartment, meaning it with every beat of my heart. My whole body hummed, every sense heightened almost to the point of pain. Being near Whit woke something in me, something I hadn't fully realized was sleeping.

He smiled and lifted each of my hands, brushing a kiss to them in turn. "Me, too. But I get it. I don't want to confuse Henry either." He gave a quick tug on my hands, knocking me off balance and straight into his arms.

I laughed softly and tilted my face up for a kiss, and he was happy to oblige.

When the kiss ended, he studied me for a long moment before saying, "Let me take you to dinner. Just you and me. We'll make a whole night of it."

I was slightly taken aback. A whole night? "Um...okay. I could ask June if she'll keep Henry for the evening."

"How about this Thursday?" he suggested. "I'll pick you up at three, we'll go to the Chateau early, avoid the crowds, and then take the night wherever it goes."

I blinked at him in disbelief. "The Chateau? You mean in Charleston?"

"Well, not the one in France. We'll save that for a weekend trip," he promised with a wink. "Will you settle for the one in Charleston?"

I'd heard about the Chateau, a French restaurant, winner of loads of foodie awards, the kind of place where a glass of water probably cost more than what I made in a day.

"Whit, I'm flattered. I'm sure it would be incredible. But..." I pulled back from him, reluctant to share my thoughts, but why bother avoiding the truth? "I've never been anywhere like that. It's not exactly the kind of place I could ever afford."

His eyes narrowed playfully. "Remember our conversation about letting me spoil you? But if it's too much, that's okay. We can go anywhere you want."

What could I say to that? That my version of spoiling myself was dinner at a chain restaurant with all you could eat salad and breadsticks and bottomless pasta bowls that would feed me for a few days if I took home leftovers? He'd go if I asked. I knew he would. But some part of me was insisting I'd be a fool to turn down something I might never have a chance to try again. Even once I was back on my feet and no longer living in Dawes House, a place like the Chateau would still be out of reach.

"I don't have anything to wear to a place like that, Whit," I said, making the last argument I could think of, even as the reality of the excuse made me a little panicky.

"We'll go shopping," he said casually, like it was nothing.

I shook my head. "Whit, that's too much. I already feel like the dinner is more than you should spend. I'm not going to let you buy me clothes like I'm a charity case you're dressing up like some modern-day Eliza Doolittle."

He chuckled. "Put in my place by literary allusions." He pursed his lips, thinking. "If I can figure out another solution that you're comfortable with, will you go?"

I took his face in my hands and kissed him slowly, savoring the moment, and murmured with a grin, "Yes. I'll go."

Henry and I had just finished our cereal the next morning when a jaunty knock on the door made us both frown.

"Who's that?" Henry asked. "It's awfully early, Mama."

I laughed. "Hey, don't grow up so fast, okay?"

I was still smiling when I opened the door to see Merilee. She walked right in and turned around, leaning on the back of the couch, grinning from ear to ear. "So, looks like we're going shopping!"

I blinked. "What?"

"For your date," she said, her smile getting a wicked slant to it. "Whit asked me to help you out."

"Thanks, Merilee," I said, surprised that she'd been brought in our plans. "But I'll figure something out. I don't really have the money to go shopping."

"Good thing we're shopping in my closet," she said. Before I could stop her, she called out, "Henry! Come on, little man. We're going to go play at my apartment. Ms. Netty can't wait to see you!"

Henry trudged into the room dutifully but looked less than thrilled. "Yes, ma'am."

"Oh, don't look *too* excited," she teased. "Of course, if you don't come with us, I don't know who is going to eat all the cookies I baked this morning..."

This brought a light to Henry's eyes. "Well, I guess I could help with that."

"Good lord, Merilee," I said as she grabbed my hand and pulled me into the hallway. "What time do you get up?"

"I can sleep when I'm dead," she called over her shoulder to me. "Close the door, Henry!"

Before I could process what was happening, we were in Merilee and Ms. Netty's apartment, Henry seated at their kitchen table, eating cookies and milk, chatting animatedly with Ms. Netty.

I took in the apartment as I followed Merilee out of the kitchen and down the hall to her bedroom. The place looked like it had been frozen in time in the 1920s or 1930s, the rooms rich with the opulence and vaguely futuristic décor of the Art Deco period—lots of mirrored or metallic surfaces and bold colors and scalloped designs and geometric patterns in the wallpaper and fabrics.

It was stunning.

When we entered Merilee's bedroom, she flung open the doors to a massive wardrobe with a flourish like a game-show hostess revealing the grand prize. A ridiculous number of dresses hung inside. "Try on anything you like!"

Still confused, I said, "Thank you so much, Merilee, but I can't imagine anything you have will fit me. I mean...you're tall and gorgeous and...I'm sure you look beautiful in everything."

She came over to me, lips pressed together, and took me by the shoulders, gently turning me around to face a full-length mirror. "Zellie Dupont, that woman right there is beautiful. All she needs is a little permission to feel it. And, Zellie-girl, *I* am giving you permission to feel it."

Emotion rose in my throat. I managed a grateful smile, not willing to trust my voice. I'd rarely experienced any sort of generosity, had no idea how to respond, how to accept even this small bit of happiness.

"So," she said, returning to her wardrobe, "we're going to find the perfect dress for you. And if you don't find one here, we'll check my other closet."

Other closet?

Still too stunned to respond, I just stood in front of the mirror as Merilee pulled out more than a dozen dresses and held them up to me and studied my reflection, my skin tone, my shoulders, sizing me up to determine which ones were the most flattering.

By the time we'd gone through her selection, she had six of them for me to try on. To my surprise, it was more fun than I'd anticipated. As I tried on each dress, pretending to model on the catwalk, Merilee would either scrunch up her face to rule them out or love-bomb me with compliments on the ones she approved of.

The last dress I tried on slid over my skin, silky soft, as I pulled it on over my head and down my torso. It clung to my curves in all the right places, fitting as if made for me. The blood-red sleeveless sheath was overlayed with a filmy black material decorated with beautifully beaded patterns, striking without being gaudy.

"This one," I whispered, staring at the mirror, finding it hard to believe that the woman I saw there was me.

Merilee handed me heels that looked like they might've come from the Art Deco period like the rest of the house. "Try these"

To my surprise, they fit perfectly, the soft leather molding to my feet.

"Hmm," she mused, narrowing her eyes, studying me. "Something's still missing."

She rummaged around in a huge jewelry case, then handed me a pair of garnet earrings. After I put them on, she fastened a matching necklace around my throat.

I brushed my fingers over the beautiful stones, marveling at how perfectly they matched the dress, how well they suited *me*.

Merilee examined me thoughtfully, then nodded. "Just one more thing."

She came up behind me and gathered my hair, twisting it into a sleek, sexy updo, then pinned it into place. When finished, she rested her hands on my shoulders, regarding my reflection in the mirror like an artist admiring a finished piece.

"Whit won't be able to take his eyes off you," she said softly.

Her fingertips drifted down my arm, a feather-light caress that brought an icy tingle to my skin, then her arms snaked around my waist, her chin settling on my shoulder. "I wore this dress one night with my lover." Her lips curved into a wicked grin. "We never made it to dinner, but we certainly danced."

As she spoke, I grew lightheaded. The room tilted. I felt drunk. Drunk like the night I'd had too much of Junior's elderberry wine. I tried to tell her that I needed to leave, that I needed to lie down until the world stopped spinning, but my tongue felt heavy.

"I don't think..." I managed, slurring.

"Shhh," she soothed. "No need to think, Zellie-girl. You'll do just fine..."

When I abruptly snapped out of my brain fog, I was sitting on the couch in my apartment while Henry played with his action figure on the coffee table. He was talking to me, telling me a story.

What was it he said? He'd mentioned Ms. Netty...

"What was that, baby?" I asked, frowning as I tried to focus despite the pounding in my head.

"Ms. Netty told me that she was supposed to be young again," he said, "but Mr. Whit wouldn't let her."

I shook my head slightly, my frown deepening. "What does that mean?" I asked. "It doesn't make any sense, does it?"

Henry shrugged. "Ms. Netty says a lot of funny things. She told me Ms. Merilee was her sister and that she didn't like her anymore."

I sighed. "Oh, baby. Ms. Netty..." How was I supposed to explain dementia to a five-year-old? "She gets confused sometimes. I'm betting she had a sister once and that Ms. Merilee just reminds Ms. Netty of her."

"Okay," Henry said with another shrug. "Maybe somebody should tell her that."

I gave him a sad smile, wishing life was as simple as it seemed through his eyes. “Maybe so.”

CHAPTER EIGHTEEN

When I awoke the next morning, the first thing I saw was the borrowed dress from Merilee hanging on my closet door, and I smiled, determined to focus on my upcoming date with Whit instead of the strange events at Merilee and Netty's apartment. I mean, it's not like I hadn't experienced things one hell of a lot stranger already at Dawes House.

There was a bounce in my step, a happiness I couldn't suppress as I left for work that morning, but the sight of Billy Wayne standing in front of the elevator doors when Henry and I came downstairs brought me up short. The man made my skin crawl. Even if I hadn't known what an asshole he was to Kitty, I wouldn't have liked him. There was something about him that was just...off. Menacing. Dangerous.

"Good morning," I said politely as we passed.

He cast a surly look my way and said nothing before stepping into the elevator.

"I think he has his grumpy pants on," Henry told me, rolling his eyes.

"Mind your manners, sir," I said with a warning look, but softening it with a grin.

Iris was already at the front desk when I left Henry with June. I wished her good morning on my way out, but then paused and turned back, needing to ask the questions that had been nagging me for days.

"I saw Billy Wayne earlier," I told her. "He was even more disgusted by my presence than usual. Is everything okay?"

Iris shook her head on a sigh. "You haven't heard yet? Their baby didn't make it. Poor little thing just wasn't strong enough."

"Oh, God, no," I breathed. "No, I hadn't heard that. How's Kitty taking it?"

Iris cast her eyes down at the paperwork on her desk and didn't immediately answer. "She was beside herself. Couldn't bear the loss."

I frowned at her, hoping I didn't understand. "What do you mean?"

"Billy Wayne went to the hospital this morning to make arrangements for her body," Iris said.

Sweet Jesus.

The shock of the truth left me speechless as I wrestled with the poor woman's tragic fate. That she had been so hopeless, so despondent… And as much as I detested Billy Wayne and how he'd treated his wife, I still hated that anyone would ever experience such heartbreaking loss.

"Is there anything I can do?" I asked. "Is there anything he needs? I know he's not my biggest fan, but I would never wish that on anyone."

Iris gave me a kind smile. "I'll let you know," she promised. "I'm sure he could use consoling from all of us."

That evening before picking up Henry from June's, I took the elevator to the third floor, intending to offer my condolences to Billy Wayne. I had no idea what I could say. There were no words that seemed adequate.

When I reached his apartment door, I lifted my fist to knock but a sudden cry in the apartment brought me up short. Then came muffled moans and gasps—a woman and a man who I assumed was Billy Wayne.

"That son of a bitch," I spat under my breath, seething for poor Kitty and her baby, not even in their graves yet. Grieving husband, my ass. He'd probably had a mistress all along. Hadn't Whit told me Billy Wayne's wandering eye was behind their screaming matches and Kitty's uncontrollable sobs?

Disgusted that the man could be such an unfeeling bastard, I marched down the stairs, needing the extra time before picking up Henry. I'd managed to tamp down my contempt by the time I reached June's door, but the woman was far too perceptive.

"What's wrong, darlin'?" she asked, taking my arm and pulling me inside. "You look like you could spit nails."

"Hi, Mama!" Henry cried, running to me and giving me a tight hug when I scooped him up and kissed his cheek. "We helped Mamaw June dig up one of the flowerbeds to get it ready for new plants!"

"Did you find any squiggly worms?" I asked, tickling his ribs.

"No!" he laughed. "But I found a treasure!"

I gasped with excitement. "You did? No way!"

"Why don't you go play with Addie for a few more minutes," June said. "Then you can show your mama what you found."

"Yes, ma'am," Henry said, squirming to be put down.

As soon as he was out of earshot, June led me into her kitchen and put on the tea kettle. It was way too hot and humid for anything warm to drink, but I wasn't going to refuse her hospitality.

I glanced around her kitchen, taking in the countless plants that filled the room, many of them hanging upside down from several lines strung across the room, drying until ready for...whatever she used them for.

"Now, tell me what's wrong," she insisted, pulling out the chair across from me and setting a teacup of pale-yellow liquid on the well-worn top of the heavy wooden farm table.

I took a sip of the tea, surprised by the spiciness but finding it unexpectedly soothing. "Iris told me about Kitty and her baby."

She nodded. "A terrible loss."

"I thought so, too," I said. "So, I went upstairs a little bit ago to offer my condolences. But..." I hesitated, cleared my throat, took another sip of the tea. "When I reached the apartment, I heard Billy Wayne having sex with someone. Loudly."

“Ah,” June said, straightening in her chair.

I shook my head. “Don’t you think it’s suspicious? Billy Wayne and Kitty had such horrible fights they’d leave her sobbing so loudly I could hear her from the floor above. Then their baby dies, and Kitty takes her own life. And now I hear him with another woman?”

“Don’t get involved, Zellie,” June warned. “It’s not your business.”

“But what if Billy Wayne did something to Kitty and the baby?” I pressed. “What if the complications were because of *him*?”

“Zellie,” June said firmly, “don’t you think the doctors would’ve reached out to the police if they’d found anything suspicious?”

She had a point, of course. But the nagging wriggle of unease at the base of my spine told me something was off. The whole situation wasn’t right. There was more to the story, I was certain. But June’s tone told me our little heart-to-heart was over.

“Now,” she said, assuming her usual pleasant tone, “drink your tea, darlin’. It’ll help you feel better.”

She wasn’t wrong. I was completely relaxed after a few more sips. “What’s in this?”

“Herbs and flowers and a few other ingredients,” she said with a smile. “Old family recipe.”

“So, tell me about Henry’s treasure,” I said, changing the subject before I made myself completely unwelcome.

“Oh, yes!” June said, her face lighting up. “Henry, my little prince, come show your mama what you found!”

“Why do you call him ‘little prince’?” I asked.

June turned to me, her smile somewhat condescending. “Well, Henry’s rather a royal name, isn’t it? It suits him, even though he obviously hasn’t been raised in wealth.”

I leveled my gaze at her, narrowing my eyes. "So, what? It's a snide joke making fun of the fact that we're poor?"

"Now, Zellie," June replied, waving off my indignation as if it were a pestering fly. "You're being too literal. And, besides, just because you're poor doesn't mean Henry always will be. Humble beginnings and all that."

I blinked at her a few times, trying to figure out what the hell she was implying. But before I could press her, Henry bounded in, Addie at his heels, her blond curls bouncing.

"We found pirate treasure!" Addie announced.

"Addie, I want to tell her!" Henry protested.

I set my tea aside and pulled Henry onto my lap. "I still don't know what it is, baby," I told him. "No need to get upset with Addie."

"Mamaw June," Henry said, his voice eager once more, "could you please show Mama?"

June rose from the table and picked up an object wrapped in a very dirty burlap cloth. Grinning, she set it on the table in front of me. "Go ahead."

Henry looked at me expectantly, his eyes shining with barely restrained excitement. "Open it, Mama!"

With a slight shake of my head, I pinched a bit of fabric and unfolded one side, then the other. I gasped when I saw Henry's "treasure."

A very old, very dirty dagger lay on the cloth, its sheath caked with mud, obscuring the designs engraved in the metal. The hilt was simple, reminding me of the pieces I'd seen in a museum display case on a school field trip, but I didn't know enough to guess how old it was or where it came from.

"Isn't that cool?" Henry asked. "Mamaw said I could have it if you were okay with it, but that you'd have to keep it put up for me until I was old enough."

All I could think of as I sat there staring down at the antique weapon was the dagger in *Macbeth*. *"Is this a dagger which I see before me, The handle toward my hand?"* In the infamous play, it had foreshadowed murder—and the beginning of the end.

When we arrived back at our apartment, I placed the dagger, still wrapped in its cloth, on top of one of the bookshelves in the living room where Henry couldn't reach it, my fingertips lingering on the bundle. Part of me wanted to examine it more closely, try to determine its origin, why it would be buried in the garden. But there was something just outside my knowing that nagged at me, an impression I couldn't quite grasp that made me shy away from thinking about it more.

Despite June's warning not to get involved, I decided to stop by Billy Wayne's apartment the next morning to tell him how sorry I was about Kitty and their son and see if I could sense anything about what had happened. But as I stepped out of the stairwell and into the third-floor hallway, Billy Wayne's apartment door opened. And Iris stepped out. Her hair was a tangled mess, her stiletto heels in her hand.

She threw her lovely head back and laughed as Billy Wayne grabbed her around the waist and pulled her roughly to him with a hungry growl. And then he grabbed her by the back of the neck and kissed her hard, making her moan.

I swallowed the bile rising in my throat, disgusted and heartbroken by the truth. How could they betray Kitty that way? Had Iris always been the other woman, or had she just moved in as soon as Kitty was out of the picture?

Furious, I hurried back to the stairwell before they could see me. I'd never liked Billy Wayne. And I wasn't a huge fan of Iris, either. Yet I somehow felt betrayed. I reminded myself that I hadn't been wronged in any way, that June was right, and it wasn't any of my business. But my image of the perfect harmony among the residents of Dawes House was tarnished. And if that had been a lie, what else wasn't as it seemed? Was *any* of it true? The friendship? The love they'd shown me and Henry?

I shook my head, forcing all the doubts away. It didn't matter. My stay at Dawes House was temporary, just a couple of months more. It was probably just as well that I'd found out about Billy Wayne and Iris. That was just two fewer people I'd miss when I was gone. Really, it was only Pearlie and Junior I'd really miss. And quirky little Addie with her unruly curls and frank, matter-of-fact way of talking. June and Earl had been kind, but I would be glad to have some distance, remind June that she wasn't Henry's grandmother, no matter what she told him to call her.

At least there was Whit. Whatever happened, whatever lies and drama lay beneath the overtures of kindness and the empty promises of "family," at least I knew what we were building was real.

When Thursday finally arrived, I was so nervous about my date with Whit, that I'd barely eaten anything and was so distracted I burned Henry's toast at breakfast, setting off the fire alarm again, much to my son's amusement.

"Are you sure you don't mind spending the night with Ms. June and Mr. Earl again?" I asked as I packed Henry's backpack for the night. "I can tell Mr. Whit that we need to be home sooner. You're more important than any fancy dinners."

Henry came to me and gave me a tight hug around my neck and kissed my cheek. "It's okay, Mama. I don't want you to be sad anymore."

"Sad?" I repeated, frowning. "What do you man, baby? I'm not sad." I gave him a playful little shake. "You make me happy every single day!"

He laughed and hugged me again. "But you were really happy when you were at Mr. Whit's house, too."

I shook my head, confused. "I've never been to Mr. Whit's house. Do you mean his apartment down the hall?"

"No," Henry said as he gathered a few of his action figures and put them in his bag. "His house by the ocean. The big one with the pointy thing." He lifted his arms over his head and pressed his palms together, simulating a triangle. "At the top of the house."

"When have *you* seen his house?" I asked, baffled.

"In my dream," he said, as if it should've been obvious. "It was me, and you, and Mr. Whit, and Addie. And we had a little puppy. She was so cute! I can't wait to see her."

Now it all made sense...

I grinned. "A puppy, huh? Did she have a name?"

He nodded, grabbing his teddy bear. "The tall lady said her name was Daisy."

"Who's the tall lady?" I asked, a ripple of unease just beneath my skin. "Is she another...friend?"

"No, ma'am," he said. "I need my toothbrush!"

Deciding "the tall lady" was a mystery to solve another day, I dropped Henry off with June and hurried back to my apartment to get ready. I'd finished doing my makeup and arranging my hair—not nearly as expertly as Merilee had, but still a decent attempt—and checked the time. Whit would be arriving any minute.

I hurried into the bedroom to slip into the dress but came to an abrupt halt as soon as I entered the room. It wasn't hanging on the door where I'd left it.

"What the heck?" I muttered.

I rushed to the closet door and swung it open, rifling through the clothes hanging there. Which was ridiculous. I knew I'd seen it hanging on the closet door just that morning. And of course, it wasn't in the closet.

Frustrated, I dropped onto the bed and covered my face with my hands, trying to retrace my steps. But that revealed nothing.

I glanced at my phone again.

"Damn it!" I pushed off the mattress but froze.

A corner of crimson fabric peeked out from under the bed.

Remembering all too well the last time I'd had to check under my bed for anything, I swallowed hard and eased down onto my knees, and then darted my hand underneath, yanking the dress out as fast as I could.

Fortunately, nothing sinister made an appearance and the dress was undamaged, just a little dusty. Trying not to think about how the hell it had ended up there, I slipped into it and added the jewelry borrowed from Merilee. I was just searching for the shoes that should've been sitting next to my closet when the doorbell rang.

Finally locating the shoes on the other side of the room as if someone had flung them there, I scooped them up and hurried to the door. "Just a sec!" I called, slipping them on.

I pulled the door open, my face flushed with excitement. But my smile faded instantly when I saw that it wasn't Whit.

The man standing there was young, Hollywood-handsome, and dressed like he was preparing to set sail on his private yacht.

"May I help you?" I asked, closing the door halfway between us.

"Just introducing myself," he said, extending a hand. "Carter Dean. I reckon you knew my grandfather."

I blinked, confused. "I didn't think Mr. Dean had any children or grandchildren. He wasn't exactly fond of kids, from what he told me."

Carter laughed lightly. "Sounds about right. We weren't particularly close, but I'm the only family left."

I could see a family resemblance. He could've been a much younger, much less bitter and cantankerous version of Old Man Dean. But something about him made me uneasy.

"I was told Mr. Dean didn't have *any* family around," I said, remembering my conversation with Whit about funeral arrangements. "Why didn't you come sooner?"

Carter shrugged. "Like I said...not close. I only found out about my inheritance when Mr. Briggs contacted me."

I frowned at the familiar name. "Mr. Briggs?"

Carter smiled, a smooth, bright smirk that hinted at silver-tongued assurances that ended in unkept promises. "Yes, my attorney. Do you know him?"

"Monty's—Mr. Proffitt's attorney was named Briggs," I told him. "What a coincidence."

"No coincidence at all," Carter explained, leaning against the doorjamb. "It's the same person. Mr. Briggs made a point of mentioning that he'd represented the late, great Mr. Proffitt." His eyes took on a predatory look as his gaze slid along my body from head to foot and back again. His voice dropped, thick with insinuation. "And *you* are...?"

"Not interested."

My attention shifted over Carter's shoulder where Whit had come up behind him and was now glaring daggers at the man's back. Carter, however, only smirked and leisurely turned to face him.

"Whit," he drawled. "A pleasure."

"What do you want?" Whit asked, stepping around Carter to stand in front of my door, putting himself between us.

"Well now," Carter drawled, "you *wound* me, Whit. I do not want anything at all except to introduce myself to this *lovely* woman. We are neighbors after all."

"Fine," Whit snapped. "You've done what you came to do. No need to stay."

Carter's smile tightened, hostile beneath the charm. "I see you all have plans, so I will excuse myself. I need to go put my grandfather's affairs in order anyway. You know how it goes, I'm sure, having so recently lost your daddy and all."

"Best get at it," Whit said, jerking his head toward the stairwell.

Carter turned back to me and gave a two-finger salute before sauntering away.

"Do you know him?" I asked. "He said he's Mr. Dean's grandson."

"Yes," Whit said, "I know him. He won't bother you anymore. I'll handle it."

I studied Whit as he stared down the hall after Carter Dean. There was clearly no love lost between them, but there was something more...*territorial* in the tension.

"He's not my type," I assured him. "I prefer tall, dark, and handsome."

A smile tugged at his mouth, and he gave a short laugh as he turned toward me. But the smile faded, and for a heartbeat I saw a flicker of light in his eyes, something primal and hungry in the way he looked at me.

It sent a shiver through me—part desire, part fear. "What's wrong?"

"My God, you're beautiful," he breathed. He stepped closer and caught my hand, drawing me to him. "I don't think I've told you that lately. I should have. I meant to."

"Well," I said, my face growing warmer from the desire I saw in his eyes, "you have now."

He brushed a soft kiss to my lips then groaned and pressed his forehead to mine. "We should go now," he murmured, his voice rough. "Otherwise, we might never leave."

I smiled. "Never leaving sounds tempting. But I didn't get all dressed up in Merilee's borrowed clothes just to sit at home." I took his hand and walked backward toward the elevator, pulling him along with me, lifting my brow in unspoken promise. "Come on, Mr. Proffitt. We can pick up this line of conversation later."

That hungry look in his eyes bordered on ravenous as we entered the elevator. He pulled me to him, his lips hovering over mine as he whispered, "You'd better believe we will..."

CHAPTER NINETEEN

I leaned my head back against the seat, my eyes closed, savoring the warmth of the evening sun on my face, pleasantly drowsy after an unbelievable meal at a restaurant that made me feel like the most important person in the room—something I'd never experienced until meeting Whit.

"You're smiling," Whit said after we'd been driving in contented silence for a while. "I hope that means you enjoyed dinner."

I opened my eyes and turned toward him, my smile widening. "It was amazing. Thank you. But it was really the company I loved most."

He brought my hand to his lips for a brief kiss. "Are you ready for your surprise?"

I sat up straighter, wondering what he could possibly have in store. "Absolutely!"

"We should be there soon," he assured me.

It was then that I realized we were driving through a remote area that looked like something straight out of the travel magazines I would flip through over and over at the library when I was a kid, dreaming of faraway places, sandy beaches, and breathtaking views of the ocean that stretched out endlessly.

We traveled for several more miles before Whit turned off onto a private road that wound through thick foliage until it opened up to a stunning three-story house. Although built in a style reminiscent of another time, it was clearly modern. Surrounded by palm trees, with a patio that spanned the width of the house and another deck in the second story, the house looked like it was meant to host elegant Charleston parties where guests sipped mint julips and chatted about the weather and the latest society gossip. Yet as charming and welcoming as it was, the house still somehow seemed *lonely*.

"Where are we?" I asked as Whit parked in the circular drive.

He stared at the house for a moment before answering, "My house."

I said nothing as Whit led me up the stairs, seeing the house with new eyes. When he opened the door, I gasped in awe at the grand spiral staircase, the crystal chandelier in the foyer, the art that was both modern and classic at once.

It was remarkable. And everywhere I looked, I saw touches of his personality.

"This is stunning," I breathed, turning in a full circle.

"Come," he said, grinning. "Let me show you around."

Although all the other rooms were just as beautiful as the foyer, nothing compared to the view. Whit led me through a massive second-floor library to French doors that opened onto a terrace with a magnificent view of the ocean. I drifted toward the railing, my breath catching as the sunset painted the sky in an explosion of color.

Whit came up behind me and wrapped his arms around my waist.

"Whit," I breathed. "This..."

"I thought you might like it," he whispered near my ear.

"I've always dreamed of living close enough to the ocean to see a sunset like this, hear the waves crashing," I confessed.

"I know," he murmured. "You told me once."

I turned enough to see his face. "I did?" I asked, frowning. "I don't remember telling you that."

He glanced down, caught my gaze briefly, then returned his attention to the sunset. "I remember. As soon as you said it, I knew I'd have to bring you here."

I remembered what Henry had said about being happy at Whit's house. Had he dreamed about Whit bringing me here? Or was it just a coincidence? "Don't suppose you have a spire, do you?"

Whit looked at me curiously. "No. Not on this house. Why?"

I snuggled back against him, smiling contentedly. Even if this wasn't the house in Henry's dream, I was definitely happy. "No reason."

As the sunset eventually slipped toward twilight, Whit stepped back and took my hand, leading me toward a small table I hadn't even noticed. Candles in the center threw shadows onto the white tablecloth, the flames dancing eerily in the gentle breeze. Two plates covered by silver domes sat beside a set of delicate wine glasses and champagne flutes. From within the library, soft music drifted out to the terrace.

"Where did these come from?" I asked with a surprised laugh.

"Butler," Whit said offhandedly, pulling out my chair. "He's nothing if not discreet." He then lifted the silver dome with a flourish. "Your dessert, mademoiselle."

My eyes widened. On the plate were three exquisite desserts that looked too beautiful to eat. "What are these?"

"Dark chocolate torte with pistachio crumble," he said, pointing to the dense triangle of chocolate. "Rhubarb and orange trifle there in the glass. And the last is my personal favorite—strawberry mille-feuille."

He then poured wine and champagne for each of us. "I hope you like these," he said. "I chose them myself."

"I'm sure I'll love them then," I told him. I lifted my champagne flute and took a sip, closing my eyes to better enjoy the experience, delighted by crisp bubbles that tickled my tongue. I grinned and licked my lips. "Delicious."

When I opened my eyes again, he was still standing beside the table, his expression a smoldering blend of pleasure and desire. "Indeed."

We took our time with dessert, the wine and champagne making me a little bolder than usual. Questions I'd been hesitant to ask no longer felt off-limits.

"This house is beautiful," I mused. "But it seems so sad, so lonely, Whit. Do you live here alone?"

He leaned back in his chair, draping his elbow over the back, and turned his attention to the ocean. "Yes, except for staff. But I rarely see them. I'd always hoped to have a wife and children here to fill the house with love and laughter. Things I didn't experience growing up."

"What do you mean?" I asked. "I can't imagine Mr. Monty not being a loving father."

Whit grunted dismissively. "I told you before, my father was not the saint you imagine, Zellie. I have no doubt he loved me in his own way, but I was raised by nannies and tutors, with an occasional visit from dear old Dad when he wasn't traveling on family business or enjoying his latest conquest."

This was all entirely at odds with the Montgomery Proffitt I'd known—a man who was kind, genuine, caring. "How could your dad and the man I knew be so different?"

Whit swirled his wine thoughtfully before answering. "I was a disappointment," he finally said. "I wasn't interested in the traditions that mattered so much to him. I didn't care about preserving his legacy. And I certainly didn't give a damn about my stepmothers who were barely around long enough to get to know, let alone care about."

"How many did you have?" I asked. "Stepmothers, I mean."

Whit shrugged. "I stopped counting."

"I thought my mom was bad with her boyfriends," I murmured. "Was he still married when he died?"

Whit shook his head. "Widowed. His wife Jessamine died after they'd only been married a few years."

"Jessamine?" I repeated, the unusual name tugging at something in my memory.

"Heard of her, have you?" he asked, catching something in my expression. Before I could respond, he added, "June and Earl don't talk much about their daughter, so I wasn't sure if they'd mentioned her."

I shook my head, then asked, "So, Addie...?"

"Is my sister," he said, lifting his glass and finishing off his wine. "June still hasn't forgiven my father for Jessamine's death, nor me by extension, I suppose."

When Whit didn't elaborate on what he meant, I let it drop, though what he'd shared explained the tension I'd sensed between him and June.

By the time we finished dessert, stars filled the sky, reminding me how remote we were. Even the *location* of the house felt lonely and withdrawn. When Whit took my hand and turned to lead me inside, I instead pulled him gently toward me and took his face in my hands.

"You've been lonely too long, Whit," I told him softly. "But you don't have to be lonely anymore."

I pulled him down to press a kiss to his lips, but that one kiss turned into another and another until we were lost in each other. At some point, we began to sway together to the music that still drifted out from the library, my head resting against his chest.

I don't know how long we danced under the stars before by unspoken agreement, we finally stepped apart. And this time when he took my hand, I let him lead me inside, through the library and down the hall. But as we passed one of the rooms, I released his hand and wandered inside.

The furniture was dark, masculine, the stark white walls and deep blue bedding and rugs a striking contrast. But there was also an airiness to the décor, the ocean breeze coming in from open French doors lifting the white gauzy bed curtains in a hypnotic ballet.

I immediately realized it was Whit's bedroom.

I don't know how. I just *knew*, like I'd been there before—perhaps in one of my *many* dreams of him. Had they actually been prophetic and not just fantasy?

I swallowed hard, erotic memories of my dreams rushing back to me.

"Zellie?"

Whit had entered the room and stood just inside the doorway, his hands deep in his pockets, his brows drawn together as if struggling against the urge to move forward, to embrace what was before him for fear of what the wrong move might cost him.

But I was tired of struggling, of denying what I wanted, what I needed.

I said nothing. Instead, I slipped one of the dress straps from my shoulder and then the other, letting the dress slide down my body.

"Zellie," he said, his voice rough, "I didn't bring you here expecting anything from you."

I held out a hand to him. "I know."

He swallowed hard, hesitating. But then he turned and gently closed the door. As he came toward me, his movements were controlled, restrained. He took my outstretched hand, pulled me to him. His eyes drank me in, exploring the lines of my face, every curve of my body. His fingertips followed, lightly skimming my shoulder, along my arm, the curve of my waist. And then, so slowly, so gently, his lips pressed against the curve of my jaw, my throat, my shoulder...

"Whit," I breathed, my fingers sliding into his hair as he kissed the valley between my breasts.

He allowed me to drag him back up, and his lips captured mine in a tender, sultry kiss so beautiful it made me shiver with emotion. At the same moment, a series of images flashed through my mind, just glimpses of being kissed the same way years before, leaning my head back as my lover traced kisses down my throat, found my breasts... A rush of emotions overwhelmed me every time I remembered that night, that cherished, magical night, when the man whose face still eluded me had made love to me so gently, like I was something fragile and precious, a treasure of unimaginable worth, and in doing so had given me the most beautiful gift of all.

But vague memories were nothing compared to the man who held me, whose kisses brought me to the brink, drove me mad with desire, filled my heart till it ached. And new erotic images played in my mind, flashes of Whit making love to me, guiding me toward heights of desire and pleasure like none I'd even dared to imagine.

But those erotic images were abruptly interrupted by a burst of pain behind my eyes. I winced and pulled back, squeezing my eyes shut as I waited for the pain to fade.

"Are you okay?" Whit asked softly. "Should we stop?"

I shook my head. "No," I said, still reeling from the brief headache that was already vanishing. "No, please don't stop. I want this, Whit. I want *you*."

He studied me for a moment longer, still hesitant, his expression so loving, so tender, my throat grew tight. Then his lips found mine in a kiss that spoke the love in his eyes, and his hands splayed across my bare back, pressing me closer. When he ended the kiss, the hunger in his eyes was both thrilling and unnerving.

But then he eased down onto his knees, pressing kisses to my belly, my hip, dragging my panties down, baring me to him. And when he lifted my leg to remove my shoe, he brushed a kiss to the inside of my thigh, repeating the whisper of a kiss on my other thigh as he removed my remaining shoe. His hands slid up my thighs to my waist as he kissed a path on my hip to my belly, pausing to lave my bellybutton. I gasped at the unexpected sensation then shivered as the rumble of his deep chuckle vibrated against my skin.

When he turned his face up to me, his wicked grin growing, I grasped his tie and urged him up the rest of the way. Then we were edging back toward his bed, slow, unhurried steps as his lips found mine again, one kiss ending and where another began.

I pulled at his tie, sliding it down his chest, letting my fingertips brush against the muscles beneath his shirt. And then I was tearing at the buttons, pushing his shirt off his shoulders, longing to touch his skin. My hands explored his chest, his back, savoring every inch, then traveled lower to his waist, undoing his belt. Then our fingers fumbled together in our haste to remove the last barrier between us.

Whit sucked in a deep breath and broke our kiss, squeezing his eyes shut as I caressed him. Emboldened by his reaction, I gently shoved his shoulder, and he obediently eased down onto the bed, pulling me with him, his fiery gaze holding mine.

With a wicked smirk, I unhooked my bra and tossed it to the floor. Then one by one, I removed the pins from my hair, letting it fall around my shoulders.

He sat up, propping himself with one elbow then grasped the back of my neck to pull me to him for a long, sultry kiss that made me shudder.

I moaned when he drew the kiss to a close, my aching need for him growing unbearable.

Without a word, he reached around me to the bedside table, searching for a few frenzied seconds before finding a condom and slipping it on. In the next moment, he grasped my hips, guiding me, easing me down, joining our bodies.

Now it was my turn to gasp. We began to move together, unhurried, giving ourselves over to the pleasure building between us with each sensual motion. I let my head fall back, closed my eyes, loving the feel of him inside me, the way he filled me—body and soul.

He sat up, pulling me against him. And when I was overtaken by that blissful release, I breathed his name, my fingernails digging into his back as I curled into him. And then I was falling, his hand gently cradling my head as he rolled me onto my back.

He peered down at me as he began to move again. I wrapped my arms around his neck and pulled him down to me, capturing his mouth, unable to get enough of him. And when he tensed and buried his face in my hair with a groan, I shuddered with him, held him close, smoothed his broad shoulders, seared the beauty of the moment into my memory so that I would never forget it when my beautiful fairytale ended.

We lay together, refusing to look at the time, fingers entwined, my head resting on his shoulder, holding onto the happiness that enveloped us.

But eventually, he sighed.

"We should probably head back to Dawes House," he said but making no move to rise.

I turned into him, snuggling closer. "I don't want to go back to Dawes House," I admitted. "If Henry wasn't there..."

His arms tightened around me. "Something tells me that the reluctance to leave isn't all to do with me. What else is going on? I thought you liked it there."

I sat up, briefly surprised that I didn't feel self-conscious when the sheets slipped down and pooled at my waist, leaving my breasts bare. He'd now known the most intimate parts of me. What was the point in hiding anything anymore? He would either accept all of me or this beautiful dream would come to an end.

"There's more to the hauntings," I said quietly. "So much more."

I told him all of it—the screaming woman in the bloody nightgown who I'd seen the first night but hadn't realized she was a spirit, the drowning woman, the woman in the wall. I told him about the drawings I'd found, the dreams of Susanna and her forced marriage to Josef Profitt, the pregnancy she'd tried to end out of terror for what she carried inside her.

"I'm so grateful for everything you've done for me, Whit, and for what the others have done," I told him. "The friendship everyone at Dawes House has shown me has meant more to me than any of them will ever know. But I can't stay there any longer than I have to. I'm afraid of what might happen to me or to Henry."

When I finished, he sat in silence, his expression unreadable. Then he reached for me, cupping my cheek. "I had no idea. Of course, you can't stay there, not with everything you've been dealing with."

A huge weight lifted. "You believe me?"

His thumb grazed my skin. "Zellie, if you tell me all these things have happened, then I believe you." He drew me back into his arms and held me for a while before speaking again. "There are other properties. You can pick whichever one you want."

"I'm not sure it will matter where I go," I admitted. "If they want to give me a message badly enough, they'll eventually find me."

"We'll figure it out," he promised. "Hell, I'll *build* you a house, if I need to."

My heart leapt at how deeply he cared, the lengths he was prepared to go to, but then my pride overtook my relief. "I appreciate that, Whit, truly. But I can't. I already feel like I've taken advantage of your generosity with Dawes House. I can't continue to live off your charity, especially *now*."

He lifted my chin. "Zellie, it's not charity. But if staying in one of the other properties makes you uncomfortable, I want you and Henry to come stay here."

I shook my head, not understanding. "What do you mean? You're offering for us to move in with you?"

"Well, yeah," he said, his lips curving into a smile. "But more than that. I'm offering you my heart, Zellie. Marry me."

I could only stare at him for a few seconds, too shocked to immediately respond. When I found my voice, my words terse, tight, as my defenses went up. "Whit…I… Don't joke about something like that."

His smile grew. "I'm not joking. I know it's sudden—"

"No kidding."

"—but I love you, Zellie. Do you love *me*?"

I blinked at him, stunned but certain. "Yes." I said it without hesitation. I loved him so much my heart ached at the thought of ever having to say goodbye again. "I do love you, Whit."

"Then why wait?"

"Why rush?"

He leveled his gaze at me, suddenly serious. "Because I'm not the only one who's been lonely too long. I just want to make you happy, give you and Henry everything you've ever wanted."

I kissed him once, twice. "You are everything I could've asked for, Whit. More than I ever expected. And no matter what happens, you will always be one of the most amazing things to happen to me."

"But?" he prompted softly.

"We barely know each other," I insisted.

A mischievous grin draped his lips. "I'd say we know each other pretty well at this point."

The way he looked at me brought a rush of heat to my skin. "You know what I mean. I've told you a lot about me, sure, but there are still things you don't know. And I know almost nothing about you."

He nodded. "Fair enough. Ask me anything."

"Okay," I said, my mind racing with all kinds of questions. So, of course, I started with a lame one. "Favorite color?"

He gave me a look. "Our entire future depends on my favorite color? No pressure."

I smacked his arm playfully. "Whit!"

He laughed. "Okay, okay." His gaze wandered to the discarded dress on the floor. "Red. Next?"

"Where did you go to school?"

"I had private tutors growing up," he said, his voice shifting into that guarded tone he used when talking about his childhood. But why where he attended school would make him uneasy was a mystery. "I went to college at Oxford."

My eyebrows shot up. "Seriously? I've always wanted to visit the UK—or anywhere, really."

"Where have you been so far?" he asked, eager to switch the focus back to me, it seemed.

I shrugged. "Well, we lived in Kentucky when I was born. Then Tennessee for a few years. South Carolina. Now Georgia."

"What about vacations?" he asked.

I shook my head. "I've never been on a vacation. We didn't even have a place to live sometimes, so the closest I ever got to a vacation was sleeping on my mom's friends' couches."

He closed his eyes briefly. "I'm sorry. That was a pretty insensitive question." He took my hand, kissed my palm. "If you could go anywhere right now, where would it be?"

I didn't hesitate. I'd imagined the place for most of my life. "A quaint seaside village in the UK where you can smell the salt in the air and feel the breeze on your face. And I'd live in a beautiful old house with a view of the water. It would have walled gardens filled with roses where we could take our tea in the afternoon or lounge in a hammock reading. And there'd be lots of room for Henry to run and play and climb trees. We'd have a dog or two and maybe some sheep."

"Well, that's certainly specific," Whit said with a warm chuckle. "Not sure we could find all of those amenities in an Airbnb."

I flushed. "Sorry—it's been a dream of mine forever. Imagining I could escape to someplace like what I read about in books helped me survive a really shitty reality."

"Then if that's your dream," he said, "I'll find it for you."

"That's sweet," I hedged, "but we were supposed to be talking about *you*, remember?"

"You don't miss a trick," he admitted with a grin. "So, what's your deal-breaker question that would prevent you from saying yes?"

Good question.

"The first time we met, I thought you could've stepped out of a Brontë novel—a Heathcliff or a Mr. Rochester," I said. "You don't happen to have a secret wife hidden somewhere in an attic, do you?"

He chuckled. "Never been married, and you and I currently live in what was once the 'attic' at Dawes House. So, no worries there."

"I've never heard you talk about what you do when you're not at Dawes House," I said. "You've only ever mentioned work. I still don't know what it is you *do.*"

"Nothing exciting at the moment," he said with a shrug. "Just managing things for my father, his properties, investments."

"What about friends?"

"What about them?"

"Do you have any? Or just those of us at Dawes House?"

He took a deep breath, taking time to consider his answer. "The people at Dawes House aren't my friends. I like some of them. Respect them as elders. But they'll always look at me as just a boy trying to fill his father's shoes, someone who needs looking after." He sighed. "And as for real friends... Not really. Not anymore."

"What about family?" I asked. "You've never really mentioned any beyond Chase, your father and various stepmothers."

"I guess I *haven't* talked much about my family," he admitted. "I'm not all that close to any of them, except my sister."

"Addie, you mean?" I asked with a grin, glad that he was finally getting to know the quirky little girl.

"Uh, no, not Addie," he said.

I raised up a little at this, surprised. "You have another sister? Really?"

"Yes, really, but I grew up with this one—more or less. We had the same mother. Pretty much the only two of my father's progeny that can claim that. I'd trust Cora with my life. And yours."

Cora. Cora Proffitt.

CP.

That explained their frequent texts. But one question still nagged in the back of my mind, one I should've asked a lot sooner.

I cleared my throat, suddenly feeling awkward. "What about...other women?"

He cupped my cheek, his eyes intense, serious. "There is only you. I will never want anyone else."

"Why?" I pressed. "I mean you must be the subject of the fantasies of many women here in Charleston or Savannah or...wherever."

His eyes went darker, flaring with desire. "Your fantasies are the only ones I care about. And I plan to help you realize every one of them. I think we should give it a try right now."

Heat pooled at the center of me, eager to take him up on his offer, but I lifted a brow. "I'll hold you to that, but you're changing the subject."

His expression grew serious again. "I've never allowed myself to get attached to anyone, Zellie. Not until you. What else can I say to convince you that my heart is yours? What else do you want to know?"

I sighed. "I've always told myself I couldn't marry anyone who had done something unforgivable. My mother...some of the men she was with..."

"What do you consider unforgivable?" he asked, his tone grave. When I didn't immediately answer, he gathered me close. "Zellie, I've told you before, I'm no saint. No one is. But I would never harm you or Henry. I would never harm anyone who didn't threaten me or the ones I love. But know this—I would *burn this world down* to protect you, rip the heart out of *anyone* who threatened you. And I wouldn't regret it for a second."

I pulled back to study his face, my heart pounding, overwhelmed by what I saw in his eyes. Fierce devotion. Genuine, unshakable love. "Ask me again."

"Zellie," Whit said, his handsome face breaking into a bright, boyish grin, "will you marry me?"

Laughing through tears, I nodded. "Yes. I'll marry you, Whit."

When we arrived at Dawes House, we strolled up the walk hand in hand, exhausted but exhilarated. I carried my shoes so I wouldn't make too much noise on the foyer tile and wake anyone, but June still met us at the door of her apartment before I even had the chance to knock.

"Looks like y'all had a fun night," she drawled, looking pointedly at Whit. Then she offered me a sweet smile. "Zellie, darlin' you go on and get some sleep. No sense waking up Henry just to carry him up to bed. You can come collect him in the morning."

"Oh, Ms. June, are you sure?" I whispered. "I feel like you already do so much for us."

She briefly pressed my hand. "We're family, darlin'. It's no trouble. Now, go on. I need to get back to my own beauty sleep."

When we reached my apartment, Whit seemed oddly awkward. "Will you be okay here by yourself? After everything you shared, I hate to leave you alone."

I nodded. "I've been by myself this long. But I'd feel much better if you stayed."

"Then I will," he said without hesitation.

"Besides," I said, grabbing his shirt and pulling him closer, "the night you first kissed me, I believe we agreed to spend more time in bed together. And now that I've had you, I don't think I can get enough of you."

Whit's eyes went darker instantly, his own desire clearly matching mine. He grasped me around the waist, lifting me off my feet, and kicked the apartment door closed. His mouth crashed down on mine, his kiss savage, hungry, as he walked me backward until we bumped against the couch. He set me down on my feet and grasped the fabric of my dress, roughly pulling it up over my hips.

Then he was down on his knees, sliding my panties off. Before I could even register what he had in mind, his mouth found the center of me, pressing into me as if he was sampling the sweetest nectar. He groaned as his tongue caressed me, making me moan and writhe against the electrifying onslaught of sensation. I gripped the back of the couch, my legs shaking as a fire blazed inside me. Suddenly, it exploded, and I cried out, not bothering to hold back, shuddering again as he drove me through my release. Then he was on his feet again and spun me around, bending me over the back of the couch.

I gasped as he pressed into me, the fullness of him from this angle bringing a new round of ecstasy. He wasn't gentle this time. He was rough, demanding. I pushed back against him, eagerly accepting each deep thrust, crying out in rhythm with the sound of flesh against flesh. And just when I didn't think I could take any more, my muscles seized, that exhilarating heat lancing through my body once more.

Then, in a frenzy, we were tearing off the rest of our clothes, tossing them aside as we made our way toward my bedroom, pausing once for him to press me against the hallway wall, capture my mouth with another savage kiss as his fingers found the bundle of nerves that made me shudder again within seconds.

My muscles were still pulsing when he hooked an arm under my knee, lifting my leg enough to open me to him. I gripped his shoulders, needing to hold onto him to brace myself as every hard thrust rocked me.

"Oh, God," I gasped as I felt my release building again. "Don't stop. Please, don't stop."

His pace increased, driving me over once more, then slowed, gentled, drawing out each thrust. And when he pulled back, I felt cold without his warmth filling me.

He braced a hand against the wall, his head down, visibly struggling.

I took his face in my hands and lifted it to accept my kisses—on his jaw, his chin, his lips. "We're not finished here," I murmured. "It's your turn."

"Zellie," he breathed, when I pressed a kiss to the side of his neck, but when no other words followed, I took his hand and led him the rest of the way to my bedroom. Seconds later, we crashed down onto my bed, losing ourselves in one another again.

Later, as early morning sunlight seeped into the room, golden and amber, glinting off the mirror in brilliant, blinding bursts that cast gems of light on the wall, a line from a Robert Frost poem intruded on my happiness, reminding me that at some point everything loses its luster and falls apart.

Nothing gold can stay.

But as I fell asleep wrapped in Whit's arms, flush with the warmth of his love, I refused to believe it.

CHAPTER TWENTY

A harsh, wracking cough woke me. I recognized the sound even before I opened my eyes.

My mother stood beside my bed, scowling down at me, rage and disapproval distorting her features, her fists balled at her sides.

I blinked a few times, squeezed my eyes shut then opened them again, confused more than startled by her sudden appearance at Dawes House.

How in the hell had she found me? How in the hell had she gotten into my apartment?

"Vivian?" I murmured, still groggy.

She moved in a blur and was suddenly inches from my face. Her expression twisted with disgust. "The devil has found you, girl," she spat. "I always knew he would."

Before I could respond, another hacking cough shook her until she gagged and gasped, and then she was gone.

I stared wide-eyed at the space where she'd been, my pulse hammering. It had been a dream. Must've been.

I glanced behind me to see Whit still sleeping soundly. Obviously, if my mother had suddenly appeared in my bedroom, spouting her usual brand of hatred and accusations, it would've awakened him as well.

Right?

I was still sitting in my bed, too stunned and confused to process what had just happened, when my cell phone rang. Whit stirred as I reached for the phone and watched me with bleary eyes as I answered.

"Is this Zellie Dupont?" a male voice asked.

I frowned. "Yes. Who is this?"

"Ms. Dupont, this is Detective Dwight Jones with the Atlanta Police Department," the clipped voice said on the other end, all business. "Are you the daughter of Vivian Dupont?"

"Yes," I replied, glancing at Whit. "She's my mother."

"Ms. Dupont, I'm sorry to inform you that your mother has died."

My stomach clenched, the reason for Vivian's "visit" now apparent. "How? When?"

"It appears to be natural causes," he told me. "But it's difficult to tell. She's been dead for quite a while."

Dead for quite a while?

My stomach dropped. Had her phone calls been her attempt to reach out after she'd *died*? It freaking figured. Even in death, Vivian had found a way to torment me.

A tentative touch on my arm startled me, and I sent a panicked glance in that direction, relieved as hell to see Whit's concerned expression.

"Ms. Dupont?"

"I'm here," I said. I reached out my hand to Whit, who immediately took it and gently squeezed, silently offering me comfort.

"We need you to come down and officially identify the body at your earliest convenience," the detective informed me.

I shook my head, forcing myself to focus on his words. "Uh, sure. Of course. I'll be there as soon as I can."

I hung up and sat motionless, trying to absorb the news that Vivian was dead. My only remaining tether to my past gone forever. I wanted to cry for her, felt that I should. But there were no tears. There was no sorrow. There was only...relief.

"Zellie?" Whit eventually asked softly. "What's happened?"

I blinked at him, having momentarily forgotten he was there. "Vivian's dead."

His eyes went wide. "Your mother?"

I nodded. "I need to go identify her body. Make arrangements."

He pulled me to him, kissed my forehead. "What can I do?"

"I'm fine," I assured him, surprised to find it was the true. "I need to go get Henry and get ready so I can go to Atlanta."

"You take a shower," Whit told me, throwing back the sheets. "I'll go get dressed and then pick up Henry. He and I can hang out while you deal with everything."

Tears of gratitude and love pricked the corners of my eyes. "Are you sure?"

He pulled me close. "Absolutely. You just tell me what you need me to do."

I took his face in my hands and kissed him. "All I need right now is you. Would you stay a little longer?"

After taking a long shower with Whit, letting the warmth of the water and of his body envelop me, I quickly got dressed and forced down a piece of toast so that my stomach wasn't completely empty when I made the drive to Atlanta. After making a few preliminary phone calls to mortuaries, I went to Whit's apartment. When he didn't answer the door, I headed downstairs, realizing he must've already gone to June and Earl's to pick up Henry.

As I approached June's door, I overheard Whit and June talking in what sounded like angry whispers. They spoke a language I didn't understand, didn't even recognize, but I definitely caught my name more than once. Then, as if they both sensed my presence at the same time, their words abruptly ceased. But then June got in the last word—in English.

"You have a duty to the family," she snapped. "Remember that." Then she came toward me, hands held out to grasp mine. "Zellie, darlin', I'm so sorry to hear about your mama. Are you all right? What can I do?"

I glanced at Whit before offering June a grateful smile. "Thank you, Ms. June. But I'm okay. I'll let you know if I need anything. Where's Henry?"

"He's just finishing up breakfast," she said. "Come on in."

Whit turned to follow her, but I grasped his arm. "What was that all about?"

"June's concerned that I'll leave before everything is finished," he said, turning once more toward the door.

"What language were you speaking?" I asked.

He paused and then turned back to me. "An old one. June isn't originally from here. Her accent is all but gone at this point, but she sometimes slips into her native language when she's angry."

"And you speak the same language?" I asked, trying to understand.

"I learned as a child," he told me. "I speak several languages." He smiled, but it seemed forced. "Private tutors, remember?"

Henry was excited to spend the day with Whit. I didn't bother telling him where I was going. What was the point? He'd heard about Vivian in that he knew that I had a mother like everyone else, but he'd never met her. To Henry, Vivian was just a nebulous concept, not really something a five-year-old would bother thinking about.

I made the drive to Atlanta, courtesy of the driver service Whit ordered. I'd protested, insisting I could drive myself, but as I sat in the backseat of the black sedan, staring out the window at the cityscape, inching along through the traffic of the clogged downtown arteries, I was grateful I didn't have to be navigating.

My guilt gnawed at me, making my conscience squirm. I should've felt *something*. Vivian had been my mother.

But the only sorrow I experienced was that she'd never known Henry, had never gotten to see what an amazing kid he was or hear his laughter or experience one of his uninhibited, fully loving hugs that always made the day better. And it was sad that she'd died alone, that no one had even noticed she was gone for who knew how long. In the end, the woman who had gone out of her way to make me feel like I was useless, worthless, something to be abhorred, had mattered to no one.

"I'm very sorry for your loss," the morgue attendant said as he ushered me into the room where a body lay on a cold steel table, a sheet draped over her face.

He lifted the sheet without ceremony, revealing a bloated, discolored version of Vivian. I nodded to him. "Yes, that's my mother. Vivian Dupont."

"Would you like a few minutes?" he asked gently.

Momentarily confused, I met his gaze—kind, compassionate. "No," I said with a shake of my head. "I'm fine."

When I arrived home that evening, I opened my apartment door to find several bouquets of flowers set out on the tables, credenza, shelves. A soft clatter in the kitchen startled a brief cry from me, and a face peeked out around the doorframe.

"Oh, I'm sorry, honey," Pearlie said, hurrying toward me, hands outstretched. "I was trying to finish up before you got home."

"Finish up?" I repeated, confused.

"Whit told us about your mother," she explained. "June and I have made you plenty of food and put it in the fridge. You might want to move some to the freezer, as usual, so it'll last you. And Merilee cut you some flowers from the garden. Lots of lavender to help you relax. Iris will be by later to drop off her cobbler. The woman's cobbler is the best is Savannah, but bless her heart, she needs to expand her repertoire."

"Oh, Ms. Pearlie," I said, my voice small, the weight of their kindness overwhelming. "This is too much. You didn't have to do all this!"

"Hush now," she replied, waving away my words. "You don't need to be worrying about anything right now. Junior and Earl did some cleaning for you, so you just focus on taking care of your mama's arrangements."

"Thank you, Ms. Pearlie," I told her. "I truly appreciate it. But Vivian and I weren't close. She wasn't really much of a mother to me. I'm honestly okay."

She put her arm around me and led me to the couch, then sat down beside me. "I'm not one to tell a person how to feel or how to grieve," she began, "but she was still your mama. And at some point, all that you've lost with her passing—whether that's something real or something wished for—will hit you. Sometimes grieving for what *could've been* is harder than grieving for what *was*."

Pearlie's words struck me more than the actual news of Vivian's death. And the tears came before I even realized it. Once the floodgates had opened, I couldn't close them again. Pearlie pulled me close, smoothing my hair, rocking me as I sobbed for all that never was and the missed opportunity to ever change it.

"There now," she murmured. "I've got you, baby. You just let it all out."

I don't know how long I cried. Probably not as long as it seemed. When I finally lifted my head, Pearlie brushed my hair from my eyes.

"Now," she said, "I'm going to get you a cloth for your face. And then you're going to go see Henry and Whit who are down at Whit's apartment making quite a mess. And you're going to let them cheer you up a little bit. You just remember we all love you, Zellie. And you might have funeral potatoes and cobbler to last you till Christmas—"

I laughed and dabbed at my eyes with the heel of my palm.

"—but you'll never be alone as long as you have us."

After applying the cool washcloth to my eyes to reduce some of the puffiness and then saying goodbye to Pearlie, I took a deep breath and forced a smile before walking down the hall to Whit's apartment. The door stood open, and I could hear Whit's deep voice and Henry's giggling.

I followed the sounds, and when I entered the bedroom where they were, I nearly burst out laughing. Whit was letting Henry "help" paint the walls. White paint was all over Whit's jeans and shoes, a large puddle on the drop cloth evidence of a spill. Henry had paint on his cheek, in his hair, and all over the back of his clothes where it looked like he'd leaned against the wet wall. He held out his hands toward Whit, palms covered in paint, pretending like he was going to wipe it on him. Whit jumped back with an exaggerated yelp, which Henry thought was the most hilarious thing he'd ever seen. He threw his head back, cackling.

And suddenly my smile was no longer forced.

"Hey there," Whit said when he noticed me. He came toward me, opening his arms to hug me, but I laughed and ducked out of his embrace.

"No way," I said, backing away, my hands held out in front of me.

"Oh, come on," Whit teased following after me. "Just a little hug?"

Henry giggled. "Yeah, Mama! Just a little hug!" He ran to me and threw his arms around me, paint-covered hands pressed against me.

"Ewww!" I laughed.

"Don't worry," Whit said, grinning. "The paint's washable."

I lifted by brows. "Oh, really? In that case..."

I wiped my hand across the wet paint on my clothes and reached toward Henry.

He giggled and ran a few feet away, out of my reach. Whit wasn't so lucky. I dabbed a bit of white on the end of his nose.

Laughing, Whit caught me around the waist and lifted me off my feet, spun me once, then set me back down, still smiling as he kissed me, the paint on the end of his nose transferring to my cheek.

Now it was Henry's turn to "Ewww!"

Whit chuckled and held me close, whispering in my ear, "I love you."

My arms around him tightened. "I love you too."

"You doing okay?" he asked softly.

I nodded. "Yeah. I am now."

I buried Vivian in a simple private burial service. I insisted on the residents of Dawes House letting me do this on my own with just Whit and Henry as support. Henry soon grew bored, though, so Whit led him away to feed the ducks at the cemetery pond while I stood alone as the attendants lowered a plain box into the plot Whit had insisted on paying for. There were no flowers. No hymns or readings. I threw in a handful of dirt on top of her coffin and then turned my back on that part of my life.

Or so I'd thought.

Most of the few possessions Vivian had in her apartment I either threw away or donated to local charities that helped victims of domestic violence, hoping that some good would come from what she'd left behind. The only things I kept were a few spiral-bound notebooks she'd written in sporadically. I should've just thrown them away with all the other trash.

But curiosity got the better of me. I don't know why, but I had to get into her head now that she was gone, try to understand why she was the way she was.

Nothing could've prepared me for the deranged scribblings of a woman who had been completely consumed by paranoia. I almost felt sorry for how terrifying her thoughts must've been—her claims of being stalked by demons, seeing their monstrous faces lurking everywhere, being tormented in her dreams by images of fire and people screaming, being accosted in her sleep by terrifying creatures who drew power from her fear.

But what was most horrifying were the ravings about Henry and me. She was obsessed with the idea that I was possessed. Nothing new there. But she was convinced my soul had been compromised, that I was a willing servant of evil, that I was colluding with demons, conspiring to kill her and feast on her entrails. In one of the entries, she recounted a dream where I was standing in a dungeon, covered in blood, wielding a knife, my face contorted with vengeance while fire raged around me.

"Zellie, baby, what's wrong?" Whit asked, coming into the living room where I sat on the floor, the notebooks scattered around me. He crouched down beside me. "I heard you crying from the kitchen."

I looked up at him, Vivian's ravings briefly tainting my vision, making the caring, handsome face of my beloved look like something out of a horror film. I gasped, shrinking back, as he reached for me.

He instantly pulled his hands back. Vivian's toxic influence immediately vanished, and he was my love, my Whit, again. "Zellie?"

Relief washed over me, and I reached for him. "I'm so sorry... What she wrote... Whit, it's so disturbing. I didn't realize she was this troubled, that she needed professional help. I should've tried to get her the help she needed."

"Disturbing how?" he asked, frowning.

I flipped back a couple of pages. "She was convinced that Henry was the son of the devil, that he was a product of a demon *seducing* me. She says she dreamed of the encounter...and she goes into great detail about that dream."

"Jesus," Whit breathed, his eyes going wide.

I held the notebook out to him.

He took it, holding my gaze for a long moment before finally turning his eyes down to the page. I watched his face as he read. His jaw tightened, the muscles twitching with strain from how hard he must've been grinding his teeth. I could see his rage growing, his expression becoming harder, the already chiseled lines of his face growing sharper. When he looked up, his eyes burned with fury.

Without a word, he gathered up the notebooks and took them into the kitchen.

"Whit?" I hurried after him when I heard him rummaging through the drawers. "What are you doing?"

"I'm destroying these," he said, his tone clipped. "Do you want me to tear them to shreds or burn them?"

"Whit—"

He turned abruptly, cutting me off. "Do you want to put yourself through more abuse? Are you going to let her do this to you even now, Zellie?"

I was conflicted. I knew he was right, but part of me wanted to finish reading them, figure out what else she'd put on those pages. "I don't know," I admitted. "I just need closure."

He gave me a curt nod and grabbed a box of matches from the drawer. "You sure as hell do." He swiped the notebooks into the empty sink with his arm then handed me the matches.

I hesitated only a moment before taking them. I looked down at the pile of notebooks. My final connection to Vivian. Her last words to me, appropriately wounding and harmful. Anger welled up in me so powerfully my hands shook as I struck a match and held it to the pages of one of the notebooks. I stared at the flame as the paper caught fire, the white pages curling upon themselves, charred and crumbling into ash as the fire spread.

It vaguely registered that the smoke alarm went off, but the strident beeping was cut short. Several minutes later, only the metal spirals and a pile of ash lay in the sink where the notebooks had been.

Whit turned on the faucet, dousing the ash. Then he pulled me into his arms, held me, wrapped me in his love. And when I lifted my face to his, he wiped the tears from my cheeks and kissed me so tenderly that my pain from the searing agony of the rejection, humiliation, and hatred from a woman who was supposed to love me, began to dissipate, supplanted by another kind of heat.

CHAPTER TWENTY-ONE

A week later, Whit and I shared our engagement with Henry, who wasn't surprised at all, just eager to tell Addie as soon as he could.

"Can we go tell her now, Mama?" he asked, bouncing on his toes. "And do I get to call you Daddy now, Mr. Whit?"

Whit's mouth opened and closed, searching for the right answer. Whit looked at me, brows raised, then back at Henry. "Well, it's up to your mama. But I would very much like that."

Henry turned hopeful eyes on me. "Can I, Mama?"

I was just as much at a loss for words as Whit, who automatically picked up Henry when he raised his arms to Whit. Seeing them like that...it just felt *right.* "I...yeah, I guess so. If that's what you want."

Henry threw his arms around Whit's neck, hugging him tightly, then kissed him on the cheek. "I always knew you were my daddy."

I flushed, confused and embarrassed. "Henry—"

"Well, I guess you were right!" Whit cut in, grinning broadly, apparently just as excited as Henry. "Should we go tell everybody?"

Panic fluttered in my chest. I wasn't sure I wanted to share our happiness just yet. But I was clearly outnumbered. Whit was already helping Henry put on his shoes.

When I hesitated, Whit cocked his head, his brows drawing together. "Zellie, honey, you okay? We can wait if you want."

"No, no," I said quickly, waving away his concern. "I just... No...it's fine."

"You sure?" he pressed. "There's no rush if you're not ready."

"Really," I said, joining them by the apartment door and slipping my arm around Whit's waist. "Just give me one more minute to have you to myself."

He held me close, kissed the top of my head. "You have me for as long as you want."

"Me too! Me too!" Henry cried, jumping up and down.

Whit released me long enough to lift Henry with one arm and then pulled me back against him. "This better?" he asked, his arm tightening around me.

I nodded. "Perfect."

Still, the thought of telling the others filled me with dread, as if somehow it would set in motion a chain of events that would destroy our happiness, shatter my dreams when they were finally within reach.

But that was ridiculous. I was being paranoid, letting my past poison my future. So, we joined the rest of our neighbors downstairs for the weekly gathering and Whit made the announcement as soon as we'd finished supper.

There were exclamations of joy, hugs for both of us. But there was something off, an undercurrent of tension that I couldn't explain. Was it just me being paranoid again? Did they think that someone like me wasn't good enough for Whit despite the hints they'd dropped that had sometimes felt like encouragement? Or was it something else entirely?

Before we left, June pulled me aside and pressed a small cloth parcel into my palm. "Add a little of this to your morning coffee every day. It will keep you healthy."

My brows came together. "What do you mean? What is it?"

"Just herbal supplements," she said. "An old recipe. The women in my family have passed it down to new brides for centuries. Babies have a way of leeching nutrients right out of you."

"Babies!" I scoffed. "That's a bit premature, Ms. June. We haven't even set a date for the wedding let alone talked about if we want children."

She curled my fingers around the bundle. "Talking isn't what gets you in a family way."

"I'm aware of how it works," I said, chuckling. "I have Henry, after all."

June gripped my hand and leaned in closer. "And do you remember how you got with *that* child?"

Insulted now by her presumptions, I pulled my hand back, but her grip was like a vice. "How do you know anything about it?"

"Take it," she said, her tone offering no room for argument. "You will thank me."

"Zellie?" Whit said, suddenly at my side. "Everything okay?"

"Yes," I said, casting a wary glance at June. "Yes, it's fine. Let's go."

As soon as we were in my apartment and Henry had gone to his room to get his pajamas, I rounded on Whit. "What the hell was that?" I demanded. "There's something *seriously* wrong with that woman! I don't need her advice. Who the hell does she think she is?"

He ran a hand through his hair, sighing. "June means well. We'll talk more about this when I get back."

"Where are you going?" I asked, my chest tightening.

Since learning of what Henry and I had experienced at Dawes House, Whit hadn't left us alone any more than absolutely necessary. We were still discussing moving to another property, weighing pros and cons for Henry, so I knew we wouldn't be at Dawes House forever. But I still felt better when he was there with us.

"I need to go out of town for a couple of days on business," he said. "I won't be gone too long. Will you be okay?"

I nodded. "When do you leave?"

"Tonight, I'm afraid." My eyes must've given away my disappointment. He took my hands in his and kissed them. "But it doesn't need to be right now."

After Henry was asleep, Whit followed me to my bed, made love to me, slowly, tenderly. Then he held me until I was asleep. I didn't feel him get out of bed; just the absence of the warmth and peace I'd already grown used to.

I tossed and turned, unable to sleep soundly, too many thoughts cycling through my brain on a continuous loop. Finally, realizing sleep was too illusive, I threw off the covers and checked on Henry, relieved to find he was sleeping peacefully and that none of the intruders had decided to torment him.

Still feeling uneasy, a nagging dread making it impossible for me to do much more than wander around the apartment, I went to the living room window and peered out into the darkness. I glanced at the time on my phone.

3 a.m.

The Devil's hour.

"Well, here we are again," I muttered, turning my attention back to the window.

There was no activity on the street, even the most hardcore bar hoppers had gone home.

I wrapped my arms around myself, suddenly cold. I could sense an intruder nearby, but it was only a faint tickle as the hair on the back of my neck reacted to the sudden influx of energy in the room. I scanned the living room, searching for even a misty haze that would give away who was visiting.

"Fine," I sighed. "Don't tell me who you are. But maybe stop the arctic blast, okay?"

I turned back to the window, wishing Whit had waited until daylight to leave, when movement in the courtyard caught my attention. I frowned, squinting to make out who it was. The night was moonless and darker than usual. The streetlights cast a muddy light, giving off a jaundiced glow that obscured the identities of the three people I saw walking toward the carriage house. It wasn't until they reached the front door that the porch light revealed who it was.

Chase and Merilee ushered a third person up the stairs. The unknown woman was dressed in a hot pink sequined miniskirt, black stiletto thigh boots, and a sheer black tank top. Her bleached blond hair had pink streaks that matched her skirt. Chase motioned the woman in with a flourish of his arm, his typical roguish smile making her drop her gaze like she was embarrassed and flattered by whatever he'd said.

Merilee stepped forward to follow them inside, but stopped, hand on the doorframe, and looked over her shoulder, her eyes lifting to the window where I stood as if she knew I was there.

And she waggled her fingers at me, waving to let me know she saw me, and gave me a sly, taunting grin.

I darted away from the window, my heart pounding at being found out. But found out doing *what*? Just looking out my window in the middle of the night? Why would *that* make me feel guilty like I had to hide?

Chastising myself for being ridiculous—Chase and Merilee's sex life wasn't any of my business, after all—I stepped back to the window. But they were gone, the door to the carriage house closed behind them.

The light from dozens of candles bathed the room in soft light creating shadows that danced eerily on the walls. I glanced around, not sure where I was. It looked like a farmhouse, maybe, the furniture and décor rustic, something from the previous century or even older. Bundles of herbs and other plants hung drying from the ceiling like those I'd seen in June's apartment. In the stone hearth hung a black cauldron, the simmering contents releasing a thick, intoxicating aroma that made my limbs feel too light, my head spin, my vision hazy and distorted.

As my eyes rolled, trying to make sense of what was happening, I realized I was lying on a table, my arm hanging off one side, something warm and sticky running down my forearm to my palm, dripping from my fingertips. Despite the fire blazing in the fireplace, I grew colder by the minute.

It was then I heard the maniacal laughter near me. I turned my head, trying to see where it was coming from. Chase and Merilee knelt beside the table, cupping their hands to gather what I realized was my blood, then smeared it over one another's faces, shoulders, arms, bare chests, abdomens in slow, sensual motions, clearly aroused.

I rolled my head away, coughing and sputtering as blood filled my throat. I choked and tried to sit up but lacked the strength.

Chase and Merilee's faces loomed over me, grinning broadly, laughing. Merilee wiped blood from my neck and held it up for Chase to see.

"We have a bleeder, baby," Chase told her. "Look at that. And still hangin' in there."

Chase grasped her hand with a groan of need and licked her skin from wrist to fingertips, then took her fingers into his mouth, sucking the blood from them, leaning his head back with a gasp of satisfaction. Then he grasped her by the back of her neck and kissed her savagely.

My vision grew dark, and I felt like I was floating, drifting away as my soul left my body. A few moments later, when I could see again, I peered down at my body and saw a naked woman with bleached blond hair with pink streaks made darker with the blood that had pooled from my slit throat.

I turned away from my lifeless body only to see Chase and Merilee lying on the floor, Merilee straddling Chase, riding him as he gripped her hips, growling with animalistic pleasure as he drove her to dramatic release. Then he rolled her over onto the blood slicked floor, and lifting her hips, slammed into her over and over as they both panted and cried out with primal abandon.

I gasped, bolting upright as I woke from the nightmare. Instinctively, I grasped my neck, expecting to find the gaping wound from my dream, then checked my forearms. When I found nothing, I collapsed onto my pillows, relief so powerful overwhelming me, I couldn't move again for several minutes.

Finally, still weak but my heart no longer hammering, I rolled over and reached for my phone. It was 7 a.m. I'd only been asleep for a few hours. Henry would be awake soon, and I'd have to pretend that nothing was wrong, that I hadn't dreamt of Chase and Merilee murdering a woman, having sex while they bathed in her blood.

My stomach rolled. I swallowed the bile rising in my throat. My fingers shaking, I tried to text Whit to tell him what I'd seen, but I deleted the message without sending it. This wasn't something I should send over text.

There was a rustle of movement in Henry's room, then the click of the light switch in the bathroom. The morning routine had begun whether I was ready or not.

"Mama!"

"Coming, baby!" I called, my mouth so dry I could barely croak out the words. I wiped the perspiration from my forehead with the back of my hand then closed my eyes, taking a few deep breaths, pulling myself together.

"Mama! I can't reach my toothbrush!"

I forced a smile, ignoring the fact that my lips trembled, and got to my feet. "My goodness, Henry James, we are *impatient* today!"

I felt like a ghost as I went through the motions of the day, taking care of Henry, working at the bookstore, trying to make sure I avoided running into Chase or Merilee. And the next day wasn't much better, but since it was my day off, Henry and I stayed inside, playing with his action figures and doing puzzles.

"This is boring," he complained. "Can't I go play with Addie?"

"Not today, baby," I told him as I swept away the last of the puzzle pieces, making sure not to lose any so Henry's favorite puppy cartoon character was complete the next time we put it together. "I wanted just the two of us to hang out today."

He heaved a disappointed sigh, his bottom lip protruding in a little pout. "Yes, ma'am." But a knock on the door brought a sudden smile to his face. "I'll get it!"

"No!" I yelled, sprinting after him. "Henry, stop!"

He halted abruptly, giving me a confused look.

"It's okay," I assured him, giving him a shaky smile. "You're not in trouble. I just don't want you opening the door. It could be a stranger."

His frown deepened. "But it's my daddy!"

Now it was my turn to frown. I peered through the peep hole in the door, tears ridiculously springing to my eyes. I swung open the door and threw my arms around Whit's neck.

"Hey, you," he murmured, holding me close.

Henry tugged my shirt. "Me too!" he insisted, bouncing.

Whit pulled back and scooped him up, giving him a squeeze. "Hi, buddy. I missed you guys." It was then I noticed Whit looked tired, his clothes uncharacteristically rumpled, his eyes slightly bloodshot as if from lack of sleep.

"Are you okay?" I asked, pulling him inside.

He kissed me tenderly but briefly. "Yeah, I'm fine. Just had a long couple of days."

"What were you working on?" I asked.

He shook his head. "Just liquidating some assets, tying up some loose ends. I'll be finished sorting everything out soon. Then it'll just be you, me, and Henry."

Later that evening, after Henry had gone to bed, I told Whit about my dream. He just stared at me in silence, his expression impossible to read.

"Whit, I'm not crazy," I insisted.

"I don't think you're crazy," he assured me, drawing a hand down his face. "I'll go talk to Chase, check out the carriage house."

I watched from the same window as I had before as Whit crossed the courtyard. Chase opened the door, looking irritated and tired, but I didn't see any evidence of the blood bath I'd dreamed about.

Although I couldn't hear their conversation, there was a visible tension between them. Whit glanced back at me, and then motioned Chase inside, closing the door behind them. I chewed the side of my thumb, worried for Whit's safety. After what I'd seen in my dream, there was no way I would ever be able to look at Chase and Merilee the same way, let alone trust them around anyone I cared about.

I don't know how long I stood there before I saw Whit leave the carriage house and cross the courtyard.

"Well?" I asked when he opened the apartment door.

He shook his head. "I didn't see any evidence of a murder, Zellie. Chase said he and Merilee did bring someone home the other night for a little *consensual* fun. But she left early the next morning. I didn't see any blood anywhere."

I shook my head. "But..."

Whit gently took hold of my arms. "Baby, I can't do anything else. If I called the police, they would find the same thing I did."

"You don't believe me," I whispered, deflated.

"I *do* believe you," he insisted. "Chase said he and Merilee saw you in the window but didn't see the need to mention anything about it to you. And there's no denying the dream you had. I just don't know if there's a connection."

I gave him a pointed look. "Then what about my dreams of Susanna Dawes? Are those just products of my imagination?"

"I really don't know, Zellie," he snapped, then immediately held up his hands. "I'm sorry. I just don't know how to help you on this one." He sighed. "Could we talk more tomorrow? I'm tired and sore—"

"Sore?" I interrupted. "What happened?"

He stiffened, his defenses going up. "From all the traveling. I'll be fine."

"When are you going to stop doing that?" I asked.

He shook his head. "Doing what?"

"Withdrawing, closing yourself off when I hit too close to home?" My tone was harsh, betraying my frustration. "Closing yourself to what, I have no idea! But if you want to marry me, Whit, you have to let me in."

He shoved his hands in his pockets, but said nothing, his jaw clenching as if he was silently working through frustrations of his own.

I sighed and shook my head, not knowing what else to say. "I'm going to bed. You're welcome to stay. If you leave, please lock the door behind you."

I was just slipping into bed when Whit appeared in my bedroom doorway. "Was that our first fight?"

I pursed my lips. "Not if you count the first couple of times I talked to you on the phone."

He chuckled and came in, stripping out of his clothes until he was down to his undershirt and boxers, then crawled under the sheets and stretched out on the bed, pulling me into his arms.

"You had every right to be angry with me then," he said, his voice soft. "I never should've allowed Briggs to talk to you without already having a solution in mind. It wasn't fair. I'm so sorry that's the first thing you remember about me."

I curled into him and hugged him tightly but immediately pulled back when he winced. "Whit, that's more than just being sore from traveling!"

"Zellie, it's fine," he sighed, the exhaustion in his tone belying his words.

Unconvinced, I sat up and lifted his shirt, gasping at the extensive bruising to his ribs. "Oh, my God! What the hell?"

He gently caught my hand and pulled his shirt back down. "Disagreement with a tenant. That's all."

"That's *all*?" I cried. "Whit! Your ribs could be broken! Who did this to you?"

"It's handled. And please don't worry. I'll be okay in the morning. Really." He gave me a tired smile and caressed the curve of my jaw with his fingertips. "I just want to hold you while I get some rest. That's all I need."

I pressed my lips together, my heart aching at the sight of him in pain. But I nodded and then laid back down, letting him draw me into the curve of his body. Seconds later, his breathing became deep and steady, his exhaustion too heavy to fight any longer.

⁂

I woke to a small hand gripping my calf, urgently shaking my leg. My eyes snapped open, startled by the sudden interruption to what had been a blissfully peaceful sleep. I expected to see Henry standing there and felt a momentary flare of panic at the thought of him seeing Whit in my bed, but the panic was instantly supplanted by something far worse.

It wasn't Henry.

A little boy stood beside the bed, his skin pale, translucent, his eyes wide with fear.

David.

He shook my leg again and glanced toward the bedroom door as if expecting someone—or something—to burst through it.

David darted toward the door, pausing to look over his shoulder at me and motion urgently for me to follow. My maternal instincts roared to life. I threw off my covers and hurried after him.

"David!" I called, catching a glimpse of him passing straight through the apartment door. "Wait!"

I yanked open the door and chased after him, not bothering to close the door behind me. He disappeared down the stairwell, glancing back once to make sure I was still following. I hurried after him, only vaguely noting each floor we passed until the stairs ended abruptly, and I realized I was in the basement.

Panting, I stood at the base of the stairs, glancing around frantically for the little boy. The lights came on in succession down the hallway, something tripping the motion sensors as it passed.

A ripple of icy fear rushed through me. I swallowed hard, hesitating.

What if the little boy wasn't really David? Or what if David wasn't actually a little boy at all? What if Vivian had been right and the intruders who sought me out *were* actually demons or malevolent spirits, this one taking the shape of a small child to play upon my maternal instincts and lure me here?

But desperation for answers propelled me forward. I sprinted down the hallway after David, reaching the laundry room just as the light came on.

He stood before the cracked section of the wall where I'd fallen against it during my terrifying encounter with the screaming woman. When he noticed me, he gestured at the hole, his eyes pleading with me to understand. This is what he wanted me to see. As soon as his intention was clear, the boy vanished.

Needing to understand why he'd brought me there, I approached the crack and squinted at the small opening the impact of my fall had created. But it was too dark to see what was inside, aside from a few broken pieces of wooden slats.

I grabbed a loose chunk of plaster and pulled it away. Then another. And another. I tore apart the wall bit by bit, determined to reveal what was hidden behind it. One stubborn section refused to budge. I adjusted my grip and pulled again, groaning with the effort. Suddenly it broke free, sending me stumbling back a few steps.

A flash of white tumbled through the hole I'd created.

"My God," I breathed, my blood turning to ice in my veins.

The skeletal hand lay palm up, the index finger curled inward as if beckoning me closer.

Slowly, I stepped forward and reached out to pull away another piece of plaster. In a blur of motion, the skeletal hand shot out and grasped my wrist, yanking me toward the wall. I stumbled and slammed into it, the impact startling a scream from me. I struggled to get away, but the bony fingers dug into my skin, drawing blood. My throat burned as another scream ripped from me.

Strong hands grabbed my upper arms, startling another scream from me, this one ending in a terrified sob.

"Zellie!"

The sound of my name jolted me out of my nightmare. The skeletal hand vanished. Whit stood in front of me, concern etched into every line of his face. I blinked several times, trying to make sense of what had just happened.

"Zellie?" he said, bending his knees a little to look me directly in the eyes. "Are you okay?"

I glanced at the wall and was shocked to see the plaster still intact. "No," I whispered. "No, I tore it open."

I grabbed a chunk of the plaster and pulled it off, then feverishly broke off one piece after another as I swore I had already. "Whit, help me!"

"Zellie," he replied, his tone maddeningly reasonable, "let's go back to bed, honey."

I threw a pleading look over my shoulder. "Whit, please!"

Without another word, he joined me, pulling off pieces of plaster and wood, tossing them to the ground, slowly revealing the space behind the wall. Just when I was starting to doubt there was anything to find, something white caught my eye.

A bone.

"Holy shit," Whit breathed.

"You see it, too?" I asked, my hair and pajama shirt soaked with sweat from my wild destruction of the wall.

He nodded. "Yeah."

He caught my hand as I reached forward. "Don't touch anything else. The police are already going to want to know how you found this."

It felt like forever before the police came and longer still until the forensics team arrived to remove the body and document any other evidence. By then, I'd already gone back upstairs to get dressed and give Henry breakfast. When I dropped off Henry at June's, the rest of the residents were hovering around the foyer, talking with each other in quiet voices, sending guarded glances my way.

I returned to the basement just as the forensics team was removing the body. Long, stringy hair clung to the skull.

"It's not a child," I murmured as they put the bones in a black zippered body bag.

"No," Whit said, pulling me close. "At least, not a small child. I guess it could be a teen. But I think it's an adult."

"This doesn't make any sense," I told him, shaking my head, confused. If it wasn't David, why had he brought me to the body? Had he known her? Was the woman his *mother*?

"How long has it been here?" Whit asked one of the forensic techs. "Are you able to tell?"

The woman shrugged. "Hard to say, but not recent." She gestured to the remains. "Her clothes look like maybe mid-twentieth century. I'll know more after we run some tests."

"But it *is* a woman?" I asked. "You do know that for sure?"

She nodded. "Yes, ma'am. Definitely. That much I can tell you."

Mid-twentieth century was too recent to be Susanna or Eliza. So, who was *this*? But I answered my own question almost as soon as it came to mind.

The lady in the wall.

I'd thought that was just what Henry had dubbed her because she'd come from inside his closet. Turns out it had been this wall all along. The one the screaming woman had startled me into falling against. Had she been trying to tell me about the bones hidden there?

The rest of the day was a blur of questions from the police asking the same things over and over, testing my story of how I knew the body was there, most likely finding my account of having a dream about it hard to believe. Fortunately, the age of the remains eliminated anyone currently living at Dawes House as a suspect in her death.

"I'm surprised someone didn't find her sooner," one of the officers said to Whit as we walked him to the main door of the building. "This place has been renovated more times than I can count. My granddaddy used to talk about how it was always being worked on when he was a kid, crews coming and going. I seem to recall the same thing when I was growing up."

Whit nodded. "Guess we just never did much in the basement. We've only recently started converting that area into additional apartments." He frowned like something had just occurred to him as he added, "It was probably only a matter of time before one of the construction crews came across the bones."

The officer shook his head. "I'm not a superstitious person, but no way in hell I'd ever be caught living here with all the history of this place. But you'd know more of the history, wouldn't ya, Mr. Proffitt?" He clapped Whit on the back and then tipped his chin down in a curt motion. "Y'all have a good day now. We'll let you know what we find out."

CHAPTER TWENTY-TWO

June was the first to visit, bringing Henry upstairs after the police had gone. "Zellie, darlin', are you alright? I can't imagine getting that kind of shock! I brought you some tea for your nerves. It's my own recipe. I want you to drink it all, now. I don't want to hear from Whit that you left a single leaf behind."

"Yes, ma'am," I said, offering her a weak smile from where I sat on the couch, my knees to my chest. "Thank you."

Whit opened the door for her, not exactly a subtle hint for her to leave.

"You know," June said, heading toward the kitchen instead, "I think I'll just go ahead and make you a cup before I go, make sure you don't forget."

"Thank you, June," Whit said, exasperation evident in his tone. "I'm sure I can manage a cup of tea if you are otherwise engaged."

She waved away his words like she was swatting a fly and addressed me instead. "It is no trouble at all. You just rest there, Zellie, darlin'. I'll have you feeling right as rain in no time."

Whit heaved a long sigh and swung the door closed none too gently.

June finally left after a couple of hours of fussing over me, making sure I had a comfy cushion behind me so my back wouldn't protest, that I had enough hot water for my tea, that Henry had a nice hot lunch like he was used to when he was with "Mamaw June."

She almost completely ignored Whit's insistence that he could capably take care of me, clucking her tongue and sending disapproving looks his way as if to imply if that were the case I wouldn't have suffered "such a shock" in the first place.

Whit had just shut the door behind her when a knock made his jaw clench and his posture go rigid. He pulled the door open with an irritated jerk of the handle only to see Pearlie standing there holding a plate of cookies.

"Oh, Zellie, honey!" Pearlie cried, brushing past Whit as if he weren't even there. She set the plate of cookies on the coffee table and held out both her hands to me. "How are you, baby?"

I took her outstretched hands, and she sat down on the couch, pulling me into her arms, rocking me gently.

"I'm okay, Ms. Pearlie," I assured her, but too comforted by her motherly concern to pull away. "I just feel awful for that poor woman."

"Whitman Montgomery Proffitt," Pearlie admonished, "why are you just standing there in the doorway? Get this poor girl some warmer blankets. She's shivering!"

I didn't know I was until Pearlie mentioned it. Then a rhythmic clacking caught my attention, and I realized it was my teeth chattering.

Whit sent Pearlie an annoyed look but obediently turned and went down the hall to grab a blanket from my bed. When he returned, Pearlie wrapped me up tightly and hugged me close.

"There now," she soothed. "That's more like it. Is that better, baby?"

I nodded, the chattering already subsiding. "Yes, ma'am."

"Why don't we go get some lunch?" Whit said, holding his hand out to Henry, ignoring the fact that June had already fed Henry not half an hour earlier.

Henry immediately hopped up from where he'd been quietly coloring. "Yes, sir." He scurried off to get his shoes but a moment later called out, "Mama! I can't find my other shoe!"

I extricated myself from my blankets despite Pearlie's protest about needing to let Whit get it. "It's okay, Ms. Pearlie. Really. I can take care of it. I'm not going to break in half." I smiled and then laughed a little shakily. "Just have to tell the bones to stop rattling, right?"

Her brows twitched together almost imperceptibly in a frown, and I didn't miss the look she cast Whit's way.

"The song?" I said, explaining the reference. "The one June taught Addie and Henry? I don't really know the words. Sorry, bad joke."

Pearlie's chuckle sounded forced. "Oh, that! Yes, I'd forgotten she'd already started teaching the children."

Unsettled for some reason, I hurried down the hall to help Henry. He was on his hands and knees, lifting up the comforter to look under his bed when I came in.

"No luck?" I asked.

He stood and frowned at me. "No, ma'am. Where did it go? I put them together in my closet just like you told me, Mama, I promise."

"I believe you, baby," I told him, tousling his hair. "We'll find it."

But another thorough search of his bedroom still didn't reveal the shoe's mystery location.

"What the heck?" I mumbled. "Henry—"

"It was in my closet!" he said, his face twisting in frustration. "I know it was! I'm not lying!"

I stared at him, too stunned at his uncharacteristic behavior to respond. But my expression must've revealed the words that were sitting on my tongue.

"I'm sorry, I'm sorry!" he said in a rush, running to me and gripping my shirt with his fists, his eyes wide with fear. "I'm sorry, Mama!"

"Henry!" I soothed, prying his fists loose from my shirt. "What's wrong, baby? Why are you so upset?"

"Everything okay?"

I turned at the sound of Whit's voice to see him standing in the doorway. "Yeah, I think we've all just had a rough morning." I smoothed Henry's hair out of his eyes and kissed his forehead. "We just can't find Henry's other shoe."

Whit strode into the room and went to Henry's bookshelf. "Is this it?" he asked, pulling the shoe from where it had been wedged in among some of the books the previous tenant had left behind.

"I didn't put it there," Henry insisted. "I promise!"

I picked him up and sat him on his bed, helping him put his shoes on. "I know. It's okay. The important thing is we have it now, right?"

"I think David hid it from me," Henry grumbled. "He's mad at me for playing with Addie more."

"I'm sure he's not mad," I assured him. "He needs to understand you have other friends."

"*I* have other friends," Henry told me. "But *he* doesn't."

That made my heart ache. Did David not have anyone else to interact with? Was being dead really so lonely, so dependent on the notice of the living for any interaction at all? The poor boy...

My musings were cut short when I entered the living room and found Pearlie had gone. "Where's Ms. Pearlie?"

Whit's jaw tightened at the question. "I assured her that I was more than capable of taking care of my future wife."

"Oh, Whit," I admonished. "I hope she wasn't offended. Pearlie's been more of a mother to me than my own mother ever was!"

He sighed, his expression contrite. "I'm sorry, baby. It's complicated. None of them had much faith in me taking over for my father, so I'm probably overly sensitive to their criticism, even if it's only my perception."

I hadn't thought about Whit's side of things. I rested my palm on his chest and turned my eyes up to him. "I have complete faith in you," I told him. "There's no one I would trust more to take care of us."

The look in his eyes told me how much my words meant. He dipped his head and brushed a brief kiss to my lips. "I love you."

"I love you, too. Now," I added, my tone light, "about that lunch..."

The next few days were a steady stream of hot meals and June's special teas and drop-in visits from all the neighbors. Even Billy Wayne stopped by to see how I was doing. And although there was still an unspoken, inexplicable tension simmering between Whit and the others, he was more welcoming. But watchful.

Soon, all of us fell back into our normal routines, although I noticed Whit spent more time with Henry, getting his "help" with the renovations on the other fourth-floor apartment, including Addie as often as June would allow. This meant Henry spent less time with June. And I can't say I minded.

For weeks, the house was quiet. I saw no intruders, heard no strange noises, had no items go missing or show up in strange places, had no disturbing dreams. For the first time since coming to Dawes House, everything felt...*normal.*

Henry continued to grow, flourish, his cheeks rosy, his energy like a normal five-year-old boy. He was *healthy.* And, as much as I hated to admit it, I owed his improvement to June's home remedies, old-world knowledge that helped him where modern medicine simply couldn't.

As the first day of school approached, Henry's excitement grew, and my job at the bookstore made it possible for me to buy school clothes and supplies and all the things he would need. It was a moment I'd dreaded, having to admit to my son that I couldn't afford to give him the same things his classmates had. But I *could*. And it felt damned *good*.

Whit had wanted to help, but I wouldn't let him. I wanted—needed—to do this on my own. In the end, though, I let him take Henry shopping for a new pair of shoes since he only had the one pair that still fit. And even though Whit bought him three pairs, I didn't care. What mattered was how happy Henry was, how much he loved Whit, and that Whit was eager to be the father Henry had never had.

Whit and I spent as much time together as possible when he wasn't traveling for business. He always came home exhausted and often bruised. And he was as evasive about why as he had been the first time, but I didn't press. I knew he would tell me more when he was ready. I could imagine that not all the tenants were thrilled with the idea of being relocated, even if (as I found out) Whit offered them all a sizable sum to help them find a better place to live and to pay for any moving expenses.

With every day, I realized how much I had misjudged Whit when we'd first spoken after Mr. Monty's death, how deep his kindness ran, how unwavering his love was for me, for Henry. And I loved him. Loved him with such intensity, it sometimes frightened me. It was as if I had already loved him for a lifetime.

That's why after one of Whit's business trips, when we lay in each other's arms in the darkness, I said, "I don't want to wait."

"Wait for what?"

I could tell he was frowning in confusion even though I couldn't see him clearly in the darkness. I just knew every line, every curve of his handsome face by then, the way his different muscles twitched or stiffened depending on his reaction.

"To get married," I told him. "I don't want a big, elaborate wedding. Who would I invite anyway? I don't have any family. And you don't have any family outside of Dawes House that you'd want to invite except Cora. So why wait?"

He chuckled, the deep rumble in his chest vibrating against my cheek. "Using my own words against me. Well played."

"Speaking of Cora, when do I get to meet her?" I pressed, eager to know this sister if she was someone important to Whit, someone who could help fill in the gaps about my beloved's past that was still something of a mystery. "Will she come to the wedding? Where does she live?"

He tilted his head, a smile tugging at the corner of his mouth. "I didn't realize you'd be so interested in her."

"Of course I'm interested! If she's important to you, then she's important to me."

He pulled me back into his arms. "Then you'll definitely get to meet her. But she lives in England, so it might be a while. And she's not a fan of Dawes House, so we'll probably have to visit her there."

"Works for me," I assured him, snuggling closer.

"Now," he prompted, "about this wedding..."

"Would you be disappointed if we didn't have anything fancy?" I asked, suddenly worried that perhaps I hadn't considered what *he* had envisioned for us.

"No," he said, drawing me closer. "How could I be disappointed? I want you to be my wife, Zellie. I don't care if we get married at the courthouse or at the cathedral in Rome. I just don't want *you* to be disappointed."

"I feel the same way," I told him. "All that matters is that we're together. The three of us." I waited a beat before adding, "That's why I also don't want to take a honeymoon just yet, if that's okay. I mean, Henry starts school next week. I don't want to disrupt his routine so soon or be away from him very long."

Whit kissed the top of my head. "Whatever you want. We can take a trip later, just the three of us. Anywhere in the world you want to go. Just tell me when and where. And I'll make it happen."

I shifted positions so that I was stretched out on top of him, and kissed him, my heart singing with joy. And when he took hold of my hips, urging me to my knees and guiding me back down slowly, I exhaled a long, satisfied sigh as I took the full length of him inside me.

Had anyone asked me years ago when I was lying on a dingey cot, cold and scared, in a church basement that doubled as a homeless shelter if I thought I would one day marry someone like Whit, that all my dreams would come true, I would've laughed in their faces—and then would've cried myself to sleep that night, angry and humiliated that they'd thought happiness was so out of my reach.

Whit was true to his word. Three weeks later as the air became a little cooler with Savannah's version of autumn, we were married in the garden of Dawes House, surrounded by the residents—our *family*—and Dottie. It was small, intimate. Perfect.

That day before, June and Earl cut dozens of flowers from their gardens, weaving garlands that she strung up around the patio and wrapped around the single lamppost in the yard, centerpieces for the bistro and picnic tables, and a small bouquet of crimson roses for me to carry. There was even a basket of crimson petals for Henry and Addie to sprinkle ahead of me as Junior led me down the walk to where Whit waited with Pearlie and June who were to perform the ceremony. The love in his eyes was so deep, my own eyes stung as tears of joy blurred my vision.

And then he took my hand and drew me to him, and—

A horrific image assaulted me so powerfully, it made me wince and suck in air through my teeth. It was Whit, bloodied, beaten, broken. Then a subsequent barrage of images followed, passing too quickly to fully understand. I could only catch glimpses—fire, hooded figures, blood on my hands.

"Zellie?" Whit whispered, his concern cutting through and pulling me back to the present.

"I'm okay," I said quickly, breathless. "I'm sorry. Sudden pain in my temple. It's gone now."

He cupped my face in his hands, searching my eyes, concerned. "Are you sure? We don't have to do this today."

I gave him a shaky smile. "Yes, we do."

He lowered his head to kiss me, but Pearlie placed a hand on his shoulder. "Hang on now. Getting a little ahead of yourselves..."

Whit chuckled and pressed his forehead against mine for a moment then straightened, smoothing the front of his suit and giving Pearlie a curt, solemn nod. "Yes, ma'am."

Pearlie lifted a long length of gauzy crimson fabric and raised it to chest level, draping it over her open palms.

"Today I bind your hands together, Whitman Proffitt and Zellie Dupont, symbolizing the union of two souls as one. May this handfasting represent the love that brought you together, the bond of the vows that unite you. May your love be strong enough to last for eternity and beyond."

She wound the material around our clasped hands so that it created the infinity symbol, a perfect figure eight.

My stomach fluttered with nerves when I momentarily forgot what was supposed to happen next. The ceremony wasn't the typical one I'd seen on TV or read about in books. Whit had shared with me that the ceremony had been passed down through generations and was part of his family's tradition, so I had readily agreed to honor that since it seemed to mean a lot to him. And although Whit was familiar with the traditions of his family, I'd never been to a Proffitt family wedding, obviously. In fact, I'd never been to *any* wedding.

But then Whit gently pressed my hand and drew me ever so slightly closer as June stepped forward to cover our hands with hers and bless our union, first in English with a prayer that evoked the creator of all, and then with an ethereal song in the language of the song she had taught Addie and Henry. I didn't understand it, but I knew it was beautiful. Whit had loosely translated it for me the previous day so that I would understand what was being said but assured me it lost something in the translation. Hearing it now, the emotion in June's voice, brought tears to my eyes.

When the song ended, June took a step back and inclined her head, signaling Whit.

He then turned his eyes to me, the love I saw there steady and sure. "Zellie Dupont, you are the one I choose to share all that I have, all that I am. You are blood of my blood, bone of my bone. My love for you is eternal."

My throat tightened with emotion as I repeated the words. "Whitman Proffitt, you are the one I choose to share all that I have, all that I am. You are blood of my blood, bone of my bone. My love for you is eternal."

Pearlie then removed the crimson ties and took the thin wedding bands of braided platinum that Whit had commissioned, pausing to hold them in her hands and offer a silent blessing upon them before handing them to us to place on the other's finger.

Whit lifted my hand and pressed a kiss to my ring, then glanced at Pearlie.

She just chuckled and waved her hand. "Yes, yes, go ahead and kiss your bride now, honey."

The rest of the day was a blur of warmth and happiness. And later that night when Whit and I stood naked on the veranda of his home near Charleston, his arms wrapped around me, letting the warm ocean breeze caress our bare skin, I finally knew the peace that I'd always dreamed of.

"I want to stay here forever," I said softly as if speaking the words too loudly would shatter some fragile dream that was too precious to last for long. "Just like this."

His arms around me tightened, and he dropped a kiss on my shoulder. "You'll get no argument from me. However, the rest of the world might have something to say about it."

I leaned into him and closed my eyes, listening to the waves break gently on the beach below. "Hmm...well, I guess we'll just have to come here and do this often."

"Well, Mrs. Proffitt," he said with a mischievous grin, "I plan to do this—" He suddenly swept me off my feet and into his arms. "—as often as I can."

I laughed as he carried me back to his bed—*our bed*—and pulled him down with me, wrapping my arms and legs around him as his lips captured mine. And when his mouth left mine to trail kisses down my throat, nip gently at my breasts, trace a path down my belly, I sighed contentedly and gave myself over to the pleasure.

"Oh, yes," I gasped as his mouth continued to explore, "definitely often."

CHAPTER TWENTY-THREE

I sat huddled in the corner of the attic, my hair a tangled mess hanging in disarray, partially obscuring my vision. But I didn't need to see everything—just the door. And I waited. For hours. Or maybe just minutes that stretched on, felt like hours. Finally, the door eased open, allowing in a young woman wearing a simple blue dress and carrying a tray with a silver dome set atop it.

"You need to eat something, Alice," the woman told me, pushing the door closed with her hip. "Your husband isn't happy with you starving yourself."

I merely stared at her, hating the sight of her because it meant I was still alive, still trapped in the damned attic, an abomination growing inside my belly.

The young woman set the tray on a plain wooden table near the wall. "Look, Alice," she said as if I were a child. "It's your favorite. And I even brought you some peach cobbler."

"I do not want it, Netty," I spat. "I do not want anything from any of them!"

Netty huffed and put her hands on her hips. "What about little David? He misses you. Please just eat something. If you do, I know Mr. Proffitt will let you come out again. Wouldn't that be nice? Sit under the tree and drink lemonade?"

I narrowed my eyes at her, briefly sorry that it had to be Netty who brought me my dinner today. She'd always been kind. But then, she wasn't one of them. *Not yet.*

"Leave it," I ordered. "You can come back for it later."

Netty looked hesitant. "I don't know, Alice..."

"Who employs you at this house, Netty?" I demanded, pushing away from the corner and slinking slowly toward her. "If you like your job, you will do what I say."

She took a few steps back, her eyes going wide. "Mr. Proffitt promised me—"

I sprung forward, coming within inches of her face. She pressed herself as flat as possible against the wall, her eyes squeezed shut, her head turned away from me.

"Do not believe a word he says," I ground out near her ear. "He'll use you as he has the rest, make you and your sister vessels for his hell spawn. Has he promised that he will always take care of you? That he will always love you? Has he fucked you yet, Netty? Has *he?"*

Netty ducked away from me and ran toward the door. But I was faster. I grabbed the silver dome and swung it, striking her in the back of her head. She crumpled to the ground, unconscious from the blow.

I tossed the dome aside and fled from the room. Turning to close the door behind me, I paused to survey the place that had been my prison. Carved into the walls over and over again until nearly all the surface was covered was my warning to anyone else who followed.

The Devil's child must die.

I crept out of the attic and down the servants' stairs to the kitchen. Finding it empty, I hurried in, snatched a knife from the table, then tiptoed back up the stairs until I reached the top floor where the nursery was located.

The Devil's child must die.

I could hear a child singing softly and went forward before I changed my mind.

The Devil's child must die.

It had to be done.

The Devil's child must die.

For his own good.

The Devil's child must die.

I couldn't let him become a monster. Not my David.

The Devil's child must die...

The nursery door was only half closed. I pushed it open slowly so as not to startle him. He sat at his little desk, drawing. His hand stilled when he saw me standing in the doorway.

He said nothing—merely watched me as I stepped inside and closed the door behind me.

I bolted upright, a scream on my lips, but I choked it back before I could make a sound. Tears streamed down my face unchecked as I scanned the room, assuring myself that I was in my apartment and not the nightmare that had intruded on sleep that had been so, so sweet since I'd married Whit.

As the adrenaline dissipated, I began to shiver, not just from my sweat-soaked pajamas and sheets, but the horror I'd witnessed in my dream.

"Zellie?" Whit reached for me, wrapping me in his arms. "What's wrong? What's happened?"

"I saw her, Whit," I sobbed. "I saw her. She killed him."

"Who, baby?"

"Her name is Alice," I said, pulling back and wiping my eyes. "She's the screaming woman, the one I keep seeing. The one I saw on the first night here."

I gasped, suddenly sensing a presence nearby. I threw off the covers and ran down the hall to the living room and pulled open the apartment door, stumbling out into the main hallway. At the far end of the hall, the door was open, the white curtains billowing in the breeze.

And then I saw her—Alice, knife in hand, blood splattered across her nightgown, her arms, her face, a macabre testament to the heartbreaking scene I'd witnessed in my dream. Her black, empty sockets where eyes had once been bored into me as if trying to communicate the pain, the desperation, the madness that had driven her to such horrific acts. Then she raised the knife and plunged it into her stomach, over and over again.

"No!" I screamed and would have lurched forward to stop her from mutilating herself if Whit hadn't wrapped his arms around me, keeping me where I was.

She lifted her crimson-drenched hands and let the knife slip from her fingers. Then she leaned back, falling out of the open doorway as if in slow motion, her apparition fading but not before her mouth opened wide in a wail of rage and grief.

"What the hell?" Whit breathed.

"You saw her?" I choked, my voice little more than a rasp from my own sorrow. "You saw her too?"

His eyes were wide as he nodded. "Yeah."

I took a step toward the open door, but Whit guided me back to the apartment door. "No, no, inside. Please, Zellie. Let's go back inside."

I glanced down the hallway again, torn. Part of me felt like I owed it to Alice to stand where she stood, understand what had driven her to murder her son, her unborn, herself. But as my adrenaline began to dissipate, my legs started shaking, so I nodded and let Whit help me inside.

He led me to the couch, then returned with two glasses and a crystal decanter of scotch that had been a wedding present from Junior and Pearlie. He poured each of us a drink and gulped his down then poured another.

We sat on the couch together in silence, neither of us sure what to say. Then he finally murmured, "My God."

I ran my hands through my hair, wiped the fresh tears from my cheeks. "It's over now, right?" I asked. "I saw what she'd wanted me to see. I saw how she died. And why. So, that's it, don't you think?"

He dragged his hand down, suddenly looking aged beyond his years. "Yeah. I would think so. I mean, this is really more your area of expertise. But...yeah."

Leaving my drink untouched, I scooted closer to Whit and curled into him when he put his arm around me and pulled me close. We sat this way until the first beams of sunlight began to peek through the blinds. Only then, too exhausted and drained to stay awake any longer, did I allow myself to sink down into a dark, dreamless sleep.

Whit and I kept what had happened to ourselves. I'd seen how everyone had reacted when I first brought up that Dawes House was haunted and knew they would never take the story seriously. At best, they'd think Whit and I had overreacted to something completely explainable. At worst, they'd think we were losing our minds.

Besides, I had concerns about the present that kept my thoughts off the distant past of Dawes House. Only a few weeks earlier, I'd cried myself into exhaustion the day I put Henry on the school bus the first time and waved goodbye, excited for him and happy to see him finally living the big day he'd anticipated for so long, but my heart broke as I watched the bus drive away. A little piece of my heart tore away with it, floating after him like a leaf on the wind, chasing after him but never quite catching up, and leaving in its place a hole that seemed both small and large at once, reminding me of the stone in Henry's favorite poem by e.e. cummings that was "as small as a world and as large as alone."

Since then, I'd tried to keep myself busy. My job at the bookstore and my class for the fall filled up my time when I wasn't with Whit and Henry, keeping my mind off how quiet it was without Henry running around the apartment and telling me about all the adventures he and Addie had shared. But the transition wore on me. I was exhausted, distracted. Eating made me nauseated. And when I actually couldn't keep food down any longer, Whit insisted I see a doctor.

"What did she say?" he asked when I returned from my appointment. He was furiously trying to finish up the last of the renovations to his apartment and was splattered with paint, giving his hair a salt and pepper look that made him look even more like his father.

"I need more vitamins," I told him.

He nodded, wiping his hands with an old rag. "Okay. That's good. I'm sure June has something she can give you to help with that."

"Well," I drawled, "June already gave me something, which might actually have played a role in what's going on."

He went still, his back rigid. "What did she give you, Zellie?"

"It's the special mixture of herbal supplements that's been passed down in her family and given to new brides," I told him. "The one she gave me the night we announced our engagement. The one meant to keep babies from leeching all the nutrients from mothers' bodies."

He stared at me, silent. But I could see his mind racing as he put it together. "Do you mean...?"

I laughed with pure joy. "Yes! I'm pregnant, Whit."

His jaw tightened, and he wiped his hands with the rags again, his attention trained intently on the paint that wasn't there. Finally, his eyes still averted, he asked, "Are you sure?"

My elation at getting the news dissipated in that instant. "This isn't really the reaction I was hoping for. I thought you'd be happy."

He ran a hand through his hair, then pulled me into his arms. "I'm sorry. I *am* happy. I really am, Zellie. It's just..."

I caught the flicker of fear in his eyes. "It's just what?"

He cupped my face in his hands. "I love you, Zellie. I love you so much. There are things I want to tell you...things you need to know. I just...I don't want to lose you."

I shook my head. "Lose me? What are you talking about? Whit, I'll be *fine*."

"I'm sure Kitty thought that, too."

I pulled him down to me and kissed him, then stood on my toes to wrap my arms around his neck. "You'll *never* lose me, Whit," I promised, hugging him tightly. "I'm not going anywhere."

What Whit's reaction to our news lacked in exuberance was made up for by the others at Dawes House. Henry was overjoyed and talked a mile a minute, planning all kinds of adventures for him and his new sibling, finally determining that they would either be astronauts or pirates, but only after they were in *at least* third grade.

There were hugs all around and lots of congratulations from the Dawes House residents—Ms. Netty was positively giddy, instantly looking a decade younger in her excitement. I could see a hint of the young woman she'd once been, the young woman in my dream.

"Well done," Ms. Pearlie said, taking Whit's face in her hands and beaming with pride. She patted his cheek. "Well done."

"Guess you took my advice," Merilee said with a sly wink. She then shared a meaningful look with Chase, some message I didn't understand clearly passing between them in a single glance.

That night, I ran my fingers through Whit's hair as he lay with his head on my lap. "What is it you wanted to tell me?"

He took my hand and pressed a kiss to my palm. "It'll keep until morning."

I don't know how long we'd been asleep when I jerked awake, every sense on alert. At first, I didn't know what my subconscious had picked up on, but then I heard it—a strange scratching sound coming from Henry's room.

"I hear it too."

I started at the sound of Whit's voice but was glad he was with me when I went to check on Henry. A jolt of panic stabbed me in the chest, causing my heart to seize painfully when I entered Henry's room and saw his bed was empty.

I nearly called out to him but then saw a thin sliver of light seeping out from below his closet door. I heaved a sigh of relief and pulled the closet door open to see Henry sitting at the desk, scribbling furiously.

"Henry?" I said softly. "What are you doing, baby? You shouldn't be up. You have school tomorrow."

"I'm drawing you and Daddy a picture," he said in a strange monotone, not looking up from his drawing.

"That's awesome," Whit replied, slipping by me into the closet to crouch down next to Henry. "But you need your sleep, buddy." He gently took the crayon from Henry's fingers and set it aside then lifted him into his arms. "Come on. Let's get you back to bed."

As Whit tucked Henry back into his bed, I picked up his picture from the little desk, my blood turning to ice water in my veins when I saw what he had drawn. There were three stick figures—a dark-haired man, a brown-haired pregnant woman with red scribbles across her belly, and a little boy with dark curly hair lying on the ground at the mother's feet, a puddle of blood beside him.

My hand went to my mouth as I raced to the bathroom, barely making it to the toilet.

"Zellie!" Whit cried, rushing in to steady me as my stomach heaved again. "I've got you, baby. It's okay."

I shook my head, a single sob escaping before I could stop it. "It's not okay, Whit. His drawing..."

My stomach heaved again.

"I've got you," he said, gently rubbing my back with one hand, holding my hair for me. And when I was able to breathe through the nausea and sit on the floor, he grabbed a washcloth and ran it under the faucet before sitting down on the floor beside me.

I leaned against him while he held the cool cloth to my forehead.

When my stomach finally settled, I let him help me to my feet. "Come with me," I croaked out. "I need to you to see what Henry drew. I need you to understand how serious this is."

His face was solemn, concerned, as he nodded. "Okay."

I led him back into Henry's room and picked up the paper where I'd dropped it in my haste.

"What the fuck?" Whit breathed. "I thought you said this was over..."

I glanced at where Henry was sleeping peacefully and motioned for Whit to follow me. "I thought it was," I told him when we were in the living room. "I don't know where this is coming from. But it scares the shit out of me, Whit! Henry...he sometimes sees things...visions. Just like me. Just like my mother, I think."

"And you think this—" he waved the paper for emphasis "—is a vision?"

"I don't know," I told him sincerely. "It could just be a nightmare. But I can't take it anymore, Whit. I thought it would be fine. It had been so quiet for a while. But we can't stay here. Please!"

"What about Henry's school?" he asked. "You said you didn't want to disrupt his routine."

I groaned, frustrated—mostly at myself for not leaving sooner when Whit had first offered, for trusting the lull in activity, for letting myself become too comfortable at Dawes House. "Then we can go live in a hotel for a couple of weeks while we find another place nearby. Or offer to drive him every day. Or something. I don't know, Whit!"

Whit gave a curt nod, his jaw set. "Okay. I'll make arrangements first thing in the morning and then we'll figure out what we want to do after that. The most important thing is that you and Henry and the baby are safe. That's all I want, Zellie. I'll do whatever I have to do to keep you safe."

The moment the promise left his lips, an entire row of books flew off the bookshelf as if someone had swept them off in a rage. I screeched and hopped out of the way as they thudded to the floor at my feet.

"Zellie!" Whit cried, sweeping me behind him in one swift motion and putting himself between the shelf and me.

I sent a frightened glance his way, but a blur of movement out of the corner of my eye snapped my attention in that direction in time to see the dagger June had given to Henry flying toward me. I gasped as the dagger suddenly stopped mere inches from my face. It took me a moment to realize the reason. Whit had somehow intercepted it, caught it with his bare hand. Droplets of blood trailed down the heel of his palm and dripped onto the floor.

When I stared at him, shocked, he cursed under his breath and snatched up the cloth the dagger had been wrapped in, hastily folding it around the weapon.

"Enough!" he roared at our unseen assailant, fury twisting his features into someone I barely recognized. "That is enough! She already knows!"

"Not everything."

I gasped at the harsh whisper near my ear and spun toward the sound but saw no one there. I turned my wary gaze back to Whit. "What does she mean? 'Not everything?'"

His brows twitched together. "What? Who?"

I tried to swallow, but my mouth was suddenly too dry. "It might be Alice. Or Susanna maybe. Or Eliza. Or the woman from the wall. Hell, I don't know! But she just told me I don't know everything. What don't I know, Whit?"

He stared at me as if weighing his words, sorrow and...*defeat?*...in his eyes. He reached out to me. "Zellie—"

I reflexively shrank back from him. The anguish that crossed his features gutted me.

"Whit, you said you had things you wanted to tell me," I reminded him, my throat tight with tears, fearing for the destruction of my perfect dream. "What did you mean?"

"Zellie, baby," he said gently, "could we just go back to bed? Let's talk more in the morning."

"No," I said, not about to let him off the hook. "Don't do that, Whit. You can't blow me off after what just happened. Please, just be honest with me."

"Okay," he agreed, so softly I almost didn't hear him. He cleared his throat, his eyes pleading for understanding. "Whoever she is, she's right. I haven't been completely honest with you."

My heart sank. My voice was barely above a whisper when I asked, "About what?"

He hesitated then finally said, "Alice."

I blinked, hoping I hadn't heard him right.

"You're not the first one to see her," he continued. "The previous tenant... She had experiences as well. Not like what you've had. She wasn't sensitive that I'm aware of. But there were plenty of things that happened that scared her. That's why she left so abruptly and didn't take anything with her expect a few things she could pack in a suitcase."

"How could you keep this from me?" I demanded, my voice shaking, fear of what else he wasn't telling squeezing my lungs, making it difficult to breathe. "How, Whit? Knowing what I've been going through?"

"I only knew about David. You didn't tell me about the others until our first night together at the beach house," he countered. "I had no idea what you'd been going through. David is just a little boy, just lonely. I was hoping that Alice and the rest would leave you alone."

I gaped at him. "The *rest*?"

Too angry to talk to him about this anymore, I strode passed him, jerking my arm away as he tried to reach for me.

"Zellie, please," he called, his voice raw. "Let me explain everything. I have so much I've wanted to tell you, things you need to know."

I threw my hands up, as if trying to block the sound of his words from reaching me as he followed me to our bedroom. "I don't want to talk to you right now," I told him. "I'm too pissed."

I expected him to enter our bedroom, but he just stood in the doorway, both hands braced on the doorframe, head hanging down. "You don't have to talk to me," he told me as I climbed into bed and rolled over, my back to him. "You have every right to be furious with me. I should've told you so much before now. But, no matter what, just know how much I love you, Zellie. How much I love Henry. *You* are my family. The only family that matters."

I frowned at his words, finding them curious, but I was too hurt to ask him what he meant by that. When he didn't join me in bed after a few minutes, I rolled over to face him, but he was no longer in the doorway.

My curiosity overriding my anger, I quietly got out of bed and went to look for him. When I didn't see him sitting in the living room on the edge of the couch in his typical withdrawn, closed off posture when he was upset, I checked the kitchen, the bathroom. I was about to go check the other apartment, but then I heard his quiet words coming from Henry's room.

I peered into the room from the doorway to see Whit sitting on Henry's bed, arms on his knees, forehead resting on his clasped hands as if in prayer. Then his head snapped up as if he'd suddenly sensed my presence.

His eyes seemed to flash briefly—a trick of the light from the hallway behind me, no doubt, but disconcerting for a moment before his expression changed, became questioning. The look in his eyes was so repentant, so full of regret and sorrow, that it broke my heart.

Without a word, I held out my hand. After only the briefest hesitation, he rose and came to me. I pulled him with me out of Henry's room, shutting the door behind us before leading him to our bedroom. There, I placed his hand on my back and stepped closer as his arm tightened around me.

I wrapped my arms round his neck and held onto him as if holding the world together in that one embrace. His breath brushed against my neck when he sighed, his relief palpable. I shuddered at the warmth, suddenly needing him urgently, desperately. He must've felt it too. He pulled back just enough to capture my mouth in a savage kiss, fingers from one hand tangling in my hair, the other hand clutching the material of my nightshirt in his fist.

I gasped when he broke away and peered down at me, his eyes questioning. In answer, I slid my hand down between us and caressed him. He squeezed his eyes shut with a groan. Then his mouth was ravaging mine again as he walked me backward to our bed, pulling my shirt over my head and tossing it aside, taking my breast into his mouth, his tongue teasing, relentless, until desire swamped all rational thought.

He yanked the comforter out of the way, and when I fell back onto the bed, he dragged my hips to the edge, plunging deep, each thrust hard, powerful, rocking me, claiming me. I dug my nails into his arms, biting back the release building inside me, until I couldn't any longer and cried out, arching off the bed. When I collapsed back onto the mattress, his pace quickened until his muscles tightened, the veins in his neck visible with the strength of his release.

We lay together afterward, still joined, panting until our breaths slowed. And then he lifted his head and looked down at me, his love so clear, so fierce, tears stung my eyes. But he gently kissed them away, kissed my lips, the salt from my own tears still on his. And then his mouth and fingertips skimmed my skin, exploring, caressing with the same care and tenderness he had shown our first night together. And this time when he made love to me, it was so gentle I almost missed the roughness of before. Because unlike the first time we were together, that beautiful, perfect night at his beach house, this felt like an end instead of a beginning.

CHAPTER TWENTY-FOUR

Whit was still face down on our bed, sleeping soundly, when I got Henry up early, hoping to avoid running into anyone else at Dawes House as we left that morning. Henry seemed blissfully unaware of anything that had happened the night before and was humming happily as he ate pancakes at the little diner where I took him for breakfast.

My cell phone rang while we were eating, the vibration traveling through the table and into my hand, drawing my attention. My eyes lingered for a few seconds on my wedding band, before checking my phone's screen. I sent the call to voicemail when I saw it was Whit—no doubt wondering where we were. He texted a moment later, confirming my suspicions.

Where are you? Please call me. I just need to know you and Henry are okay.

I almost called him then, regretting the panic he must've felt waking up to find us gone. But I knew the minute I heard his voice, my resolve would crumble, so I settled for texting him instead.

Needed time to think. Having breakfast. Taking Henry to the park then to see Dottie.

Dots appeared on the screen, telling me he was working on a response. But then they disappeared. Started again. Disappeared. Finally, a message came through.

Love you. I'll be here when you get back.

I stared at the message, torn. I wanted to tell him I loved him, too. That my heart ached so badly, I could hardly breathe. I wanted to see him, feel his arms around me. I wanted to tell him that we could handle whatever it was he wanted to tell me, that we'd be okay. I wanted to tell him I forgave him.

But I didn't say any of it. I couldn't. Not yet. I turned my phone face down on the table, ignoring it when it rang again.

That afternoon, I brought Henry to the bookstore, forcing a smile when Dottie greeted us enthusiastically. She must've immediately seen that something was off because she quickly wrapped up with the customer she'd been helping and told her other employee to take the rest of the day off.

"Oh, honey," Dottie said, taking both my hands as soon as the shop was empty. "You look as sad as a cucumber. What's wrong?"

Henry tugged the hem of my shirt. "Excuse me, Mama, could I please play with the toys?"

"Yes, baby," I said, smoothing his curls. "Go ahead. Ms. Dottie and I are going to chat for a while." I turned back to Dottie, hesitating as I tried to decide how much to tell her. "Mind if we have some tea while we talk? I think this might take a while."

After Dottie and I were tucked in with sweet tea and snacks she'd prepared, I told her about the most recent encounters with the screaming woman—with Alice—Henry's drawing, and how Whit hadn't shared that others had experienced encounters at Dawes House before me.

"Zellie, honey," Dottie said on a sigh, reaching across the bistro table to take my hand, "I'm going to ask you a question, and I want you to be honest with me—but, more importantly, with yourself."

She gave me a pointed look as if to make sure I understood the gravity of what she was about to say.

When I nodded, she took a deep breath and heaved another, dramatic sigh. "Do you really want to know the whole truth?"

"Of course. I love Whit, Dottie. I really do." I paused, taking a few seconds to swallow the tears constricting my throat. "I don't want there to be any secrets between us. I need him to be honest with me."

She peered over her glasses. "Let me remind you that you weren't completely honest with him about all you'd been seeing until recently. Why did you not tell him everything?"

"Well," I said, drawing my hand back, "I didn't want him to think I was losing it."

She leaned back in her chair and clasped her hands. "Do you think perhaps he was worried about the same thing?"

"Why would he be worried about that?" I asked. "Clearly, I already believed in the intruders, in ghosts."

She pursed her lips, then gave a curt nod. "Very well, then. I'm going to show you something. And I want you to remember this bit of conversation, all right?"

Dottie returned with an enormous, leather-bound tome. She set it on the table in front of me. "This is a Proffitt family heirloom. I was able to acquire it some years ago. Go on, now. Take a look."

I reached out to touch the book but paused, briefly reconsidering my desire to know the truth. But then I swallowed hard, promising myself that no matter what I found, it wouldn't change my love for Whit. I opened the cover and frowned. "It's a photo album."

Dottie nodded and flipped through the first couple of pages. "Mmm-hmm." She turned to another page and spun the book toward me so that I could see the photos.

I was stunned speechless as I stared down at the black and white image she tapped with one long hot-pink fingernail. It was a wedding portrait from what appeared to be the early days of photography. The 1840s, maybe? Because staring back at me from the page were faces I recognized, including that of Susanna, the forced bride of Josef Proffitt. He stood next to her, calm and stoic. The resemblance to the other men in the Proffitt family I'd known as uncanny as it had been in my dream. And Susanna looked trapped, defeated.

But they weren't the only faces I recognized. There were others. The drowned woman, Eliza, who would be Josef's next bride. And a scowling man in the background that could've been Whit's twin. My fingertips lightly grazed the man's image, marveling at how even his aloof posture was familiar, before taking in the other individuals.

Standing to one side of Josef was a woman with blond hair pulled back tightly in a severe bun who looked exactly like Iris. And there were Earl and June, glamourous and stately. And was that Chase? He wore a mustache and sideburns fashionable for the day, but there was a mischievous twinkle in his eyes that was unmistakable. There were others in the group, people I didn't recognize. But they were all clearly wealthy, smirking with some secret shared between them.

"What the hell?" I murmured, turning to another page. Josef again, this time a wedding portrait with Eliza. She appeared far happier than her sister had, but I knew her fate, had seen her death, so something certainly changed after she married her mysterious suitor. A sudden image of her lying in the water flashed in my thoughts, but I shook my head, banishing it.

I paged through several more photos, many of them featuring the others I'd seen in the first: June and Earl, Chase, Iris, the man who resembled Whit so closely it was unnerving. The locations varied, from countryside to bustling cities. The fashions evolved, representing the trends of different decades—everything from the wide hoop skirts and ridiculously tight corsets to the slimmer skirts and enormous puffed sleeves. And any wedding photos among them featured only the brides, women I didn't recognize.

The next set of photos taken in Savannah appeared to be from the 1910s and once again featured a wedding, this time the images including both bride and groom. At first glance, I thought the groom was the same man from earlier photos who looked like Whit. But then I realized the brow was too heavy, the expression too entitled to be him.

It was Josef Proffitt again.

My sense of relief at it not being the man I loved was so powerful, I almost laughed at how ridiculous it had been for me to even suspect it was Whit in the first place. Of course it wasn't him! These pictures were from over a century ago. The whole thing was absurd.

But it was no less ridiculous to assume the groom was Josef Proffitt. The photos were clearly taken—what? Fifty, sixty years apart? If that was Josef Proffitt, he looked like he hadn't aged a day. Which was impossible! The resemblance was just a coincidence. *All* of this was just a coincidence.

It had to be.

Then I saw the label beneath the photograph, scrawled in ink that had faded and nearly vanished over time. It wasn't Josef Proffitt after all. It looked like him. Exactly like him from all the photos before. But that was not the name I read.

"What?" I breathed. "No...that's not..."

Dottie tilted her head, regarding me with a sad smile. "What does it say, honey?"

I shook my head, trying to clear my vision, but the words remained the same. "Montgomery Proffitt."

"Indeed," Dottie sighed.

I frowned. "And Mary Alice Shay."

Alice. The screaming woman.

"Shay?" I mused, lifting my eyes to Dottie. "A relative of yours?"

She nodded. "Oh, yes."

I hurriedly flipped to the next page. "Montgomery, Mary Alice, and David Proffitt."

I tentatively touched the face of the small boy in the photo. It was the same boy who had peeked out from behind Henry's bed, who had led me to the body of the woman in the wall.

"David," I whispered. Then I pointed to the man in the photo. "This man looks just like Josef. But this has to be Mr. Monty's grandfather. He was probably named after him. Right?"

Dottie didn't respond. But I wasn't sure I really wanted her to, too afraid of what she might say.

The next page featured Montgomery Proffitt again, perhaps only a couple of years later, maybe the 1920's, but with another bride. And another group photo with the familiar faces of Dawes House, including a very stately looking Pearlie and Junior this time. And I recognized the young woman from my dream—Netty, but older now. Netty had to be a family name, passed down to a daughter or niece. Because *this* Netty couldn't possibly be the Ms. Netty I knew, even though I could see a resemblance. The Netty in my dream had already been a teenager, maybe even in her twenties, old enough to talk to Alice as a friend and not as her elder.

But then standing next to the younger Netty, smiling broadly, clinging to Chase's arm, was Merilee. And another man had joined the group—Carter Dean. The woman who held his arm looked familiar. She could've been Mary Alice's sister.

This album, these photos, had to be either an elaborate hoax or the most dedicated historical reenactments I'd ever seen. At least, that's what my brain kept insisting as I continued looking through the album, the photos taken through the decades—30s, 40s, 50s... Sometimes the man featured in so many of the photos was listed with a different name, but his face was always the same. The man who resembled Whit was sometimes present, sometimes not. In one photo from 1917 that I found tucked between pages, out of chronological order, he wore a US

Army uniform. In another from 1942, he was again in uniform, but his face was still young and handsome, untouched by time.

I went back through the album several times, taking in each photo, studying it, trying to force the math of the years depicted to make sense. Henry grew bored at one point, so he and Dottie disappeared upstairs to Dottie's apartment, returning with supper that I couldn't eat, my stomach in too much turmoil. Later, they returned with freshly baked cookies, which Henry insisted I try.

"Mama," Henry said, yawning, "I'm tired. When are we going home? Can I take Daddy some cookies?"

I nodded, absently. "Sure, baby." Then I raised my eyes to Dottie, encountering her sympathetic expression. "How can this be possible...?"

She gently closed the photo album. "That's probably not a question for me, honey."

The room began to spin in concert with the whirlwind of thoughts in my head, so I closed my eyes and took several deep breaths, managing to avoid tossing my actual cookies. When I opened them again, Dottie was watching me closely as if trying to determine if she needed to get more tea or grab a mop and bucket.

"May I borrow this album?" I asked, my tone flat, controlled as I tried to keep it together.

"Of course, honey," she said. "Are you okay to drive home? Would you like me to take you?"

I shook my head and hefted the album onto one hip. "No. Thank you," I said in a daze. "I'll manage. Henry, baby, come on."

I vaguely remember the short drive home. It didn't give me much time to consider possible explanations, to figure out what questions I even needed to ask, but it wouldn't have done any good to continue driving around. That only prolonged the inevitable.

As Henry and I made our way toward the elevator in Dawes House, I registered that some of the others had come out to the foyer, were greeting me, but I didn't respond. None of them were who I needed to see, who I needed to hold me and assure me that the album was just an odd prank that wasn't funny.

Whit was sitting on the couch when Henry and I entered, a glass of dark liquid in his hand, a bottle of Junior's elderberry wine sitting on the end table beside him. He didn't turn to look at us, but I could see from his profile that the proud, confident man I loved looked weary, defeated.

"Henry, baby," I said softly, "why don't you go play in your room for a while?"

He yawned but shrugged. "Yes, ma'am."

As soon as Henry was in his room, I circled around to face Whit then set the album on the coffee table and flipped it open to the first photo.

He stared at it for a moment then let out a short, bitter laugh. "Gotta hand it to Dottie," he said with mock praise, raising his wine glass in salute. "She played us all."

"Whit?" I wasn't sure what to do or say, but all my questions apparently came through in that one word.

He took another swig of his wine and heaved a sigh. "I had hoped things could be different for me," he began. "I tried to avoid my family duty, spare you from all this." He chuckled again, but this time it was heavy with sorrow. "Hell, I even eradicated family from several of our homes when they refused to support my leadership and change their ways. But this life it's..." he lifted his glass, peering at it thoughtfully. "Intoxicating."

I placed my palms on my belly where Whit's child grew in my womb. "What do you mean by 'eradicated'? Whit, are you drunk?"

He shook his head. "No. Can't be. I wish I could be. Wish I could drink myself blind, pretend the truth was just a horrible nightmare that I could wake up from to find you there beside me and hold you until the world faded away again."

"What are you talking about?" I asked, my throat tightening with my growing fear. "Baby, you're scaring me."

"No point in sugar-coating it now since Dottie's interference has ruined my chance to ease you into our world." He gestured toward the photo album and answered my unasked question. "Yes, Zellie, the people in that album are the same people you know and love. Me included."

My knees suddenly weak, I sank down onto the other couch. But I couldn't say a word.

"Some of us have been around for longer than others," Whit continued with a shrug. "My father, Pearlie, June... It was a lot easier to hide the truth in the old days, taking only in moderation mostly from those no one would really miss or ones that could be explained away. June survived I don't know how many witch trials. Pearlie moved among the royalty of Africa, Europe, England, amassing a fortune. And my father—the venerable Montgomery Proffitt as *you* would know him—has been gathering a family for longer than recorded history."

I stared at him, hoping what he was saying was just a product of too much wine, no matter how much he denied it. It must've shown in my face.

He took another sip, topped it off with more from the bottle, then sighed. "It's hard to wrap your head around, I know. Even those who have directly witnessed the truth find it impossible to believe. All the better for us, really. We had a bit of a scare in the 1600s when my father's cousin Elizabeth's insatiable appetite nearly exposed us all. All those poor young women..."

"Elizabeth?" I repeated. "Eliz— *Báthory*?"

He nodded. "I wasn't there, of course," he said. "I wasn't born until the 1700s. I was raised in this house—did you know that? Well, not *this* house. My father built the original. He was going by Thomas Montgomery then. But people start to notice our idiosyncrasies after a while, so we moved during the British occupation of Savannah. That seemed like a good time to disappear. But he loved the house, and he hates giving up what's his. That's why he married Susanna Dawes when he returned under a different name, to reclaim what was his."

"As Josef Proffitt," I murmured.

Whit nodded. "He changed his name periodically as we moved among the network of properties the family had created. Unfortunately, those moves became more frequent as time wore on and communication, the media, improved."

I pulled my hands down my face and laughed in a short burst that probably gave away how close I was to not being able to hold myself together.

Whit leaned forward to reach for me, but I shot to my feet, avoiding his touch. Needing to loosen the knot pulling tighter in my stomach, I paced the room, attempting to process everything. He was laying it out so logically, so matter-of-factly as if what he was telling me was just as ordinary as any other family's history. But some things still didn't fit.

I halted directly in front of him, keeping the coffee table between us. "Your father was an old man when I knew him, Whit. Explain that."

He'd been sitting with his head on his clasped hands like I'd found him the previous night in Henry's room. When he lifted his head at my question, the pain I saw there nearly broke me. He leaned back against the couch cushions, his hands now resting limp on his thighs.

And I realized he was *already* broken. It took every ounce of my willpower to keep my feet planted where they were and not go to him.

"We all have a choice," he explained. "Leave and become nomads, never planting roots, never experiencing the security and safety of the family, changing our identity at more frequent intervals. Or leapfrog with the others, growing old until it was time to be renewed. My father liked to mix it up to keep things interesting."

"Renewed?" I repeated softly, still refusing to connect the dots he was laying out for me.

"We need blood to survive and stay young," he said. "But if we choose to grow old, consuming enough blood erases decades. My father discovered quite by accident that the blood of pregnant women or recently pregnant women was far more potent than the blood of others. The renewal was so much quicker, so much more invigorating with them as the source."

"My God." I took an involuntary step back, my hand covering my mouth to keep the rising bile from escaping.

"Originally, my father had only resorted to this in the most extreme cases," Whit continued as if that somehow excused my former benefactor's actions. "Horrific injury, starvation, when massive amounts of blood were needed. But with the renewals, he'd found a whole new way to preserve his legacy and his stranglehold on the family. Not only would he be sowing his seed like he always had, but he'd also be ensuring the survival of his existing family."

I wrapped my arms around myself, the horror of everything he'd told me fully sinking in. "What are you?" I croaked, finally working up the courage to ask the question that burned on my tongue. "Witches? Vampires? Demons?"

Whit held my gaze, the light I thought I'd seen before—just a reflection, a spark of passion—shone there like a predator's eyeshine in the darkness. "None of these. And yet all of them." He shook his head. "We are who we are, Zellie. History and folklore have called us many things."

Part of me wanted to scream at him to stop telling me these outrageous lies. Part of me wanted to run. But another part of me, the part that had loved him so completely, still refused to believe Whit could be part of such a horrific legacy.

"I'm not like the others, Zellie," he assured me, his expression softening. "I chose to be a nomad, sticking to the shadows, trying not to be seen. I've lived so many lives, never taking more than I needed to sustain me. I would *never* harm you or Henry—I swore that to you, remember? What I am changes *nothing*."

"How can you say that?" My voice was infuriatingly faint. It should've been stronger, more forceful. But as much as I wanted to hide the fact that I was terrified, there wasn't any point in trying. Whit could read me. He knew better. Why pretend?

He set his glass aside and spread his hands in a helpless gesture. "Because it's true. That's all I can say."

A sudden, heartbreaking thought occurred to me. "Kitty? What happened to her and her child? Was she one of these sacrifices?"

Whit didn't immediately answer as if wondering if he should tell me the truth. But I saw in his expression the moment he decided that he had to tell me everything, no matter the cost.

"Not intentionally," he said. "Most of our children don't survive long because of the anemia that basically causes us to cannibalize our own blood. And the mothers have an even harder struggle. June was right, Zellie—our unborn leech so much from the mother's body, and keeping the infant healthy once it's born is a difficult balance that isn't always successful."

"That's why Kitty was so sickly," I guessed. "And her crying?"

He nodded. "Kitty was born one of us, so she knew the risks, recognized that she wasn't doing well despite all of June's remedies. She told the family that if she didn't survive she wanted to give her blood for renewal so Billy Wayne could claim it as his sacrifice and would finally get his chance to become one of us. He's human. I guess you'd call him a Renfield in pop culture parlance. Becoming will be his reward for his many years of service to the family. I'd have slit the bastard's throat years ago for his repeated infidelity to Kitty—with *Iris,* of all people, for fuck's sake. But Kitty wouldn't allow it. For some reason, she still loved him."

"Who received her...blood?" I asked. But before he could respond, I realized the answer. "Mr. Dean. Carter Dean is Old Man Dean."

Whit nodded. "His and Netty's renewal were delayed—Carter's by request so he could age with his partner. Netty's was by design, punishment from my father for letting Alice die. But I felt sorry for her, hated how my father had cursed her, letting Merilee renew, forever young, as her sister grew older and older, refusing to let her die. I promised Netty I'd find a way to help her."

I was afraid to find out where this was going, but I had to know everything. And I could feel him holding back, the worst betrayal yet to come. "How would you be able to do anything?"

"Short of allowing there to be a sacrifice for her renewal, I honestly don't know," he admitted. "I was going to try just feeding her more, maybe reverse her aging over time. But it would take a while. And it wasn't something I'd be able to do with my father's spies here at Dawes House, that's for damned sure."

"I don't understand," I said, trying to process that absolute madness of it all. "How do Henry and I factor into any of this?"

"I told you before that my father is obsessed with his legacy," Whit reminded me. "We are expected to create a life, take a life, give a life once we become adults as a pledge of loyalty and obedience."

"What the hell does that even mean?" I demanded.

"I refused," Whit assured me. "It was an antiquated tradition, my father's way of ensuring his dominance, keeping everyone in check, offering them eternal life for their fealty to him and his dark lord who'd 'blessed' us with immortality."

I felt for the couch, sinking back down onto it in a daze. My mother's words echoed in my head: *Your devil's found you.*

"I thought I could thwart that obligation," Whit continued. "He let me live despite my rebellion because I was one of his few surviving biological children and one of the only ones strong enough to take over for him from time to time. That's another reason I'm not exactly everyone's favorite. But I was determined. I even refused to have a relationship with a woman beyond an occasional encounter for fear of getting her pregnant and having to fulfill my obligation to the family. Until one day, I stopped for coffee at a little café in a shitty neighborhood near one of our properties."

My blood went cold, all the warmth draining away in an instant. "What are you talking about?"

"You quoted *Henry V*," he said.

"'Once more unto the breach, dear friends, once more,'" I murmured. "I used to say that to my teammates at the coffee shop when things got busy. How do you know that?"

"Not one of the Bard's most widely read plays," he noted, avoiding my question. "But it's always been one of my favorites. To hear a beautiful woman quoting it like that... I was utterly captivated. I came back after my meeting—"

I shook my head. "Stop it, Whit."

"—and we talked about literature until your boss kicked me out." He smiled wistfully. "But I came back the next day."

"That's not true," I insisted, my throat going tight, a sharp pain growing behind my eyes. Something in my memory rustled, trying to break free.

The sincerity in his eyes was unmistakable as he continued, "Zellie, I loved you so very much. And you loved me. For a year. We were together for a year. The best year of my very long life—until now."

I shot to my feet. "No!"

"Eventually, I told you everything," he said. "All of this. Every single ugly truth about my life, my family, who I was. And you still loved me. But we got carried away one night, weren't careful."

"No!" I said, stabbing my index finger at him. "That's not true. It's not possible."

"When I realized what I'd done, the danger I'd put you in, I panicked," he admitted. "I took your memories of us for your safety. All I left was a vague impression of what we'd had that night, what we'd shared so many nights."

I was speechless, could only stare at him, my entire body shaking with fear, rage, sorrow... Finally, I managed a very quiet, "How?"

"It's just another part of who we are," he said. "I don't know—"

"That's not what I mean," I snapped. "How could you do that to me? If it's true—how dare you take something so personal from me?"

"To save your life," Whit said simply. "And the life of our son."

My breath caught in my chest. "That's not true. You're *not* Henry's father. I don't care what kind of bullshit you're trying to feed me about stealing my memories and some *secret life* we had."

"I wasn't sure either," he admitted. "Not at first. But then I learned about Henry's anemia, the same condition that plagued the family's children. And I saw how he improved when June and Pearlie started feeding him our blood."

"Your *blood*? What the fuck are you talking about!?" I screeched, then glanced toward the hall, relieved to see Henry was still playing in his room. This was the last damned thing he needed to hear.

"Our blood has certain healing properties," he told me. "That part of the folklore is true."

"Prove it," I ordered through clenched teeth. "Prove any of this right *fucking* now!"

"I took my own memories as well," Whit told me, standing to fish his phone out of his pocket. "To keep my father from finding out about you. He couldn't make me tell him what I didn't know. I didn't even leave myself an impression like I had with you. But I left a breadcrumb."

He turned the phone around to show me. On the screen was a photo of Whit and a younger me with his arm around me, an ocean sunset behind us. We were smiling, happy.

My hand shook as I reached out and took the phone. Holding it with both hands, I stared at the image, trying to figure out where it had been edited, how he had faked it. But it was real. And dated about two months before I found out I was pregnant with Henry.

But, *how*? How could this be true? And if it wasn't, why in the hell would Whit create such a cruel story to try to make me think he was Henry's father?

"I didn't know who you were," he said, edging closer, "but I still felt longing, sadness, whenever I looked at the photo. And despite everything I'd done to shield you, my father still found you, insinuated himself into your life, insisted I bring you to Dawes House."

I lifted my eyes to his, frowning. "What the hell are you talking about? Your father died before you decided to evict me."

Whit ran his hands through his hair, then dragged his hand down his face. "No, he didn't. He went through his renewal and moved to New England."

"His renewal," I repeated. "A sacrifice."

Whit gave me a curt, solemn nod. "I don't know who."

"The woman who lived here?" I squeaked, my heart breaking into so many pieces as I had to face the truth that my hero, my guardian angel, had been a murderer.

Whit shook his head. "I don't know. I wasn't part of the ceremony. I was brought in after to take over my father's business affairs, be his puppet for a few years until he could resurface and take it back over. It was only after I saw you that first night here at Dawes House that I realized you were the same woman in the photo. That somehow, he had found you and would expect me to honor my obligation."

"Kill me, you mean," I said. "Then raise our son as one of you."

He nodded and turned his back to me, laughing bitterly as he snatched up his wine glass. "He even brought the rest of the family at Dawes House in on it." He turned back to me as he said it, gesturing with his glass and sloshing some of its contents onto the rug. "Oh, not the part about you and I having a past together. He only told June and Pearlie about that bit. The rest of them just thought he'd brought you here so I could prove I was finally the dutiful son and seduce you, impregnate you." He eyes blazed, bright with rage as he ground out through clenched teeth, "And, yes, murder you."

I could only stare at him, so many emotions competing for dominance.

Whit downed the last of his wine. "So, I went to New England to have a little chat with dear old Dad, set him straight. I demanded to know what game he was playing." The muscle in his jaw twitched, betraying how furious he was even just remembering the conversation. "Turns out you were an experiment, Zellie. You survived your pregnancy with Henry so well, you were so strong, and Henry was stronger than he had a right to be without any supplements. It was similar to how my mother had been when pregnant with me and how I was as a child. Genetics, maybe? Your abilities are hereditary, so maybe it made you different in other ways as well. He wanted to study you, study Henry, figure out how to replicate the success."

I shook my head. "No. That's not true. I wasn't just some experiment!"

"Not to me, Zellie. *Never* to me." Whit's expression grew dark. "I told him to go to hell and that I'd kill any bastard who tried to take either one of you away from me. That didn't exactly go well, as you can imagine."

"And?" I prompted, although not sure I wanted to know the rest.

Whit set his glass on the table then shrugged nonchalantly. "And I ripped his heart from his chest before he could mine."

I stared at him, eyes wide. "You killed him."

"I did," he confirmed without a hint of remorse in his voice. "I told you I would protect you no matter the cost."

"And your trips up north?" I managed. "The injuries, the bruises?"

"Asserting myself as head of the family," he said without elaborating.

I'd always heard that when watching a horror movie, a director will leave the monster unseen, letting the audience's minds fill in the gaps with their own imagination, often with images more horrifying than anything that would've been on film. But somehow, I didn't think that was the case this time. I had a feeling that my imagination couldn't even begin to do justice to what my beloved had wrought. To protect me. To protect Henry.

My God.

"Give them back," I ordered, my voice little more than a whisper. "My memories. I want them back. I need to know what you're saying is true."

"I can't," he said. "Not just by wanting to."

"Then how do you have yours?" I pressed, my anger returning in a rush.

"They came back when I killed my father," he replied without hesitation. "I don't know how or why. Maybe it was the fact that my subconscious realized the main threat to you and Henry was gone at that point. Or at least I thought it was."

"Was everything a lie, Whit?" I asked, afraid to know the answer but needing to hear it anyway. "Why did you allow Henry and me to stay here? Why did you fucking *marry me?*"

"Everything I feel for you—felt for you even before I had my memories back—is true. It was *never* a lie, Zellie." He came toward me, eyes pleading for understanding, but halted when I flinched at his sudden movement. "I thought I could protect you better if you were here, keep anyone outside of Dawes House from trying anything as a way to get to me. I made it very clear that you and Henry weren't to be touched without my permission."

"Why would they listen to you?" I asked, eying him warily.

"Because I'm head of the family now," he said. "We have rules, customs. They're centuries old and run deep. Which is partly why June and Pearlie weren't going to let me forget that the role comes with one critical responsibility. June was impatient for me to get on with it, but I think Pearlie hoped you would become one of us instead."

The full magnitude of the betrayal hit me, knocking the air from my lungs, crushing me. My so-called family at Dawes House who had seemed to love and embrace me as one of their own had all been a ruse.

Whit's phone buzzed with a text message from CP.

Cora. Was she a part of all of this, too? His sister I hadn't even met?

I set his phone on the coffee table and stepped back.

"We need to go, Zellie," Whit announced with a glance at the message, his tone abrupt. "I've made arrangements for us, security until I can completely cement my place as head of the family, abolish the reprehensible practices that have gone on for far too long."

I nodded and slowly edged backward toward the hallway.

He had to be out of his fucking mind.

If even half of what he was saying was true, there was no way in hell I was going anywhere with him. I pivoted and rushed to Henry's room, then grabbed the duffle bag that was in the top of his closet and started pulling clothes from his drawers and shoving them into the bag.

"Mama?" Henry asked cautiously. "Are we leaving?"

"Yes, baby," I said, sniffing as I wiped the tears that were streaming down my cheeks. "We're going to go visit Ms. Dottie again, okay? Can you grab some of your favorite toys?"

He nodded, his eyes wide, and gathered up his action figures and teddy bear and put them in his puppy backpack.

I took his hand and pulled him with me into my bedroom, where I grabbed a few clothes that would still fit into the duffle, leaving the rest behind. "Let's go, baby."

He jogged along beside me. "Mama, is Daddy coming? Does he have his bag already?"

Stifling a sob, I wiped my cheek on my shoulder. "No, baby. Not right now."

I snatched up my purse and pulled the strap over my head and shoulder, and took a step toward the door, but froze when I saw that Whit was now standing in front of it.

Henry let go of my hand and ran to Whit, who scooped him up in his arms. "Why aren't you going with us?"

"I'll be there later," Whit told him. "I have to deal with a few things first. But you take care of your mama, okay? Keep her safe until I get there."

Henry nodded. "Yes, sir." Then he hugged Whit tightly around the neck and whispered, "Don't let the monsters get you, Daddy."

Whit's eyes darted to me, held my gaze before he set Henry down. "Don't you worry. I won't."

I was just opening my mouth to tell Whit not to try to stop us when he held out his car keys. "Take mine. It's more reliable." He gave me a quick, sad smile. "I'd planned to get you a new one as soon as you'd let me."

I nodded and cautiously reached out to take the keys. My fingers brushed his, the same explosion of sensation and desire as I always experienced when we touched racing up my arm.

"I love you, Zellie," he said. "More than my life."

His expression was so full of emotion—love, sorrow, regret—it almost made me reconsider leaving.

Almost.

When I said nothing, he stepped away from the door. Without even sparing a glance his way for fear that I'd change my mind, I took Henry's hand and rushed to the elevator.

As soon as we reached the ground floor, I had to force myself not to hurry toward the front door, not wanting to draw attention to us, but my stomach clenched in sudden fear when I saw Iris sitting at her desk.

"Now, where are y'all off to?" she asked with a grin, getting up and coming around the desk to greet us. It was the same grin she'd always had, but instead of welcoming and friendly, it now seemed sinister.

I forced a smile, hoping my lips weren't trembling as much it felt like they were. "I'm taking Henry to the house in Charleston," I lied. "Whit's coming later after he takes care of some business."

I took a step toward the door, but Iris deftly slid in front of me to block the exit, still wearing that chilling smile. "It seems an odd time of day to be making that trip," she said, her voice louder than it had been, echoing off the walls. "Is everything alright, honey?"

"Yes, of course," I assured her, trying to keep my voice light, registering movement in my peripheral vision. "Now, if you'll excuse me, Ms. Iris."

I tried to take another step to go around her, but she moved with me, continuing to block our escape. "Now, *Zellie*," she said, an undercurrent of warning in her voice, "I would hate for you to rush off without saying goodbye to the family."

I pulled Henry closer, curling him into my body protectively, and turned my head slowly to survey the foyer. The other residents of Dawes House had exited their apartments and were drifting into the foyer, spreading out around the perimeter, effectively blocking any possible means of escape. As I looked at them, their eyes began to glow amber, their faces taking on a feral, savage appearance, their features stretched taut on their bones.

"Get out of the way, Iris," I ordered, trying to keep my voice even but letting her know I was not about to go slinking back to my apartment to wait for...whatever it was they had in store for Henry and me.

Iris's lips curled into a broad smile, her teeth extending to become a maw of horrifying fangs. She stretched her mouth wide, emitting an ear-splitting screech, then it was as if time had slowed to a crawl, my instincts instantly identifying a threat in that second Iris's pupils dilated, and her shoulders rolled forward.

But before she could lunge at me, a booming voice bellowed something in that strange language I'd heard before, bringing her up short, and she jerked back, sending a startled glance up to the fourth-floor balcony. The predator had suddenly become the prey.

My head whipped around to where her gaze was fixed. There, crouching on the balcony railing was Whit, his own features distorted like theirs, his expression deadly.

Beside me, closer than she'd been before, June spat something back at him then darted toward me. I cried out as her fingers curved into long talons, and she growled—fucking *growled*. But then something blurred between us, and her growl cut off abruptly.

I stared at her, my eyes wide with terror and confusion as she grasped her throat, gurgling as blood spurted between her fingers. And then I saw Whit, blood dripping from his own talons, a deep growl rumbling in his chest as his furious gaze slowly swept the room, daring the others to make a move.

Iris hissed at him, and before I could even react, Whit was standing between us, only inches from her face, his fangs bared in warning. She screeched at him angrily but dropped her eyes in submission and stepped away from the door.

Movement behind me brought my attention back to the rest of the group, who were closing in, stalking closer inch by inch.

"Whit..." I warned, my voice tight with fear as I hugged Henry closer.

Whit pivoted, spreading his arms wide, blocking Henry and me from the others, and hissed in warning. But emboldened by their numbers, they continued to close in around us, their shoulders rolling forward, fangs bared as they prepared to attack.

"Run," he ordered in a gravelly snarl that sent fear lancing through me. But it wasn't fear of him. It was fear *for* him.

I hesitated, my love for Whit and concern for his safety twisting my heart. I grasped the back of his shirt, trying to pull him along with us. "Come on! Whit—"

"Run!" he bellowed just as Earl lunged forward.

I spun around with Henry and threw open the door, racing down the steps and into the street. When we reached Whit's car, I helped Henry scramble in and threw our stuff into the front seat, glancing over my shoulder at the horrific screeching and growls coming from the house.

I ran around the hood to the other side of the car and dove into the driver's seat, sending one more glance toward Dawes House, desperately hoping to see Whit running toward us. But one glimpse of Henry's wide, terrified eyes, and I threw the car into gear and stomped the accelerator.

My hands trembled so badly, I had to grip the steering wheel until my knuckles were white to keep from sideswiping cars parked along the street. I checked the rearview mirror again and again, terrified that one of them would be following us but still hoping I'd see Whit somehow. After driving several blocks without anyone pursuing us, I forced myself to slow to the speed limit and wiped tears with a shaking hand.

"Mama?" came Henry's voice from the backseat, small, afraid.

I sniffed and cleared my throat, trying to compose myself for Henry's sake before answering. "Yes, baby?"

He made a little mewling sound before a hard sob shook him. "I think the monsters got Daddy."

The tears I'd been crying quietly now overtook me, and I had to pull over as the sobs I'd been holding back wracked my body. I gripped the steering wheel and rested my forehead against it, sinking into my soul-crushing sorrow. It was as if someone had physically ripped my heart from *my* body as Whit had done his father's. The grief of losing the family we'd built at Dawes House shattered me.

And my heart ached for poor little Addie. She was an innocent as well. What horror was that quirky, sweet little girl going to find when she went looking for her grandmother?

And Whit.

My love. My heart. The man who'd made me feel so precious and cherished. Who'd brought such joy to our lives. Who'd made me believe in love that could last forever.

Could he really be gone? Had Henry somehow sensed something? Or was it just fear? The same fear that now gripped me so intensely that I wanted to turn the car around and fight to the death for the man I loved but that also made me want to race away from all of them as far and as fast I could?

And yet I could still *feel* Whit. It was as if there was a tether between his heart and mine—pulled taut, stretched almost to a breaking point, but still intact, binding our souls together.

Could he still be alive?

The glimmer of hope made me straighten and wipe the tears from my cheeks. "No," I said to Henry who was still crying quietly in the backseat. "They didn't get him, baby. I don't believe that."

Henry threw off his seatbelt and scrambled into the front seat and into my lap, squeezing me tightly around the neck. "Are you sure?"

I hugged him for a long moment before pulling back and forcing a smile as I wiped his cheeks. "Yeah, I am. I can feel him, Henry. I don't know how, but I can. Can you?" When he frowned, his eyes turned up as if searching for something far away, I added, "It's like a little pull right here." I touched the center of his chest. "Do you feel it?"

Henry's eyes went wide, and a smile broke across his face. "Yes! I can, Mama!" But then his smile dimmed a little. "Can we go back and get him?"

I smoothed his curls away from his forehead. "I don't think so, baby. At least, not you. I need to find us a safe place for a little while. Then, I promise, I'll go back for Daddy."

It was the first time I'd called Whit that. Even though Henry had immediately embraced the idea, I still hadn't referred to Whit that way. But the moment I said it aloud, I knew it was true. I'd felt it even as he was confessing the full truth to me, as if something had triggered a long-forgotten secret that haunted me at the edge of my consciousness.

My promise gave Henry the assurances he needed, and he climbed back into his booster seat and buckled in.

"Where are we going, Mama?" he asked as I pulled out into the street.

"We're still going to see Ms. Dottie," I told him.

Where else *could* I go? The few friends I'd had from my old job were hours away, and I'd barely spoken to any of them since I'd moved. Showing up on their doorstep with a "Hey, I know I haven't been a great friend since leaving, but can you watch my kid while I go fight—*vampires?*—and rescue my husband" seemed a little presumptuous.

A hotel, maybe? But the thought of being alone made me feel too vulnerable, too exposed. Whit had said he'd made arrangements for our protection, but I had no idea who he'd contacted or even how to find out. We hadn't had time yet to go over all the particulars now that our lives had been combined.

No, we'd go to Dottie's tonight. And then I'd figure out the rest later. There was no other option. Besides, Dottie was my friend, my confidante, and, quite literally, the only other person I knew in the city. And she clearly knew more about the residents of Dawes House than she'd let on.

It was only when she opened her upstairs apartment door and ushered us in without a single question did I begin to wonder why.

CHAPTER TWENTY-FIVE

It was the first time I'd been in Dottie's apartment above the bookshop, but it was as cozy and inviting as the shop itself and just as eclectic. I sat at her little round wooden table in the kitchen, gripping a mug of tea she'd prepared, letting it warm my cold fingers.

"Drink your tea, honey," she urged softly, joining me at the table with a cup of her own and a plate of cookies. "It'll help you feel so much better. It's my own special blend of herbal teas. I've used it for years to calm my nerves."

I dutifully took a sip and gave her a shaky smile. "Thank you, Dottie. I'm so sorry to intrude on you like this."

"Don't you fret over it," she assured me, patting my arm. "I'd hoped you would come to me."

I took another sip of tea. It really was as delicious and soothing as Dottie had promised. "What do you mean?"

I peeked out of the kitchen to the red velvet couch where Henry lay on his stomach, sleeping soundly. My poor baby. He was so emotionally exhausted, he'd fallen fast asleep within minutes of finishing the hot chocolate Dottie had made for him.

"Well," she said, "you seemed so distraught when you left earlier. I was worried about you, honey."

I experienced such a powerful surge of gratitude and relief that I nearly allowed my barely restrained tears to start flowing again. "Thank you, Dottie. I didn't know where else to go."

"Why don't you tell me what happened," she suggested. "That might help."

I started to tell her she wouldn't believe me but reminded myself that she'd been the one to show me the photo album, so she'd had to have at least suspected something was going on at Dawes House.

So, I told her everything. From the ghostly intruder at our previous house to the full story of the intruders at Dawes House to the attempted assault on Henry and me by our supposed "family" to my conflicted emotions about Whit's betrayal and my love for him.

Dottie listened, making no comment, taking it all in stride. When I finished my story and my tea, Dottie took my mug and set it in the sink before returning and taking my hand. "You poor dear," she said, her voice soft, hypnotic. "Why don't you come into the living room to get some rest?"

Rest? I wasn't sure I could ever rest again after what had happened! And I needed to go back for Whit as I'd promised Henry. But I didn't know what to do, who to call. If I called the police, would they believe me that anything had happened? They hadn't seemed too concerned when I'd called about Kitty and look how that had panned out.

Still, I had to do *something*. "Thanks, Dottie," I told her. "But I have to go. I can't leave Whit there. God knows what will happen to him."

Dottie nodded. "I understand," she said. "There was a man I loved like that. I still do. There's nothing I wouldn't do for him. Or him for me."

I gave her a grateful smile for understanding and stood up to tell Henry where I was going, but the room started spinning. I gripped the table to steady myself, grateful Dottie grabbed my arm to keep me from falling.

"What the hell?" I mumbled.

I tried to take a step, but my legs were like lead weights, and I collapsed back into the chair. I blinked several times, trying to clear my blurry vision, keep everything in the room from distorting cartoonishly. It reminded me of when I'd had too much of Junior's elderberry wine.

I turned my eyes to Dottie, her face swimming before me. "What did you give me?"

I tried again to get up, determined to get the hell out of there, but fell against the table, nearly knocking it over.

"What's happening to me?" I demanded.

Dottie grinned. "You're *becoming*, honey."

I stared at her, trying to make sense of what she was saying. "Becoming *what*?"

Dottie put her arm around me and gave me a squeeze. "Everything you were meant to be."

Fear shot through my veins. I launched myself from the table and took several stumbling steps out of the kitchen toward Henry, groping along the wall, using it for support to stay upright.

"There's nowhere to go, Zellie, honey," she called after me. "There's more to the family than just what lives at Dawes House."

Running out of wall, I launched myself toward Henry, but tripped over my own feet, my legs suddenly going numb, and landed sprawled out on Dottie's Persian rug. I tried to get up, my will to reach my son, to save him from Dottie's betrayal, giving me enough adrenaline to drag myself forward a few feet before I collapsed again.

I stretched out a hand toward him, willing my arm to work, but it flopped onto the floor, useless. "Henry," I called, but my voice was faint, hardly a whisper.

Dottie's face appeared before me. Now on her hands and knees, she bent forward to look into my eyes. "I knew I could count on Pearlie and June to try to make you one of us when they realized what was happening between you and Whit," she said, her grin triumphant. "They've always been so *dedicated* to keeping the line going. Clearly, they've been prepping your system for all these months. I'm just speeding things along, honey. Don't fight the transformation when it's offered, Zellie. It'll be better for both you and Henry if you just accept it. They'll only offer once."

Transformation? What the fuck?

I wanted to scream at her, demand she tell me what the hell she was talking about, but I could no longer speak.

"I'm sorry, honey," Dottie said, gently wiping away the single tear that slid along my cheek toward my nose. "I truly am. But they have to die for what they did to my sister. I allowed myself to become part of the family and so did my lover, just to wait until the perfect moment. You see, if *I* were to do it, I'd be hated, hunted, and then where would I be? I've tried to get others to avenge Alice's death for me, but they just didn't possess the talents you do. Or the connection to Whit. Who knew that would be the key to their undoing?"

I narrowed my eyes at her, hoping she could see how furious I was.

She just smiled and patted my cheek. "Yes, that's it, honey," she encouraged. "Use that hatred and rage. You're going to need it. You can do this. I have faith in you. Oh, you might not be able to get them all, but any will do. You're a good mama, Zellie. I know you'll do whatever you have to do to protect Henry. Whit has already removed June for you, so that's one less to worry about. Isn't that nice? Just take out as many of them as you can for me before they kill you."

"Dottie, darlin', we should go."

That voice. I recognized it.

"We don't want to be here when they arrive."

I gasped, suddenly realizing who Dottie's lover was.

Carter Dean. Dottie *had been the woman on his arm in the wedding photo!*

"Help me," I tried to cry out, hoping perhaps Mr. Dean would put an end to this madness and be a voice of reason, assure Dottie that she was only leaving Henry and me to the mercy of the very monsters she despised.

But before I could plead with him to help us, my world went dark.

The voices sounded muffled, far away. But I was still cautious when I opened my eyes just enough to see without alerting anyone that I was awake. I was in a basement. But not at Dawes House.

The carriage house? Some other property entirely?

I moved my eyes ever so slightly, searching for Henry. He lay on a low table or bench that was draped with a black cloth, still asleep from what Dottie had given him or newly dosed with something from our captors.

The room was dim, lit only by flickering candlelight that cast dancing shadows upon elaborate tapestries covering the walls. And then I saw them. Several people dressed in crimson robes, standing in a circle across from me. Candelabras like what I'd seen in my dream of Chase and Merilee were arranged around the edges of the room.

Oh, God.

As my brain came back online, my thoughts began to race, searching for a way to grab Henry and escape before they noticed I was awake.

But before I could react, someone grabbed my elbow and dragged me to my feet, clamping my wrists in manacles that hung from a beam. I struggled to get away, pulling against the heavy iron restraints. When that didn't work, I kicked out at the person who stood before me, nailing him in the crotch.

He cursed and pulled back his hood, his eyes blazing with fury as he took hold of my throat.

Chase.

"Not yet, baby," Merilee called out, interrupting what most likely would've been my crushed windpipe.

He cursed again and shoved me away before stepping aside, revealing Merilee in her crimson robe, sitting on the bench where I'd seen Henry. She now held him on her lap, cradling him against her as she rocked gently.

She grinned at me. "Welcome back, Zellie-girl. We were worried you might miss everything. But don't worry—you woke up just in time."

"Please, Merilee," I pleaded, tears in my voice. "Please just let Henry go. I'll do whatever you want."

Chase gripped my face in his punishing grasp, his laughter filling me with terror. "Let him go?" he repeated. "Why, Zellie, he's one of us. Seems my clever cousin hid him from us all these years."

"Oh, don't you worry, Zellie," Merilee said, her grin widening to reveal her maw of fangs. She kissed Henry on the top of his head, then added, "We'll take good care of your sweet boy. Raise him right."

Furious at the thought of these assholes raising my son, warping him into a monster, I renewed my struggle against the manacles, punctuating my struggles with a guttural scream of frustration when they failed to give.

Chase's cruel laughter crept along my skin, making the hair stand on end.

"That's enough."

Pearlie.

Pearlie nodded toward stairs across the room. "Take Henry to Netty, Merilee. We can manage."

"No!" I screamed, twisting and pulling against my restraints as Merilee climb the steps. "Please! Merilee!"

"Hush now, Zellie," Pearlie said from where she stood in the shadows, using the same tone I'd once found so soothing. "Henry won't be harmed as long as you cooperate."

"Go to hell," I spat, my voice breaking.

Pearlie stepped out of the shadows then, giving me a reproachful look. "I hope you'll change your mind."

I turned my face away, refusing to acknowledge her, blinking away the tears that stung my eyes.

She sighed. "Perhaps Whit can persuade you."

"What have you done with him?" I demanded, panic seizing my heart. But then a rush of warmth flooded my veins and the tug in my chest grew stronger. He was nearby, but where?

Pearlie gestured toward the shadows. My head snapped in that direction, hope surging only to come crashing down again.

Earl emerged, dragging Whit by one arm, leaving a sickening smear of blood on the floor. Once they were in the center of the room, Earl flung Whit's arm away, rolling him onto his back. Whit arched off the ground, sucking air in through his teeth, clearly in pain.

It was then that I saw the full extent of his injuries. He'd been savagely slashed across his chest and abdomen, his wounds gaping, so I assumed his back was in similar shape. A flash of white ribs showed where his shirt had been ripped open. His arms and legs bore more wounds, his clothes torn and blood-soaked. And a jagged cut ran from his temple to chin, the wound recent, blood trailing down his cheek to his neck.

My chest tightened painfully, the sight of him suffering both breaking my heart and filling me with rage. I clenched my jaw, biting back the tears that strangled me, refusing to give the others the satisfaction of knowing how deeply it affected me. Well, except for my fury. I wanted them to see every single fucking ounce of that.

I turned my murderous glare on the woman I'd loved like a mother and whose betrayal absolutely gutted me. "I'm going to kill every damned one of you for this."

"I think that might be bit difficult, given your circumstances, darlin'," Earl drawled.

"And I think I'll start with you, Earl, you pretentious prick," I ground out, perfectly fine with Earl knowing that I planned to rip his throat out as soon as I was free of the restraints.

"Settle down, Zellie," Pearlie soothed. "We don't want to kill you or Henry. We *love* you. You're *family*." She sighed and cast a sorrowful look toward Whit. "I had hoped we could all be happy together. But betrayal can't go unpunished, no matter how much we love the betrayer."

I looked to Whit, my desperation ratcheting to a new level. They were going to kill him. Right there in front of me.

"No, please," I pleaded. "*Pearlie...*"

She offered me a sad smile. "It's up to you, Zellie. I will give you a choice, but it's one we can only offer once."

"What choice?" I asked, dreading the answer.

She stepped closer and took my face in her hands, her eyes gleaming. "You've been consuming our blood for months in everything we've ever fed you, every sip of tea, lemonade, priming you for this. Dottie probably gave you a bit too much today, but it won't matter soon. We want you to become one of *us*, Zellie."

This must've been the offer Dottie was talking about.

"You are *so* strong," Pearlie continued, "such a good mama to Henry. And your abilities... Well, there's no telling what you'll be like once you *become*! You're already feeling it, aren't you? That surge of power?"

I continued to glare at her, refusing to admit to anything. Even if it was true.

Pearlie stepped back and drew a dagger from the folds of her robe. She held it out to me with both hands. The blade was covered in an intricate design that I immediately recognized. It was the same as what decorated the elevator and the blade of the dagger June had given Henry.

"All you have to do," Junior said, stepping up to stand near where Whit lay, "is make your first sacrifice to pledge your loyalty to the family. Then we can share our blood openly and you yours. You will fully *become*. And it will be *glorious*."

He gestured toward Whit. It was then that I realized Earl had dragged Whit into a circle formed by ancient symbols carved into the floor, the concrete darkened by the blood of countless before. The implication was clear. If I didn't kill Whit, we both would die.

Whit lifted his eyes just enough to meet mine, his expression filled with love and an unspoken plea for forgiveness. He'd resigned himself to his fate. After all, he'd sworn to me that he'd do anything to keep Henry and me safe, that he'd die for us. And now he intended to make good on that promise.

I broke our connection and lifted my chin, attempting to make my expression as stony and disinterested as possible while I tried to determine if the offer was actually sincere or if they were just bullshitting me, hoping to entice me to murder my husband as a particularly shitty *fuck you* to the man who'd betrayed them.

"If I do this," I began, carefully enunciating each word for emphasis, "do you swear to me that Henry and I will be safe?"

"Of course, darlin'," Earl responded quickly. "You'll officially be family, Zellie. You'll have everything you could possibly want. All you have to do is kill the son of a bitch who killed my June."

I turned to Pearlie who nodded, her kind and loving smile absurdly ironic.

I searched the rest of their faces again—Junior, Iris, Chase—trying to stall, my mind racing. There was no escape. No other way. That's what Whit had tried to communicate to me in the look we'd shared. He wasn't just asking for my forgiveness for everything that had happened. He was letting me know he'd already forgiven *me* for what he knew I had to do to save our son.

I just hoped he could read what was in my eyes as easily as I could his.

My heart pounded, my blood rushing in my ears as the full realization of what was about to happen hit me. I swallowed hard and nodded. "I'll do it."

"Sorry, Cousin," Chase drawled with a wicked chuckle, coming forward to release my hands.

As he unlocked the manacles, the others' eyes began to glow amber, their excitement and blood lust growing in anticipation of what was to come. I caught motion out of the corner of my eye, and fixed my attention elsewhere, focusing on my captors. But that glimpse of movement had been enough for me to see Whit slowly dragging himself to his feet, his face twisting with rage.

I inhaled deeply as I reached for the dagger in Pearlie's hands, my gaze briefly meeting Whit's where he was creeping in the shadows, unnoticed, then exhaled slowly and stepped past Pearlie into the circle.

At the same moment they all realized he wasn't where Earl had dropped him, Whit lunged forward, ripping out Earl's throat in one swift motion. But before Whit could turn toward me, Chase tackled him, taking him down, his talons slashing at Whit, who parried his arm away, barely managing to avoid his own throat being torn open.

"Kill him, Zellie!" Pearlie commanded, her voice edged with maniacal fervor.

I took a quick step forward as if to join the battle between Whit and Chase, but pivoted back toward Pearlie, swinging my arm as I spun and slashing her throat with the dagger she'd handed me.

Pearlie grabbed her neck with both hands in a vain attempt to staunch the blood spurting from the artery I'd opened, the hurt and betrayal in her eyes opening up a wound deep inside me that I doubt will ever close. But not waiting for her to recover from the unexpected assault, I slashed again, tearing open her stomach, spilling her entrails.

Her eyes bulged and a gurgle of blood sprayed from her mouth as she stumbled back, knocking over one of the candelabras. The fire caught her robes in a flare of light. Her scream was so shrill, I winced and covered my ears, but the distraction was enough.

A hand grasped my hair and jerked me off my feet, flinging me to one side, and sending me slamming into the bench where Henry had been. It upended, tipping over as I fell, catching me in the ribs and stealing my breath.

I pressed a hand to my side and pushed myself up with the other. As I turned to intercept Iris's next attack, I saw Junior had rushed to Pearlie and was trying to strip her robes from her, but the material had melted to her skin, was melting to his hands. He roared with pain from the fire and heartache as Pearlie dropped to the ground, completely consumed by flames. But by then, his own robes had caught fire. He flailed wildly, trying to extricate himself from the burning mantle, but stumbled, knocking over another candelabra, the candle's flames catching his robes and racing up his back to meet the fire already consuming him.

It all happened in the space of a few seconds, but it was enough. A searing pain in my ribs as talons ripped into my skin drew a scream of agony from my lungs, and I reflexively spun around, slicing with the dagger. The blade caught Iris across the abdomen. Not deep enough to disembowel her as I'd done Pearlie, but enough to bring her up short. I lunged for one of the candles in the circle and tossed it at her feet, the flame fizzling at the hem but not catching as I'd hoped.

When she screamed in rage and lunged at me, her face twisting with hatred, I rushed toward her instead of standing my ground, the move catching her by surprise. I brought the dagger down with both hands, burying it in her chest.

She gasped and blinked at me several times as if she didn't know what had occurred, then dropped to her knees. I pulled another candelabra over, this time igniting her robe. Within seconds, the flames spread up to her shoulders before completely engulfing her as she fell to one side.

I glanced down at where her talons had sliced into my skin, relieved to see the wounds weren't deep. Fortunately for me, her rage-fueled attack was sloppy, and she'd merely grazed me, only one of the cuts more serious than a cat scratch. I heaved a ragged sigh, my relief cut short when a hand came down onto my shoulder. I spun around, dagger raised and brought it down toward my attacker, but he intercepted my wrist, stopping me from driving the blade into his heart.

A single sob shook me when I recognized the beloved face before me even through the blood and gore that covered it. "Whit."

I threw my arms around his neck, holding him for a moment, his weight heavy when he sagged against me, his strength waning. When I released him, he took my face in his hands and kissed me, the salt on my lips—whether from his tears or mine, I couldn't be sure—stinging where my lip had split at some point.

"I love you," I said, my words confirming what my heart already knew.

He kissed me again, long and hard, then took my hand and pulled me with him toward the basement stairs. The fire had spread to the tapestries and was now catching the wooden beams above us. But as we attempted to ascend the stairs, his knees buckled and he stumbled, landing hard on the steps.

"Come on," I urged, squinting against the smoke that burned my eyes, assaulted my lungs. I grabbed his arm and pulled it over my shoulders. Still gripping the dagger, I wrapped my other arm around his waist, trying to avoid the worst of his wounds and keep from adding to them. "Don't you dare give up on me now."

We'd just reached the top of the stairs when a hulking figure appeared in the doorway, blocking our escape.

Billy Wayne.

With a low growl, Whit sprang up the last few steps, taking down Billy Wayne before the man could react. "Go!" Whit shouted. "Run!"

This time, the word was like the crack of a starter's gun. I shot forward but only made it up a single step before a hand grabbed my ankle and yanked my foot out from under me. I fell against the steps, lightning hot pain radiating from my shoulder.

I tried to pull my foot free, but the grasp only tightened and dragged me down two steps before I could roll over and kick with my other leg, nailing Chase in the face. He snarled and lunged upward at me at the same moment I brought my dagger down, driving it through his skull.

Not bothering to retrieve the weapon, I raced up the rest of the stairs. Billy Wayne lay motionless on the ground, his head twisted at an awkward angle.

Whit pushed himself up from his hands and knees, his head hanging between his shoulders as he tried to stand on shaky legs.

I rushed to him and grabbed him around the waist, pulling his arm over my shoulders again, hurrying him toward the door of what I now realized was the carriage house. When we were safely outside and in the night air of the courtyard, a different kind of terror enveloped me.

"Merilee has Henry," I told Whit, frantic. "She was taking him to Netty."

"Zellie," Whit said, his voice thin with pain.

"I don't know why," I continued without missing a beat. "We have to get to him before she does anything to him—"

"Zellie."

This time, his voice was harsh, bringing me up short. "You have to keep going," I told him. "I can't do this without you."

His lips curved up in one corner in a weak smile. "I think you can do just about anything after what I saw in there."

I shook my head. "No, I need you, Whit. I don't know what to do, how to stop her."

I started forward, but he resisted. "I've lost too much blood, Zellie. I have to replace it to heal."

I searched his face in confusion. Then understanding sunk in. "You need *my* blood."

He nodded, his legs buckling and making us both stumble. I landed hard on my knees and nearly fell onto him but somehow kept from toppling over.

"Okay," I said with a determined nod, desperate to save him. "Okay, what do I do?"

His eyes flicked toward my forearm. Without hesitating, I held it out to him. He took hold of my hand gently and held my gaze as if asking my permission, making sure I was okay with what was about to happen.

I swallowed hard, my pulse kicking up with fear, but nodded.

In the next moment, his fangs sank into my skin, and his lips latched on around the wound, gently suckling. I gasped, the sensation surprisingly erotic and one I would've been happy to sink into if our son wasn't being held hostage by a murderous bitch.

He released me abruptly just a few seconds later. His head fell back, his eyes closed as he let my blood do its work.

"Now me," I whispered.

His eyes snapped open, the bright amber glow taking me off-guard. "I can't reverse what will happen," he told me. "They've been prepping you for months. And now that I've taken your blood, as soon as you take mine, it's forever."

Instead of answering, I bent forward, intending to take blood from one of his open wounds, but he stopped me and shook his head. "It isn't clean." Then he punctured his wrist and held it out to me.

The moment he offered his arm, I knew an urgent hunger, a deep, soul shaking need I'd never experienced. I grasped his arm and drank in greedy gulps. When he groaned as if in pain, I abruptly broke away on a gasp. Heat flooded my body, the gift he'd given me buzzing like electricity in my veins. But there was more than that. All of the memories Whit had taken to protect Henry and me came back all at once like a movie reel playing at warp speed.

And I *knew*. Everything he'd said about our past together was true. And the rush of emotion that hit me nearly knocked me on my ass.

"My God," I breathed.

"You'll need more to fully become," he panted, perhaps not realizing what had just occurred with my memories, "but I'm too weak to give you any more right now. That will be enough to make you stronger. Just find Henry."

I nodded then kissed him briefly. I'd tell him about my memories returning later, after we got Henry back. I pressed my forehead to his and closed my eyes, letting my mind drift, instinctively reaching out for our son. And then I saw him in my mind, a bright light guiding my way.

Suddenly sensing we were no longer alone, my eyes snapped open, drawn to the doorway of Dawes House. There, staring back at me, was Alice, her expression at last at peace, her eyes no longer vacant, black holes, but wide blue eyes filled with purpose. She turned around and walked back into the house.

"I know where Henry is," I told Whit. "I have to follow her."

He nodded. "Go. I'll be right behind you."

I scrambled to my feet and ran after Alice, the pounding of my heart a deafening war drum.

Once more unto the breach, dear friends...

When I entered the foyer, I took in the area with a rapid glance, searching for where Alice had gone. And then I saw her slowly ascending the stairs, her fingertips brushing along the banister, leaving a trail of fire in their wake.

"Oh, shit."

My stomach sank as I realized what was happening. She was planning to burn down the house like one of her predecessors had done with the first house that had stood on these grounds.

I ran up the stairs behind her, passed her, not stopping until I'd made it to Merilee's and Netty's apartment. I was just reaching for the knob, when the door flung open with such force, it tore from the hinges. There was Merilee on the couch, Henry in her lap, now wide awake and crying quietly.

"Henry!" I called, my voice hoarse with emotion.

When he saw me, he tried to leap from Merilee's lap and run to me, but she easily kept him where he was.

"Mama!" he sobbed, reaching for me with both arms.

I shook with rage and frustration, my thoughts racing as I tried to figure out what to do, how I could kill that fucking bitch without harming Henry.

Then Merilee's mouth curved into a knowing grin. "Why, Zellie-girl," she drawled, "you've *changed*."

"Let him go," I ground out, my hands balling into fists at my side.

"Or what?" she laughed. "Do you really think you can best me? I've lived for over a hundred years, Zellie-girl. You've been one of us for, what? Five minutes?"

As I glared at her, trying to figure out which option I was going to choose from the violent ideas I had for tearing her apart, a swirl of white mist began to form behind Merilee, and then another and another until there were too many to count. Within the mist, faces took form. I recognized Susanna and Eliza Dawes, the lady in the wall, and the woman who I'd seen murdered in my dream. But there were many others—nameless, forgotten.

Suddenly, their faces twisted into terrifying death masks, rotten, putrid, screaming with vengeance. I gasped, and stumbled back a few steps, my eyes going wide.

Merilee's brows twitched together in a confused frown when she saw my reaction. "What the—"

Whatever she'd planned to say was abruptly cut short by a ragged scream as the spirits of the victims of the horrors at Dawes House attacked, tearing into her with ghostly fingers. She released Henry to claw at her skin, ripping off her own flesh in her frenzied attempt to pull her assailants off her.

Henry vaulted from her lap and ran to me. I scooped him up and pivoted to run from the apartment, but caught sight of Ms. Netty, sitting in her wheelchair in the doorway of her bedroom.

Her shoulders sagged, her eyes taking in the scene with detached resignation. She turned her head to me and held my gaze briefly. "Run, girl," she told me, her voice flat, emotionless. "Go now before it's too late."

I'd come back for her, I decided. As soon as I got Henry to safety, I'd come back.

I raced down the servants' stairs, reaching the foyer as the floors above began to creak and collapse, the flames spreading with unnatural speed. I ran with Henry to June and Earl's apartment. Finding the door standing open, the doorframe splintered from someone breaking in, I rushed inside, yelling for Addie, but not finding her in her bedroom.

"Addie, honey!" I screamed. "Where are you?"

"Outside, Mama!" Henry told me, bouncing a little in my arms, urging me back toward the doorway.

Not stopping to question his assertion, I hurried out of the house and down the steps. Addie stood at the gate to the yard, holding a little stuffed doll in her arms and sobbing. My heart fluttered with relief at seeing her safe. I rushed to her and dropped to my knees, gathering her close.

"It's okay, baby," I assured her. "I've got you. It's okay."

In the distance, sirens rapidly approached. I looked around, searching for Whit.

"Addie, where's Whit? Did you see him?"

She nodded, hiccupping as her sobs slowed. "He brought me here. Then he went to look for you and Henry."

My head snapped back toward the house, now completely engulfed. "No," I breathed, fear squeezing my heart. "Oh, God, no."

Then motion at the door on the fourth floor caught my attention. Ms. Netty stood in the open doorway, flames already catching her clothes and hair. Before I could do more than cry out, she spread her arms and fell forward—just as Alice had done so many decades before.

I turned the kids into me, shielding them from the end of Netty's suffering.

"Ma'am!" someone called, pulling gently at my arm, helping me to my feet. "Ma'am, you need to come with me."

As the firefighter dragged me away, I stared at the conflagration consuming Dawes House, the carriage house. They were already collapsing in upon themselves as the structures weakened and gave way. I craned my neck around the fire equipment, straining to see what was happening, hoping that at any moment, Whit would emerge unscathed, that he would pull us into his arms and tell us it was over, that everything would be fine now. Even as Henry and Addie and I were loaded into the ambulances and treated for shock and smoke inhalation, I searched for him, insisting that they keep the ambulance door open for just a few more minutes.

But he never came.

"We need to take you to the hospital now, ma'am," one of the paramedics said gently.

As we drove away, I stared out the back window, tears streaming silently down my cheeks, watching the flames dance like a million little rejoicing devils, and mourned the dreams that died along with the family I'd always wanted, thought I finally had.

As we turned the corner, I closed my eyes and focused on the tug at the center of my chest, praying it was real and not a manifestation of hope that refused to die.

CHAPTER TWENTY-SIX

I sat on a chair in the hospital room where Henry and Addie slept, the sedatives the doctors had given them allowing them at least a little relief from the horrors of their new reality.

I pulled the blanket wrapped around my shoulders a little tighter and stared at Henry's face, wondering how I'd never noticed the resemblance to Whit before. Tears stung my eyes, blurring my vision, and I blinked them away, not wanting the children to see me crying if they should wake up.

A quiet creak of the door opening brought my head around. For one joyful heartbeat, I expected to see Whit standing there, but it was the doctor, wearing that "poor Zellie" look I'd hoped to never see again.

"Have you heard from my husband?" I asked. But I knew the answer before she shook her head.

"I'm so sorry," she told me. "But I do have some good news for you. All your tests came back okay. The baby is fine despite the puncture wound to your abdomen and the cracked rib. You were very lucky."

I forced a grateful smile, not betraying the fact that the wounds she'd spoken of were already mostly healed. "Thank you."

She took a deep breath, clearly stalling the delivery of something else she needed to say, before announcing, "The police have arrived. They want to speak with you about what happened. And, when you're ready, they will need you to identify the bodies."

I glanced at Henry and Addie. "I can do that now while they're sleeping," I told her. "I want to be here when they're awake."

An hour later, I'd given my statement to the police, explaining the blood all over my clothes, my arms, my face, were the result of escaping from the murderous cult that had been living at Dawes House. Given the body they'd found in the basement wall, the story wasn't even questioned. The fire? An accident that started in the struggle. They seemed to accept the facts much easier than I'd anticipated.

Then I was led to the basement of the hospital, to the morgue where several bodies lay covered by sheets. The first they revealed was Netty. But the others, burned almost beyond recognition, were harder to identify. The women were all there—Iris, June, Pearlie, Merilee. I was able to determine which was which based on what I could make out about their height, a wedding band, a strand of hair that was somehow untouched. My dagger was no longer lodged in Chase's skull, but the hole in the top of his head made his identification easy. Billy Wayne with his broken neck. I held my breath as the attendant peeled back the next sheet and let it out on a harsh sigh of relief.

"That's Junior Johnson," I told the attendant who was taking notes, then turned to the final three bodies.

Three.

I wrapped my arms around myself as they pulled back the sheet on the next slab. "Earl Forester."

"We have a Carter Dean listed as a resident," the attendant said, checking his notes.

I turned with dread toward the final two bodies. "You won't find him," I announced, my voice flat. "He left town with my boss, Dottie Shay, before anything happened at Dawes House."

The attendant checked off another name on the tablet he carried. "Well, that's all then. Thank you, Mrs. Proffitt."

My head snapped up. "What?"

He nodded at one of the remaining bodies. "That's just bones the firefighters found at the bottom of a well in the basement of the main house."

No wonder I'd been drawn to that stupid well.

"You'll probably discover that they're old," I told him, suddenly certain I knew who it was. "It's most likely one of the former residents. A woman named Eliza Dawes Proffitt. She drowned."

He scribbled it down. "Thanks. We'll look into that. If they bring in anyone else, we'll be in touch."

"What about the other one?" I asked, unable to look away from the sheet-covered body on the remaining slab.

"Oh, that's from another incident."

I collapsed to the floor with the enormity of my relief, not bothering to hold back the sobs that wracked my body.

It wasn't Whit. He was alive. He had *to be.*

That's all I needed to know.

The next day, we sat in the chairs at the hospital entrance, Henry and Addie quietly snuggled up against me, while we waited for the police officer who was to pick us up and take us to Dottie's to retrieve Whit's car and what remained of our belongings. After that? I had no idea where the hell we were going to go.

A quiet swoosh of the automatic doors drew my attention to the entrance. A statuesque woman strode in, each purposeful step echoing in the silence of the hospital waiting room. She was dressed all in black, wearing black combat boots and dark shades, her short dark hair slicked back.

Henry sat up straight, his smile beaming. "Hi, Cora!" he called. "We've been waiting for you!"

This brought a smile to the woman's face, softening her harsh features in an instant. "Hello, Henry. I'm delighted to finally meet you." Then she offered an incline of her head to Addie. "Adelaide."

When she turned her attention to me, she clasped her hands in front of her, then bent her head forward briefly. "It's good to finally meet you, Zellie," Cora said. "Whit has told me so much about you."

"You're Whit's sister," I said. I'd sensed it the moment she'd walked in, before Henry had greeted her by name. Maybe it had been something he'd told me *before.* Maybe he'd shown me photos. Some of the memories were still a little foggy. I had so much to learn about him even after all my returned memories came into focus. I shook my head slightly. "Addie's sister too, I guess."

Cora nodded. "Yes," she answered simply. "I've come to take you home."

"I don't have a home," I told her. "Are you taking us to the house in Charleston?"

She shook her head. "No, Whit had arranged for another house before the unfortunate events of the last two days. I had already planned to arrive today to escort you to safety should anyone try to stop you from leaving. I'm sorry I didn't arrive sooner."

There was genuine regret in her voice. And of course it was Cora that Whit had brought in on his plans. Hadn't he told me that she was the only one he would trust with our safety?

I rose to my feet, a ghost myself as I drifted out to the car waiting for us, my emotions flat, deadened—perhaps a side effect of the shock. Or maybe a defense mechanism to keep the grief and despair from overwhelming me. I didn't care where we were going. It didn't matter anymore. As long as Henry and Addie were safe, I didn't care.

So, I didn't ask any questions as we drove to the airport or during our flight on the Proffitts' private jet. Not even when we sat in the car that drove us to the countryside of what I soon recognized from various signs we passed as somewhere in England. But when the driver finally turned off onto a winding road, I could smell the ocean, feel the salt in the air. And soon after, a house came into view—a two story manor with a walled garden with plenty of room for Henry and Addie to run and play. And a spire.

"Good evening, Ms. Proffitt," a man in a uniform wished Cora as we exited the car. "The manor has been prepared according to your specifications with the additional security measures put in place."

I heard Cora respond, but the yipping of a puppy drew my attention away. A little brown and black dog that couldn't have been more than a few months old came bounding out of the house and straight for Henry.

"Daisy!" he cried, scooping her up into his arms, struggling to hold onto her as she squirmed with excitement, eager to cover his face with puppy kisses. Addie giggled and ran over to Henry to snuggle with their new friend.

"Whit," I whispered as I entered the house, taking it all in. I closed my eyes for a few seconds to keep the tears at bay, then climbed the stairs to the second floor, peering into each of the bedrooms before finding the master suite. Off to one side of the room, a set of doors opened out onto a balcony that afforded a view of the rose gardens and beyond to an expanse of land that ended at cliffs overlooking the ocean.

He'd found it. My dream. The house we were supposed to live in together as a family. I placed my palm flat against my chest, searching for the faint connection. It was so weak, struggling. It was then that the pain of losing him, the fear of never seeing him again overtook me, and I sank down against the balcony railing, my sorrow too heavy to hold as I grieved for not just the loss of what *was* but for what *could've been*.

I don't know what drew me outside that morning three months later. There was something in the air, something that made me restless, that made sitting still impossible.

"Are you alright?" Cora asked, joining me on the porch, coffee mug in hand.

I pulled my cardigan tighter around me and nodded. "Where are Henry and Addie?"

"The nanny is getting them dressed and ready for their lessons," Cora replied, her brow furrowed much like her brother's did when he was concerned about me.

I nodded, distracted, but then turned back to Cora and offered her a grateful smile. "Thanks, Cora. For everything. I don't know what we would've done without you."

It was true. Cora had become a trusted friend and sister to me, a loving aunt to Henry, helping me navigate our new reality. She'd taken care of finding tutors and a nanny who were still loyal to Whit and could be trusted. Whit had made a lot of enemies, Cora explained, and our safety was her chief concern. She'd assured me Whit would come to us when it was safe to do so. And after he'd healed.

She hadn't needed to elaborate on that part. I knew what Whit needed. I tried not to think about the fact that it would be someone else's blood helping him heal—even if it was just what he could access from a supplier who'd already gathered it from a willing donor.

I'd finished my final class and received my degree. And with Cora's help, I began sourcing used books for the bookstore I planned to open in the quaint little village where we now lived.

A few weeks earlier, when we were in London at my first auction, I thought I saw Dottie and Carter Dean among those in attendance. Dottie was young again, *renewed*, but her quirky fashion sense and cat-eye glasses had given her away.

Or maybe I'd just imagined that our gazes had met from across the room because when I was able to squeeze through the crowd to where they'd been standing, they were gone. Or maybe it was just paranoia that Whit's enemies would find us, that Cora and our rapidly growing puppy Daisy wouldn't be enough to protect us. That I'd have to kill again to protect my family.

My *true* family.

But that morning, the restlessness didn't feel sinister. There was an ache, deep in my bones, urging my legs to move. But it wasn't painful. It was more like...anticipation. Like something was coming.

An intruder? Or *visitors*, as I call them now that I'm no longer afraid. I'd had several come to me since arriving at the manor, souls who needed my help to tell their stories, mostly women whose voices had been silenced and needed me to speak for them, help them find peace.

But I felt like a fraud some days. How could I help them find peace, when my own soul ached for the vital piece that was still missing?

"Where are you going?" Cora called. "Take Daisy with you!"

Until she'd spoken, I hadn't even noticed that I'd left the porch and was making my way down the drive. My heart pounded as I increased my pace, bracing my barely rounded belly so as not to jostle the baby when I broke into a jog.

And then I saw him. Walking on the road toward me.

He looked tired, worn down, and his beautiful dark hair now showed hints of gray, but his stride was the same, his smile when he saw me so filled with relief and love that I would've known him from a mile away. But it was only when he rushed to me and gathered me into his arms, holding me like he'd never let me go, that I finally dared to believe he wasn't just an apparition who'd come to taunt me.

And then he was kissing me, over and over, as if reassuring himself that *I* was truly there in his arms, until there was only one kiss, tender, loving, perfect. And my heart was whole, my soul complete once more.

Finally, Whit took my face in his hands and pressed his forehead to mine. I placed my hands over his and closed my eyes, letting his love envelop me, no longer afraid. There was much to tell, much to discuss, much to work through, but it could wait. This moment, having him with us again, was all that mattered.

"I'm home, Zellie," Whit whispered as if saying it louder would shatter our happiness.

Home.

As we strolled back to the house, Whit's arm around me, holding me close, I finally knew what that meant.

ACKNOWLEDGEMENTS

Every novel is a journey, and this one began after a family vacation to Savannah, GA, in 2022. I'd always wanted to visit the city, and it did not disappoint. My family and I had a wonderful trip—and I came home with the beginnings of *Among Her Bones* already taking shape in my mind.

It took a year to write the first draft, another year of revisions, beta reads, and discussions with my agent about the best path for this story, and yet another year of fine-tuning the text between other projects to bring the novel to its next stage. I'm so excited to finally be able to share Zellie and Whit's story with you!

I'd be remiss if I didn't say a huge THANK YOU to the many people who were right there with me along the way.

First and foremost, thank you to my family—especially Zach and the boys. Your unwavering encouragement and support keep me going. You are my sun, moon, and stars. Thank you to my sisters who prop me up when I need it most. Hugs to Cecy, Beth, and Amanda. Your friendship keeps me sane.

Thank you to my amazing agent, Nicole Resciniti, for her constant guidance and friendship. A special shout-out to my assistant, Kimberly, who has been an incredible partner in this wild industry. Many thanks as well to my beta readers and everyone else who played a role in bringing this novel to fruition.

And thank you to my own Mamaw, whose kitchen was the epicenter of our family gatherings and whose dining room table always had an extra chair waiting for anyone who stopped by.

Thank you to Dee, Kathy, Grace, Hilene, and so many other mentors who taught me how to dig deep, both as a reader and as a writer. To the women who came before me, whose stories have shaped and inspired so many, thank you for paving the way. And to the women who will come after—keep moving forward on your own journeys. And never let your voice be silenced.

Kate SeRine (pronounced *serene)* writes award-winning paranormal romance, urban fantasy, romantic suspense, and horror—because what's love without a little darkness? Though she's a steadfast believer in soul-deep love and happily-ever-afters, her characters are guaranteed to experience blood, bones, and heartbreak along the way.

When she isn't writing books that keep readers up way past bedtime, Kate can be found antiquing, browsing used bookstores, or scouting out local coffee shops. She lives in a smallish, quintessentially Midwestern town with her husband, two sons, and an extremely judgmental cat.

Kate never tires of creating new worlds to share and is even now working on her next project—probably while consuming way too much coffee.

Connect with Kate at:

www.kateserine.com

Facebook: @kateserine

Instagram: @kateserine_author

Threads: @kateserine_author

TikTok: @kate_serine

Goodreads.com/kateserine

Don't miss the other award-winning novels by Kate SeRine...

The Transplanted Tales series

RED

Grimm Consequences

The Better to See You

Along Came a Spider

Ever After

Better Watch Out

Dark Alliance series

Deceived

Concealed

Protect & Serve series

Torn (in *Way of the Warrior* anthology)

Stop at Nothing

Safe from Harm

www.ingramcontent.com/pod-product-compliance
Lightning Source LLC
LaVergne TN
LVHW090550110826
845146LV00001B/87
* 9 7 9 8 9 9 4 8 8 7 1 1 0 *